Footprints on the African Savanna

A Historical fiction novel of the journey and adventures of a Sikh Woman in Somalia, Kenya and Tanganyika

Pally Dhillon

Copyright © 2018 Pally Dhillon
All rights reserved

ISBN-13: 978-1985784604
ISBN-10: 1985784602

DISCLAIMER

Footprints on the African Savanna is a work of fiction. While portions may be based on real events or extracted from the author's memoirs, for dramatic and narrative purposes, the book contains fictionalized scenes, representative characters and dialogue, and time compression. Names of historical figures are interspersed throughout the manuscript for fictional purposes and should not be considered factually accurate. The views and opinions expressed in the book are those of the characters only and do not necessarily reflect or represent the views and opinions held by individuals on which those characters are based.

DEDICATION

*"My mother was the most beautiful woman I ever saw.
All I am I owe to my mother. I attribute my success in life
To the moral, intellectual, and physical education
I received from her."*
GEORGE WASHINGTON

This manuscript is dedicated to my mother, Amrita Kaur Dhillon, who wrote fifty pages in her own handwriting about her childhood and life in East Africa. Unfortunately, she passed away before she could complete and publish her story.

My mother belonged to a generation of pioneering Sikh women in East Africa who were born there in the early part of the twentieth century, and worked tirelessly to raise their families. This is her story, from birth to a glorious childhood which ended abruptly when she was married at the age of fourteen and thrust into the busy and demanding life of a large Sikh family who were one of the early settlers in East Africa.

Here you will read of the intriguing life experiences of my mother's father and father-in-law, who were pioneers, professionals, hunters and business owners and you will also learn of my mother's struggles, hardships and daring adventures as she attempts to support her husband, his family and her own children in the vast, raw and often turbulent countries of Kenya and Tanganyika. She was a big game hunter, ran businesses in the nomadic Maasailand and drove large trucks to transport goods through the roughest terrains in East Africa.

I hope my mother is happy with the completed manuscript you hold in your hands. May it bring you many hours of thrills and enjoyment.

OTHER BOOKS BY PALLY DHILLON

Kijabe (2001)   Amazon.com
Surkh Haneri (2005)   Amazon.com
Walk with Pride (2008)   Amazon.com
Whispers from the Heart (2012)   Amazon.com

ADVANCE PRAISE FOR FOOTPRINTS ON THE AFRICAN SAVANNA

Get ready to put your khaki safari suit on as Pally takes you on a cultural journey with Footprints on the African Savanna. The depictive narrative makes you experience the dry dust of the desert, tribal customs and traditions and most importantly, struggles of migrant families. With conspiracies and secrets you won't want to put this read down. The main character, Amrita Kaur Dhillon, empowers you to break all social or gender boundaries to succeed. She is an inspiration to the reader to dust yourself off and never give up. Today she would be proud of her son's achievement in completing and publishing her gripping and intriguing novel.

POONAM MAJHU

With great detail and imagination, Pally continues the saga of his mother's written account of her family's new life in East Africa. The drama of their lives is portrayed in a captivating and creative way. The tapestry Pally weaves of daily hardships, government and political turmoil and jealousy within the family are all brought together in Footprints on the African Savanna. Pally's writing skills and his interesting story telling techniques makes for this suspenseful historical fiction novel. A book you won't want to stop reading.

SAMUEL ZANOTTI

Footprints on the African Savanna is author Pally Dhillon's latest historical novel. This book was inspired by a series of notes and recollections compiled by his mother Amrita Dhillon. The information she recorded reflects many of her life experiences from childhood through adulthood while living in Kenya and Tanzania. The author uses his mother's information as the basis for this compelling novel. The Sikh woman in the story is confronted with a sequence of seemingly insurmountable obstacles that she faces throughout her life. Her story is one of courage, character and the inner strength necessary that enabled Amrita to not permit these many hardships from fulfilling her life's dreams and aspirations. Amrita would be extremely proud of her son's effort to tell her story in such a moving and captivating manner.

DOCTOR ROBERT ZANOTTI

Pally Dhillon's latest book, Footprints on the African Savanna, depicts the tragedies and triumphs of a family from India who moves to East Africa in order to improve their livelihood. Mr. Dhillon succeeds in telling his family's journey through letters and stories he found after his mother's death. Amrita Dhillon is a courageous and intelligent woman who has no fear of powerful conflicts or obstacles that confront her when it comes to the survival of the family. One of the most frustrating issues revolves around a family member's betrayal and his endless efforts to destroy everything that Amrita and her husband have worked so hard to acquire. The settings of the lush African Savanna, the descriptions of the various tribes of people, and yet dangerous environment, is so richly put into words that you feel you are actually there! Amrita's experiences compel the reader to appreciate and admire the inner strength of this successful woman and her will for survival and that of her family. In the end they too leave their Footprints on the African Savanna.

WINIFRED ZANOTTI

WITH GRATITUDE

I am thankful to my mother who hand wrote fifty pages outlining her life before she passed away. I used that as the basis for this manuscript and hopefully enriched it with my experiences, my memories and stories that were told by family members when I was younger and hope I did justice to her story.

My sincere thanks to Winnie, Bob and Sam Zanotti, my daughter Salena, my brother Satpal and to Poonam Majhu for their continuous encouragement and persistence in helping me complete this emotional manuscript for me and then doing the arduous task of editing it. Their feedback and support in completing this project was invaluable.

SIKHISM

Sikhism, the youngest of the world religions, is barely five hundred years old. Its founder, Guru Nanak, was born in 1469. Guru Nanak spread a simple message of *"Ek On Kar"*: we are all one, created by the One Creator of all Creation. This was at a time when castes, sectarianism, religious factions and fanaticism were tearing India apart. He aligned with no religion, and respected all religions. He expressed the reality that there is one God and many paths, and the Name of God is Truth, *"Sat Nam"*.

He opposed superstition, rituals, social inequality and injustice, renunciation and hypocrisy and inspired seekers by singing divine songs which touched the hearts of the most callous listeners. These songs were recorded, and formed the beginnings of the Sikhs' sacred writings, later to become the *"Siri Guru Granth Sahib"*. Sikhism is well suited to the needs of modern life.

In Sikhism, women have equal status with men. In the fourteenth century, Indian women were severely degraded and oppressed in their society. Given no education or freedom to make decisions, their presence in religious, political, social, cultural and economic affairs was virtually non-existent. The first Sikh Guru, Sri Guru Nanak Dev Ji, the first of ten, intended to give women a sense of self-respect and warrior ethos. Guru Nanak broke the shackles of women by admitting them into the *Sangat*, congregation, without any restrictions or reservations. The equality of both genders was the tradition set by the founder of Sikhism.

Guru Gobind Singh was the last Guru of the Sikhs. He created the *Khalsa*, a spiritual brotherhood and sisterhood devoted to purity of thought and action. He gave the *Khalsa* a distinctive external form to remind them of their commitment, and to help them maintain an elevated state of consciousness. Guru Gobind Singh introduced Kaur and Singh, when he administered *Amrit*, baptism, to both male and female Sikhs. All female Sikhs were asked to use the name Kaur meaning princess after their forename and males were to use the name Singh, meaning lion. Kaur or Singh is a name that can be used as either a middle or last name. Having a common surname in the form of Singh or Kaur served the main purpose of removing caste differences signified by caste based surnames.

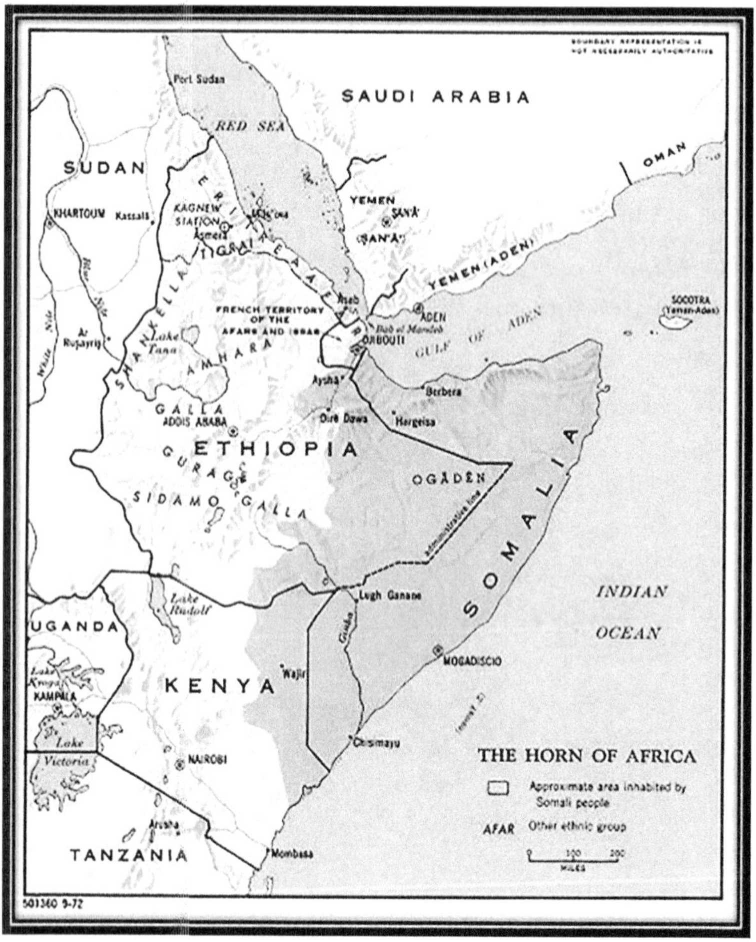

THE HORN OF AFRICA

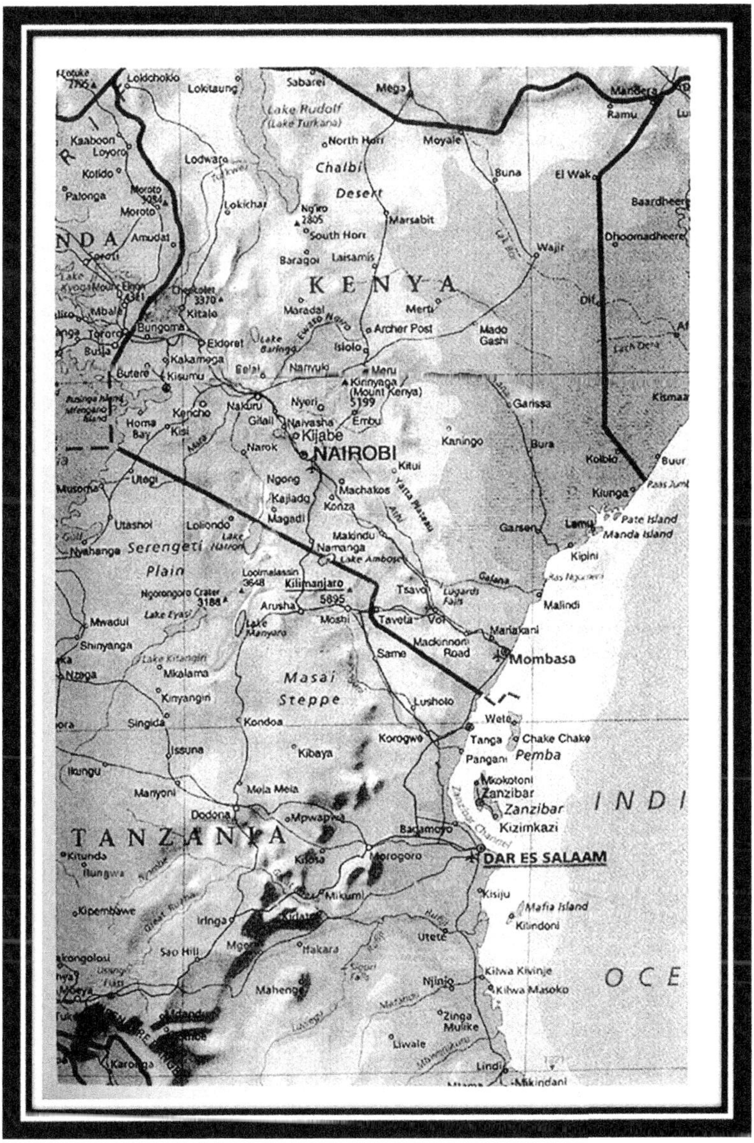

Lokichokio
Lokitaung
Sabarei
Mega
Mandera
Ramu
Lake Rudolf
(Lake Turkana)
North Horr
Moyale
Kaabong
Loyoro
Kotido
Lodwar
Chalbi
Desert
Buna
El Wak
Moroto
Lokichar
Marsabit
Baardheere
Amudat
South Horr
Wajir
Dhoomadheere
Baragoi
Laisamis
K E N Y A
Maralal
Merti
Dif
Kitale
Archer Post
Mado Gashi
Tororo
Bungoma
Eldoret
Lake Baringo
Isiolo
Busia
Kakamega
Meru
Butere
Kisumu
Nanyuki
Kirinyaga
(Mount Kenya)
5199
Nakuru
Nyeri
Garissa
Homa Bay
Kericho
Kisii
Gilgil
Naivasha
Embu
Kijabe
Kaningo
Bura
Narok
NAIROBI
Kolbio
Buur
Kitui
Musoma
Utegi
Ngong
Machakos
Kiunga
Kajiado
Konza
Magadi
Pate Island
Utashoi
Loliondo
Lamu
Manda Island
Garsen
Makindu
Lake Natron
Nyahanga
Serengeti
Plain
Namanga
Lake Amboseli
Kipini
Ngorongoro Crater
3188
Kilimanjaro
5895
Tsavo
Lugards Falls
Malindi
Arusha
Lake Eyasi
Moshi
Taveta
Voi
Mwadui
Lake Manyara
Mariakani
Shinyanga
Same
Mackinnon Road
Mombasa
Mkalama
Nzega
Masai
Steppe
Kinyangiri
Lushoto
Singida
Kondoa
Wete
Tanga
Chake Chake
Korogwe
Issuna
Kibaya
Pangani
Pemba
Mkokotoni
Manyoni
Mpwapwa
Zanzibar
Mkwa Mela
Dodoma
Zanzibar
I N D I
TANZANIA
Bagamoyo
Kizimkazi
Kitunda
Kilosa
Morogoro
DAR ES SALAAM
Mikumi
Kisiju
Kipembawe
Mafia Island
Iringa
Kilindoni
Utete
Hakara
Sao Hill
Kilwa Kivinje
O C E
Mahenge
Njinjo
Kilwa Masoko
Zinga
Mulike
Liwale
Karonga
Lindi
Mikindani

GLOSSARY OF CHARACTERS

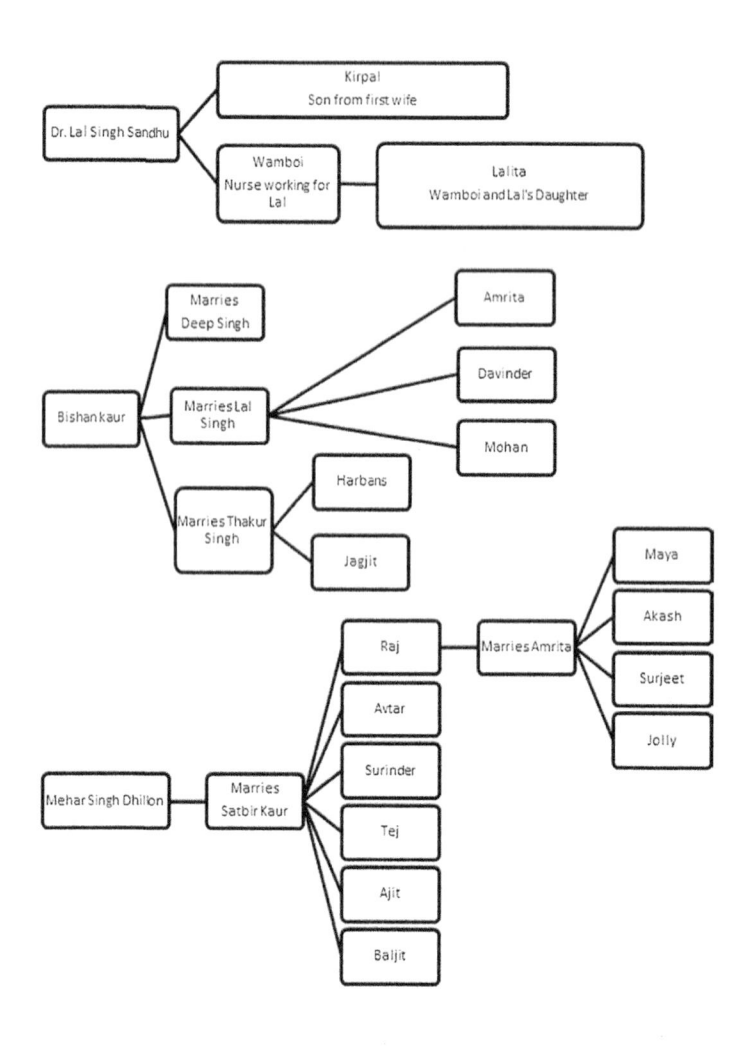

- Dr. Lal Singh Sandhu
  - Kirpal — Son from first wife
  - Wamboi — Nurse working for Lal
    - Lalita — Wamboi and Lal's Daughter

- Bishan kaur
  - Marries Deep Singh
  - Marries Lal Singh
    - Amrita
    - Davinder
    - Mohan
  - Marries Thakur Singh
    - Harbans
    - Jagjit

- Mehar Singh Dhillon
  - Marries Satbir Kaur
    - Raj
      - Marries Amrita
        - Maya
        - Akash
        - Surjeet
        - Jolly
    - Avtar
    - Surinder
    - Tej
    - Ajit
    - Baljit

GLOSSARY OF AFRICAN AND PUNJABI WORDS

Aaram :	Rest
Allah-ho-Akbar:	God is great
Amrit:	Sikh holy water
Anand Karaj:	Sikh wedding
Ardaas:	Punjabi word for a Sikh's prayer
Asante:	Thanks
Askari:	African Policeman
Ayah:	African baby sitter or maid
Baisakhi:	Festival in the Punjab when harvesting is done
Bauld:	Bullock
Beta:	Parents refer to a child
Bhangra:	Vigorous dance in the Punjab
Boma:	Maasai enclosure made of sticks and shrubs
Bui-Bui:	Piece of black cloth worn as a shawl by Moslem women
Chai:	Tea
Chui:	Leopard
Chunni:	A long scarf that is worn by many Indian women on their heads
Dactari:	Doctor
Desi Daru:	Local liquor in the villages
Dhols:	Drums

Dhurra:	Sorghum widely cultivated in Africa and Asia also called Egyptian corn
Dudus:	Termites
Duka:	Swahili word for a small shop
Ek Onkar:	One god
Granth Sahib:	Book of holy Sikh scriptures
Granthi:	Reader of the Granth Sahib
Gurbani:	Sacred hymns
Gurudwara:	Sikh temple
Gyani:	Sikh Priest
In-sha-allah:	God willing
Jambo:	Swahili greeting
Jats:	Sikhs encompassing members of the farmer subgroup
Jibba:	A long coat worn by Moslem men
Kada:	Steel bangle worn on the arm by Sikhs
Kanzu:	Long robe
Karibu:	Welcome in Swahili
Keekar:	Acacia tree
Keffiyeh:	A Bedouin Arab's kerchief worn as a headdress.
Kibui:	Made out of Olive Wood which is stripped clean on the inside and is used to store milk or blood by Maasai
Kirtan:	Sikh Prayers
Kofia:	Caps
Laiboni:	Maasai chief
Lambardar:	Village elder
Lassi:	Butter milk
Makuki:	Maasai spear

Manyatta:	Maasai village
Matatu:	Swahili word for Taxi
Mbogo:	Buffalo
Mehndi:	Henna
Moraan:	Maasai warrior or young man
Mto-wa-Tembo	River of the elephants
Mubarak:	Congratulations and celebrations
Muhindis:	Indians
Mullah:	Muslim priest
Mwanandas:	Maasai cattle auction
Mzee:	Respectable name for an elder
Ngombe:	Cattle
Ol-Dubai	Like a sisal plant
Ol-maati:	Locust
Panga:	A big knife used by tribal natives
Pombe:	Liquor in Swahili
Posho:	Maize
Ramgharia:	Sikhs encompassing members of the carpenter subgroup
Rotees or chapattis:	Round Indian bread made of corn or wheat flour
Rungu:	Round wooden stick like a baseball bat
Saag:	Spinach
Salwar Kameez:	Punjabi dress for women
Sangat:	Sikh congregation
Saree:	Traditional Indian dress
Shabads:	Holy hymns
Shukas:	Cotton sheets
Siangiki:	Young Maasai woman
Sidai:	Good in Maasai

Simba:	Lion
Simmi:	Maasai Sharp knife
Tabla :	Drums
Toba:	Village pond
Toto:	Young boy
Ugali:	Porridge made of maize
Uhuru Sasa:	Freedom now
Wah-e-guru:	Punjabi word praising god as being great
Wanainchi:	Swahili word for locals
Zanana:	Part of a house which is reserved for the women of the household

BOOK I
Doctor Lal Singh Sandhu

"There is one God
He is the Supreme Truth
He, the Creator, is without Fear or Enmity
He, the Omnipresent, pervades the Universe
He, being unborn, cannot die to be born again
Through His Grace, All may worship Him."

THE MOOL MANTRA, GURU NANAK DEV JEE

Amrita was sitting in a rocking chair in the garden outside the red tiled roof house in Pangani, a suburb on the northern side of Nairobi. It was getting hot as the afternoon sun shone brightly overhead, but inside her eleven-year-old heart it felt like dusk. Dark clouds threatened in the distance. She tucked her tan legs and feet beneath her off green skirt and crossed her arms over the sleeveless white top and sweater she was wearing.

"Why don't we go inside," Lalita, her friend, asked her.

She had known her fair skinned Kikuyu friend, Lalita, ever since she could remember while living in Nyeri.

"No, wait, I want to stay out here for a while, it just feels better."

Lalita had come to Nairobi from Nyeri with her mother, Wamboi, as soon as they heard the tragic news of Amrita's father, Lal Singh's death from Doctor Kohli. They wanted to see Lal Singh for the last time and also wanted to be there to console Amrita and her brothers, Davinder and Mohan.

Amrita rubbed her swollen eyes and kept them closed for a moment. She was hurting from all of the crying after seeing her father's lifeless body. Despite her best efforts to curb her grief, the initial shock wave of hearing of her father's passing, refused to ebb. How peaceful his face had been as his head lay on the wooden platform made especially for him. The memory was vivid of the men covering her dad's face and laying his body on the funeral pyre. It was so quiet; she felt so alone. There was no one to look after her now. Her father had been her life. He'd cherished her more than anything he owned. Now, she faced a lifetime without him and the responsibility of caring for her two younger brothers.

The day had started with a typical morning chill, which quickly gave way to the dull, humid heat. As the sun steamed down, her mind kept drifting back to the good days in Nyeri with her father, who spoiled her as best he could. She was so carefree back then, constantly daydreaming.

In Nyeri, she would run into the yard and pause to breathe in the cool, sharp-scented breeze of the African morning. The crested hoopoes would call and the birds flapped leisurely about, hunting worms and lizards on the lawn. She would often end up outstretched in her father's zebra skinned brown leather recliner, staring out of the large picture window toward the snowy, twin peaks of Mount Kenya, in the distance. In the early evening, the houseboy would try to pad soundlessly into the room on bare feet and light the hurricane lamps. She sat there hoping to catch the sunset. It was sometimes called the *"Mountain of the Ostrich"* by the Kikuyus because of the pure whiteness of its crown against the stark blackness of the rocks below which made it look like an ostrich's plumage. Amrita found the contrast of the flat, arid grasslands and sparse wooded plains against the mountain and Kenyan Highlands to be completely mesmerizing.

Amrita was born in Nyeri, a small town about a four-hour drive north of Kenya's capital, Nairobi. Nyeri is situated in the densely populated and fertile Kenyan Central Highlands, lying between the base of the Aberdare Mountain range on the eastern end of the Great Rift Valley and the western slopes of Mount Kenya.

It was here that Amrita's father, Doctor Lal Singh Sandhu, decided to settle and start his medical practice after moving from Somalia in the early part of the twentieth century. Amrita's second-story bedroom allowed her to peer out at the magnificent twin peaks of Mount Kenya as she lay in bed, sometimes gazing at the beautiful landmark for hours on end.

That setting, that house, and that father of hers, were the closest she would ever get to paradise. And now she longed for those happy, carefree days once again. Nights were more difficult as she turned the lamp lower and tucked herself under the colorful, soft quilt that her father had brought from Somalia and lay there feeling stunned and wishing that it was a bad dream. Lalita and Wamboi were leaving early in the morning to go back to Nyeri and that made her sadder, almost wishing to go with them to her birth place. Shadows came creeping and sighing over her bed as she thought of how quickly her whole life had shifted away from under her, never to return.

Amrita's mother Bishan Kaur opened the living room door and shouted,

"Amrita, I was looking for you. Come inside now. It's late and it is cold outside."

"Oh, I will be there in a minute," Amrita responded without looking at her mother.

"You have noticed that everything an Indian does is in a circle, and that is because the Power of the World always works in circles, and everything tries to be round. The Sky is round, and I have heard that the earth is round like a ball, and so are all the stars. The wind, in its greatest power, whirls. Birds make their nest in circles, for theirs is the same religion as ours. Even the seasons form a great circle in their changing, and always come back again to where they were. The life of a man is a circle from childhood to childhood, and so it is in everything where power moves."

BLACK ELK OGLALA SIOUX HOLY MAN

Bishan Kaur Saran, Amrita's mother, was born in Punjab, India in the small village of Jasowal. She was the only child of Harmeet Singh, a Sikh *Jat* farmer. Just turning fourteen, she had grown into a tall and slender beauty, with long black hair, huge tilted eyes with a hint of green, slender nose and a face that was long and perfect in its symmetry. She had inherited the facial features from her father but her complexion and straight black hair were from her mother, Baldev Kaur. Her skin was porcelain and she had a tattoo on her chin shaped with the Sikh *Ek-onkar* sign, which means one god and another bigger one on her forearm with her name written in Punjabi. This was common in India at that time, making girls who got lost or kidnapped traceable. She had been strictly disciplined by her father after she had the sign on her chin engraved, but it was too late to take the engravings off. She had a small gap between her front teeth, just wide enough to make it conspicuously attractive.

Growing up in a small farming village in the Punjab, Bishan and the other children were blessed with a simple, carefree life of plenty in terms of food. Surrounded by fertile farmlands, the village of Jasowal was inhabited by a population of about five hundred Sikhs, Hindus and Moslems. It sits just southwest of Ludhiana, in the uppermost reaches of Northwest India. Narrow and unpaved streets wound their way through the village and between the flat roofed houses and low walled courtyards. Alleys, bordered by gutters overflowed with the slush of brown waste, alternate with still narrower lanes leading to footpaths that ended in the silky wheat fields. To the south, a row of broken mud walls culminated in the village pond, the *toba*, ringed by banyan and acacia *keekar* trees.

The mundane and routine daily life in the small village started as the sun stretched its first rays into the early dawn, so too did the *Mullah* rise, bathe and reach out towards Mecca. His long sonorous notes of *Allah-ho-Akbar*—God Is Great— not only called the faithful Moslems to prayer, but rousted the Sikh *Gyani* from his cot across the street in his *Gurudwara*, the Sikh place of worship. After dousing himself with a bucket of cold water freshly drawn from the courtyard well, he too began his morning prayers. Down the street at the remaining house of worship, and throughout the village before their home shrines, the Hindu residents of Jasowal also began their day. As both ancient history and modern-day newscasts illustrate, Moslems, Sikhs and Hindus have not always lived so simply, even comfortably, side by side. But, as always, children made the exception. Harmeet and all the other villagers were also awakened, like an alarm clock, by the holy men doing their morning prayers.

In any other place and time, Bishan may never have sat together at the feet of the Hindu Brahmin schoolmaster, with her friends, Sharmeen and Hardev, scratching out their daily lessons with nibs of chalk on well-worn slates. In any other place and time they might not have raced together through the village and beyond, flying their single-string paper and bamboo kites which were decorated with shards of colored glass meant for slicing the lines of their competitors. In any other place and time they might not have spent hours chewing on long pieces of grass, watching the dairy cattle graze, or spending spontaneous afternoons watching the boys riding buffaloes into the *toba* pond before they jumped into the tepid, muddy waters, or chased each other to collect peacock feathers.

But in this village, just before the turn of the century, just before the height of British Imperialism and Colonization, the carefree children were free to be children. They were free to revel in their sameness and not their differences, and together they would decide to forge a future none could foresee.

In the mundane life of a Punjab villager, days turned into weeks and months of a routine, that varied little. By mid-morning, the men took to the fields dressed traditionally in either *kurtas*, long, straight-cut loose shirts paired with pyjamas, baggy *salwar* trousers or a type of sarong known either as a *loongi* or *tehmat*. Each proudly displayed his "crowning glory," his turban, indicating his religious affiliation by the way he tied it. The Hindu and Moslem turbans were tied in looser configuration than the Sikhs. In winter, they wore colorful sweaters knitted by wives, sisters and mothers, topped by equally colorful blankets slung over the shoulder.

Meanwhile all Punjabi women, regardless of their faith went about their chores dressed very much alike. They topped their *salwars* with a *kameez*—a versatile garment that could be fitted close like a dress or loose like a *kurta*. Each added a personal touch with her choice of *chunni* or *duppatta*, the difference between the two being merely linguistic, a rectangular scarf draped across their chests and shoulders. Often, in the winter, they used a wide variety of passionately collected woolen shawls to further distinguish themselves. Only the presence of a *kada*—a steel bangle worn on the arm—indicated whether a woman was of a Sikh family.

At lunchtime, Harmeet and all the other men farmers returned home for nourishment, *aaram* and the traditional village hot meal of *rotees* and spiced *saag*, spinach or vegetables. Besides Indian tea known as *"Chai"*, they drank *Lassi*, made from a mixture of warm milk and yoghurt, sometimes sweetened and sometimes salted; always the most popular drink on the farms of India. On a hot sunny day, it was only natural to quench one's thirst with a tall glass of *Lassi*. As the older members of the village congregated on platforms in the shade of the sacred *Peepal* tree, they talked, gossiped and dozed. While their elders rested, boys romped in the lake with their buffaloes or chased kites in the afternoon wind. Young girls played quietly in the shade while their mothers rubbed each other's hair with mustard seed oil. When necessary, they corralled the children to remove lice from their tresses, all the while, never missing a beat in the never-ending song of village gossip.

The setting sun cued the farmers to round up the cattle for their final milking and the women to begin preparing the evening meal, usually a combination of vegetables grown near the wells—carrots, radishes, cabbage and cauliflower—as well as freshly baked *chapatis*, simple fried discs of bread, and warm creamy milk served in large copper tumblers.

In summer, gathered on their rooftops to take advantage of the cool evening breezes, families would await the tones of the Mullah's final *Al-lah-ho-Akbar* of the evening. As the faithful nodded their amen, the Sikh *Gyani* murmured the evening prayer to a semi-circle of drowsy old men and women, while the crows cawed softly from the *Keekar* trees. As it got dark, the stars twinkled overhead, mosquitoes sang through the hot air while the village dogs barked at imaginary adversaries.

Customarily, young girls were married in their early or middle teens and Bishan's father had already been approached by a neighboring village farmer whose son had just turned nineteen and was ready to get married.

Bishan's parents, Harmeet Singh and Baldev Kaur, greeted the men from the neighboring village who had come to finalize the wedding arrangements. As traditions went in Punjab, the arranged marriage had been initiated by a mutual friend, a *bachola*. The ceremony was to take place in three weeks at the village Sikh Gurudwara in Jasowal with Harmeet Singh giving the customary dowry. The groom, Deep Singh worked in the farm with his father along with three of his brothers. He was the youngest brother. Deep was tall and lanky and tied his turban very loosely as if it was going to come off when he took the next step. He had a short beard, dark complexion and deep set brown eyes. Having the older brothers who were married now, he was dominated by their presence, and timidly never looked up when he spoke.

Baldev Kaur, accompanied by the women and girls in the village, had spent the last few mornings practically living at the community *tandoor*, baking piles of *mathians* and *rotees*, small snackable breads for the wedding party. At home, Bishan and the younger girls helped their older sisters mix semolina and lentils with sugar and nuts into baseball-sized sweet *pinias*. The night before, the women got together, singing, dancing and getting *Mehndi* applied to their hands and feet. It is traditional for brides in India to apply different designs of *Mehndi* as a celebratory gesture.

At last, on a dry, bright Sunday as the sun rose on the dusty Punjab, the families and neighbors gathered at the Sikh Gurudwara. The people from Deep Singh's village had turned up to join the wedding party. They were all seated facing the Guru Granth Sahib, the women seated to the left of the groom and the men on the right, in their very best *salwaar kameez* and new shiny *pazaibs*. The groom and bride were seated in the front watching, wide-eyed as the *Gyani* described the Sikh *Anand Karaj* ceremony. The words literally translated as "Blissful union". A Sikh marriage was not merely a physical and legal contract, but a holy union between two souls, that appeared physically as two individual bodies that in fact were united as one.

The trio of long bearded, blue turbaned, *Ragees*, wearing white outfits, sang the *Keetaa Loree-ai Kam*, accompanied by the beat from the *Tabla* drums and the harmoniums, a small keyboard instrument. This Shabad emphasized the Sikh tradition of beginning each new venture followed by *ardaas*, the word being derived from the Persian word '*Araz-dashat*', meaning a prayer and a special request for blessings made by the immediate families of the couple. The mother of the groom had presented the *palaa*, the shawl that joined the couple, and placed it over the shoulder of her son and handed him the right end to hold, before everyone sat down in front of the Guru Granth Sahib. As the Ragis continued to sing, in turn, Harmeet Singh got up and wrapped the shawl around his daughters' shoulders and placed the remaining end of the *palaa* into her hands, signifying the giving of the bride.

The couple performed the traditional four circles around the Sri Guru Granth, while the *ragis* sang the four *lavans* followed by the *Viaa hoa mere baabolaa*. On the fourth *Lavan*, family and friends showered the couple with flower petals. Almost giggling and chatting with her girlfriend, Sharmeen, Bishan accepted the fruit her betrothed fed her and returned the favor, still not quite understanding what she considered to be an elaborate game of dress-up at her tender age. Having witnessed the eating of the shared fruit, the *ragis* concluded with the *Anand Sahib* prayer.

On cue, two young men, dressed in brightly colored and starched turbans and shiny waistcoats, started playing the *dhols*. They feasted, danced, hugged, and even cried, late into the afternoon. Finally, the village elders and family members placed flower garlands on the couple. The newlyweds, Bishan and Deep Singh, touched the feet of their parents and the elders to receive their blessings. The elders patted their heads.

Villagers also blessed them and handed nominal amounts of money, *Shagans*, as token gifts. Amid more tears and hugs from her mother and relatives, Bishan finally climbed aboard the *bauld* drawn buggy destined for a new start in life with Deep Singh. The procession of buggies formed an impressive line as they trekked from one village to the other.

"He who has no faith in himself can never have faith in god."
SRI GURU NANAK DEV JEE

After the two hour ride, Bishan's wedding party arrived at her husband, Deep Singh's village. Her in-laws had gone ahead and were waiting outside. The *Gyani* conducted a prayer before they entered the rustic looking brick fenced compound. The houses in the village were made of clay and wood, the inner walls painted with a mixture of water and coloring. Each room had a simple wooden door, a window and flat roof made of wooden beams. The roofs were used to dry grain and for sleeping in the hot and muggy months.

The mother-in-law poured ghee in the entrance as a sign of good luck before she accompanied them inside, throwing rose petals on the newly married couple. Women sang Punjabi traditional wedding songs to the accompaniment of the *Dholki* drum. The men went out towards the *peepal* trees on the edge of the wheat farm where food was laid out on the wooden tables along with bottles of homemade liquor, *Desi Daru*, traditionally prepared from a procedure that has been passed down in the villages for centuries. It is fermented and distilled from molasses - a byproduct of sugarcane.

Men sang, told jokes, drank and danced the Punjabi *Bhangra*, late into the night, with each other and away from the women. It was close to nine when the women took Bishan to her bedroom and dressed her in anticipation of Deep Singh coming to see her. Bishan sat on the bed with her wedding dress, her heavy gold earrings, a golden *Tikka* in the middle of her forehead and a heavy gold necklace. She waited for what seemed like an eternity and finally dozed off. It was close to midnight when she was woken by Deep Singh stumbling and crawling into the room after having fallen outside the door. His drunkenness and loud breathing scared Bishan. But before she could get up and check, he collapsed in front of the bed and passed out. She undressed herself, disappointed as to how her married life and wedding night had started. She got up in the morning while he was still snoring on the floor and joined her mother-in-law and others in the yard.

"Well, how was it, tell us all about the night," the women teased her.

Bishan quietly kept her head down, careful not to show any emotion or sadness.

The next night was almost a repetition but he did manage to climb and collapse onto the bed before falling asleep. It was almost a week before he lay next to her and touched her and made an effort to consummate the marriage. He fumbled, trying to hug his wife, take her clothes off, not knowing what to do and was unable to perform. Deep had been injured when he was twelve. He had been attacked by a buffalo, protecting her calf, near the village *Toba*. He had survived but not without serious damage to his manhood.

In the villages it was not uncommon when other members of the male family took advantage of the daughter-in-laws or other wives. This had been going on as long as anyone could remember. It was only a question of time before it happened to Bishan. The oldest brother, Gurmail got Deep Singh drunk late one night and came. He barged into the unlocked Bishan's bedroom and closed the door. When she realized that it wasn't her husband, she tried to run out into the courtyard, but he grabbed her by the waist and put his hand on her mouth and raised a finger to his lips telling her to keep quiet.

She fought fiercely with Gurmail, digging her nails deep into his back and scratching his face, pulling on his beard, biting his forearm. She managed to get away and ran to the door but before she could unlock it, he was there and backhanded a slap on her face followed by punches to the mouth and stomach. The tall and muscular, Gurmail, was just too strong and pushed her back onto the bed, holding her hands down. He had done this before and knew what to do, quickly tying a cloth around her mouth. This was her first sexual experience, she tried to scream with the pain but the muffled noise was hardly audible. The stench of stale sweat permeating and the foul smell of alcohol from the man on top made her want to vomit. She closed her eyes. It seemed to go on forever, an endless nightmare of pain and humiliation. When it was over, he mumbled something and rolled over the bloody sheet and out of the bed. He warned her,

"You better keep quiet about this or I will come back and finish you, understand."

He banged the door shut and stepped into the yard. She sat on the edge of the bed, sobbing, trembling, finally getting up after he left and locked the door. She untied the cloth around her mouth. Her clothes were bloody, her body aching, face swollen, pain in her stomach and the lower part of her body completely numb. She wanted to run out and tell someone, her in-laws, anyone, but she knew exactly how they would react and protect their son and probably blame her for something. She managed to get out of bed, cleaned herself slowly, wiped the blood from her wounds and changed clothes.

After a sleepless night and teary eyed, she joined her mother-in-law and other women to make breakfast. Everyone got up early in the villages so they could go to the farms before it was too hot. Her mother-in-law and the couple of other women who were servants looked at her a few times, noticing the bruises and swollen eyes. They knew what had happened, but they carried on with their chores. They weren't going to ask questions and interfere. Bishan knew there wasn't going to be any discussion on this. She was on her own.

Working in the farms, the three older brothers talked and laughed about this and a week later the other brother, Sham, tried to open the locked door. Bishan started locking the door at night and only opened it for Deep.

"Who is it?" She asked.

"This is Sham, I want to talk to Deep, open the door."

"He is not here."

Sham pushed the door open which wasn't very robust and barged in, closing the door behind him.

"If you make any noise, you know what is going to happen. Just let me do what Deep should be doing."

This almost became a weekly routine with Deep Singh staying away and the punches becoming more aggressive and painful whenever she resisted. She wanted to run away but the gates to their compound were always shut and very rarely did her mother-in-law leave the house. The other women were always around helping with the buffalos, milking the cows, sweeping the yard. She had no way of sending a message to her village or the parents. She was imprisoned in her own bedroom and the compound. Her mother-in-law would force Bishan to dress up and accompany her to the Gurudwara once a week on Sunday mornings, but she was never alone there to talk to anyone. Bishan's routine was to help make breakfast, lunch and dinner and serve the men. Then she would do the laundry and in between the chores, stayed in her room. Once in a while, the mother-in-law would ask her to take lunch for the boys in the wheat fields accompanied by one of the other women servants. Food was prepared for the father-in-law and the four boys. The brothers would stare at her, laugh out loud and whisper to each other.

As luck would have it, eight weeks later, her Moslem friend Sharmeen from the village came to visit. She was on her way to Ludhiana and stopped by the village to see Bishan. She was shocked to see the bruises on her arms, legs, neck and face. Her eyes were red and swollen; Bishan just sat, clasping her hands with her head down.

"What is the matter, something is wrong. Tell me?" Sharmeen asked.

"I fell, it was a bad fall. I landed on my face," Bishan brushed it away thinking of the seed that was growing in her womb.

That didn't explain the bruises on the arms and legs. Her hands and feet still had light traces of *Mehndi* from her wedding. But from her tone, Sharmeen knew that something was wrong. On her return to the village, she went straight to Harmeet's house and told him about the visit. After discussing that with his village elders, Harmeet returned to Deep Singh's village accompanied by the village *Lambardar* and others. They sat around the ancient banyan tree, in the middle of the village, where the branches were being supported by pillar like aerial roots, appearing to have shot up from the ground instead of the other way around. One of the elders went to Deep Singh's house and explained why they were there and requested them to bring Bishan with them to the banyan tree.

Harmeet was shocked to see the state his daughter was in. She was limping, could barely stand and was being helped by some women from the village as she approached her father. He tried to speak to Bishan; initially she just kept sobbing and looking away but when he persisted, she broke down with tears running down her fair cheeks. Harmeet walked over and hugged his daughter, holding her up before she collapsed onto her knees. Teary eyed and shaking she begged her father to take her home.

"I am abused physically and mentally on a regular basis, this is not the life I expected. Please, please take me home dad."

The elders spoke to Deep and his father. The father denied that there was an issue at all.

"She is making this all up," he said.

When questioned, Deep had nothing to say, just stood there with his head bowed. But Harmeet knew his daughter wouldn't lie.

Harmeet decided,

"I am taking her back and will return everything you gave us in the wedding. I don't want to see you people anymore and hope god forgives you for what you have done to my daughter."

Deep's father threatened Bishan's father and the village elders but they stood firm and helped her on to the *bauld* drawn buggy and took her home. The baby, a boy, was stillborn, five months later.

"Not everything that can be counted counts,
and not everything that counts can be counted."
ALBERT EINSTEIN

A surgeon, Dr. Lal Singh Sandhu from the Punjab in the north of India had gone to Somaliland on the horn of Africa in the early part of the twentieth century to serve in the British Army. He had been recruited in India by the ruling British, who had colonized most of Eastern Africa. At the time, he was in his late forties and had been practicing medicine successfully for some time.

Lal, born in Punjab, was tall and strong, an erect back, a thin aquiline nose, classic Roman face and eyes that were dark brown and deeply set with neat eye brows. His beard was long, a hint of grey, but always neatly groomed. In the Sikh tradition, he wore a turban, normally white in color, neatly wrapped around his long hair, tucked tightly in a round bun and a thick steel *Kada* on his right wrist.

Lal had made the three day journey by train from his village, Bopa Rai, in Punjab, to the western Indian port of Bombay. The railway system which had been a significant contribution from the British rulers in India linked the four corners of the Sub-continent. The British imperialists had set up an infrastructure in India that enabled them to rule efficiently and effectively. With each stop, the southbound trams were swelling with young men going to Bombay or joining others in seeking to make their fortunes in Africa.

Lal's first image of the vast, picturesque harbor in Bombay was one of bustling with activity. Its docks hosted some four dozen coconut wood and teak masts, emerging from an assortment of dhows and dinghies. The high-peaked triangular lateen sails flapped noisily in the early morning wind. Workers called to one another in half a dozen languages. The whole colorful, upbeat scene mirrored the excitement beating in his heart. He couldn't wait to jump aboard the vessel that would set his life on a brand new course on another continent.

Thirty minutes of winding his way through the maze of piers finally yielded his quest, the boat that would take him to Africa, *Shah-en-shah*. Its captain, Kabir Mohammed, a squat man as broad as a *peepal* tree, with skin the color and texture of the finest teak, barked orders in an accent borne of a life on the sea. He greeted everyone the same:

"You there, bags below, then get yourself up on deck!"

Lal wove his way through the throng of confusion until he finally found the hatch that led him to the sleeping quarters. He searched for a safe place to lay his few belongings and leather medicine case. Then he headed back up on deck where he saw a man heading toward him with a distinct limp that reminded him of his friend, Sati Sharma, from his adjacent village.

"Sati, Sati Sharma,? Is that you?" he called.

The man looked up as he squinted in the brightness, shading his eyes with his left hand,

"Lal Singh? Yes, it's me, my friend."

"Thank God! Am I glad to see you. I don't believe this. Where are you heading?"

"Somalia and Mogadishu," Sati said. "I have a posting there with the government. What about you?"

"I have the same assignment at the British Hospital in Mogadishu! This is awesome!"

Sati was born in Ludhiana in the Punjab to a Hindu family and had an older sister. His father worked for a bank and lived in a moderate two bedroomed apartment just off the GT road in Ludhiana. Sati was quite an athlete playing cricket and hockey till he had the auto accident. He was a teenager in Ludhiana, India, when a bus hit him and damaged his right leg. Sati had been crossing the road to go home when the GT Punjab Express hit him. He was left with an awkward limp ever since. He had a difficult time adjusting but eventually finished school and was accepted into the medical school in Lahore.

Lal and Sati graduated from Lahore Medical School, later named King Edward Medical College. They were working in Punjab in separate towns and villages when they heard about the opportunities overseas. The British rulers actively advertised and promoted the assignments and benefits. Lal and Sati had no hesitation in signing up because of the challenge, adventure and the money.

"You've never been on a boat before, have you?" asked Lal.

"No. Never seen the ocean either," Sati said. "Have you?"

"Sati, my friend, I have had only the same opportunities as you until now. But I've been listening to the other sailors. They talk of a sickness that comes with the waves for all the new hands. I've heard the best way to avoid it is to volunteer to work at night. If we do that, we might gain favor with the Captain, since most of the new recruits still think they should sleep at night. It'll also keep us out of the sun during the hottest part of the day."

"I'm game." Sati chuckled. "I'm so excited, I don't think I could sleep anyway!"

"We're in this together," Lal said. "We'll volunteer for night watch. We'll clean decks, repair sails, shuffle freight around if the seas get bad. Mostly we'll stand around waiting for the Captain to tell us what to do."

He motioned to the main deck. "Ready to head back up? Our belongings will be fine here."

The journey went well, until they were halfway across the Indian Ocean, known in India as "The black water". The first squall struck suddenly and fiercely, pummeling the vessel, and forcing it to rip through the water at breakneck speed. Before the sailors could shorten the sails to reduce the effect of the wind, a gust tore through the lateen sail, rocking the boat and flooding the deck with almost three feet of water. As the current raged, the Captain roared above the howling wind for anyone who wasn't reining in a sheet.

"Bail! Bail! Bail! Quick as you can mates."

It was a mighty struggle to keep the vessel on course. Sharks rammed the boat from various angles, nearly capsizing it. In competition with the wind, a cacophony of fervent voices rose to the heavens, as each man prayed to his own god, in his own language. Within time, their prayers were answered. The storm abated. In silence, the exhausted crew retreated and limped back to their bunks or back to their regular duties.

Lal and Sati gave thanks as they remembered why they'd taken the risk to cross the sea in the first place. Life in India had been good and, perhaps it could have improved, but they wanted something more than the sedate life their fathers and grandfathers had known. They wanted a life they knew was out there, a life that would make the blood in their veins sing, and give them an opportunity to practice the professions they felt stirring in their souls.

Slowly, their days turned into weeks. The night sky grew even more broad and clear as they sailed south. The sun rose and they went to sleep; the sun set and they reported for duty —until the day they approached The Seychelles Islands. They'd been promised a stopover, for supplies and some well-deserved recreation. The archipelago of more than a hundred islands stretching over hundreds of miles in the middle of the Indian Ocean was known as A Paradise on Earth. There, time was meaningless. Its tall, graceful palm trees bent over from the strong winds of the Indian Ocean. Still a thousand miles from Africa, the scenic islands boasted warm waters and a friendly population, graced by beautiful fair-skinned, blue-eyed women.

Finally in port, the friends made their way through the crowded docks, which were overflowing with men selling everything from fish to pearls. Feeling young, impetuous, and invincible, Lal and Sati savored the exotic aromas, flavors, and sensations, both of the food and of the environment. In no time, they had made the acquaintance of a breathtaking bevy of locals, and secured rooms for the four-day layover. It was a glorious time that went by way too fast.

Back out on the sparkling, phosphorescent ocean six weeks later, the vessel hugged the East African coast and turned south around the horn of Somalia. A perfumed wind blew off the desert and brushed the water. They could smell Africa. Before the *Shah-en-shah* turned into port in Mogadishu, the sea changed color and temperament. The ocean lost the sapphire sparkle of deep water and became sullen; the swells were steeper and they ran before the wind in closer ranks. Clumps of seaweed and other flotsam drifted aimlessly with the current. Seabirds hovered over the seething shoals, dove, and splashed for small fish.

Slowly, the ship eased into dock between two taller ships. The white sandy beaches glistened beneath the burning sun, looking like paradise. The rich green landscape on the shoreline was broken here and there by the shining roof of a European-style mansion or the glint of a tin-roofed shed.

On the beach in Mogadishu the mid-afternoon sun was so bright it was as if the aperture of the sun was stuck wide open. From a distance, the ancient port city had an auburn hue, its streets the color of ocher, its rooftops made of Spanish tile and rusted corrugated tin, sunlight glinting off the corrugation. Scrub trees dotted the landscape, and high stone walls were streaked with traces of yellow, pink, and grey. The ornate white towers of mosques towered above everything, acknowledging that Islam was the only religion Somalis held sacred.

Down on the wharf, chaos reined as the sweating workers on ships from many countries hurriedly unloaded cargoes of ironwork, cloth, olive oil, and a multitude of other commodities that were in demand by the Somalis. Standing with the stocky captain, the two Punjabis took in the scene from the deck of the dhow. Sailors, traders, and businessmen from all over the world shouted back and forth in a dizzying array of languages, their only common bond being the money and goods they exchanged. Groups of men, most wearing *Kofia* caps and *Kanzu* robes, sat talking in any shade they could find.

Through an archaed gateway, affluent Somalis sat in their lavish verandah where they could see off into the harbor where lateen rigged dhows bobbed up and down in the shimmering water. Women, some covered head to toe in black *Bui-buis* that revealed little more than their eyes, hastened by and disappeared into the narrow alleyways. A call to afternoon prayer from a nearby mosque echoed over the din of voices, braying animals, and clattering hooves.

Exhilarated, the two friends sensed the unlimited potential and opportunity in this unsettled land. They heard men talking of small fortunes being turned into large ones without ever leaving port. They would have to work hard to build their future. Lal hoped this country would make a better life for him, something he'd dreamed of from the moment he'd heard that he'd been approved as a medical doctor in Somalia.

After unloading their belongings from the dhow, the two split off from the others, wanting to find a place to stay for the night before reporting for duty. Dozens of Somalis sat anchored in the harbor, rocking with the current.

Lal noted that the Somalis were quite tall and wiry in stature, with sharp features, elongated heads, and light brown to black skin. Somali women were generally tall, sharp featured and well-known for their beauty. Unmarried or young women, however, do not always cover their heads. Traditional Arabian garb such as the *Hijab* is also commonly worn. Additionally, Somali women have a long tradition of wearing gold and silver jewelry, particularly bangles. During weddings, the bride is frequently adorned in gold.

Arabs introduced the Islamic faith to Africa beginning in the 7th century. By the 10th century, Arab trading posts thrived in southern Somalia along the Indian Ocean. These included Mogadishu established as the first Arab settlement in East Africa. The city was at the height of its influence and wealth during the 13th century, when it controlled the gold trade on the East African coast.

Most Somalis converted to Islam in the 12th century. They joined with the Arabs in fighting the Islamic holy wars against Ethiopian Christians. By the 18th century the Somalis had defeated the Oromo people, who had threatened both Muslims and Christians in Ethiopia and Somalia. The Somalis became the dominant people of the land.

The two Indian Doctors climbed aboard an oxen-driven cart and set off toward the city. Stunted trees, cacti, and shrubs cast scant shadows along the dusty landscape. Closer to the city, they passed a stream of donkey carts driven by shirtless Somali boys wearing tattered shorts, heading in the same direction. The flat, wooden platforms of the carts were laden with bananas, papayas, watermelons, and bags of charcoal; their large wooden wheels churned up reddish dirt on the unpaved road. They were both a little nervous anticipating the challenge and uncertainty that was ahead of them in Somalia.

Sati looked at Lal and whispered,

"This is so different than our country, I have no idea what to expect."

"Me too, but at least we are together."

*"There is never a time or place for true love.
It happens accidentally, in a heartbeat, in a single flashing,
throbbing moment."*
SARAH DESSEN

On the outskirts of Mogadishu, Lal and Sati ran into a roadblock with a large Somali party of turbaned, bearded men standing around and some sitting on horses and camels. The men looked strong and menacing, with sculptured features, armed with rifles and ammunition belts strapped around their chests. The horsemen had swords and shields tied to their animals, and had formed a sloppy circle. Their leather shields were made from the cured hides of giraffes — the toughest of all wild game, yet not as heavy as that of buffalo or hippos. The round shields were adorned with images, marked only by the blade of the enemy, or the claw and fang of the chase.

Blade-honing was a favorite and essential pastime of the locals, as much a part of their lives as breathing, and more so than eating or drinking. Each blade was sharp, double-edged, and about three-and-a-half feet long. The lightest stroke could split hide and hair, flesh and sinew to the deepest bone. A full stroke could divide an enemy at the waist, cutting him in two as easy as a ripe pomegranate.

The Somalis were stopping everyone, asking where they were from, and where they were going. The Indians grew nervous, realizing something out of the ordinary was about to greet them.

Lal looked at the man in the middle of the armed group, who appeared to be the leader. As the man reined in his steed, he cut a romantic, heroic figure. He held a green turban in his hand. His thick black hair was parted down the middle and drawn into a long plait that hung down to the blue silk sash strapped around the waist of his ornately patched *jibba* — a long, collarless smock worn by Moslems. His neatly trimmed beard was lustrous and wavy, giving him a stark look of distinction.

The leader held the scabbard of his broadsword clamped under his right knee against the saddle; its hilt exquisitely fashioned from rhinoceros horn, its blade inlaid with gold and silver. Under the fine, loose cloth of his bone white *jibba*, his body was lean and wiry, the muscles of his legs and arms like the sinews of a bowstring. He wore a thick and shining golden chain around his neck. His eyes were large and dark, with thick, curled lashes similar to that of a beautiful Somali woman, but his features were rugged and boney, except for his long, fine nose.

When he swung down from the saddle, he stood tall beside his horse's head and stared toward the men and women approaching them from the direction of the harbor.

The Somali riders were travelling with several slave women. One of them knelt before the leader with a dish of water, on which oleander petals floated. The man dipped water from it and made the ritual gestures, then dismissed the woman with a nonchalant wave. Another tall voluptuous slave girl, brought a silver tray with a long-stemmed silver cup, filled with lemon sherbet. He sipped and drank half of it. A third girl knelt to offer him a scented silk cloth with which to dab his lips.

Two of his men shouted and ran toward him, pushing Lal and Sati in front of them.

"Sire, we found these two men," one of them said.

"They are Hindi, and they claim to be doctors. I think they can help us."

"Oh yes?"

The tall Somali leader turned toward the Indians.

"You are medical doctors, is that so?"

Sati answered softly almost whispering, "Yes, we both are."

"I can't hear you."

The Indian repeated and made sure he was loud enough.

"I am Muhammad Abdallah Hassan—"

The instant the man shouted his name Lal recalled all he had learned about the freedom fighter who stood before him. This was an unprecedented time in Somalian history, and this man, Muhammad Abdallah Hasan, had been extremely active in fighting the British.

Born in the valley of Sa'Madeeq, Muhammad Abdallah Hassan rose up to become a prominent religious and patriotic leader in Somali. Referred to as *"Mad Mahdi"* by the British, Hassan established the Dervish State in Somalia that fought the twenty-year Somaliland campaign against British, Italian, and Ethiopian forces.

In several of his poems and speeches, Hassan said the British,

"Have destroyed our religion and made our children their children, and they are bent upon plundering the political and religious freedom of the Somali nation."

He soon emerged as a champion of his country's political and religious freedom, defending it to his supporters against all Christian invaders. He issued a religious ordinance that any Somali who did not accept his goal and would not join his Salihiyya brotherhood would be considered an infidel.

"They call me the Mahdi — messenger of god." Hassan's words snapped Lal back to reality.

"We are fighting the imperialists, the British, who we will get rid of very soon and be free of them forever. My son, Mustafa, has been badly wounded fighting the infidels and needs treatment and quickly. Can you treat him?"

Lal and Sati looked at each other and nodded, realizing their options.

"I have been looking for someone like you," Hassan said. "Both of you, come with us now."

The two Indians peered at each other again, obviously perplexed by the sudden developments, but well aware of their predicament.

"We are physicians," Lal said. "If we can help, we will."

"Time is of the essence, we have to hurry."

Hassan placed his turban on his head and swiftly mounted his tanned stallion in a single, graceful movement. Without a word, the others tightened their girths and did the same. Hassan lifted his rifle with one hand and pointed it at the sky. Grey gun smoke blasted high into the air like the breath of a breaching sperm whale and the sound of the gunshot followed seconds later. A mighty shout went up from the Dervish ranks, "*La ilaha illallah*! There is but one god!"

The echoes shouted back, "*Allah! Allah! Allah!*"

The Somalis mounted their horses and camels. With the cracking of whiplashes they urged their mounts into a gallop. Lal and Sati had never ridden horses in their lives. They struggled to secure their luggage and medicine bags, then got help from the Somalis to mount the creatures. Before they even knew what to do with the reins, the horses galloped off following the Mahdi in a cloud of dust toward the northwest. Several of the Somalis saw the danger and raced up next to the Indians' mounts and grabbed the reins. Eventually, they all came to a stop, including the lead group. As they did, Sati fell from his mount into the dust.

"We have no time to teach them how to ride horses!" the Mahdi shouted.

"I hope they know how to be doctors. Tell them to jump on with the nearest rider, we must hurry, we are losing time."

They ended up sharing horses with the Somalis, winding down the slope of the valley, traversing through the open Savannah, where the stately, flat-topped acacias stood along the banks of the Shabelle River. They had ridden a couple of hours under the hot midday sun when they dismounted beside one of the deep green pools. The elephants had been there before them, filled their bellies with water, and then bathed riotously, hosing powerful jets from their trunks over their backs and into the surrounding sandbanks. The large animals had scooped up the thick black mud and plastered it on their heads and backs as protection against the sun and the swarms of biting insects. The ground was marked with large piles of bright and fresh yellow dung on the sandbank. The Somalis filled their water skins and rested in the shade as the horses drank, then mounted up and followed the trail through the open acacia forest.

They entered the desert and, as luck would have it, one of the nastiest *khamseen*, a dry, hot, sandy windstorm, in years began to blow through. This one filled the air with fine red sand that covered everything in its path. Everyone rushed to cover their faces with scarves, blankets, and anything they could get their hands on. The lucky ones had goggles over their eyes and striped head-coverings known as *keffiyeh* tied around their throats and covering the faces. Areas of exposed skin felt as if it was being scoured raw by the stinging grains of sand. The riders gathered in a circle, their horses bucking, trying to look for cover, but there wasn't any. They were forced to duck down and hold on until the *khamseen* subsided.

After what seemed like forever, the wind hushed. Their mouths were filled with sand, their noses stuffed with it, and a rancid odor hung in the air. They dusted off best they could and began to ride again. For two hours they made their way through the desert and sand dunes, which were soft and fleshy, the color of pale ivory, and difficult to traverse.

There was not the faintest hint of greenery anywhere. The sand sparkled like a trove of diamonds when the sun caught the grains of silica in it. Eventually, out of the shimmering heat, a mirage resembling a range of blue hills rose up before them. As they drew closer, Lal saw tucked away amongst the rugged hills a startling green garden. There were groves of palms and orange trees. He thought for a moment that he was seeing things. Beds of melon and maize were irrigated from furrows of running water. The Dervish village was just across the river and in the shade of a hillock.

Their spirits lifted as they made it to the riverbank, but then they realized they had to cross the river; the current was swift, and the body of water was wide. The lead Somalis rode up and down along the bank, evaluating the depth, and descended into the water until they found a shallow area where they were able to cross safely.

The collection of huts looked like exaggerated anthills. They were made of wattle, woven into mat-type structures with covers on top, and supported by sticks acting as pillars. Each hut had one door, all of four feet high, and was surrounded by a tall fence made out of acacias and thorn trees. Lal and Sati later found out these were portable homes that could be set on a camel's hump and moved to different pastoral areas. The huts provided shelter for babies, shade from the midday sun, and storage space for fresh milk. When the migration took place, the babies and small children rode on top of the camels alongside the portable huts. The collection of huts, *bomas*, was surrounded by high thorn fences.

To the west of the complex, there were camels tied in two corrals — one for females and one for the young; this was to prevent the young from drinking all the females' milk as they fed each morning. Up on the steep hillside were many stone buildings. Atop the largest of these was the distinctive cupola and minaret of a mosque. Adjoining this was a large, shapeless building which sprawled down the slope, seemingly without design or purpose. This was the Mahdi's residence.

When they reached the compound, its gates opened from within and the journeymen rode through a paved courtyard, in the center of which grew a tall acacia which shaded a small group of veiled women and young children. Upon their arrival, a number of male slaves in long white robes ran down to meet them with baskets of cool damp clothes for them to refresh themselves. Pitchers of milk and orange juice sherbet were passed about.

Lal knew that milk from camels, goats, and cows was a major food for Somali herdsmen and nomadic families. Young men tending camel herds during the rainy season drank up to five quarts of milk a day. At times, aging camels were slaughtered for their meat, especially when guests were expected for a celebration. The fatty camel's hump was considered a delicacy.

Meat, including liver from sheep and goats, was also popular, but Lal knew meat was only served several times a month, usually on special occasions. He learned later that some of the main food staples for nomads included honey, dates, rice, tea, and a grain sorghum known as *durra*.

Farmers in southern Somalia grew corn, beans, sorghum, millet, squash, and a few other vegetables and fruits. Boiled millet and rice were staples, but the rice had to be imported. The most popular bread was *muufo,* a flatbread made from ground corn flour. Somalis were known to season their food with butter and ghee, the clear liquid skimmed from melted butter. They also sweetened foods with sugar, sorghum, and honey. A holdover from Italian occupation in the south was a love for pasta and marinara sauce. Although fish was plentiful in the waters off the Somali coast, the locals generally did not care for fish. In accordance with the Muslim faith, they did not eat pork or drink alcohol. Milk, tea, coffee, and water were favorite beverages.

"Hurry, get the doctors to Mustafa," the Mahdi shouted.

Lal and Sati were rushed to the flat roof of a house where a man was lying on a low *angareb,* a bed frame traditionally made of wood, having four legs with the sleeping part of bed made of a woven rope. The bed was covered with a silk prayer rug and strewn with cushions.

Five scowling guards stood around him; they wore Dervish *jibba* and were armed with swords and rifles. A screen of reed matting covered the terrace to shield out the sun, but the sides were open, enabling the cool breeze from the river to blow through, and provide a view of the vast plain beyond. The man cringed in pain every time he moved. A thick bandage caked in dried blood was wrapped below his left shoulder.

The Mahdi rushed in.

"Now, Hindi, do what you are supposed to do. Just make sure he is alive by tomorrow. If not, you will be joining him."

"Who are these people?" the wounded man whispered, in obvious pain as he tried to lift himself from the couch.

"Mustafa, my son, they are Hindi doctors," the Mahdi said. "They are on their way to Mogadishu to work for the *ferengis*. We brought them to look at your shoulder. *In-sha-allah*, they will take care of you. Not to worry."

The young Indian doctors looked at each other and wanted to pray. The Mahdi stood behind them and Lal could almost feel the heat from his body.

"We need water," Sati blurted. "To wash our hands. Hot water for him, too."

"And we'll need some clean sheets as well," Lal addressed the Mahdi.

"Let them have whatever they need — and quickly, hurry, hurry," the Mahdi said.

The Indians examined the wound and spoke softly to each other. A bullet was entrenched deep in his shoulder. It had to be removed, soon.

The Mahdi headed for the exit.

"Just make sure when I come back, I want to see you, and my son — alive!"

> *"I'm so fast that last night
> I turned off the light switch
> in my hotel room and was in bed
> before the room was dark."*
>
> **MUHAMMAD ALI**

The Mahdi returned to his enclosure the size of a small village known as a *zanana*, where all the women in his harem lived. There was only one gate leading into the *zanana*, which was enclosed by a ten-foot wall of mud and brick. Inside the compound were a number of thatched huts housing all the Mahdi's wives, concubines, children, slaves, and servants. The women were fed from the communal kitchen, but it was a monotonous diet of *dhurra* grain and river fish fried in ghee, clarified butter, and blindingly hot chili.

The women were classified as senior wives and ranked concubines. The senior wives had up to three female house slaves to attend to them, and were privileged to have their food, such as large fish, caught and brought to them straight from the river. They were treated to calabashes of soured milk, bowls of wild desert honey still in the comb, the most tender cuts of mutton, legs of venison, live chicken, and fresh eggs served in generous portions.

It was not possible for a Somali woman to arrange her hair alone. It was a social enterprise that involved all her close companions. The styling was elaborate and could take two or three days of patient, skilled creation. First, the hair had to be combed out. It was usually wiry, matted, and twisted into tight curls from its previous dressing. A long skewer was used to separate the strands. Then a coarse wooden comb was used to bring some order to the dense tresses. The hair was then twisted into tiny tight plaits and set with a liberal application of Arabic sticky gum and *dhurra* paste. This was allowed to dry until it was stiff as toffee. On the final day, each tiny plait was carefully unpicked with the long tortoise shell skewer and allowed to stand on its own, free and proud, so the woman's head appeared twice its normal size. In ten days, the process would be repeated.

The Mahdi had the privilege of selecting a wife from his harem that he wanted for the night. The selected woman felt honored. She would be washed and dressed with new clothes and jewelry by their slaves, and delivered to his quarters. If he liked a particular concubine, then she was asked to come on a regular basis until he decided otherwise. Once he decided he didn't care for a particular concubine she would end up spending the rest of her life in the *zanana* with her children. She would probably die without ever seeing him again or leaving the compound. The Mahdi loved his harem; women fascinated him, and he spent as much time as possible with them. Women were dazzled by his height, his grace, his fine features, his perfume, and the angelic smile that disguised his true emotions.

The Mahdi had been thinking about Jamila for the past twenty four hours, and requested her presence. She was the newest teenaged concubine from the south of Sudan, a gift from one of the Somali war lords. Her six-foot frame with unusually long legs, gorgeous facial features and soft skin was not unusual for that tribe.

The Mahdi headed toward his private living quarters. The massive entrance was heralded by a tall pair of elephant tusks, mounted on the far wall. The rest of the living room walls were covered with magnificently woven Persian and Turkish carpets, and dozens of murky yellowing photographs in dark wooden frames. More thick carpets covered the floors and situated romantically within a curtained recess sat a large *angareb* bed, spread with golden leopard skins, dappled with black rosettes. A row of rifles and muzzle-loading guns stood on a rack between the curves of the thick yellow tusks, and an array of double-edged swords were displayed as well.

Hassan kicked off his boots, laid back on the vast *angareb*, and sipped fresh pomegranate juice, his heartbeat kicking up a notch as he licked his lips and awaited the entrance of the young Sudanese woman, Jamila.

Mustafa was in tremendous pain; not surprising given the damage a gunshot wound causes to the shoulder. Lal and Sati were fortunate to have morphine and ether in their medical bags. Lal gave the man a dose of each, and very soon it calmed Mustafa considerably. Sati cleaned the wounded area as best he could and sterilized the medical instruments with alcohol.

Lal performed an incision around the wound and found the location of the bullet. To their pleasant surprise, it remained outside the humerus. The axillary artery and major nerves were spared. Lal expanded the incision and slowly with his soft and experienced hands removed the bullet using tweezers. It turned out to be a .303 caliber rifle bullet that had lodged just below the right collarbone. Lal used the needle to suture the wound, sewing it into a ten-point star before pulling it closed, which would allow it to heal more quickly. Sati added more alcohol and bandaged the wound with medical gauze to keep it clean. After several more doses of morphine, Mustafa had calmed down considerably. He was groggy and began dozing off. Temporarily, his arm was going to be of little use and would remain in a sling for many weeks.

Lal and Sati looked at each other and breathed a long sigh, washed their hands, and collapsed on the nearest chairs. They would live to see another day. After a couple of hours rest, they called for the Mahdi to come and see for himself.

A runner delivered the good news to the Mahdi's quarters that Mustafa would live, but would need extensive rehabilitation. The leader, wearing no clothes, dropped to his knees, faced Mecca, and gave thanks to Allah. He abruptly dismissed the young woman from the *zanana*, got dressed, and rushed back to where his son was sleeping. The two doctors came out to greet Hassan, whose arms were outstretched; he hugged them warmly. The doctors told him Mustafa would be waking soon and they asked him to wait outside. He said he would, but also said he needed to see Mustafa before he was convinced the doctors had done their job well. They sat down on the long sofa covered with smooth blankets and soft animal skins. Hassan told the male slave to get some fresh fruit juices for everyone.

A tall, scantily clad black Nilotic slave girl brought the hookah and placed it in front of the Mahdi, who was restlessly waiting to talk to his son. Slavery in Somalia existed as a part of the Arab slave trade. To meet the demand for menial labor, Bantu tribesmen from southeastern Africa captured by Arab slave traders were sold in cumulatively large numbers over the centuries to customers in Somalia and other areas in Northeast Africa and Asia. People captured locally during wars and raids, were also often enslaved by Somalis.

With silver tongs, the girl — who was barely in her high teens — lifted a live coal from the clay fire pot and placed it carefully on top of the black tobacco packed into the bowl of the pipe. She sucked on the ivory mouthpiece until the smoke flowed freely, coughing on the powerful fumes before she passed the mouthpiece to her master. The water in the tall glass jar bubbled blue as he drew the smoke through it deep into his lungs and held it while passing the mouthpiece to Lal.

Lal held his hands in front of his face and politely said,

"I am sorry, I don't smoke. It is against my Sikh religion."

"What religion? I don't understand this, everyone smokes," the Mahdi said.

"Who are these Sikhs? They don't smoke? How about your friend, is he a Sikh too?"

Sati, a Hindu, wanted to avoid confrontation with the unpredictable Somali.

"I will try it," he said.

Sati took the pipe, puffed several times, and then bent over coughing as he politely passed the Hookah back to the Somali leader.

"Sire," a slave girl appeared from Mustafa's bedside. "Your son is awake. He tried to get up, but we need him to stay still. Can you come see him?"

Hassan was on his feet in a split-second. He rushed over and sat next to Mustafa, holding and caressing his hand. He looked up at the ceiling and shouted,

"*Allah-u-Akbar*! Thank you my god for saving my son, my life."

He called the doctors over.

"You have done well gentlemen! My son lives and I can't thank you enough. You know that now you have saved your lives too. How long before he can ride by my side against the *ferrangi* Europeans?"

Lal thought about it, because he wanted to answer the question carefully, knowing the Mahdi would hold him to it.

"His wound was quite deep," Lal said, "We were lucky in getting the bullet out. But the recovery will take a while. He is going to be just fine. It will take several months."

"*In-sha-allah*," Hassan said. "If that is god's wish, then let it be."

The Mahdi pointed a finger to an older man with a long white beard and loosely tied turban; he was the person who looked after the valuables.

"Ibrahim, go and get two good-sized clear diamonds and give one to each of these Indians. They saved my son's life and deserve a gift."

Lal and Sati looked at each other and smiled. Maybe it was all worth it.

"Now, you two will be able to go, my guards will accompany you to the city." Hassan said.

"I wish you well on your journeys and god willing I won't see you or need your services again."

The Indians were fed bowls of roasted goat, fresh dates, oranges, pomegranates, and a jug of lemon sherbet, and then they were escorted to some horses. They rode with two of Hassan's Somali men to the outskirts of the city, collected their belongings and began walking the rest of the way to Mogadishu.

"Thank god, I thought we would never get away from them," Lal spoke to Sati.

"We were very lucky, he would have killed us if we could not save his son," Sati replied as he sighed.

Somalis affectionately remember Muhammad Abdallah Hasan as the instigator of bloody interclan warfare. He was also the defender of their cultural and religious authenticity as well as the proto-nationalist hero of their anti-colonial resistance. His powerful poetic legacy proved that he was all of this, and more. In his farewell poem he wrote, "If I failed to have a flag flown for me from here to Nairobi, did I fail to win honor in paradise ..."

*"I just want to do god's will.
And he's allowed me to go to the mountain.
And I've looked over, and I've seen the promised land!
I may not get there with you, but I want you to know tonight
that we as a people will get to the promised land."*
DR. MARTIN LUTHER KING, JR.

On the outskirts of the city, Lal and Sati walked through a conglomeration of shacks and hovels, each had thatched and corrugated iron roofs. The walls were built of sun-dried clay bricks and painted in a motley array of colors. Strolling the streets of Mogadishu, the tired Indians could still hear the constant roar of the Indian Ocean, breaking over the coral reef. Walking beneath the coconut palms, they felt the fresh sea air, tainted with the faint scent of the brilliant purple bougainvillea that grew in proliferation in the rich African soil.

Tall men in long white gowns like nightshirts screamed admonitions in an unfamiliar language as the nearly naked Somali boys shouted insults in return as they scampered about. Local Moslem women, veiled in black and swathed head-to-toe black *buibuis,* appeared mysterious and exotic. They lounged beneath the mango trees, listening to the eerie melody coming from an Arab flute played by a local musician somewhere nearby. Pushcarts were loaded impossibly high with bananas, bricks and melons. A veiled stooped old woman walked by with a smoldering charcoal stove on her head. Although the features of the Moslem women were veiled, one could feel their sensuousness. This clashed with the raucous noise from the wharves, just as the stench of rotting fish vied with the smell of fresh coffee drying in the sun, and the cloying sweetness of jasmine. The air was hot and thick with humidity and, getting deeper into the city, the air was tinged with a faintly foul odor.

Although Lal and Sati had been accustomed to cramped spaces in India, the narrow alleyways and overhanging balconies seemed to box them in from all sides. The towers and minarets of the mosques rose high above the lower buildings, proclaiming the heavy Arabic influence on the island.

In the center of the city, where the alleys narrowed at points to the width of a man's shoulders, you could walk as if in a dream, never certain of what might appear around the next sharp bend. It could be a bare-chested man with a silver swordfish flung over his thin black back, or a shoal of children reciting the Quran from their wooden slates. Through the confined passageways, scores of Arab traders moved slowly, jamming the alleys with donkey trainers, hand-pulled carts, and caravans of camels moving no more than two abreast. In these close quarters, the smells of animals mixed with those of dried fish, curry, cinnamon, and unleavened bread baking in nearby houses and shops left an indelible mark on the senses.

Some of the larger houses, belonging to the elite in Mogadishu, had intricately carved wooden doors that were arched at the top; some had been transported all the way from Zanzibar. The salt air from the Indian Ocean caused the white wash on the concrete buildings to flake. They passed Somali women, tall and graceful in their walk, clothed in brightly colored ankle length dresses, heads and shoulders covered with transparent scarves.

Finally, they came across a sign indicating "Rooms Available." After bargaining for what they considered to be a fair rate, Lal and Sati checked into the small, rusty building. The Punjabis chose to share the small room with two beds. Indeed, any sort of bedding would be luxurious after the journey on the dhow. Completely exhausted, they wasted no time in cleaning the sea from their bodies and washing clothes with water they brought up in buckets from a courtyard well. Once clean, they descended on the town in search of sustenance. Wandering through the narrow streets, the sweet, tangy smells led them to a small café where they tasted their first African meal and raised their glasses to the new continent, which would now be their home.

The next morning, after a traditional Somali breakfast of eggs, beans, and local *injera* bread, they headed off to check out their assignments with the British. Again, the sky was bright and watery turquoise blue. Somali men sleeping by the roadside began to rouse, their afro hairstyles full of sand. Some men walked hand-in-hand wearing large threaded turbans and beautiful ivory daggers in their belts, as they hustled to the markets on camels. Men and boys shuffled past ferrying all kinds of things on their heads and in their hands, from fruits and vegetables, to breads and meats, and crusty loaves of flatbread tucked under their arms like newspapers hot off the press. Butterflies danced about, enjoying their morning flutter before the day turned unbearably hot.

The doctors reported for duty at the British Army barracks where the King George Hospital was set up. The high rock wall enclosed the hospital grounds and hid the buildings from the road. Eucalyptus towered over the wall, and where there was no eucalyptus there were firs and jacaranda and acacia. Green bottle shards poked up from the mortar at the top of the wall to dissuade intruders, robbery and petty theft being rampant in the city, though the site of roses lapping over the wall softened this deterrent. The wrought iron gate covered with sheet metal was normally kept closed, opened by a guard, and pedestrians were admitted through the smaller, hinged door in the gate. Across the garden, there were bougainvillea and camphor trees. The veranda was filled with many huge pots of colorful flowers.

The facility housed seventy five beds with a large lush garden on the sides and in the backyard. There were ten Somali nurses and four doctors were already there, two from England, one from Ireland, and one from Wales.

"We have been waiting for the both of you for some time now, we are very busy and need all the help we can get," Doctor Gareth Williams, the Welsh chief of staff at the hospital greeted them.

Lal and Sati were each assigned lodgings that included a bedroom, kitchen, small bathroom and a living area. The living rooms had couches in the middle that were slanted, as if dropped there by accident. The rooms were hot and smelled musty. Everything was coated in a layer of dust. The bedrooms featured a bed, chest of drawers, a small table and loosely carpeted floors. The Indians shopped for pans and utensils, and then found a store run by an Indian Gujarati where they picked up a variety of spices; soon they were cooking their own meals and some limited Indian dishes. The evenings were warm and relaxing, air carrying the repetitive croaking of frogs and the scents of jasmine and dust.

Their medical assignments were fairly routine, treating locals, British Consulate staff, and British soldiers for everything from common colds and bullet wounds, to cholera, malaria, and sicknesses requiring minor surgeries such as appendectomy, peptic ulcers, hernia repairs and subtotal thyroid resections.

Lal and Sati were excited to receive their first paychecks. Most of the money was sent home to support their families in India. Lal had been married, with two sons, until an epidemic swept India and took his wife and older son. His younger son, Kirpal, a toddler at the time, was now being cared for by Lal's brother. The plan was for Lal to settle down in Africa then return and take Kirpal back with him.

As a surgeon, Lal was well known for his speed, courage, daring, boldness, inventiveness, and calmness under duress. These were skills he'd honed on a trusting and uncomplaining population, briefly in India and then refined in Somalia.

During their stay in Mogadishu, the two friends took excursions to smaller towns surrounding the capital, especially when they were invited by friends and patients. The Somali houses were irregularly strewn on the bare ground and looked as if they had been nailed together with a bushel of four-inch nails to last for a week. It was a surprising thing, when you entered one of them, to find vessels of brass and silver, and swords with ivory hilts and noble blades and scented with Arab incenses. The Somali women themselves, had dignified, gentle ways and were hospitable and happy. For transportation, they had little grey donkeys while some had camels.

When Lal and Sati were invited to a Somali wedding as guests of honor they learned that wedding ceremonies were not primarily about the bride and groom in Somalia; they focused more on the extended families. The couple being married — an intern named Suleiman and his bride Farida — took a backseat to the two heads of the families.

The wedding had two parts: *Nikah* was the ceremony, and *Aroos* was the party. According to Islamic law, the ceremony was to be performed by a Muslim Sheikh. It was essentially a marriage contract between the families of the bride and groom. The marriages in Somaliland are arranged by the elders of the families with consideration as to the birth, wealth and reputation of the young people. In the best families the bride and groom do not see one another till the wedding day. The main part of the contract covered the bride's price, which the groom's family paid. The dowry, *Meher*, was given by Suleiman to Farida as her personal possession. The bride's price included camels, goats, and clothing. It reminded Lal of his wedding, which was quite similar, except for the contract.

When Lal and Sati arrived at Farida's house, her extended family had already gathered. The men were talking in the living room, while the women sang and danced at a neighbor's house. Meanwhile, the bride was in a bedroom opposite where the men gathered; several close friends were with her, doing make-up and hair. Other women prepared snacks for the wedding party, including a table of sweets and pastries set up out in the yard. A typical dish for a Somali wedding was the Somali *Halwa*, a sweet, oily confection served on biscuits.

As the groom's family arrived along with the Sheikh, the women gathered in the yard to offer a song of welcome. Interestingly, some of Farida's extended family members were not pleased with the price for the bride and were arguing for more. The bride stayed in the bedroom out of sight but close enough to hear any discussion from the men. The elders gathered around the Sheikh. There was some negotiation and eventually an arrangement was reached. The Sheikh sat down with the men and confirmed the details of the wedding contract, drafted a document and read it aloud. This pronounced the marriage, which was followed by a prayer of blessing.

After soft drinks and snacks were distributed, and the groom's family made their exit, the bride's *Abti*, maternal uncle — who served as a sort of godfather in the arrangement — reported to Farida on the ceremony and informed her that she was now married. The celebration party took place that same evening. Being quite religious, Farida opted to have only women at the party. She wore a traditional Somali white *guntino* dress, specially made for a bride, along with beaded jewelry with her hair let down. Female guests wore colorful dresses and scarves. Farida sat in a chair in front of the room watching her guests dance, feast, and celebrate. Toward the end of the evening, Suleiman showed up to pick up Farida and take her home before they left on their honeymoon. Lal and Sati congratulated the newlyweds and headed for home.

*"Clouds come floating into my life,
no longer to carry rain or usher storm,
but to add color to my sunset sky."*
RABINDRANATH TAGORE

After four years working in Mogadishu, Lal was growing impatient and somewhat fed up with his British subordinates, who treated him as inferior, even though he was the best surgeon on the team. Lal was extremely busy as he could successfully perform most surgical operations. His disrespectful British counterparts even had the audacity to call him a "wog," a derogatory word for people with dark skins. The British had made the term popular in India where they ruled over the dark-skinned people. Needless to say, Lal was ready for a change of scenery.

That's when he received a letter from his old friend Ram Chand from Nairobi, telling him about an exciting opportunity for a surgeon to start a new practice in the small town of Nyeri, Kenya. Ram had graduated from the same medical college with Lal in India, moved to Kenya, and ran his own practice in the capital. The timing was amazing and Lal's heart leapt with hope when he read the letter. He grabbed pen and paper, and immediately wrote back to Ram that he could be in Nyeri in two months. Sati was disappointed to hear the news,

"I am going to miss you. Now I have to deal with these arrogant British guys on my own."

"Let me get to Kenya, surely I will find a place for you there," Lal assured him.

Lal packed up and boarded an Arab boat that would ultimately take him from Mogadishu to the coast of Kenya but first it went south to the island of Zanzibar, just off the coast of Tanganyika, north of the capital of Dar-es-Salaam, then north onto Mombasa.

Lal had read some history on Zanzibar. It was an old stone town that jutted into the Indian Ocean. Beyond its coral houses were many mud-and-thatch dwellings. Zanzibar was also a center for exploration, as men like Livingstone, Stanley, Burton, and other western explorers recruited porters and guides, as well as stocked up on supplies and trade goods. Then they set off in search of the source of the River Nile.

Long before the Kenya-to-Uganda railway and its world famous man-eating lions, a railway line in Zanzibar had run on the lure of beautiful women fetched from afar to entertain an erotic Arab Sultan. The fourteen kilometer line, which ran from the Sultan's palace at Stone Town to Chukwani had 'trains' and Pullman cars, pulled by mules until the steam tank locomotives imported from India came onto the scene.

Located meters away from the sea to take advantage of the abundant breeze, the Mahrubi palace had several bedrooms for women and a sitting room where they assembled after bathing in any of the compounds three swimming pools. Women selected by the sultan for the day's sexual pleasure bathed in one pool, then another for further clean up, before heading to a room upstairs where the Sultan would be waiting after his massage and exercise session.

Standing at the harbor, Lal realized he had been daydreaming as a haze drifted over the shimmering sea. Half a dozen small dhows were beached below with their sails down, waiting for the tide to rise. A covered cart pulled by a donkey loaded with salt, creaked its way across the wet sand to meet them. Men in long white robes and some with bunches of bananas on their shoulders dashed through the narrow streets. Other men pulled rickshaws with tourists or locals aboard who could afford to be whisked through the narrow alleys. Come evening, Lal thought, those dhows would rise with the tide and sail for Mombasa, Pemba, and other destinations.

Lal learned a lot on his journey, and was determined to soak it all in. Several days later, he finally arrived in Mombasa, a peninsula connected to the mainland of Africa by a precarious looking causeway with its main port of Kilindini. Mombasa was the largest city in Kenya at that time. As the boat slowly approached its final destination, after seven days on the Indian Ocean, the view of Kilindini harbor was stunning. Green coconut palms and a scattering of white buildings emerged in the near distance.

The ancient Portuguese fort was accented by clusters of palm trees. Hundreds of black porters, some in red fez hats, thronged the harbor, along with white traders in sharp-peaked caps. Kenya's most solid monument, Fort Jesus, was the focal point of the landscape, having been built by the Portuguese at the end of the 16th century. Lal soon learned about the fort's gruesome history of sieges, captures, recaptures, massacres, and murders, which punctuated three centuries of struggle between the Arabs and the Portuguese for possession of Mombasa and the East African coast.

As Lal disembarked the sailing vessel, everything around him was fresh and green; the island had an oriental glamour about it. The old town was bathed in brilliant sunshine and reflected itself lazily on the motionless sea. Its flat roofs and dazzlingly white walls peeped out dreamily between waving palm, lofty coconut, and flourishing mango trees.

The harbor, dotted with the white sails of Arab dhows, soaring like the wings of huge prehistoric birds, and the tropic surroundings brought to mind visions of stirring adventures and the reckless doings of pirates and slave-traders. The port was full of cargo vessels and fishing dinghies, their flat decks hung with curled, drying shark meat or buckets of eels. The smell of fish, of salt and acrid wood smoke and sewage blended with dust and dung throbbed in the air. Lal wanted to get to Kilindini, "*the place of deep waters*," and search for the Mombasa trolleys, which shuttled passengers from port to the railway station, propelled by teams of chanting Africans in sailor suits. Everyone knew of the trolleys and Lal soon found them — six small wagons rattling on narrow-gauge rails, each topped by a striped canvas sun roof, and seating passengers on back-to-back benches facing fore and aft.

Baggage in hand, Lal jogged alongside, and then hopped on board as the trolley coasted by. The overloaded wagon glided away toward the railway station at Kilindini. Lal was joined on the trolley by a large group of English pioneers. He came to find out they had traveled from Britain on another ship with the hope of buying land in the Kenyan highlands, and starting new lives as farmers.

The British, with Lord Delamere leading them, had begun allocating the prime farm land to British settlers, while Indians were forbidden by the British government from buying any land in the highlands. Delamere had arrived in Kenya in the late 1890's and managed to get a lease on one hundred thousand acres of land near Naivasha. He started cattle and sheep ranches as well as dairy farms. Delamere soon became an influential leader for the British farmers in Kenya and communicated directly with the home offices in England. He was a keen hunter and was mauled by an attacking lion. As a result, he limped for the rest of his life. He is also credited for coining the term "white hunter".

The Indians were only allowed to buy land within the town centers. It struck Lal as ironic that the British had brought more than thirty thousand Indian coolies to East Africa to build the railway, during which, thousands of them had died on the job. The British had allowed the better caste of Indians to set up in businesses, but they were denied the real riches: land. The Kenyan highlands, later known as the "White Highlands", were cool, green, healthy, and ideal for farming wheat and raising sheep, with the potential to grow tea and coffee at the right altitude.

The peninsula of Mombasa waited for Lal and the other passengers like a dusty toad resting by the side of the road, low and wide. Sewage, spoiled food, and old garbage gave up their odors. A nearby well, already burdened with unmentionable contributions, was filled to the brim with thick shark oil, useful for hardening work boots and protecting the bottoms of Arab dhows against boring worms.

The trolley dropped its passengers in the main street near the railway station. As soon as they stepped down, they were engulfed by native Indians and Arabs rushing to sell their wares. A tall, handsome Arab, with a beard so red with henna that it looked like blood, burst through the crowd and guided the passengers to a canopy of shade in an alley off the main road. He was chewing and spitting out jets of red betel nut into the street, barely showing his gold-trimmed teeth,

"My name is Sultan," he whispered.

"I have to show you something, you will like it. It won't take long. You won't be sorry."

Dave, the tall Englishman, said to the others with a heavy cockney accent,

"There are ten of us, we have nothing to lose. Let's go see what he has. This is the land of opportunity for all of us. That's why we're here!"

"I don't know," one of the others replied. "He seems a little sleazy."

"We are going. Come on." Dave led the others with authority. Lal decided to tag along, figuring it would be an experience and taking solace in the fact that he wasn't alone.

Back in the dusty street, Sultan led the group to a long, narrow warehouse. He banged on the brass-studded door and the group was admitted by an aged Arab with a wide, pointy beard and loosely tied off white turban.

"I am Ali Musa Dawood." The old man said, exposing a gold tooth and another jet black one side-by-side in the front of his lower jaw. A scar on his forehead extended to his right eye, forcing it to cover half of it. Wearing a white gown, belted with a silk sash, he held an oil lamp over-head while he examined the visitors.

"Just follow me closely, and please don't touch anything and I will show you something special."

With limited lighting, they followed the Arab into a warehouse. Lal's eyes adjusted and he noticed rows of iron rings set into the walls and extending down the length of the vast structure. Rusted chains and hinged manacles dangled from the rings. Some hung low to the ground, with lighter manacles suitable for children. Shallow stone troughs ran along each wall near the ground, reminding Lal of a milking barn.

"Slaves," the Arab said with an old smile that showcased his two remaining teeth.

"Those slaves were black gold, wish for those times again but they may be gone forever."

From a hook on the wall he lifted a long whip that narrowed to a hard-edged point.

"My father cut this from the tail of a devilfish, a giant ray." He flicked his wrist. A cloud of dust exploded as the whip snapped, then echoed like a gunshot.

"In my father's day," the old man gestured with the weapon, "these troughs ran with thick gruel. No drop was wasted. Every place was taken, hundreds. Only when the fast dhows with slaves came from Zanzibar were the irons cold. But then the Queen of England stopped the trade. Now we only have white gold, ivory, which you can have, now."

He raised the lamp toward the ceiling. Bats fluttered to distant corners. The light fell on row after row of ivory tusks, arrayed like slender ghosts, white in the shadows. There were hundreds and hundreds, some piled ten deep. The longest were stacked like sheaves of wheat in huge bundles, standing on broad hollow ends. The pieces of ivory were as varied as people, Lal thought, some fat, some short, others lean. A few were stained yellow or brownish grey, like the teeth of an old pipe smoker. The ends of some were chipped, some rounded. Forty yards down the lanes of ivory, Lal saw polishing wheels, worktables, and soft wooden vises gripping the tasks patiently awaiting chisel and knife.

Dawood turned and proudly displayed his finest pair, almost perfectly matched, exceptionally long and thick. The thickest two feet or base of the tusks were lighter and courser than the rest.

"That part was inside the face," the Arab explained.

The balance of the tooth was almost exactly Lal's height: six-feet, one-inch. The Arab invited the Sikh to lift it.

Lal hefted the tusk in both hands, surprised by its weight,

"Hundred and eighty pounds," Dawood said.

As Lal stroked it, feeling the pearl like smoothness, the lines and grain, the ivory seemed alive beneath his hand. Chilled and feeling disrespectful, he turned his mind to the elephants themselves. What would those giants be like without their tusks? What if all the elephants whose tusks were in that room could be walking the earth again, hundreds of them, making their way slowly through the forests, bellies rumbling, snapping branches, and sniffing with their trunks, trumpeting calmly while they followed the matriarchs.

Dave, Lal and the foreigners retreated quickly for the door. Dave promised the Arab that he and the group would discuss and be back to negotiate a shipment, but everyone knew none of them were interested in buying the tusks.

"Hold up. Wait! I can make a deal," Dawood said. "You won't see these anywhere else."

They left. The bright light back out on the street made them all squint and shield their eyes, as they were mobbed once again by the locals.

"Money, money. I have rupees, I have pounds," cried an Indian amid the swirling chaos of Mombasa Station. He got right in their faces and said the same thing, repeatedly. All Lal could think about was getting cleaned up, finding something to eat, and boarding the train to Nairobi.

"During my life I have dedicated myself to this struggle of the African people. I have fought against white domination, and I have fought against black domination. I have cherished the idea of a democratic and free society in which all persons live together in harmony and with equal opportunities. It is an ideal which I hope to live for and to achieve. But if needs be, it is an ideal for which I am prepared to die."
NELSON MANDELA

Passengers arrived at Mombasa Railway Station in old Lorries and ox driven wagons. The station was nothing special, basic construction with a simple façade, a station sign, and another notice indicating, "Upper Class Passengers and Luggage." The local train staff, wearing crisp white cotton uniforms and red fezzes, sold first-class tickets for carriages that were catering Europeans. Porters jumped down from the gravel platform to lend assistance. African women hawked mangoes, pawpaws, oranges, and bananas from their wide flat baskets.

Lal bought a ticket for the second-class carriage and boarded the train for the 330-mile journey to Nairobi. His carriage was at the back of the train. It turned out there were three classes: first, for white senior civil servants who travelled free, and for rich Europeans; second, for all the other Europeans and Indians; and third, for Africans who packed the train cars with babies, children, and food.

On the crowded boat train, occupants either had to share bunks or sleep upright on the thirty-hour run to Nairobi. Each compartment unfolded into four bunks, but instead of spending money on a bunk bed, Lal got out his colored thick Somali blanket and decided to sleep in his seat.

Steam churned between the great wheels of the American Baldwin locomotive as it prepared to pull out across the causeway. The engine whistled twice, the couplings groaned, and slowly the train began heading toward the mainland. It steadily wound upward through beautifully-wooded, park-like country. Peering out of the carriage window, Lal got periodic glimpses of Mombasa and Kilindini and, beyond that, the Indian Ocean sparkling blue in the glorious sunshine as far as the eye could see.

The elevation increased incrementally with each mile as they passed mango trees and coconut plantations. After the summit of the Rabali hills, the train rolled onto the expanse of the Taru desert, a wilderness covered with poor scrub and stunted trees, and carpeted with a layer of the red dust.

The railway line, also known as the "*Lunatic Express*," was built in the early 1900s and stretched from Mombasa on the east coast, across nearly six hundred miles, to the shores of Lake Victoria in the west. Never before had a railway crossed such varied and often perilous terrain, spanning jungle, desert, mountains, plains, forest, and swamplands. It climbed from the coast to around eight thousand feet above sea level. Thirty two thousand Indian workers were sent from India by the British to lay its tracks, quite a few of whom died of heatstroke, malaria, typhoid, or were devoured by man-eating lions in Tsavo.

The journey was exciting as they left Mombasa and traveled on the Savannah. The track was only one meter wide and mostly single track to help facilitate the steepness of the climb. Wood burning steam engines belched black smoke and frequent stops were required to refill the train's boilers with water. All the while, they passed through small towns that had sprouted up adjacent to the railway stations.

Lal saw a range of wild animals en route. There were more antelopes than people. A herd of zebras scattered in front of the train, at random, some of them deciding to keep pace with the train, which wasn't very difficult to do. On steep slopes the poor old engine could have been outrun by a child. But on the plains, the zebra made an event of it, tossing their short manes and snorting as they ran alongside. They were so close that Lal could almost put a hand out and touch their striped, shining coats. The animals kicked up clouds of fine red dust that settled in the passenger's mouths and ears. They could smell the zebra, propelling a horsey odor of sweat, grass, and something musty as they rode just underneath, clusters of thorn bushes and umbrella-like trees that sprinkled the patchy, coarse grassland. A family of warthogs, grey and solid, trotted off in a tight, regimented line, with heads and tails held proudly in the air. The three youngsters darted down a hole. Their parents followed, entering backwards, the prickly old boar going last.

Dust was the bane of the journey. It was so fine, it drifted into the compartments no matter how hard one tried to exclude it. And in the heat of the Taru desert, to keep the windows tightly shut would have been like consigning oneself to an oven. The dust got into everything, including noses, eyes, ears, and clothing. When the passengers arrived in Nairobi, their faces were brick red and their hair and clothes were stiff with the red powder. Unfortunately, the last cars, where Lal was sitting, got most of the dust.

For much of the route, the tracks were laid with insufficient blast to stabilize the ride. In the wet seasons, farther inland, Lal was told, the train sprayed arcs of mud as it rocked from side to side, pounding the rails into the murky black soil that turned into swamp in the rains. All the flowers on the plains, and upon the creepers and liana in the native forest, were diminutive, like flowers of the downs. However, in the beginning of the long rainy season, there were several heavy-scented Lilies that sprouted up to massive size and with brilliant colors.

In the dry season, the same ground hardened to a corrugated rock-like surface that caused the wheels to bounce violently. In the dry weather, crossing the red lateritic soil of the Taru Desert, the penetrating red earth arose and painted the inside of the old carriages, even with the windows sealed shut. The last cars got the most dust, enveloping the rear passengers in blinding clouds for miles at a time. Sitting at the back of the train, Lal's grey and white turban had turned a dark shade of red, as had his beard and clothing, from head to toe.

The train climbed through forest and red rock to the great plain that sloped from one thousand to six thousand feet above sea level, at the foot of the Kenyan highlands. The locomotive showed its age as it climbed onto the coastal plateau. Forever thirsty, inefficient in converting firewood to steam, the old engine challenged its engineer. They passed blackened patches of bush where the sparks of locomotives had previously started grass fires.

The engineer braked for a water stop at the one hundred-mile cistern. Lal saw a long pipe descending from a waterhole ninety yards away. It supplied a raised wooden tank near the track. The firemen, pouring with sweat from stroking the furnace, jumped down to fill the engine. Doors opened all along the train. Passengers stepped down from the footboards onto the hard earth to stretch. For most of them, it was their first taste of the African bush. They savored the pungent smell, the fresh brush-scented wind, like sage, and the clean fragrance of the dust.

Three hours later, at sunset, they pulled into the station at Voi, a small town made up of a cluster of single-story buildings. Voi was one of four sparsely settled landmarks between Mombasa and Nairobi. Lal walked away from the carriage and watched another train chug away, growing smaller and smaller against the immensity of the African night. Gazing up, awed by the depth of the blue-black sky, dazzled by the intensity and individuality of each star, he thought he had never truly observed the night until that moment. He heard the distinctive high and breathy whining of a hyena nearby with another answering the call and hurried inside.

The air was muffled by the incessant buzz of mosquitoes. He was being bitten by these little blood thirsty bugs, he waved some of them away but they had inflicted enough for him to start scratching. He ran into the diner quickly and met the Goan proprietor, Marcus De'souza, who bowed and stretched his arms wide when Lal and several other travelers entered. Smartly dressed Indian stewards with white gloves served the hungry passengers a variety of Indian and European dishes. They enjoyed samosas as appetizers, entrees selected from chopped mutton, roast guinea fowl, and stew with goat meat; the meal ended with a selection of fresh pawpaws, bananas, pomegranate, and oranges and spiced Indian *Masala* tea.

The train came to the Tsavo River, its swift waters bordered by the thorny branches of lofty mimosas. The fast, cool flowing stream was an exceptional attribute to rivers in East Africa. The lofty green trees along the banks formed a welcome relief to the monotony of the landscape, which featured a range of leafless dwarf trees as far as they eye could see. The scene was broken here and there by ridges of dark red, heat-blistered rocks jutting out above the jungle.

They stopped at the edge of the small town for a hearty English breakfast of fresh warm bread, spicy omelets, and crisp sausages from Limuru. To the east, Lal made out the grey and white tip of a mountain, hiding in the distant western cloud line. It was the famous 19,000-foot majestic Kilimanjaro, with its snowy crown dominating the southern horizon, across the border in Tanganyika.

Lal recalled hearing of the man-eating lions of Tsavo, which had killed a large number of Indians working on the railway line project. The lions were finally shot by Colonel Patterson, chief engineer at Tsavo.

A tall, lean, stooped young Englishman with a moustache, Patterson was raised in India. He wrote in his book:

"I was aroused at daybreak and told that one of my *jemadars*, a rank in the British Indian army, a fine powerful Sikh named Ranjit Singh, had been seized in his tent during the night, dragged off, and eaten. On reaching the spot where the body had been devoured, a dreadful spectacle presented itself. The ground was covered with blood and morsels of flesh and bones, but the unfortunate *jemadar's* head remained intact."

Night after night, in an attempt to trap the lions, Patterson crouched in trees near their most recent kills. But the lions invariably chose other railroad camps to prey upon. Changing his tactics, he tried poison. The lions avoided the bait. When he had a trap built, it remained empty. The two man-eaters of Tsavo had transformed the dense, sun-drenched landscape into a waking nightmare for every worker within ten miles of the railroad. Nobody — white, black, or brown — knew when the ferocious jaws might seize him, and drag him to death. Patterson continued to maintain his grueling twenty-four hour watch. One particular night, the brutes seized a man from the railway station, brought him close to Patterson's camp, and devoured him there. He could hear them crunching the bones and the sound of their dreadful purring filled the air.

Luck changed for the Englishman, on the night of December 10th, from his rickety ten-foot-high platform, Patterson fired four shots at a dun form. The next morning, on that spot, he found one dead man-eater. Months later, he fired six slugs from a .303 rifle into its mate as it was dragging another worker into the bush.

Out of the infernal silence came voices and lights, flames from torches, lanterns swinging in the fine night air. Men danced all around Patterson, their hero. Africans beat drums and Indians arose, fell, and prostrated themselves before him, chanting congratulations in unison with voices both sad and joyous,

"*Mubarak, Mubarak, Mubarak!*"

They had lived for so long in a prison of terror, and now, thanks to the English *Sahib*, they were free again. Life finally returned to normal in the railway camps. The celebration and drumbeat of Indians, Europeans, and Africans continued for days, with deserters streaming back from the coast, and visitors converging from all along the line to see with their own eyes the carcasses and badly scarred skins.

Twenty five years later, Patterson's floor rugs, the lions' skins were sold to the Chicago Field Museum of Natural History for a sum of five thousand U.S. dollars. Although the skins arrived at the museum in poor condition, they were refurbished and the lions were reconstructed, and are on display there today along with their original skulls.

The locomotive did not take easily to the climb toward Nairobi. It was a struggle between rushing descents and dragging climbs. Approaching to the top of a steep climb, the passengers felt the engine lose power, drag, and begin to slip backwards. Lal heard the wheels screech as the engineer tightened the brakes. As the wheels locked, the train glided slowly backwards toward the valley floor. Some of the women and children screamed and hugged each other. Half of the passengers were demanding to get off the train. The engineer reversed power and the train backed up the preceding slope. With a swooping rush it descended again and slowly started climbing the hill. Walking rapidly along the tracks, the passengers caught up to the train and jumped quickly back on board. To complete the trip to Nairobi, the goods car was eventually uncoupled and shunted aside at the next station, Kibwezi, where another train would pick it up.

Ten miles from Ulu, the last fuel stop before Nairobi, the train screeched and braked again and all the passengers seated next to the windows leaned out to see what was happening. Sadly, a giraffe lay dead across the tracks. Copper telegraph wire was tangled insanely about its neck. The firemen and every able-bodied passenger jumped down. Hauling on the legs, the men and women dragged the two thousand pound animal to the side. Firewood was loaded at Ulu and it was off again.

The train raced through the Athi Plains and over Athi River for its final run into the capital. The town had been formed accidentally when the railway line was being forged between Mombasa and Lake Victoria. A flimsy headquarter had gone up, then an anchovy tin shack, then more shacks and tents followed by tin roofed *dukas*. The grey-green landscape was sprinkled with acacia trees and animals everywhere, from ostriches and giraffes to zebras, impalas, and Thomson's gazelles. A few of the zebras paired off and stood side-by-side with their heads pointing in opposite directions. The diagonal effect of black and white in a broad "U" pattern was dizzying, and confused and scared predators, because it made the zebras look larger than they were. A zebra let out a quick bleat, followed by others; then they all began snorting like horses. Their actions warned the other animals of approaching danger. A herd of Grants' gazelles stopped grazing and flicked their heads en masse, in a single direction, looking for any sign of a predator. Seeing no danger, they went back to their grazing.

It was several minutes past noon when the train chugged into the capital, its steam whistle shrieking. Smoke chuffed and streamed out behind, marring the skyline. Its passengers were covered in the red dust of the burnished rocks from the long trek. Lal was immensely weary, and the thin air of the high altitude only added to his tiredness. Friends and families crowded the platform, welcoming the passengers beneath the beating sun. Beyond them, it seemed that all of Nairobi gathered around the little station, in wagons, on horseback, and on foot, in open cars, and in rickshaws.

Nairobi, which meant "place of cold water" in the Maasai dialect, had blossomed from a muddy tent town in the late 1800s to a place of business and civilization. It was busy and growing gateway to a still new country, an almost unknown country. It lay snugly against the Athi Plains at the foot of the rolling Kikuyu Hills looking north to Mount Kenya and south to Mount Kilimanjaro in Tanganyika. The flat town, coated in red dust, looked as if it had been scooped up somewhere in India and plunked down in the middle of the African Savannah. Its streets were teeming with people of every description. Purposeful Indian clerks jostled with the darker-skinned native Africans, who moved with slow grace through the throng of people. Some of the natives were laden with bundles of fruits and firewood on their way to meet up with hawkers in the general market, also known as *Skoni,* where they could barter their goods. There were even white faces here and there, most meticulously guarded from the equatorial sun by hats or umbrellas. The white folks were the only ones who strode freely, keeping to the fitful shade from the blue gum trees that lined the streets, as the Indians and Africans all stepped quickly out of the colonial's way to walk in the sun.

Nairobi was a town where you could buy things, hear news or the Europeans could dine at some of the hotels. The new Government House was built, a stately cool house with a fine ballroom and a pretty garden. Colorful birds perched on the trees along the paved roadside. Several automobiles darted about, but the streets were mostly choked with oxcarts and rickshaws, which scuttled by, leaving the pushcarts to trundle in their wake and slogging through mule dung and rotting fruit. A donkey stumbled under the weight of a cart piled high with green and yellow bananas and oranges, the few cars around beeped their horns as they waited for the road to clear. The air was pungent with mule dung and rotting fruit combined with the smell of wood smoke, gum leaves, and the sunburned red soil to give Africa its unique perfume. Some of the Indians in Nairobi dominated the big native business quarter of the Bazaar and had their little villas just outside of the town. Jevanjee, Suleiman Virjee, Allidina Visram were some of them. They gave extensive tea parties in their gardens with Indian sweets and pastries

Lal, taller than most searched the crowd for his friend Ram, and then heard a familiar voice call from behind.

"Lal, over here!" Indeed, it was Ram.

He appeared small in the crowd, waving his arms and quickly dodging people to get to Lal.

"I thought you'd never get here," Ram shouted, as they affectionately hugged one other. Ram's skin was dark brown, like polished wood, and the lines on his forehead were light. He was medium height, slim and compact, and dressed casually with brown leather slippers.

"It's great to see you, friend," Lal said. "I'm so glad to be out of Somalia. It's hard to believe I'm starting a new life here."

"You won't regret it my friend," Ram said. "Kenya is nothing like Somalia. And Nyeri is one of the best places to settle. It is so picturesque. They need someone like you, badly. You're going to love the climate there."

"Let me enjoy Nairobi first then we will think about Nyeri." They both laughed.

> "To a sprinter, the hundred-yard dash is over in three seconds, not nine or ten. The first 'second' is when you come out of the blocks. The next is when you look up and take your first few strides to attain gain position. By that time the race is actually about half over. The final 'second' – the longest slice of time in the world for an athlete – is that last half of the race, when you really bear down and see what you're made of. It seems to take an eternity, yet is all over before you can think what's happening."

JESSE OWENS

Lal and Ram spent the next ten days sightseeing, visiting the Sikh Gurudwaras and Hindu Temples and traveling around Nairobi. Then, Ram decided to accompany Lal to Nyeri. For a while now, the automobile had been active, but not common, in the bush in Kenya — not only for transport, but as a substitute for horseback. So, the two doctors engaged a driver to take them to Nyeri.

The drive from Nairobi to Nyeri was breathtaking. As far as the eye could see, the vast land was dotted with trees in the Savannah. Then, spanning the view from left to right, slashing the surface of the earth in a vast crater, was The Great Rift Valley. Deep in the heart of this great divide, the grass waved in the wind and its immense green carpet was colored by herds of zebras, wildebeest, and gazelles, with the occasional herd of elephants — and unseen predators lurking in the brush.

From the early 1800s to the late 1920s, when Europeans began to penetrate the interior of East Africa, animals were in such plenty that elephant herds foraged by the hundreds. At times, antelopes covered the plains like a carpet. Lions were literally pests, and it was not unusual to see a hundred rhinos at once. Giraffes and elephants were the animals of paradise. To the European hunter, Africa was Eden. Indeed, once people got there, many stayed until the end of their lives.

Lal rode along in awe of the beauty, so overjoyed that he would now be part of this picturesque landscape. Soon they passed fields that were reddened with ripe berries, as well as rows of coffee trees that looked like brown patches on the sloping green hills. Women and children, *Totos, were* called upon to pick the coffee off the trees along with the men. Then wagons and carts brought the coffee beans down to the factory near the river.

They passed Kikuyu women heading back to their huts, their backs bent low under enormous burdens of firewood, which were suspended by leather straps that bit into their sloping foreheads. They wore pointed leather aprons and trudged along, looking like brown snails. Some women carried babies in slings on their backs, in addition to their loads. Infants' shiny heads bobbed about between the mothers' bent shoulders like polished skittle balls. Meanwhile, little Kikuyu *totos* dashed about, herding their fathers' cows and goats back to their *bomas*. A young *toto* walked in the middle of the road in front of the cows and behind a herd of goats. A stick rested across his shoulders. The goats stood bleating in the road, until the boy beat the earth around them and they stirred into a scattered motion. A donkey grazed on the side of the road, black barrels strapped to its sides, and beside him under a lone tree, an old Kikuyu man was resting. Clusters of green leaves emerged from the tangle of white thorns above him. His clothes were torn and tattered and a shining *Panga* strung from his belt.

Higher still, Lal spotted the massive blackness of the grazing buffalo along the slopes. He could smell the distinct stench of the herd. The drive continued through the valleys leading up to Nyeri. To one side, the hills rolled, and to the other, it fell away to an endless open horizon and the vastness of the Savannah. The last village they passed sat adjacent to a clear flowing stream with fresh water from the heights of Mount Kenya. An old Kikuyu woman surrounded by a handful of chickens and goats was milking a cow and smiled and waved at them displaying what was left of her front teeth. Further down the stream, a group of younger women were squatting and washing laundry against the rocks before heading back with buckets of fresh water.

Nyeri is situated in the country's densely populated and fertile Kenya Central Highlands, lying between the eastern base of the Aberdare Range, which forms part of the eastern end of the Great Rift Valley, and the western slopes of Mount Kenya.

Lal had done his homework. He knew that, toward the end of 1902, the British were establishing their colonial presence. They marched in a strong military column while meeting spirited resistance from the native Kikuyu warriors, led by Wangombe Wa Ihura. The Kikuyu were eventually defeated.

After that victory, a decision was reached to site a British post close to a little hill on the slopes of Mt. Kenya. The Kikuyu called the hill *Kia-Nyiri*, while their Maasai neighbors called it *Na-aier*. In 1902, Nyeri was founded. Shortly after the establishment of the post, a trickle of European settlers, missionaries, and Indian merchants began migrating into Nyeri and surrounding areas. The town soon burgeoned into a trading center for white settlers who raised cattle, and farmed wheat and coffee. Although the First World War had ended tragically for many, for East Africa it held great prospect for fabulous wealth, grand estates, and limitless opportunity, due to the vast resources of the land.

Lal rented a small house close to the practice he had set up on the main street, Kaburini Road. He found the fresh sun-warmed days and cool evenings the perfect climate. The air glowed about him as he walked. The scents shifted with each breeze. The dirt roads in Nyeri — lower in the center and bordered by high banks on the sides — were pitted with deep holes, set with stones, and carpeted with six inches of red dust.

Once word got around about Lal's practice and his exceptional skill and expertise as a surgeon, his mild and cheerful demeanor, his business flourished. Town's people loved the amount of time he spent patiently working with the sick. It didn't take long before he needed to expand to a larger facility, and soon he was asked to perform surgeries at the government hospitals in Nyeri and the next nearby town, Nanyuki. Lal hired a couple of local qualified Kikuyus as his assistants.

Lal was in his practice on a rainy Tuesday morning, when he heard some commotion outside; two young Kikuyu men were carrying someone into the hallway. He rushed out, a woman, wearing an off white dress which had turned a dark shade of red with blood, was half hanging down off a wooden makeshift stretcher. Lal instructed the men to rush and bring her in and lay her down on the operating table. After examining her, he saw a deep bullet wound just below her breast on the right side. It was still bleeding. Lal gave her laudanum, cleaned the wound and struggled to stop the bleeding.

"What happened to her, " Lal inquired as he continued working.

"There was a fight in the village and she was accidentally shot."

"Who shot her, what is her name,"

"She is Wamboi. Some men from Nanyuki had come to Nyeri to steal the goats and visited a number of surrounding villages. At dawn there was an altercation between the intruders and our villagers. She stepped out to see what was going on, was just standing there with her mother when the shooting started. Her mother didn't survive but we were able to rush Wamboi here on a pickup truck. The intruders set fire to some of the huts, including hers before they left."

"Did someone inform the police?"

"I don't think so we were just busy picking up the pieces."

"Never mind that for now. It doesn't look good, but let me work on her."

Lal performed an incision around the wound and found the location of the bullet. To his pleasant surprise, the major nerves were spared. Lal expanded the incision and worked slowly with his soft and experienced hands. It turned out to be a revolver bullet. Working with his assistant, the surgery had taken a couple of hours. He was able to get the bullet out using tweezers. Lal stitched her with a hooked needle and thick black thread. The thick steel bangle, *Kada*, on his right wrist, a symbol of his Sikh religion rocked up and down as he stitched the wound. Hardly conscious Wamboi moaned as she felt the pushing and pulling of the needle.

After Lal had completed his operation, she was moved to another room.

Wamboi had no home or hut to go back to now, her mother was gone. She was homeless. Her father had died when she was very young.

After he learned of her situation, Lal hesitated briefly before deciding,

"You can recover at my house, I have spare rooms. Stay there till you feel strong enough to move."

*"God counts our tears and knows our misery
Ah weep not, take thy Qur'an and recite
Litanies infinite, and weep no more."*
PERSIAN POET HAFIZ

Lal had his house servant, Makora, look after and feed Wamboi. Lal bought new clothes for Wamboi and would check on her when he got home and made sure the wound was healing properly. He started learning and practicing the Kikuyu language with Wamboi.

A few weeks passed and Wamboi was back on her feet. She spoke to the doctor and decided to move in with her cousin in the village. On Saturday evenings, Lal would stay home and cook or go hunting with his single 7-mm Mauser. Wamboi never married and had looked after her mother being the only child. She offered to cook for Lal and would stop by his house on weekends and keep him company.

Lal suggested to her that she should start working in his practice and train to be a nurse. She was ecstatic. Being a sharp student she soon became a part of his staff, helping and learning. She was in her late twenties, had a stunning figure topped by an attractive Kikuyu featured face with curly hair. She had a kind of understated beauty; perhaps it was because she was so disarmingly and innocently unaware of her prettiness. Her black skin was completely flawless. It was her inner beauty that lit her round black eyes and softened her features. When she smiled, her eyes lit up. With her loud laughter one couldn't help but smile along too, even if it was just on the inside.

She started visiting him frequently, staying late and some overnights. They talked through the nights. With her tuition, he was becoming fluent in the Kikuyu and Swahili dialects. The strong physical attraction between the two was evident and eventually was leading them to an intimate relationship.

On the weekends that Lal went hunting, Ram would sometimes join him from Nairobi. On one of these trips, they drove to the base of Mount Kenya on a dusty road that ran through a mixture of bush and native *shambas*.

Shaven headed Kikuyu women wearing beads and leather aprons weeded, dug, and drew water from the swampy stream in gourds or in *debes* — four-gallon paraffin tins that served as universal water-vessels. For the most part, the road ran across a plain whose spoil largely included murram, a coarse red gravel that baked hard and supported only thin, wiry grass. The maize in the small Kikuyu owned plots grew up higher than your head as you walked on the narrow hard-trampled footpaths in between the tall green rustling regiments. Each Kikuyu family had a small round peaked hut and a storage hut. The space between the huts was a lively place. This is where the maize was ground, the goats milked and children played. In the colder weather, they carried live coals in small wicker baskets with them from the huts, sometimes causing big grass fires which were disastrous.

Once the road came to an end the hunters walked in silence, following the Kikuyu guide named Karanja, a quiet, middle-aged man who wore an old brown tweed coat that had been given to him by a Scottish farmer. He wore a khaki hat that had seen better days, along with trousers heavily patched on the knees, and a red ragged shirt. His face was networked with wrinkles and his shrewd active black eyes darted about like a forest rat. The lobes of his ears were distended with small wooden cylinders, set with beads.

They walked past tapered anthills whose spires resembled castle ruins, thrusting themselves above the grass bush that was as hard as sandstone and the same color. These spires were the craft of termites. Deep inside each was a fat slug white queen. It would resemble a large sausage. The queen manufactured egg after egg for years on end.

Entering the forest, Lal noticed the high sweet-smelling canopy of chestnut, cedar, and camphor; underfoot, the spongy damp mulch of fallen leaves and evergreen needles greeted them. The rifle was comfortable in Lal's hands. It had the clean oily smell and feel of a well-tended weapon. He checked the barrel and saw the brilliant sky and canopy of trees above, through the spotless rifled tunnel of the gun metal.

Lal was surprised by the variety of thorns that attacked his clothes, each little plant devilishly clever and defiant. He looked up and saw a patch of white swinging monkeys in the branches, one after the other. The shifting cries came again and again while one troop after another resumed the refrain. Coming to a ravine that sliced through the ridge, a pool appeared before them. To their right was a thin waterfall dropping fifty feet from the rocks.

They spotted fresh elephant tracks on the edge of the swamp. Lal observed the small mounds of sand gathered by ants within them as nature began to reclaim the path. Fragments of acacia bark and broken benches lay along the route, the leaves already shriveled, amber sap had leaked from the wounds of the branches. This was obviously the route for the elephant herds that regularly came down the slopes of Mount Kenya and headed toward the planes before they turned round and went back up the slopes. Just to be careful, Karanja looked for saliva on the twigs and acacia pods, which the elephants chewed. If he found wetness, they knew the elephants were extremely close. He did indeed find wetness, he said, but wasn't sure if it was from elephants or recent rains. But soon they came across massive mounds of fresh dung, with clouds of butterflies hovering above them. A number of dung beetles were busy transporting as much of the dung as they could. The forest is darker and colder than one can imagine. The undergrowth is dense and the sun scarcely penetrates onto the forest floor.

The wide stream was full of rainwater from the slopes of Mount Kenya. Karanja looked up. Lal followed his glance thirty yards across the river where an elephant stood at the edge of the water. The sound of the large animal's advance was drowned out by the stream and the small waterfall. Slowly, it flapped its ears. Dust rose from its shoulders as the uneven ears slapped against them, loose sails rippling against a mast. Unhurriedly and apparently hearing no disturbing sound, the animal raised its trunk. It directed the curving tip first upstream, then down, casting for scent. The massive animal had sensed some form of danger, probably the scent of humans.

The wind direction had changed and something at the limit of the elephant's vision had caught its attention. He paused often, swinging his great grey head from side to side, his ears held out like sounding boards, his small weak eyes gleaming. Suddenly, the bull shook his head so violently that its ears slapped thunderously against its shoulders raising an enormous cloud of dust from the dry mud that coated his body. He flared his ears widely and stared directly toward the spot where Lal and his party were hiding. Dense lashes surrounded his small amber eyes. The elephant stared for what seemed like forever then bent down to continue munching on leaves.

Lal's heart practically stopped as he, Ram, and Karanja stood still as statues, watching a line of followers shuffle down to the water, huge grey blocks moving in the evening light, their pace stately, unlike any other animal on an unending majestic and dignified march. The big females entered the water to their knees. They dipped their trunks, flushing them with a fine spray. Then they drank. The very young elephants moved in among them, leaning against the legs of the females, splashing, and experimenting with their thin bugle-like trunks. Like a gunshot, a tree snapped behind where they crouched, and Lal froze.

"*Tembo Hapo*," Karanja whispered, lifting a finger to his lips, and pointed to an area behind them. More elephants were behind them, heading for the river. Karanja motioned and quickly led the hunting party to a spot behind thicker vegetation, away from the path of the herd. They laid down on their stomachs.

While the elephants advanced through the forest, Lal heard measured shuffling and snapping branches as the smaller trees were pushed aside. A deep rumbling, the relaxed sound of digestion, came to them. A cow led her young calf into the glade before them, occasionally shepherding the calf with the gentle stroking movements of her trunk.

As they lay there, barely breathing, the enormous grey tower of a wrinkled leg swung past them. They saw the front rim of four wide toenails meet the ground when the ankle flexed. Lal inhaled the rich musk-sweet odor of an elephant. The mother touched her baby's sides and forehead with her trunk as it staggered about between her front legs. The chin and upper forelegs of the calf bristled with stiff hairs. The mother slipped the tip of her trunk into the calf's mouth. The young elephant moved under its mother and began to suckle. Behind the mother, other elephants walked calmly through the cedars, like old farmers at home in a field of tall corn.

After the last elephant passed them, Karanja directed everyone to follow him, away from the herd and onto the other side of the river. They walked in silence.

"Fresh Topi tracks," Karanja whispered.

With the fresh breeze in their faces, Lal knew the antelope could not smell them. Then they saw it, about a hundred yards off; a large male, nearly four feet tall at the shoulders, thick-ridged horns, with a glossy rufous coat, which casted a purplish hue.

"I want to bag that one, he is priceless," Lal whispered to Ram.

They waited patiently as the animal grazed away from them. The Topi raised its head from time to time, and scraped the ground with a front hoof. Lal crawled to his left until an acacia bush separated him from the antelope. He stalked slowly forward in the cover of the plant totally concentrating on the task at hand. Lal was aware of each branch, every smell, and each movement of the Topi.

Whenever the Topi grazed, Lal advanced. If the Topi paused, Lal lay still, always reacting to the animal's movements. Finally, fifty yards away, Lal quietly slipped off the rifle's safety catch. Kneeling, waiting for the antelope to turn, he pressed the Mauser into his shoulder and found the animal in the rifle's site. The Topi stepped once and forked up the ground with a front hoof. It turned in profile and raised its head. Lal took a deep breath, exhaled, and squeezed the trigger. The gunshot rang in his ears, while smoke from the gun filled his nostrils. He watched as the antelope stumbled, paused, and fell.

The Kikuyu servant skinned the Topi and butchered it. They packed the meat to be transported home. Lal was pleased with his kill and was excited to enjoy his first taste of the antelope.

Along the journey back, Lal contemplated that it had been five years since he had sailed from Bombay. He wished his son, Kirpal, had been with him on his hunting excursions. His son was grown up and could join him in the hunt. Perhaps now that his practice was humming along successfully, it was time to go back to his village Bopa Rai in Punjab and get his son, and bring him to Kenya — where they would be together. Unknown to him, Wamboi was pregnant with his child.

> *"The worst thing that colonialism did was to cloud our view of our past."*

**PRESIDENT BARACK OBAMA
DREAMS FROM MY FATHER: A STORY OF RACE AND INHERITANCE**

As Lal made plans to bring Kirpal back to Kenya, he soon learned that fate had other things in store. Thinking that Lal needed a wife and a mother to help him raise Kirpal, Lal's older brother, Sham Singh, had arranged for Lal to marry a beautiful young Sikh girl from the neighboring village of Jasowal. Lal was almost fifty now and finding a bride was not easy. Sham Singh had approached his friend Harmeet Singh, whose daughter Bishan had been married, had a still born child, but now had been living at home for the past four years. Since she had been married once and had lost a child, it was almost impossible to find a young match in the surrounding villages.

Once Lal arrived in Punjab, he wasn't sure about the marriage proposal. He had his independence in Nyeri and Wamboi was there too. Life was fairly comfortable but a mother would be good for Kirpal. He discussed the proposal with his brother, and reluctantly agreed to the marriage. At the same time, he agreed to send his brother's two sons to be educated in England. The plan was for the two boys to work hard and return to India as qualified doctors. The prospective bride, Bishan, had reservations also.

"I will never see you again and will be so far away," Bishan pleaded to her father.

"This is the best thing as you will be going to another country, another continent, where no one will know you."

"He is so much older than me."

"I know, but you will have a comfortable life with the doctor."

He also told her about Lal's son, Kirpal and how he would be going back with them. She hesitated but agreed knowing there was no future here for her and a new country might be the right thing.

Life had been tough for Bishan after she had been rescued from Deep Singh. She just stayed home, learned to sew and hardly went out. She stopped going out completely after the women in the village stared at her and whispered to each other. Bishan knew what they were thinking but was helpless to respond to any of the taunts. In the eyes of the villagers, she was the odd one out, the one to be pitied and condescended and to be looked down upon.

At her second marriage ceremony now, her status as a bride dictated that she keep her head face covered with a cloth made of *malmal*, called a "*chunni*". She breathed a bit easier knowing in a few hours Lal would realize just what a shy girl he'd married. Hopefully, her expressions and voice would be able to hide the memories of her first nightmare. She carefully tried to peek through the *chunni* without being noticed, to catch a glimpse of her betrothed, who she knew was older than her. She wasn't able to see his face clearly. Lal caught her doing so quite a few times, and smiled.

Kirpal was at the wedding and pushed his way through everyone so he could get a glimpse of his stepmother for the first time. She wasn't that much older than him. After the marriage ceremony, all the villagers enjoyed the elaborate feast with spiced Indian dishes and spent some time socializing and finally, everyone left them alone for their first night together. It was awkward at first, introducing himself to his new bride.

Finally, he got close to her, she moved away as the nearness of a man now scared her. He kept talking and slowly held her face in his hands and lifted the *chunni* off her face and head. She looked away from him. He felt warmth that encircled his heart. Bishan was by far the most beautiful woman that he had ever beheld. She had loveliness beyond imagining. He missed a couple of heartbeats as her facial beauty stunned him and his lips were eager to touch hers. He hugged and held her but she surprised him by not hugging back. They stayed in that position for a few minutes.

To ease the tension between them, he began by telling her stories about his life in Africa and the things he had seen and done. Bishan listened intently to his voice and hardly spoke. She kept looking at her hands and nails and wouldn't lift her eyes to look at him. She knew he was older but had no idea what he looked like. She was anxious and tried to peek but every time she tried, her shyness prevented that. He talked late into the night, as it was important to him that she knew everything about their new life. At last, just a few hours before dawn, they drifted off to sleep on opposite sides of the bed. It had been a long day. She was up early while he was still fast asleep. She moved over and saw his face for the first time, she was pleased.

After the two month stay in the Punjab, the newlyweds sailed back to Mombasa accompanied by Kirpal. While the couple spent some time acquainting themselves with one another, Ram used a variety of contacts to arrange a surprise celebration in Nyeri. Bishan had started becoming slightly more comfortable with Lal around her. There was still a lack of communication because of the age difference and interests.

Ram had invited Wamboi but she chose not to attend the celebration.

Lal and Bishan made their way for the first time as husband and wife, up the winding gravel road to the mansion. They both looked on in awe as they rounded the final turn. Lal was taken aback at the jumble of carts, military jeeps, official sedans and horses strewn across the plateau surrounding the main house. Ram had contacted the English District Commissioner for Nyeri and arranged the welcome party at his official residence.

Unbeknown to the Sandhus, the Kikuyu chiefs from the local *Bomas*, most of the Indian traders in Nyeri and surrounding small towns, the Sikhs from the Nairobi and Nyeri Temples, and some of the Kikuyu politicians had gathered to welcome the newlyweds. After what seemed like hours of hugs and well wishes, Lal could see that Bishan was overwhelmed. Encouraging his friends and colleagues to tap the kegs of dark beer and scotch, he whisked her inside for a quick moment alone.

Refreshed, the bride and groom made their way back to the lawn where they rejoined the guests. The trays of curried vegetables, exotic meats and succulent fruits were enjoyed by all. The Bhangra dancers kept the party alive to the sounds of the *boliyan* and *dhols* until the moon rose high and the last star twinkled above.

Lal went back to his practice the next day and Wamboi was there. She was seven months pregnant.

"Missed you at the party,"

Then he looked at her closely. She had tears in her eyes and Lal could see the bulge in her belly. He gave her a warm hug as he looked down at her.

"I didn't know about the pregnancy, I shouldn't have gotten married. I am sorry. Why didn't you tell me or send a message?"

"I wanted to but just couldn't do it. It doesn't matter anymore, now you can start a new life with your wife."

"This is going to be so difficult now, with Bishan, you and the baby."

Wamboi gave birth to a daughter Lalita. The mother named her after the doctor. Lal went to see them and looked at his daughter for the first time. The baby had light tanned skin, sharp facial features and curly hair.

"She is so beautiful, just like her mother," Lal said as he looked at Wamboi.

He promised Wamboi that he would financially take care of her and she could come back to the practice when she was ready.

Time passed quickly as Lal focused on his practice and his "new" family. A few years passed and the business was well established and successful. Wamboi still worked there and she would bring Lalita with her at times and Lal would get a chance to pamper the child, play with her and buy her new clothes and toys. He had introduced Lalita to Kirpal as Wamboi's daughter. The doctor's feelings for Wamboi were still there, but he tried to force himself to act on a professional level when he was around the nurse.

Lal picked a spot of land on which to build an elaborate house. It was a ten-acre plot overlooking a stream and was next to a coffee farm. On part of the land, he had a multitude of fruit trees including orange, banana, guava, peach, plum, and pomegranate. The five-bedroom mansion turned out to be one of the largest in the area at the time. Next to the house, on the banks of the river at the waterfall, he set up a maize mill, driven by two steam engines which became the beating heart of the mill.

First, the maize was sorted to make sure it was clean. The next step was to remove the hard cover from the maize. The maize jam went to the cattle. Then the clean maize was ground into flour and packed into sacks. The grinding process at the mill was an extremely dusty endeavor. Everything around the mill was covered in a white dust. Soon after the mill was functioning, you could see a line of flat oxen-driven wagons full of maize, mingled with the Kikuyus walking and carrying sacks of maize on their heads and shoulders, all going to the mill. The mill ran all day from dawn to dusk, and the number of workers quickly doubled.

The view from Lal's new mansion and estate was breathtaking. The forest extended across the undulating land to the base of Mount Kenya.

A mosaic of square Kikuyu maize fields and banana groves, dotted with native villages, sprang to life with tufts of smoke from the rounded huts. Smoke would float up from fires that smoldered among the flat cooking stones. The most diligent observer could even make out the colored blanket skirts of the Kikuyu women, whose arms and legs, wound in decorative copper bangles which glinted in the morning sun. Boys sat by watching the cattle. Kikuyu men hung around the round straw thatched huts. They waited for their wives to bring them gourds of the thick mead, *Njohi,* fermented with honey, water, and various fruits, spices, grains, and hops.

Lal's main house was shaded by tall jacaranda and eucalyptus trees and surrounded by overgrown gardens. Its old colonial style was smoothly thatched with combed grass, and covered with bougainvillea. A long porch swept all the way around the entire house. It was built on a hillside overlooking a stream that ran down from the nearby mountain, carrying crystal clear water. The stream flowed year-round. On the other side of the stream were broken valleys that sloped steeply down into a larger valley. Heavy growths of trees filled the valleys, and there were grassy slopes on the ridges, and a thick bamboo forest further up the mountain. Three to four times a week, Lal would go into Nyeri to visit an Indian grocery store run by a Gujarati, where he selected all of his favorite Indian spices.

Smoke from the cooking fires blued the air over the servant's quarters and the sound of someone chopping wood seemed to always carry faintly across the farm. Inside the house, the main living area was huge, as the doctor enjoyed entertaining. It seemed he always invited his African Kikuyu friends to mingle with European and South African acquaintances. Also included were his Indian and Sikh friends from Nairobi and Nanyuki. Layers of tan Indian mats, with fine splinter-free Bengalis on top covered the wooden floor. Embroidered cushions and plump spangled bolsters lay along each wall, which sparkled elegantly with many colored African beads, some facing a low copper table.

The windows in the house were larger than average, allowing light to brighten the house from virtually every direction. A massive stone fireplace dominated the living area and was lit frequently as the temperature dipped precipitously in the evenings. Overstuffed chairs flanked the hearth. The verandah in front was sizeable, with rocking chairs and mahogany tables. Standing out on the porch, the distinct smell of dust and eucalyptus was quite prevalent. There were thick draperies at every window. Flowers in vases and flowers in bowls were on the table.

Having become an active hunter, Lal collected a number of trophy heads, which were mounted on the Verandah walls. A row of animal horns rose above the surface of the bar. Some were straight and some spiraled, others were delicate or monstrous. All the others emerged hard and dark from the trim white bone plates of their foreheads. The trophies, all of them staring down with glassy eyes from the walls, ranged from impala, buffalo, kongonis, elands, and even a rhino head, with its' enormous two horns in place. The massive black buffalo head, shot in northern Tanganyika, scowled down from the wall with its massive horns spread a near-record forty nine inches.

The guesthouse was a white stucco cottage with a red-tiled roof, surrounded by pink and orange bougainvillea. It featured a sitting room with a small table swathed in a vermillion and yellow, a bright kitchen with a Dutch door, and a bedroom with its own bathroom. The floor was polished wood in an intricate parquet pattern. The walls were off white and beautifully decorated with paintings from India, and from local artists.

The maize mill proved to be a success. Locals mostly from the Kikuyu tribe, traveled long distances to bring their maize and wheat on their backs in sacks to be ground into flour at the mill. Bishan, with the help of servants, took care of the mill while Dr. Lal Singh carried on with his practice at the hospital.

Since Bishan was educated only in Punjabi, she had some difficulty understanding a number of the farmers from South Africa who spoke English when they brought their crops to be ground into flour. The locals also brought their modest crops and since they only spoke Swahili or Kikuyu, it was difficult for her to communicate with them too. Lal decided to hire a Persian tutor named Sohrab, who came every day for several hours to help Bishan learn English and Swahili. In a few months, she could partake in a reasonable conversation in English and Swahili. Bishan was able to run the mill business much more proficiently.

Some things everyone needed to avoid in those days were the *ticks* and *jiggas*. The area around Nyeri was infested with *ticks*, which were known for crawling up your leg, boring into the skin, and causing extreme itching. The *jiggas* were also plentiful. They were known to burrow under the toenails, lay their eggs, and create a swollen, red, itchy, tormenting sore on the toe. To extract the *jigga*, you had to wait until the sore was ripe, then hold a needle to a match flame and plunge the needle into the area to clear a pathway so you could extract a tiny white sack, about the size of an onion seed that contained the eggs. The painful toe would then be disinfected and bandaged.

As time passed, Lal, Bishan and Kirpal did well and prospered in their new home and life together. Bishan gave birth to a baby girl, Amrita. Lalita was five years older than Amrita. Lal was ecstatic and arranged for a party in which he hosted more than two hundred guests from all walks of life. Tables were laid out in the spacious garden and varieties of Indian, European, and Kikuyu cuisines were served. Bars were set up in two corners and drinks were served all evening by two Kikuyus dressed in white with red fez caps.

As life went on, Lal would come home early from work to feed the baby and play with her for what seemed like hours. Everyone seemed happy in their own little worlds. Lalita was always there playing with baby Amrita.

Three years passed and Amrita had a baby brother, Davinder. There was an even bigger party for him! Some of the English and South African farmers were invited along with local African friends. The celebrations were excessive, with exquisite food and an assortment of drinks, combined with Indian and African singing and dancing. The party lasted into the night. Lal loved to dance the *Bhangra* and was on the dance floor with everyone for most of the night, celebrating his son's birth. Bishan was shy and almost never joined him, partly because she was so much younger and felt embarrassed.

Lal loved his children and wanted to spend as much time as he could with them. He enjoyed shopping for their clothes and toys, some of which were brand names and were ordered from Britain. The next five years were pleasant and went by quickly. The family took vacations to the coast and spent time on the beach in Mombasa. They traveled by train and sat in first-class with all the amenities. Lal took the two younger children when he went hunting for antelopes; at times the Kikuyu servants had to carry the children when they got tired. It was a childhood that was carefree and filled with lots of love from their father, with no limit on expenses. Bishan, on the other hand, was almost thirty years younger than Lal, and lack of communication was becoming a serious issue between them. She spent most of her time aloof and on her own. She wasn't one to cuddle and love the children like he was. They would all sit on the dinner table with dinner, served by Mwangi, the Kikuyu house servant. The children would talk, mainly to their father while Bishan just ate quietly. Lal had to struggle to say something interesting to his wife, something that would make her look up from the plate. She would just nod or deliberately be brief in her response.

Amrita spent most of her spare time with Lalita, catching small birds and letting them go and they even tried fishing in the streams around the house. Lal tried his best to be a father to Kirpal, Lalita, Amrita and Davinder. It wasn't easy as his relationship was different with each one of them. The children had no idea of the connections. When he could,

Lal would go and visit Wamboi and Lalita in their modest accommodation in the village and made sure they were appropriately provided with all the necessities. On some of the visits, Wamboi would cook chicken and *ugali* with corn and the two of them would sit outside and enjoy the meal while watching Lalita run around in the village chasing chickens. Lal tried his best to spend as much time as he could with both his families, in the village and in the mansion. Lal felt very comfortable with Wamboi as he could talk to her for hours whereas it was so tiresome and awkward to try and engage Bishan in any meaningful dialogue. There were times that he wished he had not gone to India and married Bishan.

"Courage is grace under pressure."
ERNEST HEMINGWAY

The Mau Mau independence movement in Kenya is remembered for its guerrilla struggles against the British rulers fought in the countryside. It began as an urban movement that came out of trade unions in the capital, Nairobi. Makhan Singh was an Indian-born labor union leader who is credited with establishing the foundations of trade unionism in Kenya.

Born in India, Makhan spent his early life in utter poverty and extremely difficult circumstances. He had a generous heart, a strong will and applied all his energy to tackling social problems. He joined his father's printing business when he first came to Nairobi. Soon, he started taking an interest in politics and the local Labor Trade Union movement and founded The Kenya Labor Trade Union and became its first Honorable Secretary. On his return to India, Makhan was arrested for political dissent and for being a communist. He was held in prison for two and a half years, followed by a type of house arrest within his own village. After his release from prison and after serving a further restriction in his village he returned to Kenya and resumed his efforts to reorganize The East African Trade Union Congress, which became the most important militant vehicle for championing African aspirations of freedom. He had the courage to publicly proclaim *Uhuru Sasa*, Freedom now.

Mau Mau leader Bildad Kaggia wrote in his autobiography that he was disillusioned with the main nationalist organization, Jomo Kenyatta's Kenya African Union, which he felt was lifeless. But then he heard Makhan speak at a trade union rally, "He had the fire I admired and was a real revolutionary". Both Kaggia and Fred Kubai, Mau Mau's other main urban leader, worked with Makhan in the trade union movement.

As a trade union organizer Makhan tried to break down the divisions between the Indians, who made up the majority of the organized workers, and the African workers. It was a hard struggle with the colonial authorities' divide and rule strategy aimed to set the two groups against each other. He attempted to show how unity would benefit all workers. He was the key to organizing strikes that won shorter hours and significant pay rises for workers. His role as the leader of the Labor Trade Union of East Africa pushed him to national influence. He toured the country making speeches on the way to achieving freedom from the British.

Lal was in Nairobi and attended the political town meeting at the Kaloleni Hall, where Makhan addressed a crowd of over five hundred;

"The time has come for the people of Kenya to unite. To demand, together, in a single, clear voice that this country is ours."

Cheers almost drowned out his words.

"Remember, my friends, no foreign power has the right to rule over us. We, and only we, will set the standards and the rules and laws of this country."

Again, waves of ascension, louder than the first, rolled through the audience.

"The Time is now."

Though Makhan set the ball rolling for eventual independence from the British colonists, he continued to spend a fair amount of time under arrest for an array of trumped up charges—each one ultimately being dismissed or ending in acquittal. Lal was very impressed with Makhan's drive and commitment to the cause and invited him to come visit him in Nyeri. Makhan brought some of his Kikuyu friends to Nyeri and stayed for a week at Lal's residence. There would be long discussions into the night about getting rid of the British and how to make Kenya independent. They discussed the leaders that were in Kenya, Jomo Kenyatta, Harry Thuku, Bildad Kaggia, Fred Kubai and others.

Lalita was fascinated by all this. She would stay up late, cuddled up against the sofa and listened, absorbing and asking detailed questions. By the time Makhan left, he had a financial commitment from Lal to support the movement, but unknown to him he had converted Lalita to become a dedicated freedom fighter.

*"It is better to lead from behind and to put others in front,
Especially when you celebrate victory when nice things occur.
You take the front line when there is danger.
Then people will appreciate your leadership."*
NELSON MANDELA

Life in Lal's household in Nyeri was about to change dramatically. On a sunny morning in August, a handsome young Sikh turned up at the mill to get some maize ground for his workers. Thakur Singh Kundi had a neatly trimmed beard, blue turban, and tall, well-built frame. His smile was charming, soft-spoken with an infectious sense of humor and he soon became a regular customer who would stop in often for conversations with the doctor's wife, Bishan, who worked at the mill most days. Soon, Thakur became a close family friend. He lived alone and was frequently invited by the doctor for dinners at the mansion. In those days, there were very few Indians in East Africa, so whenever a Sikh came across a fellow Sikh, he was welcomed with open arms.

At this stage, the elder son, Kirpal, began complaining that his stepmother, Bishan, was neglecting him in favor of the two smaller children, and had even struck him several times. This infuriated Lal, and the house was suddenly filled with arguments and strife. Lal decided it would be best for Kirpal if he were sent to a boarding school. The only school in Nyeri was the Catholic Mission School a few miles from the house. Kirpal was admitted there and only came home on weekends or every fortnight.

With Kirpal gone and Amrita and Davinder playing outside or napping much of the day, Bishan began inviting Thakur for frequent visits to the house for tea while the doctor was away in surgery. With no one to disturb them, the visits gradually took a nasty turn. The Kikuyu house servant, Makora, observed the developing relationship on a daily basis and hinted to Wamboi that there was an affair going on. He noticed Thakur and Bishan would be hugging, holding hands and talking for hours. They were similar in age and the physical and emotional attraction between them was quite evident. Thakur was already married with a wife and two sons still in India. He sent money back to the village in India every month to support them.

Initially, Lal didn't believe Wamboi, but after he was told the same thing on a regular basis, he became suspicious and started coming home at different times. It was inevitable. The doctor saw Thakur's pickup truck in the driveway. Bishan and Thakur had become quite careless in their relationship. Their bedroom door was open and Lal walked in on them. Fuming, speechless, and almost ready to kill the younger man, Lal reached for the shotgun hanging on the wall and quickly grabbed the box of cartridges next to it on a shelf. Realizing what was about to happen, Bishan quickly jumped out of bed and wrapped herself in the bed sheet, ran and stood in front of Thakur, daring the doctor to shoot. Lal aimed the gun at Thakur, but his arms were shaking violently. He knew he would throw his life away if he pulled the trigger and killed his wife.

Instead, he threw the gun on the bed and pointed a finger at Thakur.

"If I ever see you again in this house or anywhere near it, I will kill you for sure, now get out of here."

Then he turned his fiery eyes to his wife,

"I am ashamed of you. How could you do this? You will no longer be going to the mill or anywhere. You are staying at home — from now on and not contacting that man again."

But Lal knew that he had lost his young wife and that what he had said was an idle threat. Predictably, his scolding did not stop Thakur and Bishan from seeing each other. Life became unbearable for Lal and his wife. They argued constantly. There was no peace in the house anymore. Their life and their children's world had changed for the worse, forevermore.

After this turn of events, Lal made a decision to sell the flour mill business and concentrate on his medical profession. His two younger children, Amrita and Davinder, were growing up and would soon be sent to school. There weren't any good schools in Nyeri, except for the Catholic Mission. Lal visited the Mission regularly, treating them and giving them advice on various business dealings while he visited his eldest son, Kirpal, who still attended the school. On one of his trips there, Lal noticed a group of local Kikuyus gathered in the bushes, carrying a sick female.

The doctor stopped his car and asked what was going on.

"This woman is dead," one of the Kikuyus replied.

"She has no hope of recovering. She will be burned. Her hut, *in the boma*, will also be burnt. Then the germs will disappear."

After a long argument, the doctor talked them into letting him examine the woman. As he'd suspected, she was alive, shivering and an extremely high temperature, probably malaria which was common in these areas. He asked them to take her back to the *Boma*, and promised to do what he could to treat her. After several weeks under the doctor's care, the woman was sitting up and talking, still very weak but gradually regaining enough strength to soon be up and about.

The Kikuyu villagers were extremely happy and named Dr. Lal

Singh their *"witch"* doctor, as they only had faith in witchcraft and did not believe or trust modern medicines. From that day forth, the doctor was their "god" and every morning five to six pints of milk were sent to his house as a gesture of thanks. Frequently, they would send a goat or two as well.

Lal had very strict rules about health and time keeping. Every morning he would grind almonds, which had been hand-soaked in water the night before. He then added butter and sugar to make a paste. The children were each given a desert spoonful before breakfast. In the evening, they would have a bowl of chicken soup before dinner. Everyone sat down at the dinner table before the evening meal and discussed their day's activities with the doctor taking pleasure in teaching them lessons about life. Once in a while, he would invite Wamboi and Lalita to also join them at the dinner table, Wamboi helped out by making some exquisite native dishes.

When the two younger children grew up and were ready for school, Lal rented a house in the capital, Nairobi. He wanted the best for them and selected the mission school in Nairobi. Although non-white children were not allowed in the English School, since Lal was a doctor for the Mission at Nyeri, Amrita and Davinder were admitted to The Loreto Convent School in Parklands, Nairobi. The tuition fees were extremely high, but he only wanted what was the very best for his two children.

The doctor proved time and again to be a caring and generous father who genuinely loved his children. He paid a good sum for their education, although they were just starting school. The maid, *Ayah*, named Joannie, took them to school and picked them up.

The nuns at the school were very kind. The doctor still practiced in Nyeri, while the children lived with their mother in Nairobi, so they could attend the prestigious school. Bishan was happy too, being away from the doctor. Lal would come for a few days to Nairobi and spend time with them. In later years, the children's memories of their father were extremely pleasant in that he made sure they were brought up and lived like royalty. Their toys and clothes were imported from England. He took great interest in the way they were fed and dressed. They were his pride and joy.

Davinder was the only child in Nairobi with a pedal car. In those days there were very few Indians in Kenya. Everyone knew each other. Scarcely was a vehicle seen on the road in those days. Davinder played with his toy car on the main street and in front of the house. When a car drove by, the driver would stop and let him cross.

Wamboi still worked at the practice and Lalita had been attending the local school in Nyeri, thanks to the Doctor paying all the expenses. Now, she had grown up to be a tall, thin, attractive teenager.

"Our time is limited, so don't waste it living someone else's life. Don't be trapped by dogma - which is living with the results of other people's thinking. Don't let the noise of others' opinions drown out your own inner voice.
And most important, have the courage to follow your heart and intuition."

STEVE JOBS

With his family in Nairobi, Lal grew increasingly lonely and decided to move from Nyeri to the capital. He wasn't spending any time with Wamboi at his house. He purchased five acres of land in Pangani, Nairobi, where he built a house and decided to go into farming. Kirpal, Bishan and the two children moved from the rental unit into the large house. On the property, he planted fruit trees, vegetables, and maize, which were then sold at the market. Amrita and Davinder went to the Catholic school, while Kirpal lived at home. But he told his father that there was constant tension between him and his stepmother, Bishan, because she was always sarcastic and critical of him. When he couldn't take it anymore, Kirpal finally left home.

Lal also purchased a hundred acres of land, fifty in Kibos and fifty in Miwani, on the shores of Lake Victoria. This was the only area in

Kenya where Indians were allowed to buy land for farming. The British had reserved the prime land in the "*White Highlands*" for themselves, to plant tea and coffee. The Kibos area was almost swamp-like and heavily infested with mosquitoes; malaria being prevalent.

The sugar-cane growing areas in Kenya were on the lake and the coastal regions that experienced high temperatures throughout the year and conditions favorable for growing cane. With the high rainfalls and no real distinct dry season, the region had deep fertile soils, which were well-drained. The land also had a good flat infrastructural base for transporting cane to factories. Dry and sunny harvesting spells during the year allowed for maximum accumulation of sucrose. This enabled the harvesting and transportation of cane.

The area around Lake Victoria had a dense population of the Jaluo tribe that provided labor for sugar growing, which was labor intensive. Manual work was needed for planting, weeding, fertilizing, and harvesting. The land was first cleared, ploughed, and then re-ploughed. The harrowing of the ploughed field came next. Cuttings from young cane plants were planted. Buds from the cuttings sprouted in a few days to form new stalks. The plants were regularly weeded. Gapping was done in those initial stages.

Later, very little work was required on the farms as the crops grew. Harvesting was done by hand after eighteen months using sharp *pangas*. The cane was then loaded onto tractor-pulled trailers and transported to a factory in Miwani ten miles away. The farm turned out to be quite lucrative.

Meanwhile, Lal had sold his medical practice to another Sikh doctor, Satinder Kohli, and retired from his practice in Nyeri. The agreement was that Wamboi could carry on working for Doctor Kohli. That's when Lal began concentrating on the sugarcane farms, and spent a lot of time away from home. He built a comfortable farm house in Kibos where he could spend time and take care of the farm.

With him away, Bishan once again had time to spend with her man, Thakur. They began seeing each other even more than before.

Each holiday term, Lal took the children to the farm at Kibos, which was a tremendous experience for them. They traveled by train from Nairobi to Kisumu, which reminded Lal of his trip from Mombasa to Nairobi when he first landed in Kenya, and met Ram with a head full of dreams. Now, he had lost his wife to Thakur. The only consolation was that he had met Wamboi and also had three beautiful younger children.

The trains they rode were run on power that came from coal and from logs. If one got to see the outside traveling next to a window, coal bits might fly up and hit you in the face and eyes. Most of the drivers and conductors were Indians or Sikhs. They all knew Dr. Singh, and they would let his children wander to other carriages. In those days, one could go from one compartment to the other.

The train from Nairobi stopped at a number of smaller railway stations on the way to Kisumu. Kijabe was one of the smaller ones, high on the escarpment and had sulphurous hot springs. People came from all over Kenya to partake of the medicinal waters at the natural spa. On one of the trips to Kisumu, Lal stopped at Kijabe and decided to take Amrita and Davinder to the springs. A local Sikh trader, Mehar Singh, who lived in Kijabe, had constructed concrete areas around the springs where hot water accumulated and the visitors could step down and sit. On that day, Mehar happened to be at the springs. Seeing a fellow turbaned Sikh, Mehar introduced himself and invited Lal and the children to his house which was about a mile away. His house was a mansion spread out on large lot. Mehar's wife Satbir Kaur cooked an exquisite Indian meal and the Doctor and Mehar Singh talked for hours, exchanging stories about Somalia, their journeys from India to Africa and others. Amrita and Davinder enjoyed playing hide and seek with Mehar's children, Raj, Avtar and Surinder. Back on the train, Lal was ecstatic to have met another pioneer and how much he enjoyed the conversations.

Their train journey ended in Kisumu, where they would be picked up by an oxen drawn cart to go the next few miles to Kibos. The roads were extremely rough and, because it rained a lot near the lake, the soil was always black, muddy, and sticky. The roads were often impassable. Wagon wheels would get stuck in the mud and the more the oxen tried to pull, the deeper the wheels went into the sinking ground. Men would try pushing and eventually give up and walk the remaining distance, carrying children on their shoulders. They would come back later when it was drier to get the wagons.

Out on Lal's farm, the workers let Amrita and Davinder ride the tractors, chew on fresh sugarcane, and taste the ripe mangoes, oranges, guava, and the *jamun* fruit, called Indian blackberry. This was a popular seasonal fruit in India that had been introduced in Africa by the pioneers. Most of the farms in the Kibos area had rows of trees with *jamuns* hanging off the branches. Their deep purple color and strikingly sweet-sour taste made the fruit popular with virtually everyone, and it was most desirable because it was loaded with nutrients that worked collectively toward improving health.

Kibos had always been heavily infested with mosquitoes. The children caught Malaria, which no modern medicine could help at that time. They were given Quinine. But when they went back to school in Nairobi, each morning, they would begin shivering by midday, and would be brought home with high temperatures and sent straight to bed. They suffered for a whole year until a friend of Bishan's recommended an herbal treatment, which did the trick, and finally led them to recovery.

Lal decided it was time to have another child, thinking that might bring him and Bishan back together, and make her forget about Thakur. A second son, Mohan, was born. Again, Lal was delighted. But Bishan showed no emotions, and felt even more burdened than ever, now with three children to look after. The new baby did not help the marriage, and the nasty arguments between husband and wife continued.

Lal's hard work was going to come to an end one more time. The night had been quiet. He was at the farm in Kibos, at midnight, dogs started barking, some friends and the workers from neighboring farms came shouting and knocking at the door.

"Doc, come out! Quickly!" they shouted. "Your farm is on fire!"

Most of the labor workforce in Miwani and Kibos was from the local tribe, Jaluos. They were tall, well built, and physically strong. After Lal fired one of the workers, named Odhiambo, for insubordination, the African came back late that night and set fire to the Kibos sugarcane farm, which was almost ready to be harvested.

The dry cane made the fire spread rapidly. The nearest fire truck was in Kisumu, miles away. It was dark. The only way to fight the fire was with buckets of water filled from rainwater tanks that were built on stilts. Men and youngsters also used sticks and dug ditches around the flames, but to no avail. Lal suffered severe burns on his legs and arms trying to put out the blaze; he was never able to recover from the devastation to his farm that night. He had no choice but move to the farm in Miwani, which had modest housing.

Thakur continued visiting Bishan, and one morning they both disappeared, leaving Amrita, seven years, Davinder, four, and Mohan, a baby, at home alone in the big house with the servant. The couple had escaped on a holiday to India.

Luckily, the same morning, Bishan's brother, Bhagwan, came to visit.

"Where is your mother?" he asked the children. "Why are you alone?"

"We don't know. She left while we were sleeping. Mohan has been crying all day," Amrita replied.

Bhagwan was older than his sister, a stocky man with hard features, and a long black beard with silver gray streaks to go with his white Sikh turban. Quickly, he hurried off to investigate his sister's whereabouts, and found out she had gone with a man-friend to the train station; he also learned "the couple" had plans to ride the rail to Mombasa, where they would hop a ship bound for India. Bhagwan raced back and took the baby. He located his sister at the railway station, and handed the baby over to Bishan.

The couple stayed in India for a whole year, visiting holy shrines, sightseeing, and lodging in expensive hotels. Meanwhile, Amrita and Davinder continued their schooling in Nairobi, where they were looked after by the African *Ayah*. Amrita had very long hair and the maid had no idea how to comb it, clean it, or tie it into a braid. As a result, Amrita got lice and constantly scratched her head. One day the teacher noticed, examined her scalp, and sent her home.

When Bhagwan returned to check on the children, he was informed that Amrita had been expelled from school because of her hair. Bhagwan repeatedly wrote to his sister explaining the situation and, finally, Bishan returned. Using home remedies, she was able to get rid of the lice, but it took months.

Whenever Lal came to Nairobi to visit the children, the arguments would start again. The atmosphere was unbearable for everyone. Bishan had no genuine love for her children, only for Thakur. The children were growing up without the natural love a mother normally gives her children.

> *"When the missionaries came to Africa*
> *they had the Bible and we had the land.*
> *They said 'Let us pray.' We closed our eyes.*
> *When we opened them, we had the Bible and they had the land."*
> **DESMOND TUTU**

As the days passed, Bishan refused to see Lal and would go out of the house whenever he visited them in Nairobi. Lal spent most of his time at the farm house in Miwani, when he was diagnosed with Pulmonary Tuberculosis, probably caused by contagious bacteria. He must have been in contact with someone while treating his patients in Nyeri. His coughing was sometimes blood-tinged. He had difficulty breathing, was losing weight and had a high fever. He made frequent visits to the Government Hospital in Kisumu where he was treated by the specialists, but his health continued to fail. Now, the disease had started spreading to other organs. He knew the end was near.

The ailing doctor still made an appearance in court in order to settle an argument he had with another Sikh businessman. The man was suing him for funds he claimed Lal owed him over a dispute concerning sugarcane that had been sold.

That morning Lal went to the bank, took out all his jewelry and withdrew a considerable amount of money. He sold the jewelry then went to court. As he stood sweating, in the box in court, he nearly passed out. The judge ordered a chair and asked him to sit down; they got him some water to drink. In the evening, he arrived home, critically ill. He asked the neighbor, Mota Singh, to make some soup and look after him. Then he whispered to Mota:

"Will you please go to Nairobi and fetch Amrita, my daughter. I have to see her."

Lal wanted to give Amrita the jewelry that was left after paying his debts. Mota drove to Nairobi at night and told Bishan that Lal wanted to see Amrita, who was ten at the time.

"No, she can't go, she has school here," Bishan said stubbornly despite repeated pleas and refused to let Amrita go.

Mota Singh drove five hours back to Miwani,

"Bishan won't let your daughter come to see you, I am sorry, she is a real bitch."

This broke Lal's heart and he went to bed early. In the early hours of the morning, Lal had a lot of difficulty breathing and was coughing continuously. He tried to call for help but was too weak. He passed away, all alone. The house servant found him in the morning and ran to Mota Singh's farm,

"*Dactari* is gone, come quick."

Mota Singh sent a telegram informing Bhagwan in Nairobi of the tragic news. Bishan's brother came to her house to relay the news. The moment the children heard, Amrita, the oldest, realizing the severity, screamed and broke down in tears. Bishan showed no emotion and quietly went to her room. Amrita closed the door and sat on her bed. From the darkness, she saw shapes beginning to emerge and strange sounds filling her ears. She felt dizzy and her senses blurred. There was no form or coherence. Everything seemed to be in a state of utter confusion. The younger two children were scared, not knowing exactly what had happened. The mother made no effort to console her children.

Bhagwan took Kirpal with him and drove to the farm in Miwani to arrange for the body to be sent to Nairobi. Kirpal, as expected was devastated and was quiet on the long drive to go and get his father. Amrita looked after her little brother, Mohan and stayed with him day and night. Davinder was at the age where he wasn't too sure what had just transpired.

At the crematorium in Karioker, a suburb of Nairobi, a close family friend, Chanda Singh, approached Amrita.

"Come on *Beta*," he said.

"Come and pay your respects for the last time to your dad."

Amrita refused, not wanting to see her father lying there in that state. She couldn't bear to see his lifeless face. But Chanda Singh persisted and Amrita finally agreed. Holding hands with her two brothers, Davinder and Mohan, she walked over to the coffin to see her dad for the last time. Amrita's heart ached; tears were just below the surface. She was determined to be brave. The children caught a glimpse of their father's body lying on the wooden platform made especially for him; it would soon be laid on the fire. They observed the little dents on his nose where his reading glasses rested, his beard, all white with patches where the hair had fallen out, but still neatly trimmed; his moustache was slightly shaggy and in death the lines of his brow were relaxed at last. His turban was neatly tied and gave him a calm serene look. Amrita bent down and gently stroked her father's cheek and kissed his forehead. The younger two, not sure what to do or understanding the finality of the situation, followed Amrita and did what she did. Lalita held Wamboi's hand as they paid their final respects. The young children Amrita, Lalita, Davinder and Mohan all hugged each other. Teary eyed, Lalita had no idea that this was her father too.

Dr. Lal Singh had been known throughout Kenya. Sikhs, Gujaratis,

Hindus, Moslems, Africans, and Europeans from all over Kenya came to pay their respects. Government Officials, British and Kikuyu, and those from other tribes also came. His Indian doctor friends, Ram and Sati, were there as well.

The body on the wooden platform was laid on the specially constructed pyre. Liters of ghee were poured on the dry wood. In Sikh tradition, the oldest son, in this case, Kirpal, lit the pyre by placing a lit torch on the ghee-soaked pyre. The fire crackled and popped as the flames took hold and shivered up the tower of logs, licking at the linen shroud. Chanda Singh led the children away from the fire.

Wamboi went back to Nyeri with Dr. Kohli and Lalita. She knew that from now on the monthly allowances from Lal would stop and she was really on her own. Amrita also knew her life had changed for the worse.

After the cremation, Bishan and the children went to live at a family friend's house in Nairobi. She was an older lady named Karam Kaur, who refused to let them go back to their own house.

The next day, Kirpal came to see the family. He was married now. He sat down and talked to everyone and, after a while, asked Bishan if he could take Amrita to live with his family, because he sensed the bleak future that was facing Amrita and her brothers without the doctor. Since there was no love lost between Bishan and Kirpal, she refused to let Amrita leave.

Bishan and the three children continued living in the Pangani house. Bhagwan came by regularly to check on the children. He worked at Athi River and drove a truck transporting sand for Hari Chand and Company. His friend, Amar Singh, also worked there, driving another truck. They lived together. Each time Amar Singh or Bhagwan came to Nairobi they brought Indian sweets and presents for the three youngsters. They would also have breakfast with them and drive them to school in the big trucks with high seats. The children loved being that high that since they could see all the other cars and pedestrians.

Temperamental Bishan was frustrated, having to keep track of three little children; she would have much preferred to get rid of them so she could be with her love, Thakur. Whenever she lost her temper, she would beat the children with whatever "weapon" was handy at the time, a hockey stick, a rolling pin, a broom or just a good swift kick. She hit Amrita on the forehead with a rolling pin, leaving a splinter of wood in the wound. It bled a lot. She cleaned the wound, but the splinter did not come out. After two weeks, Amrita was in constant and severe pain, with a high temperature, and an infected wound. She was taken to surgery to have the splinter removed. The scar that formed on her forehead would always serve as a reminder of her mother and the unpleasant memories of childhood.

Lal's farms in Kibos and Miwani were taken over by his neighboring Sikh farmer, Jagat Singh. He bribed the local Jaluos administrators, and using forged papers and signatures claimed Lal had approved the sale before he died for money owed. His estate, which included the land in Nairobi and the residential property, was worth quite a bit, ultimately these funds paid for the children's Catholic school fees, Amrita's piano lessons, and Bishan's extravagant lifestyle. In addition, she loaned the proceeds from the sale of the land to Thakur, who never repaid the loans. Soon, the piano lessons, expensive clothes, and European foods, all stopped. It was becoming increasingly difficult for Bishan to maintain the house in which they lived. She had to sell the property and was forced to rent a smaller house. Bishan started doing some sewing for people to earn money. They barely survived. The children were taken out of the mission school. The Khalsa School offered to educate Amrita and Davinder in Punjabi, if Amrita agreed to teach English to the nursery school children, which she did.

In desperation, everyone moved back to Nyeri and Thakur's house. Soon after that, Bishan and Thakur were married at home in a Sikh wedding ceremony performed by one of Thakur's friends. The Sikh temple refused to perform the ceremony, because they were from different casts; she was a *jat,* a farmer, and he was a *ramgharia,* carpenter. In those days, inter marriages within casts amongst Sikhs were not acceptable.

A year went by and Bishan gave birth to a daughter, Harbans. Amrita was now the designated *Ayah* — washing nappies, learning to cook, and feeding the baby. Since Bishan now had a new love in her life, the baby, even less attention was given to Amrita and her brothers. Neighboring women would stop by and see Amrita washing nappies at the tap.

"Poor girl, look what she is put through," they whispered.

"What a pity. If the Doctor could see Amrita now, she was his princess, the poor thing. If only he was around. It is so sad."

Bishan liked to pamper herself. She would sit in the living room for hours, covering herself with a shawl and admiring her jewelry and the tattoos on her hands and arms. The Asian community in Nyeri was fairly small. So everyone knew the gossip about the new marriage, and baby.

"Not bad for Thakur, huh?" they would laugh and joke.

"He got what he wanted; he's adopted a readymade family!"

Bishan heard the comments and eventually stopped taking the children out of the house to the Sikh temples and shops. Amrita had a friend next door, Zeenat, an Ismaili girl, who used to come and visit her whenever Bishan was not around; they would sit and talk for hours. If Bishan was around, Zeenat was always driven away so Amrita could tend to her chores.

On one of her visits, Zeenat saw Amrita crying while Davinder played outside. She sat down and asked what had happened. Zeenat was the only person in which Amrita would confide.

"They have gone and left me with the baby again," Amrita said.

"My slippers are broken; they won't buy me a new pair. Thakur says I don't know how to walk, and that I break too many slippers and my clothes wear out too quickly. They've given me two outfits, both made out of material he used to cushion the chairs. The material is thick like tarpaulin. It's so rough, I had to soak it in soapy water and scrub it with a brush. If only my father was alive. Oh, how I miss him. He would never see me like this." Amrita sobbed.

One day the servant, Makora, had put the washing out to dry, some on the line and some scattered on the lawn, and two baby snakes slithered into the clothes. In the evening, Bishan told Amrita to fetch the washing. She brought it in and left it on the bed next to where Bishan was resting. The baby, Mohan, was asleep next to her. Suddenly, Bishan spotted the head of a snake on the bed. She screamed and ran out, leaving the baby on the bed. She yelled for a servant, but no one was nearby. Amrita heard her shouting and came running. Mother told Amrita about the snakes.

"Where is Mohan?"

Bishan pointed to where the snakes were.

"Go and get him mother!"

"I am not going in there," she replied.

Infuriated, Amrita took a deep breath and ran into the bedroom, looking everywhere for the snakes. She tossed the sheets from the bed to the floor, and then saw the snakes, some distance from the bed. She snatched Mohan, dashed back out, and shut the door. Makora returned later to kill the snakes.

BOOK II
Mehar Singh Dhillon

> *"In the End, we will remember not the words of our enemies, but the silence of our friends."*
> **MARTIN LUTHER KING JR.**

In the early part of the twentieth century, in the Punjab, a number of teenage boys heard British rulers were looking for young men to work. The recruiters would give them a few rupees and they happily went off not fully knowing the risk, without even telling their parents. Little did they know they would be marched onto boats in Karachi. They thought they were heading for other parts of India, but the sail and wind-driven dhows landed them on a different continent and in the city of Mombasa, Kenya months later. During the journey, the boys were beaten and some were thrown over if they dared argue with the British captains. They were never given answers when asking where they were being taken. They couldn't speak or understand English. Some were forced to accept sex to survive. Some killed themselves. They felt a surge of pleasure and relief after their hellish journey ended on the East coast of Kenya.

Mehar Singh Dhillon, was one of the lucky ones who was not a slave; instead, he'd volunteered in his village in the Punjab along with a number of his friends when the British advertised and recruited young men to go work on a railway project in Kenya. The youngsters signed up and boarded a train from the Punjab to Karachi.

Arriving in Karachi, almost giddy with anticipation, Mehar and friends, Nanak Chand and Shahbaz Khan, could barely contain themselves as they raced each other up the last hill before the harbor. Cresting it first, Shahbaz came to an abrupt halt, his breath momentarily taken away. Bustling with activity, the docks below hosted an assortment of sailing ships. He turned to the panting Mehar and Nanak, whose eyes were wide with the view, and realized he needn't say a word. Silently they nodded, their faces expressing their gratefulness for each other, and for the opportunity before them.

An hour of winding their way through the maze of piers finally yielded their quest: The *Shahbanu*. They found the captain, Amir Shah, a short, grumpy old man, with skin the color of wheat, ordering everyone in a squeaky voice.

"You three," he greeted them and pointed to an area on the boat, "Go store the baggage over there."

On the voyage, seasickness was common — and Shahbaz certainly got the part about the seasickness right. All three of them spent the first several days hanging onto the ship's rails for dear life, barely able to keep water in their mouths — and that was under the mild conditions of light winds and gentle seas; what would happen when it got rough? They soon found their sea legs and, to the captain's delight, became an integral part of his favorite crew. He admired their hard work and limitless energy, so much so that on occasion he even slipped them extra sweets during the darkest part of night as the boat sailed anonymously through the waves.

After eight weeks, they finally saw the African coastline. The sun rising huge and heavy from the horizon and through a screen of mist they could make out the shadow of Mombasa Island. After docking, they stepped giddily down the gangplank into a city that smelled of fish, of acrid wood smoke and sewage. They were left sweating for a few hours in the sweltering heat of the customs sheds before being released onto the small crowded streets of the Kenyan port. The locals shouting up their greetings in Swahili, "*Karibu,*" welcome. Bougainvillea's tumbled over white walls, purple, orange, crimson red, amidst the trumpets of white flowers and clusters of pink hibiscus. Dhow captains spread their intricately woven carpets on the street for sale, beating out dust in thick clouds. Porters in bare feet and white *lunghis* pad across the hot cobbles.

They spent several good nights resting and sightseeing before they jumped aboard one of the ox carts that took newly arrived Indian workers towards the inland railway camps.

On the tenth day, makeshift tents of the base camp rose from the banks of the Tsavo River. As they got closer, the boys could see the black iron of the tracks snaking toward Nairobi, and smell the vile stench of human sweat, decaying food, and stale cooking spices. Flies barely outnumbered the workers in the overcrowded barracks where bundles of personal belongings, cooking utensils, boxes, and bags were scattered in and among the tents.

For the first time since the storm on the Indian Ocean, the boys exchanged worried glances, but each kept his own counsel. They were here now and would need to make the best of things. The four of them were bundled into an overcrowded tent with four other Indian workers. The tents were barely large enough for three or four occupants.

They quickly learned of the current assignment: build a bridge across the zigzagging Tsavo River to carry the railway tracks. As on the dhow, everyone worked in shifts depending on their role in the haphazard melee of nationalities and skills. Even the cooks worked in shifts, preparing communal meals for the workers, conforming to the dietary restrictions of the Sikh, Hindu, and Moslem cultures.

The 582-mile railway line was going *to* connect Mombasa on the coast to Kisumu on the shores of Lake Victoria. Along with up to thirty thousand other Indians, Mehar worked on the project for three years before arriving in Nairobi. Living conditions were so harsh on the plains that some of the workers returned to India, while others succumbed to malaria, yellow fever, typhoid, cholera, and other tropical illnesses.

The work crews had grown smaller, leaving more work for the ones left behind. The staple diet of the Indian workers was dried beans, lentils, and rice. They had to be inventive, placing an aluminum pan in a thick turban to cook the rice and lentils, *khichri*, in a hole covered with leaves and soil. A fire was lit on top and the grains cooked slowly.

Quite a few of the workers were mauled by the man-eating lions of Tsavo. Others were killed when the local Maasai attacked the workers. A major incident was the Kedong Massacre, when the Maasai attacked a railway worker's caravan, killing around two hundred people, because two of the Maasai *siangikis* had been raped. Englishman Andrew Dick led a counter-attack against them, but ran out of ammunition and was speared to death by the Maasai.

A telegraph line followed the rails to Kisumu. The posts were there and the wire too, but rhinos took sensual and sadistic pleasure in scratching their considerable hulks against telegraph posts. Baboons could not resist swinging from suspended wires. Often a herd of giraffe found it expedient to cross the railroad tracks but would not condescend to bow to the elevated metal strands. As a result many telegrams from Mombasa to Kisumu or the other way around were intercepted with their cryptic dots and dashes frozen in a festoon of golden wire dangling from one or another of the longest necks in Africa.

As the years passed and the workers got acclimated, a small number of railway Indians deliberately 'disappeared' and after cutting off contact with their home villages, started new families with African women in remote places.

Mehar Singh sensed the multitude of opportunities to be successful and make money in this new land of opportunity. He decided to stop working for the railways. Several Indian companies had been contracted by the British government in Kenya to supply cut logs to be used as sleepers for the rail line. Mehar Singh found a distant relative, Prem Singh, who owned one of the companies, and joined him in his work. He bought a wagon and ten oxen to start supplying the logs.

Mehar Singh finally ended up in Kijabe, high on the escarpment. He fell in love with the small village, located about forty miles from Nairobi, and about sixty from Narok in Maasailand. The outpost was on the railway route between Nairobi and Kisumu, on the lake. At the base of the escarpment, Kijabe had sulphurous hot springs. People came from all over Kenya to partake of the medicinal waters at the natural spa.

Mehar Singh grew tired of the railroad business after six years and decided to open a small general store, known as a *duka* in the local Swahili language. He chose the town of Ruaraka, about twenty miles from Nairobi, and started dealing mainly in staples such as groceries, fruit, vegetables, blankets, sugar, and flour. He had trouble learning Swahili, which was a fairly new dialect that originated on the coast, and was made up of elements combining Hindi, Arabic, and English, as well as several African languages. Mehar Singh hired a tutor to come in twice a week to teach him Swahili and English.

The shop in Ruaraka did well from the start, with locals loving being around the shop to buy maize meal, sugar, and tea, but also simply to visit. They would sit around the shop, laughing, joking, and drinking Indian ginger tea with the tall Sikh.

Mehar Singh returned to India to get his wife and bring her back to Africa. His marriage to Satbir Kaur had been arranged by his father before he had left for India to work on the railway line. She had only been ten years old at the time, but now was in her late teens and would be able to travel back with him. Satbir was a small, fine-boned woman with skin that was fair and tiny hands and feet. Her face was small and angular, the regularity of its features being marred only a slight blemish in the alignment of her right eye. She had a voice that was always firm, loud and generated attention.

Mehar Singh also talked to some of the younger men in the village in India and encouraged some of them to go back with him to try their luck in Africa.

Kapoor Singh was one of the men who wanted to go with Mehar Singh. Unfortunately, his mother was quite ill. Elders in the village told him to go and find a cow that was completely black and donate it to the local temple. According to old Indian superstitions, donating a black cow would help heal the sick. Kapoor Singh really wanted to leave India and join Mehar Singh, but he couldn't, as long his mother was alive. Daily he went out half-heartedly in search of a black cow, knowing that if he delayed long enough his mother would pass and he could go to Africa.

Sure enough, two weeks later Kapoor Singh's mother passed away and he joined Mehar Singh, Satbir Kaur, and others on the trip to Kenya. For some unknown reason, Satbir Kaur told Kapoor that his name would be Isher Singh from that day forward, and it stuck for the rest of his life.

After several years passed, Mehar Singh felt the urge to explore. He had his sights set on another adventure. The British government announced the decision to allow Indian traders to start doing business in the nomadic Maasai district. That part of Kenya and Tanganyika was unsettled, and the British were hoping the Indians would develop it for them. Mehar knew he had to explore the untapped market.

Mehar and friends came up with the idea of a traveling *duka*, so rather than having a fixed location where the natives had to come to them, they set up a shop on wheels. He set up his base camp in Kijabe as it was on the way from Nairobi to Narok and Maasailand. He bought a driven cart, from an Irish farmer that would be pulled by twenty oxen;

the cart could carry up to two tons of merchandise. As they traveled through the Maasai district, they would make stops at designated areas, towns, and at the Maasai *Manyattas*. The Maasai district stretched from the outskirts of Kijabe to Namanga, and northern Tanganyika in the south, to Maasai Mara and the Mara River to the west. He planned to take the shop through the sand drifts and mud of the narrow, winding, broken roads, up into the mountains to the nomadic Maasai, rather than rely on them to come to him.

The Maasai men, stereotypically known for wearing red capes, balancing on one leg, holding a long spear and staring into the distance. They originated from Southern Sudan and emigrated along the African Rift Valley. Maasai live in a patriarchal society, with a governing body of older men, and in some cases retired elders, who made most decisions for each Maasai group. If a transgression was committed, tribal leaders made a decision as to what reparations must be made. Normally, compensation was paid in a number of cattle.

The Maasai were monotheistic, worshiping only one god known as *Engai* or *Enkai*. The home of the god was known as *Ol Doinyo Lengai* or 'Mountain of God,' and was located in the northern part of Tanganyika. In traditional Maasai tribes, the priest was known as a *laiboni*.

The traditional Maasai lifestyle revolved around their herds of cattle, which were their primary source of food. Wealth in Maasai society was measured by the number of cattle and children a man had. A 'respectable' amount was fifty head of cattle. If a man had many cattle, but few children, or many children and few cattle, he was still considered poor. As soon as the boys could walk, they were sent out to look after the young calves and lambs or goats of the herd. While most of their time was spent playing, they were also given ritual beatings to test their courage and endurance. The girls spent their time being taught by their mothers to cook and milk animals.

Approximately every fifteen years, all the boys aged twelve to twenty five, who were not in the previous generation, and had reached puberty, were initiated as Moraans or *Il-murran*, warriors. In the coming of age ceremony, the boys were circumcised by a village elder, and were forbidden from crying out.

When Maasai died, their bodies were left as food for scavengers, like hyenas. If the body was not eaten, it could be interpreted as a social disgrace. To avoid this insult, they would cover the body in fat and blood from a slaughtered ox. Only the greatest chieftains were buried, as the Maasai believed the soil was damaged by burial.

The tribal Maasai — with dappled, multicolored cattle, wide horns, and humped backs — grazed alongside the zebras and wildebeest against backdrop of flat-topped acacia trees and golden savannah grasslands. The Maasai set fire to the dry plains to get new green grass for their cattle with the first rain. Thanks to the help of the rains, grass began growing again soon after the fires. Physically, the Maasai were among some of the handsomest of people, with slender bones, narrow hips, and shoulders, and beautifully rounded muscles and limbs.

The *Manyattas*, village huts, were fenced and built with huts in round circles, with lots of room in the middle for cattle and goats — designed to protect the animals from predators. Big bonfires were lit in the middle. The women folk did all the chores, like building the huts, cooking, and milking the cows. The young lads, called *Lionis*, took the cattle herds to graze and to the watering holes.

Mehar Singh and the other Sikh traders in Maasailand wore loosely tied turbans around their proudly held heads and had beards that were never trimmed. They wore high faded black boots and khaki suits almost like an army uniform with an inordinate number of pockets. Some had roses attached to their lapels.

On his trips to Maasailand, Mehar would leave his home base in Kijabe, which had transformed from the tent he started in to a large, gated mansion complete with workers' quarters. The house was raised on stilts with wooden structures and corrugated roofs. He installed a large aluminum tank in front of the house where rainwater was collected, and used for drinking. The five-acre plot was fenced in with wooden stakes and the front had a tall, wide iron gate that was locked and opened by a Kikuyu guard who camped outside the house along with the two Alsatian dogs.

Mehar traveled south toward Narok. Carefully, he would maneuver the ox-driven wagons down the dangerous escarpment in Kijabe and over the steep slopes in Siabei, through a landscape of small, open plains dotted with silvery-white *leleshwa* bushes.

Mehar and his men camped at night, using some of the drier bushes for firewood, the *leleshwa* giving off a pleasant odor as it burned. After the oxen were untied and let loose to graze at night, huge fires were built around the camp and the animals were moved to the middle for protection from predators and poachers. A ring of tenacious, thorny acacia bushes were placed around the camp.

Along with his friends, Mehar spoke fluent Swahili but now he learned the Maasai dialect while making stops in the *Manyattas*, Maasai villages. There, the residents fashioned huts made of fine twigs and *leleshwa* or sage, shaped them into dome-like structures, covered them with a layer of grass and leaves, and finally plastered them with fresh cow dung. There were three entrances to the *Manyatta*, and these "gates" were opened at dawn and closed at dusk. The gates were made of thorny acacia bushes that were laid to block the entrances. The nomadic Maasai burnt their *Manyattas* to the ground when they moved to greener locations.

Mehar traded blankets, sugar, matches, wires of copper and steel, red ochre, beads, flour, and pieces of tires that were used by the tribe to make sandals. The natives had no concept of money and, instead, bartered using goats, sheep, skins, and hides. Mehar Singh would take the hides and leave them with the Maasai *Laibonis* to be picked up on the trip back to Kijabe.

The Maasai lived on milk and cow blood; it was perhaps this diet that gave their skin its wonderful smoothness and silkiness. Their Nilotic facial features, with high cheekbones and boldly swung jawbones, were sleek, without a line or groove in them. The young warriors, Moraans, walked swiftly, placing one slim foot straight in front of the other; but their movements of arm, wrist, and hand were very supple.

Some of the Sikh traders couldn't afford the ox-driven wagons. So, they would walk miles, herding goats and sheep that they bought from one location and sold at another. Over time, they worked hard and made enough money to afford the wagon trains, and eventually built shops. The Dhillon house in Kijabe started resembling a small railway station, with traders stopping in as they passed on their way to and from Nairobi or Narok. The warm hospitality and exquisite cuisine that was offered tempted traders to make an effort to make the stops.

Soon, Mehar Singh had started a string of businesses throughout Maasailand, in Kenya and Tanganyika, with trading shops that were used as small warehouses. The trading stores were spread throughout the Maasai district. Supplies were taken from Nairobi and Kijabe and were transported to remote locations using ox-driven wagons.

Mehar Singh constructed stores in Narok, Endulele, Narosura, Wasonyeiro, and Moricho. He assigned the stores to relatives from his village, who had worked on the railway line or had joined their relatives in Nairobi. The Sikh traders were easily recognizable with their white turbans, khaki suits, and high brown boots. The traders always carried barrels on the wagons and at the various stops on their travels throughout Maasailand, would turn the taps on the barrels to enjoy the dark navy rum.

During the First World War, the Maasai warriors had started looting and burning some of the Indian trader's stores in an effort to get rid of the foreigners. Mehar Singh sent word to all his trading stores requesting that everyone temporarily move to the main location at Wasonyeiro, for safety's sake. All the Sikh traders agreed to come and stay there. Each night, two or three of the Sikhs stood guard. The Maasai frequently attacked the store, but were driven off every time.

There was a tall Acacia tree in front of the store at Wasonyeiro, and Mehar Singh constructed a long ladder to climb the tree. Then he built a small platform up in the tree and covered it with a Tarpaulin roof. During the hostilities, the women and children would climb the ladder after dusk and sleep on the platform. The Sikhs would fire shots into the air before they went to sleep to warn the Maasai. The British district commissioner came and spoke to all the traders and warned them that the situation was getting dangerous, and that they should all move to Narok where an army unit was stationed. But the Sikhs refused and continued their stay at Wasonyeiro. After a time, things settled down and there was peace, at least between the Maasai and the Sikhs.

In 1928, there was an outbreak of foot and mouth disease, so the British set up quarantine, and cattle were forbidden to cross to the other side of the designated boundary. Mehar Singh, being the entrepreneur and leader he was, organized the supply wagons into two groups, so one crew would drop supplies at the border and the other would pick it up. The Africans named the exchange post Karatina.

Mehar Singh encouraged the other traders, who were mainly from his village in the Punjab, to get their own stores so they could establish themselves. One of them, Pritam Singh, approached Mr. Jackson, the district commissioner in Narok, to get a plot of land where he could build a shop.

"There is nothing available at the present time," Jackson told him.

But Pritam Singh persisted, and finally the commissioner assigned him a location.

When the other traders found out, one of them, Hari Singh, met with Jackson to seek his own location, but he was told there was nothing available in Narok. Hari Singh questioned why his friend Pritam had been allocated one.

"You have been coming to me for months complaining that Pritam Singh was helping the Maasai fight the Sikhs and the British," said the district commissioner.

"So, now I have him here at Narok, close to me so I can keep an eye on him."

Hari Singh went back quite disgruntled, and cursing the British.

In the late 1930s, the British opened up Tanganyika so the Indians could open trading shops. After some years of travel in the wilderness, Mehar Singh's wagons had been battered. Many of the wheel spokes had been temporarily replaced with raw native timber, the canopies were patched until little of the canvas was visible. Mehar Singh took time in Nairobi to get the parts, and had the wagons repaired in Kijabe before he started a store in Loliondo, which was about twenty miles from the Kenya and Tanganyika border, four thousand feet above sea level.

The spot was picturesque, high upon a hill overlooking the surrounding green valleys, which were covered with dense and high altitude forests. There were cedar and wild olive trees in proliferation, as well as the wood Loliondo from which the place took its name. As far as the eye could see there was nothing but greenery and dark brown rocks. Mehar built a shop and residential rooms with wooden frames made out of local Loliondo wood and roofs that were corrugated. The structure was raised on stilts to avoid snakes and other creepers. On the main road, opposite the shop, he hung a large sign displaying Johnnie Walker Whisky. It was large enough to be seen from a distance and became a landmark in that part of Tanganyika.

The main inhabitants in that area were three clans of the Maasai: the Loita, Purko, and Leitayo. The shop was primarily stocked for the Maasai, but also catered to the Europeans, as all whites were called. It offered beer, spirits, sodas, cheeses, olives, bread, tea, coffee, macaroni, marmalade, ham, and other meats. Also available were delicacies such as Ovaltine, Milo and Waterbury's Compound, and Horlick's. The khaki-clad Europeans would trundle down from their farms or government offices in their dust-draped four-wheel-drive vehicles and pickups to stop and selected groceries while they enjoyed a beer or two with the Dhillons.

Mehar Singh had also set up a *posho* mill to grind locally-grown corn into flour, providing additional income. East Africa's staple food was maize, which was ground into flour and boiled into a kind of dense cake called *Ugali*, a type of porridge made of maize; the staple meal for most East Africans. The land was so fertile that the maize grew taller than peoples' heads as they walked on the narrow hard-trampled footpaths in between the tall green rustling regiments. The Dhillons would buy the corn and then sell the flour to the Maasai.

Things were going well for the Dhillons with all four of his sons helping Mehar in the expanding businesses.

"Now, as a nation, we don't promise equal outcomes, but we were founded on the idea everybody should have an equal opportunity to succeed. No matter who you are, what you look like, where you come from, you can make it. That is an essential promise of America. Where you start should not determine where you end up."

PRESIDENT BARACK OBAMA

Mehar Singh wanted to diversify his businesses. He met with an Englishman named Michael Newton who was in the lumber business, and they discussed a mutual partnership. Eventually, they formed a new company, bought two old railway engines, fitted them with pulleys and started a saw mill at a remote jungle outpost at Mau Narok, in the Aberdare region. On the way to Mau Narok from Kijabe or Nairobi, the Dhillons would stop in Elmenteita where Mehar Singh's good friend, Moolraj had a grocery store catering to the Asians as well as the European farmers in the nearby towns Molo, Njoro and Mau Narok. Shiv Moolraj, the father, had a loud infectious laugh coupled with a sense of humour that everyone loved. The popular Hindu spoke fluent English, Swahili, Gujarati and Hindi, so was easily able to handle the Europeans, Asians and Africans.

The altitude at all these "white highland" towns was around ten thousand feet with cool breezy mornings, sparkling crisp skies and high clouds. Driving from Gilgil as one began the climb, the greening rim of the Mau Forest at the escarpment's far side with dense trees and knuckled ridges was spectacular. The drive from Elmenteita to Mau Narok went through extensive wheat farms owned by the white Europeans and South Africans. Woolly sheep grazing on low, misted hillsides added to the amazing green scenery. Ever the entrepreneur, Mehar Singh was able to negotiate a contract with the District Commissioner in Narok to clear cedar trees within three hundred feet, both sides of the road from Mau Narok to Narok, as long as he could keep the logs for his saw mill.

With the saw mill being operated by steam engines, it was the cheapest form of energy for that type of work. Since there was no natural spring or river nearby, water had to be brought from Kijabe, thirty five miles away. They drafted a contract with Messi Express Transport in Nairobi to supply the operation with five thousand gallons of water a month. Next, they purchased huge water tanks from Hartz and Bell in Nairobi, and had them transported to Mau Narok.

They received an exclusive contract to transport by road all the timber from Mau Narok to Kijabe and carry water on the return trip. The lumber was then transported from Kijabe on the railway line to Nairobi. The next year, a *posho*, maize, mill was installed at the shop in Endulele and also in Maasailand to grind the local maize and supply flour to the local Maasai in the district.

Mehar Singh enjoyed hunting and, at times, would take off in search of antelopes, zebras, wildebeest, and predator cats. On one of his expeditions, he was challenged by another trader to see if he could shoot more than one lion at a time; they bet a case of Dimple Scotch Whiskey on it. Mehar Singh first shot two zebras to use as bait to lure the pride of lions, which was in the area. He surrounded himself with rocks and hid behind the cover of some bushes. The dead zebras were tied and hung from a tall Acacia tree, directly in front of him. Night fell, and in the fading light the lions approached the fresh meat. As they neared their waiting feast, he noticed there were an unusual number of males among them. They circled the bait cautiously, and then pounced on the hanging corpses, rending the flesh from the zebra's carcasses.

Mehar Singh had two loaded rifles with him. Once the dangerous predators were busy tearing the zebras apart, he could barely see them in the fading evening light. He quietly stepped out into the open and started firing. He was a good shot and before he was done he had killed seven of the males. He returned to camp a happy man and enjoyed the whiskey, a reward of his bet, around the campfire.

BOOK III
Amrita Kaur Dhillon

"When you follow in the path of your father, you learn to walk like him."

ASHANTI AFRICAN PROVERB

As soon as Amrita turned thirteen, Bishan began looking for a match for her. In her way of thinking, finding a match for Amrita would make people stop gossiping about her and Thakur. Bishan, herself had been married very young and could never forget the trauma she went through with her husband's brothers. She deliberated if she could marry her daughter at such a young age, but her selfishness and desire to be with the man she loved overshadowed any logic or feeling towards such an arrangement.

But she had a difficult time finding a suitable match, because marriage to an Indian family was not only a private matter between two individuals, but it concerned the families and extended families. A great deal of thought and planning went into the marriage arrangement. The families could not be related in any way and needed to be of the same caste.

Finally, Bishan approached a friend of Lal's named Nika Singh. He was a friend of a man named Mehar Singh Dhillon, who he was obligated to because of an incident that took place at Mehar Singh's house.

Nika Singh had been at Mehar Singh's house and had grabbed a shotgun hanging on the wall, and began pointing it around the room as if he was shooting. But the gun accidentally went off and hit Mehar in the leg. Nika Singh wanted to repay Mehar Singh for not reporting the incident to the police.

So, Nika went to see Mehar, because he knew the man's eldest son was twenty four and well educated. As it turned out, the son was already engaged to a girl in Nairobi. After listening to the whole tragic story of Amrita's life, Mehar Singh said,

"I will accept this girl for one of my sons."

But Bishan insisted on the oldest son, because the others were not educated. The oldest son, Raj, had finished his high school education at the Government High school in Ngara. That in itself was quite an achievement in those days within the Indian community. As a result, Raj's existing engagement was terminated. When Mehar Singh's friends found out about the new engagement, they came to his house and were livid.

"How can you bring this girl into your family," said one. "Her mother has disgraced the community,"

While another said,

"She is a different caste and you know she had an affair while married to our respected doctor!"

In those days it was considered a disgrace for a Sikh farmer's girl to marry a carpenter's son, or vice-a-versa. That was the reason Amrita's mother could not find a farmer's son for her — even though her father had been a prominent part of the *Jat* Sikh community.

But Mehar Singh stood his ground.

"This is the difference in your thinking and mine," he said.

"Some of you are doctors, lawyers, and also a magistrate. Now listen carefully. What wrong has the poor girl done to suffer for her mother's doings? In addition, this stepfather of hers will marry her to a boy of his own caste; he is trying to do that now. Then will you all be happy? I have accepted this girl for my oldest son and that's that. Besides, I knew Lal Singh and I want his daughter in my house."

Amrita was married into the Dhillon family at the tender age of fourteen to Raj Singh Dhillon, and would ever be eternally grateful to her father-in-law, Mehar Singh, for rescuing her from Bishan. Raj was of medium height, with a chiseled face and finely shaped brown eyes. He was muscular with a straight back and strong arms.

Amrita thought often of how unfortunate she had been to lose her loving father at such an early age. She believed that this was her *kismet* and was meant to be for her. Her father had taken her to the Dhillon's house in Kijabe from the hot water springs and she had met Mehar Singh and Satbir Kaur. She had in fact met her future husband that day playing in the yard. If her father had lived, she and her siblings would have had a good education and possibly entered the medical or some other profession. Her life was about to make another major turn, as she had just become a member of a large pioneering family. Sadly, she was leaving her two younger brothers all alone with their mother, who cared nothing for them. Amrita had no idea how the next chapter in her life would play out, but she was relieved to be out from beneath the rule of Bishan.

> *"Real happiness comes from within and when we help someone, care for someone, love someone, it makes the difference between existence and living."*
>
> **MEHAR SINGH**

The freedom movement in Kenya was gaining strength in each succeeding day. The British Government was becoming stricter in their arrests of suspected Kikuyus and Mau Mau sympathizers. Hundreds of innocent men and women were being arrested and moved to enclosed, secured detention camps.

"I am going to leave home and join the movement," Lalita surprised her mother, one late night as they sat around the fire pit in the village.

"Why, it is not safe. You know that and I will be all alone then."

"Since I met the Sikh, Makhan, I have been meaning to do this for me, for my country and fight to get rid of the British colonialists. I have made up my mind and am leaving with a couple of other young men from the village. We are going to Nairobi and then meeting with others to go to the Aberdares."

"If you have to, then I won't stop you. Go after Amrita's wedding takes place. We owe it to her."

"I will wait a week and then leave."

Amrita's marriage proved a festive occasion, with over a hundred guests traveling from Kijabe to Nairobi and then onto Nyeri riding on the back of trucks and buses. They arrived four days before the wedding, large tents were pitched for their accommodation. There was singing, drinking, and dancing — and more drinking. When the Sikh wedding took place, it was all like a dream to the fourteen-year-old Amrita; almost like a game for her. The ceremony was performed by the local *Gyani* in Nyeri. As it is customary, the Sikh bride is given away by the father or a close relative. Amrita was reluctant but had no say in stopping Thakur giving her away. She would rather have Doctor Kohli perform the ceremony. Thakur wrapped the shawl around her shoulders and placed the remaining end of the *palaa* into her hands. Tears flowed freely as she thought of how her dad should have been there, performing this special Sikh ceremony and not her mother's lover.

On the second morning, after the ceremony Amrita, Raj and all the guests headed back to Nairobi, some continuing the celebration all the way in the back of the five-ton trucks. Wamboi and Lalita were at the wedding and promised Amrita to keep in touch even though she would be far away in Kijabe.

The Sikh tradition is that when a bride goes back to her in-laws' house, her younger brother goes with her for several days to look after her, so Davinder accompanied Amrita. She found herself in an extremely large family. After a day stop in Nairobi, the newlyweds arrived in Kijabe. Suddenly she had three brother-in-laws and two sister-in-laws. Raj, the oldest brother, was the first to marry.

The big house in Kijabe had a number of rooms, some bedrooms and other extended living areas. Raj was assigned one of the larger bedrooms. They were together in bed alone for the first time in Kijabe. Since they had been married they slept separately with family members always being around.

While at home, Amrita was just like one of the children. She played card games, gin rummy, spade, and others with her sister-in-laws, Surinder and Baljit, and brother-in-laws, Tej and Ajit. They played hide and seek outside in the big yard at Kijabe. The older brother-in-law, Avtar, worked on business ventures away from the house.

Amrita had never cooked in her life, but soon her mother-in-law began teaching her the basics of Indian cooking. On the days her mother-in-law went out, Amrita was expected to do the cooking. Being just fourteen, she would sometimes leave dishes on the hot stove, go play cards with the rest of the kids, and forget about what was cooking in the kitchen. Sometimes the food would be burned. Fortunately, a Kikuyu servant, Ndarango, was in and out to check on Amrita. He had been with the family thirty years and continually came to Amrita's rescue, often saving the day and the food, which everyone loved. Ndarango taught Amrita to cook and helped her prepare fresh dishes — and get rid of the burnt ones without the mother-in-law finding out. The Kikuyu cooked often, he was an expert in making Indian dishes. Whenever he cooked, you could hear the lids clanging on and off the pots, onions being chopped along with tomatoes, green chilies, tiny mounds of ginger and garlic stacked and fresh coriander being prepared. The strong odor of onions being fried along with ginger and garlic could be smelled even in the yard. Spices comprising of turmeric, cloves, cinnamon, mustard seed were stored in tiny stainless steel bowls within a large mother platter. After the onions were brown, mustard seeds were added that exploded in the hot oil. He held a lid over the pan to fend off the missiles. Cumin seeds were added next which sizzled, darken and crackled. Next came tomatoes and chilies followed by the goat or chicken meat and a variety of spices from the stainless steel platter.

However, often the mother-in-law would get home sooner than expected and smell the burnt evidence.

"What happened?" she would say.

"I smell something... did something burn?"

She was both strict and kind at the same time, and knew someone had helped whenever Amrita cooked, to cover the smell — probably Ndarango.

Davinder had ended up staying in Nairobi when he came back with Amrita after the wedding, because the schools were better there, enrolling in the Khalsa School. He lived with one of Mehar Singh's relatives in Eastleigh. Davinder did not concentrate much on his education, and had little tolerance for the taunting he endured daily from his class mates.

"Oh what are you talking about. Look at your mother. She married someone from a lower caste."

Every time he would try and defend himself, they would shut him down. He was always in fights, trying to defend himself. When he turned sixteen he joined the British Army.

After spending sometime in Kijabe, her father-in-law asked Amrita to join Raj in Loliondo to help run the businesses there. That was an opportunity for her to get away from the family in Kijabe and to be with her husband. She was excited and enthusiastically made the move. Although she only spoke Swahili, it wasn't long before she picked up the Maasai dialect, dealing with them on a daily basis at the shop. Now, she was fluent in speaking English, Punjabi, Kikuyu, Swahili and Maasai.

To improve the mill's efficiency, Mehar Singh had repaired an old Dodge engine, attached a pulley to it, and coupled it to the grinding mill. The engine ran on *'voco,'* a mixture of diesel and kerosene. He bought over a hundred cattle and set up a ranch outside his Loliondo shop. He also bought a large number of wide-horned brown oxen, bred from sturdy South African stock. The herd was kept in the corral next to the house. He hired two young Maasai Moraan herdsmen who took them out every morning and milked the cows. The Dhillon herd went out and grazed alongside the Maasai cattle and the wild zebras and wildebeest.

The Dhillon cattle were well fed on cottonseeds. After a few months the cattle started looking healthier and in better shape than the Maasai herds. The Maasai pride themselves on the quantity and quality of their cattle, believing all the cattle on earth belong to them, and that they had the right to rustle and keep them. They constantly bargain, sell, and buy to replenish their stock. Most trades take place at cattle auctions, or *mwanandas,* festive occasions held at different places within the district.

Indian traders would camp outside these *mwanandas* and display beads, spears, simmis, and almost everything normally sold at the store. This was a major social event, during which the Maasai reunited with their friends and relatives, and met Indian traders. The Sikhs would gather around in the evenings, drinking barrels of scotch whiskey and discussing their businesses, as well as local news, and happenings in India.

The auctions took place in a specially constructed compound. A high platform was built for the auctioneer, the district officer, the Maasai *laibonis,* witch doctors, and other officials. Cattle were channeled through a narrow alley into a circle enclosed by concrete blocks. The Maasai constantly chewed tobacco and spit, and there was a prominent smell of cow dung. Buyers and sellers pointed at the cattle they chose with long sticks, and the auctioneer sanctioned the trades. Once a trade was complete, the sold cattle were channeled through the alley on the opposite side of the entrance.

The Maasai had become quite envious of the Dhillon cattle, and planned rustling raids. However, the Dhillons got wind of the scheme and Mehar Singh's younger son Tej began carrying a .303 rifle as he accompanied the herdsmen when they went grazing during the day.

Tej was tall, over six feet, slightly shorter than his father but as strong. He had a temper that was unpredictable and quite violent at times. He loved to hunt ever since he was a teenager and had gone hunting with his African teen friends using bows and arrows. They would look for rabbits, small antelopes like *dik diks* and guinea fowls.

Tej and the herdsmen would normally graze the cattle about three miles from the shop in Loliondo, over hills covered with rich rain fed green grass, and across from a river bed which had running water year-round. The Dhillon cattle worked on the farm, pulling the ploughs in the morning and in the afternoon were taken to graze and to the watering hole. The Maasai observed this pattern and planned their rustling strategy accordingly.

One late afternoon while Raj was on a safari, the Maasai Moraans picked a strategic spot and waited in ambush. They attacked Tej and the African, Kipragut. The herdsman ran away as soon as he saw the Moraans coming. But Tej was not so lucky, and was captured before he could fire his gun. He was held down by three of the Maasai. The leader of the Maasai struck him on the head with a wooden club known by the Africans as a "*rungu*." Tej fell and lay still on the ground. Lucky for him, being a Sikh, he wore a turban that helped brace the blow. He was still conscious as he lay there and listened to the Maasai talking in their native dialect. Tej was fluent in the Maasai language and could understand the conversation.

"He is not dead, let me use my *simmi* and cut his head off," said one of the shorter, stockier Moraans.

There was a long pause and the leader spoke.

"Let me hit him on the head again with the *rungu*, and if he moves, he is all yours."

They all agreed to the plan. Tej braced himself for the blow and prayed he could remain motionless when he was struck. The Maasai warrior struck him hard on the back of his head. Tej almost cringed, but did his best to hold back the pain and play dead.

The leader looked down at the Sikh again.

"He's dead. Let's take the cattle before someone comes looking for him."

The Maasai left him on the ground, grabbed his rifle, and took off with the cattle. Bleeding profusely and close to losing consciousness, Tej realized that if he stayed until nightfall, the hyenas or other night predators would almost certainly finish him off. He had to get to the shop before it got too dark. Tej knew he was strong, despite the pain and bleeding. He began crawling, getting up, and walking slowly toward the shop in Loliondo, at the opposite end of the hill. He fell frequently, got up, and started all over again. In his mind, it seemed an eternity.

Amrita was alone at the shop and was getting worried. Tej should have been back with the cattle several hours ago. She grabbed her shotgun and, along with a couple of the African servants, started walking in the direction where the cattle were normally taken. It was nearing dusk and she knew they had to rush or it might be too late to find him. After about a mile, with night falling, in the distance they spotted a figure coming toward them. Using her binoculars, she found Tej, stumbling, getting up, waving his hands, and whistling. Tej was a master at whistling; in good health he could whistle quite a few tunes. He could also make a piercing, high-pitched single note that carried well across the plains. The rescue party heard the sharp whistles and sprinted toward him.

Tej was barely conscious. He collapsed as soon as he recognized Amrita. She held his head in her lap and poured water on him while she examined his head wound. It was still bleeding. They untied his bloody red turban, cleaned the wound, rearranged his long hair, and wrapped the turban again tightly around his head. The servants carried him back to the house. They quickly arranged to have him transported to the government hospital in Narok, a three-hour drive. He was drugged for the journey, because traveling over the rough terrain would be extremely painful.

A bed was placed in the back of the truck and the African house boys helped situate Tej in it. Amrita drove him to Narok, where a Scottish doctor examined him and patched him up. Tej was lucky. The doctor said he would have bled to death in a few more hours. It took Tej months to recover. In the meantime, all the cattle had vanished, and Amrita and Raj were forced to give up the farm. Only years later were the Maasai Moraans finally arrested, tried, fined, and jailed.

> "Muhammad, the Prophet, In the name of Allah,
> Most Gracious, Most Merciful. Those who reject Allah and hinder
> men from the Path of Allah,
> Their deeds will Allah bring to naught. But those
> Who believe and work deeds of Righteousness,
> And believe in the Revelation sent down to Muhammad –
> For it is the Truth from their Lord,
> He will remove from them their ills and improve Their condition."

THE HOLY QUR-AN

Amrita and Raj sat glued to their RCA radio listening to Alvar Lidell broadcasting on the BBC World News in the living room of their store in Loliondo.

"At 11:15 a.m. today," Alvar announced, "The Prime Minister, Mr. Chamberlain, broadcast to the nation the following statement announcing that a state of war existed between Britain and Germany."

The prime minister was then heard:

"This morning the British Ambassador in Berlin handed the German government a final note stating that, unless we heard from them by 11 o'clock that the Germans were prepared at once to withdraw their troops from Poland, a state of war would exist between Britain and Germany.

I have to tell you now that no such undertaking has been received and that; consequently, this country is at war with Germany. You can imagine what a bitter blow it is to me that my long struggle to win peace has failed. Yet I cannot believe that there is anything more or anything different that I could have done, and that would have been successful."

That same year, Amrita, gave birth to her first child, a daughter named Maya. The family wanted a grandson, and they were all disappointed. There were subdued celebrations in the Dhillon household. The next year, Amrita lost twin boys.

The war continued in 1940, bringing rationing in Britain early in the New Year, but little happened in Western Europe until the spring. On May 10, the same day Winston Churchill replaced Neville Chamberlain as Prime Minister of the UK, Germany invaded France, Belgium, and Holland, and Western Europe encountered the *Blitzkrieg* — also known as the "lightning war."

On New Year's Eve of 1944, Raj had prepared for a journey to Loliondo from Kijabe and was planning to leave the following morning. Although the truck was loaded and all set for the trip, he was told by his mother to take the truck, and go fetch the midwife from the Mission Hospital about ten miles up on the Escarpment in Kijabe as Amrita was in labor. Raj did as his mother suggested and the nursing mother arrived about midday. There were no means of medicine to relieve Amrita's pain or hasten the delivery. It was left to nature. Amrita was exhausted and given hot drinks. Then on new year's day at 4 a.m. she gave birth to a son, Akash — a Dhillon grandson — with the help of the nursing sister from the Mission Hospital.

Amrita was twenty one years old now and had grown to five-feet, eight-inches tall; she was an attractive young woman and mother. Amrita's mother-in-law was over the moon having her first grandson. It was a great and festive occasion. Amrita's two sister-in-laws were so happy that none of them wanted to go to Loliondo. They wanted to be with the baby all the time. There was a boy in the family after twenty years. Grandmother hosted a large gathering for the religious Sikh ceremonies to celebrate in front of a *Gyani* and served gobs of Indian food, sweets, and beverages.

Things took a turn for the worse when Akash was just twenty days old. He caught a cold and the doctor was called but the cold worsened. He had difficulty breathing. One of his father's sisters, Surinder, went to the temple next door in Kijabe, to get some holy water. The other sister, Baljit, got some Eucalyptus leaves from a tree down the hill. She crushed the leaves, wrapped them in a muslin cloth, and made the boy smell them every thirty minutes. The treatment helped and he began breathing more easily. Akash was a weak baby and was fed on Cow and Gate brand powdered milk, because Amrita didn't have enough breast milk to feed him.

Mehar Singh loved his grandson and, although there were quite a few ladies around to take care of him and feed the baby he would ask repeatedly,

"Has he been fed properly?"

The whole family would gather around the dinner table, with Akash sitting in the middle, and they would play with him. The uncles — Avtar, Tej, and Ajit — taught him all sorts of habits and words, which weren't necessarily the best for a young boy.

After a few months, Amrita returned to Loliondo, her sister-in-law Baljit went with her to assist and to look after Akash while Amrita did all the house work and helped at the store. Although there were servants to do the washing and cleaning, the women of the house did all the cooking and supervised the servants.

In 1945, the New Year saw the Soviet liberation of Auschwitz, and the revelation of the sickening obscenity of the Holocaust, its scale becoming clearer as more camps were liberated in the following months. The Soviet army continued its offensive from the east, while in March from the west the Allies established a bridge across the Rhine at

Remagen. While the bombing campaigns of the Blitz were over, German V1 and V2 rockets continued to drop on London. The return bombing raids on Dresden, which devastated the city in a huge firestorm, were often considered misguided.

In the meantime, the Western Allies raced the Russians to be the first into Berlin. The Russians won, reaching the capital on April 21st. Hitler killed himself on April 30th; two days after Mussolini had been captured and hanged by Italian partisans. Germany surrendered unconditionally on May 7th. The war in Europe was over.

Another eighteen months passed and a second daughter was born to Amrita in Loliondo. A Kikuyu midwife attended the birth. Amrita named the baby Surjeet. This time, Amrita's father-in-law, Mehar Singh, visited. Seeing that Amrita's hands were full, he ordered to have a servant for each chore and an *Ayah* to help look after the kids. The *Ayah*, Nazeera, was a teenage Arab girl from the coast. Her father was a cook at the district officer's house. She slept with the young ones in their room. Nazeera stayed with the Dhillons until the age of twenty and then got married. She was treated like family and given a dowry that included clothes, utensils, and bedding.

The Dhillon shop at Loliondo was a store that catered to the local Maasai. They were supplied with blankets and cotton sheets called *Shukas*. They would dip the sheets in red ochre mixed with water before drying them in the sun. They claimed this made the bad foreign smell disappear. The Maasai did not like the smell of soap. Some of the Maasai came to England and America, only to return after getting their academic qualifications. The first few days they came to the store, they spoke good English and would dress up in shirts and trousers. But after a month or so, they would come back dressed in the traditional shuka dipped in red ochre. When asked why, they would reply,

"My wife does not like the smell of my western clothes and I don't like it either."

The shop also sold cornmeal, beads, sugar, and tobacco. Some western groceries were stocked for the district commissioners, district officers, and the police force — items such as cheese, bread, jam, Scotch, beer, soft drinks, and gin.

When he was five, Akash accompanied his father on hunting trips and sometimes even visited the Maasai *Manyattas*. On one trip, Amrita went with Akash and Raj on a visit to the local *Manyatta* near Loliondo. *Laiboni* Roma felt it was his special duty as a friend of the Dhillons to pay his respects to their family by baptizing Akash. He sat Akash down on a small stool while he sat on a taller one in the middle of the village. His enormous pot belly hung over his red blanket. His two front teeth were missing, like most Maasai. There was an unsightly mole about the size of a dime on his right cheek which drew attention whenever one looked at his face. When the big *Laiboni* would speak, spit would fly freely in all directions through the gap.

Roma blew his nose by blocking one nostril with his thumb and shooting a shaft of silver mucus onto the grass through the other. He wiped the residue from his upper lip with the palm of his hand. Then he rubbed Akash's face with his bare hands and started spitting onto the young face, rubbing the spit all over his face while he recited the words of a ritual in the Maasai language. With tears in his eyes, Akash pleadingly looked at Amrita for permission to get up. She nodded back that he should just keep still, bear it and avoid upsetting the Maasai leader.

Roma prayed for Akash's good health, his sexual prowess, and for him to grow up respecting fellow humans and the animals in the Serengeti. He followed by picking up a handful of red soil, rubbing it on Akash's face, and spitting several times more onto his face. Then he rubbed the spit and dirt all over Akash's cheeks, lips, forehead, and mouth. The ritual continued for about ten minutes, while Akash was trying desperately not to throw up. Finally, Roma stopped and held Akash by the shoulders and helped him stand up. Roma wanted to circumcise Akash as well, but Raj told him it was against the Sikh religion. To further honor the Dhillons, Roma offered one of his daughters as a bride for Akash. Raj again intervened and said they should defer that for a while. This gesture by Roma was considered to be the ultimate in respect, coming from a *Laiboni*.

Akash and Maya moved to Kijabe now and were admitted to the local school. They lived there under their grandmother's supervision and with their aunts, Surinder and Baljit.

On some of the trips, Akash would join his uncle, Tej, when he went to the saw mill at Mau Narok. He could roam around and watch the trees being sawed down and then the logs transported to the saw mill. On one of these outings, he had wondered off on the main Mau Narok to Narok road where the trees were being cleared on both sides of the road per the agreement between Mehar Singh and the District Commissioner for Maasailand. Not really paying any attention, he didn't hear the Kikuyu workers shouting at him as a tall wide cedar tree fell right in front of him, just missing him. He looked up and somehow for a young lad had the foresight to get under the fallen log before a second tree fell right on top of the first log. The Africans panicked and ran towards Akash from all sides, fearing the worst. He just crawled out from under the first log and stood in the middle of the road with green leaves all over his face and clothes. The shocked natives thanked god and carried the young boy back to his uncle Tej who severely reprimanded him for wondering and getting in danger and ordered him to stay around the house from now on.

Even though he was confined to the area around the house and the saw mill, a week later, Akash wondered off around the mill. The workers were sawing the logs and tossing the small cut pieces in a pile about ten feet away, he wasn't looking and one of the sharp wooden pieces, the size of a brick, hit him on the temple. One of the Africans saw the boy go down and ran to him. The bleeding had to be stopped, so they shut the engines off and carried him back to the house. Tej was furious and called for the local compounder to come and apply stiches to the right side of Akash's head.

That was enough for Tej and he sent his nephew on the next truck taking logs back to Kijabe.

> *"I swear that I will fight for the African soil that the white man has stolen from us. I swear that I will always try to trick a white man and any imperialist into accompanying me, strangle him, and take his gun and any valuables he may be carrying. I swear that I will offer all available help and further the cause of Mau Mau. I swear that I will kill, if necessary, anybody opposed to this organization."*

OATH TAKEN BY THE MAU MAU FREEDOM FIGHTERS

In the early 1950s, the Mau Mau freedom movement in Kenya was in full swing. Lord Delamere, now a member of the Kenyan Parliament, had rushed legislation through which was written solely to benefit the whites. With his Soldier Settlement Scheme, British veterans were allocated farms at low prices. During clamorous public meetings held in London and Nairobi, names and numbers were chosen from revolving drums to select the winners of the farms from among thousands of eager applicants.

Lord Delamere's mandate was that no African or Asian would be permitted to own any of the land known as the white highlands. Four-fifths of the best land in Kenya was owned by less than five thousand whites, and one million Kikuyu were expected to use the other one-fifth that had generously been set aside for them. Many of the Kikuyus hurt by this injustice joined what was known as the Land Freedom Army Movement. The Kikuyus were denied any major additions to their reserve and they were never reconciled for the loss of their original lands of birth.

Resentment grew, and the militant faction, Mau Mau, began gathering strength under Dedan Kimathi, who had given himself the title, Field Marshal Dedan Kimathi. He always wore a leopard skin cloak to disguise himself in the forest. Upon their initiation into the movement, the Kikuyus had to swear an oath stating:

"I swear that I will fight for the African soil that the white man has stolen from us. I swear that I will always try to trick a white man and any imperialist into accompanying me, strangle him, and take his gun and any valuables he may be carrying. I swear that I will offer all available help and further the cause of Mau Mau. I swear that I will kill, if necessary, anybody opposed to this organization."

The Mau Mau started setting fires to homes and huts and killing livestock belonging to European farmers. They fought the British from the Aberdare Forest in organized raids on European settlers. They also organized attacks on Kikuyus who were loyal to the British and also invaded small shops owned by Asians in remote areas. Their technique was highly developed. At dusk they would poison the dogs and cut the telephone wires and, as darkness fell, they would walk into the farm-houses and attack the occupants. When the Kikuyus heard that Dedan Kimathi had gone to the forest to fight, they would sing in fanatical support:

When our Kimathi went up
To the mountain alone
He was given strength and courage
To defeat the white people.
We cry because we are black people
And we are not white

Nor are we beneficiaries of their blessings
Ngai, our god is our leader
He said all the footsteps
That I have taken
You must take them too
And drink from the same cups.
Do not let persecution make you afraid
Not even to be sent into detention camps
Nor to be robbed or t o be killed
With Ngai in our leadership.

The British administration declared a state of emergency. The European settlers took to carrying loaded revolvers wherever they went, placing them out on their dinner tables, the time of day when most of the attacks took place. The Kikuyus, which comprised the bulk of the movement, lived in huts deep in the forests. They conducted gruesome initiation ceremonies for new members, supervised by their witch doctors. They would chop the legs off cows and sheep belonging to Europeans and the animals would be left to crawl helpless on the ground, with only one or two limbs remaining on each. Occasionally, English farmwomen were raped, grossly mutilated, and tortured before they were killed. Initiation ceremonies included drinking blood mixed with urine, animal brains, and other revolting things.

Lalita had moved away from Nyeri and now was in the Aberdares, near Elmenteita. She took the Mau Mau oath and joined the fighters there. The role of women in the freedom movement was significant. They served as couriers, the only means of reliable communication within the organization in the forests and reservations. A number of cases were reported where their efficiency averted disasters which could have wiped out individual groups or freedom fighters. Lalita wanted to be on the front line and fight alongside the men.

Lalita met Kirit Ole Kisio alias Sungura, a Maasai, one of the very few who wasn't a Kikuyu and had joined in the struggle. Sungura is the Swahili word for rabbit and he had been nick named that by his father. He was attractive, tall like most Maasai Moraans and very efficient fighting on the front. He moved naturally like a cheetah. Sungura had decided that Kenya should be free and rid of the British rulers and he would do anything to help that cause. He had some Kikuyu friends and they together went to the Aberdares. It wasn't long before Sungura was one of the leaders with his own gang.

The fighters had transformed some naturally occurring caves in the forests to strategic hiding spots and bases. The caves, at the foot of Mount Kenya open out to a beautiful waterfall and pass though rocks on the Burguret River. These served as hospitals for the wounded fighters and home to others. The entrance to these hideouts was accessible by using dangling roots that acted as ropes and ladders. The nights were perilous in the dark, bat-infested caves. Some of the caves had rivers running through long tunnels which also became safe havens for the Mau Mau.

Lalita was assigned to Sungura's gang and started developing her fighting skills under his guidance. She was trained in the use of guns, bows and arrows, hiding in the forest and in the ability to move quickly through the Aberdare forest. Lalita and Sungura spent a lot of time together, discussing the fight for freedom. They were almost inseparable day and night. She would lie in his lap for hours in one of the caves and talk.

"Tell me all about the Maasai ceremonies, I know you have so many of these," Lalita asked Sungura.

He would explain in great detail the Maasai ceremonies from childhood, boys and girls circumcisions, to teen years to Moraans manhood and then to being an elder. She was fascinated as the Kikuyus had their rites but the Maasai life seemed so much more interesting. Then she would ask about the freedom movement, how it started, the leaders and strategies. He was patient and took his time explaining.

Their first mission together was to attack a young English farmer

John Egerton and his doctor wife, Virginia, who lived in Njoro with their six year old son. Under the cover of darkness, just before dawn, Lalita, Sungura and three others descended down the steep green hills and to the wheat farm. One of the Kikuyus crawled on his knees and elbows and baited the two Alsatian dogs with some poisoned rabbit meat. Within thirty minutes the group was in the house and in the bedrooms. Sungura was the first one in and went straight to the main bedroom and shot John at point blank range before slashing Virginia to death with his deadly panga. The other Kikuyus entered the son's room. The boy was fast asleep while they shot him. Lalita just stood there, shocked, this was her first experience and it was traumatic. She was shaking and crying, having no idea of the cruelty that she was witnessing.

"Come on woman, come on, what are you waiting for, get any guns you find, food and bullets, we have to take the cows and sheep as well, hurry," Sungura shouted at Lalita.

She stumbled forward and started going through the house looking for items to take back with them. They rounded up the cattle and goats before setting the house on fire. On their way back to the hideout, Sungura calmed Lalita down.

"Stop crying. It is difficult the first time. You will get used to this. You know we have to do, what we have to. Next time will be a lot easier for you. You will have to participate, more than you did tonight."

It was ironic that the slain doctor had opened a free surgery center for the Africans and his front door was always open, expecting to find a patient needing urgent treatment. These killings were followed with Lalita involved in attacks on an English family on their farm near Mau Narok and the killing of a Kikuyu village leader who had openly been sympathetic to the British.

Wamboi was still working for Doctor Kohli in Nyeri. She came down with a severe bout of pneumonia which became worse and both her lungs contained air sacs and became infected. Kohli visited Wamboi in the village on a daily basis to treat her but her health was failing fast, she could hardly breathe. His prognosis was that it was caused by a virus. She had been on antibiotics for a while now, but still wasn't getting enough oxygen. That was starting to cause damage to her kidneys and the heart.

Kohli sent a message to Amrita in Kijabe to come and see Wamboi, not knowing Amrita was in Loliondo. As soon as Amrita received the telegram from her sister-in-laws in Kijabe about Wamboi's health, she drove to Nairobi and then onto Nyeri accompanied by a driver.

Kohli had no idea how to inform Lalita as it was rumored that she was now in the Aberdares but no one knew exactly where. So Kohli informed the men in the village,

"Please try and find her, send a message with anyone who might know her whereabouts. She should come right away."

Unknown to Kohli and most of the people in Nyeri, Lalita had influenced quite a few men in the village with her fanaticism to free Kenya. It didn't take long for the message to get to Lalita about Wamboi, but to get to Nyeri she had to be very careful. She had to get past the British military made up of British Soldiers, The Kings African Rifle soldiers, The Home Guards and the Kenya Police. She used different disguises and travelled on the crowded *matatu* pickups driven by the Kikuyus. Unfortunately for her, Lalita had picked the wrong time and the wrong route.

Like most Innocent Kikuyus, she got caught in 'Operation Anvil', the code name, organized by the British to roundup Kikuyu suspects who may be Mau Mau fighters or helping them. In Nairobi, British troops and home guard units circled the suburbs. Every road, track and path was sealed and no African was allowed to leave or enter the city. Barbed wire enclosures were quickly set up with machine gunners taking strategic positions on roof tops, their ghostly silhouettes barely visible in the early morning light. The city of Nairobi remained a 'closed district' for a month at the end of which, thousands of Africans in the city were screened, but only the Kikuyus were detained.

She was stopped at the roadblock just outside Limuru and ordered to squat on the tarmac street among the others already gathered there. Hours went by in the scorching sun. Her legs were numb and throat parched. Finally, they were ordered into Lorries and driven to a detention camp in Karioker, cordoned by a high barbed wire enclosure. Once again, they squatted for hours, waiting, for what they did not know.

In the interrogation process designed to identify important suspects who belonged to the Mau Mau movement, or sympathized with them, *Gikunias*, hooded Kikuyu informants, sat quietly watching the multitudes being shepherded past them. They were questioned, to determine if they had taken the oath, knew any Mau Mau suspects or their operations or locations. From time to time, the informants would spit on the ground and lean forward to whisper into the ear of a British officer, giving him the name and alleged offense of the activist they had noticed or suspected. African *Askaris* walked between the rows, prodding the squatting detainees with their rifles and kicking anyone who moved a muscle.

When her turn came, nervously, she kept her head down, hoping that the *Gikunias*, Kikuyu informers, would not recognize or pick her. One of the taller Jaluo *Askaris* looked at her and slapped her, knocking her down. She made the mistake of looking back at him. This time he kicked catching her just below the stomach. She doubled over in pain.

"Get up woman, quick, get over there," he shouted.

She was questioned over and over about her connections to the freedom movement and if she had known any of them. She kept her head down and had no response for them. The Jaluo pointed to the others to drag her onto the waiting Lorries and take her to prison, in Kimathi, just outside Nairobi.

In the meantime Amrita reached Nyeri. She went to see Doctor Kohli first before going to the village.

"How bad is it, you have to tell me?" she asked Kohli.

"Her pneumonia is past the stage where we can save her. She has been going downhill for the past month. It is too late. I am so sorry."

Amrita drove down to the village and Wamboi's hut. Wamboi was lying on a wooden bed, covered with a light mattress. She had a couple of heavy greenish blankets covering her but was still shivering. Her eyes were closed.

"It is me, Amrita, I am here," as she walked closer to the bed.

Wamboi tried to open her eyes, hardly recognizing the visitor.

Amrita repeated that she was next to her. Wamboi made an effort, lifted her head, touched the visitor's face and finally recognized her friend. She was relieved that someone from the past was there to see her. She whispered,

"Oh, my friend, come closer to me, thanks so much for coming, I have been waiting for you and Lalita. Where is my daughter, is she here?"

Amrita leaned towards Wamboi so she could hear better,

"I am here, Lalita will be coming soon," Amrita assured her.

Amrita sat next to her bed on a small wooden bench and held her friend's hand,

"You are going to be fine. Be strong."

Wamboi was more realistic and shook her head,

"No, I know my time is up. This is bad. I have never felt this sick in my life. Even Doctor Kohli has told me that. But, I called you here as I have something important to tell you Amrita, it is about Lalita."

"What is it?"

Slowly and almost in a whisper, Wamboi started relating the whole scenario to Amrita, about her being shot years ago in the village by people from Nanyuki who had come to steal the goats, stopping several times as she had difficulty breathing. She told Amrita how Lal treated her and took care of her. She had moved into his house to recuperate. She stayed with him for weeks and fell in love with him.

"I, I loved your father from the day I saw him. He was so handsome and caring and loving. We spent so much time together, days and nights. We would talk till late at night, teaching each other different things. It was wonderful, what memories. This will surprise you I know, but Lalita is your half-sister."

"What? Oh my god, I had no idea, that explains why Lalita is so fair, her curly hair and even a lot of her mannerisms resemble mine and of my, of our dad. I can't believe this."

Amrita was shocked and sat in silence for quite a while, still holding Wamboi's hand.

"That clears up a lot, I always wondered about our closeness and my love for you and Lalita."

Wamboi gently squeezed Amrita's hand and pleaded,

"I want you to promise to look after Lalita after I am gone. She is your sister and blood and really has no one else in this world. Now, she is with the Mau Mau and that scares me even more. You have to promise."

"Wamboi, I promise, I will. That is the last thing you have to worry about."

Amrita tearfully left Nyeri and Wamboi, her birthplace with sweet memories of her life with her father Lal, Lalita, Bishan, Davinder and Wamboi. The memories were bitter sweet with Bishan but the other remaining memories were priceless.

At the prison in Kamiti, the detainees were brutally tortured and beaten by the black *Askaris* as well as the British soldiers and policemen using electric shocks, cigarette burns and broken bottles, gun barrels, knives and snakes thrust up men and women's private parts. Lalita was beaten up on a regular basis but finally released from Kamiti prison as they couldn't pin anything on her and she was getting weaker by the day.

She managed to get to Nairobi and jumped on a bus to Nyeri, hoping to see her mother. She needed help to get onto the bus with her injuries sustained at the hands of the Askaris and the British interrogators. She arrived too late. Wamboi had passed away two days earlier, dying of respiratory failure. Lalita sat in front of Wamboi's hut, her head in her hands, tears flowing down her cheeks. The villagers tried to comfort her. Wamboi had been buried in the forest the day after her death. Lalita was taken to the grave by the women so she could pay her last respects. She was there for hours. It got dark before the villagers persuaded her to come back to the village.

Sadly, she thought, if it wasn't for the screening she could have seen her mother, one more time. This reinforced Lalita's willpower to fight the British, they had detained her and she had missed the chance to say goodbye to her mother. She left her birthplace, Nyeri, for the last time and headed back to the Aberdare Forest and back to her love, Sungura. At least he was there for her.

"When the character of a man is not clear to you, look at his friends."
JAPANESE PROVERB

At the store in Loliondo, the main trade was in cattle skins or hides and sheep in addition to the grocery items. Mehar Singh started buying sheep and when the stock reached two or three hundred, they would be taken into Narok and other areas to be auctioned. The sheep were kept in an enclosed yard next to the shop. One night a leopard jumped over the fence and slaughtered a number of these animals before carrying one over the fence.

The following morning, Mehar reported the incident to the district office and got his permission to kill the leopard, if it returned. This turned out to be quite a cunning animal to capture or kill. Although the forests and plains surrounding the complex were searched for two weeks there was no sign of the predator. Around the same time, one of the family's Alsatians delivered a litter of puppies. A small box was made for the pups where the mother would come and feed them. The night after the puppies were born, the leopard returned. It leapt over the fence and got inside the compound. As the bitch slept, the leopard grabbed her by the neck, nearly killing her then took off with two of the puppies.

It was about 11:30 at night when Mehar Singh and the boys heard the dog screaming. First on the scene were Tej and Ajit who ran into the yard to check on the commotion. They found the bitch badly mauled, hardly breathing, moaning, nearly lifeless. The Sikhs were furious and were determined more than ever to kill the leopard. The next morning, a trap was set inside the courtyard: the trap was baited with fresh goat meat tied to a wooden pole and small bells were tied on strings wrapped around the meat.

The leopard showed up on the third night and grabbed the bait. Ajit, the younger brother, was on watch, he heard the bells ring when the leopard grabbed the goat meat. Moving quietly, he carefully aimed at the leopard's heart and fired. The animal was wounded slightly but managed to jump over the fence and out into the bushes. It was too dark and dangerous for Ajit to track the animal in the dark. He cursed the leopard, but there was nothing he could do until morning, so he went back to bed.

Early, next morning, the herdsman Juma, came to take the cattle out of the stock yard. As he approached the fenced *"boma"*, where the animals were corralled, he saw the spotted leopard hiding behind some gasoline drums. Juma back tracked and quietly walked over to the courtyard and shouted for Tej to wake up and come outside.

He told Tej,

"*Chui* is hiding about one hundred yards over there," pointing towards the drums.

Tej was unaware that his brother had wounded the leopard the night before. He loaded his shot gun and approached the *boma*. He heard the animal's hoarse, sawing bark before he saw the spotted predator. As soon as he was within range, he aimed and fired. There was no charge from the gun and no shot rang out. He fired the second bullet, but the same thing, nothing happened. By this time, the leopard had seen him and came out charging at the young Sikh. Tej quickly reloaded his gun with a new set of bullets but the leopard was too quick and pounced on him, Tej thrust the gun barrel into the animal's mouth and fired, there was no sound. The bullets he was using were old British army stock and were defective. In loud Punjabi, he shouted for help while cursing the British, the makers of the bullets, the makers of the rifle and anyone else he could think of.

While the struggle between the tall strong Sikh with the gun in the leopard's mouth and the huge cat trying to get to Tej's face was going on, Juma caught hold of the leopard's tail and chopped it in half with his sharp "*simmi*" long knife. Enraged the leopard turned away from Tej and started charging towards the young African. The herdsman ran as fast as he could with the animal in hot pursuit and hid in a wooden shed that stored equipment for the farm and closed the door shut.

With the African out of reach, the leopard turned back towards Tej and jumped on him. The young Sikh pitted his strength against that of the vicious animal. They wrestled in the dust and on the dried grass, Tej trying to avoid the slashing claws and razor-like teeth of the leopard.

Ajit heard the growling beast and the cries of his brother for help, he noticed the open door. He let a cry of alarm to alert the rest of the household and ran with his rifle to the yard, where he saw his brother struggling with the leopard. Ajit waited and aimed his rifle carefully, looking for an opening where he could shoot at the animal without hitting his brother.

Tej seemed to get a better grip on the leopard's coat and lifted the animal off his chest by brute willpower and strength. Ajit only had a moment, but it was all the time he needed. He slowly let out the breath he he'd been holding and gently squeezed the trigger. There was a sharp noise, and the force of the bullet knocked the leopard out of Tej's grasp and into the dust beside him. The leopard was dead before it hit the ground; it was quite a sight to see the beautiful animal next to the bleeding, injured but still breathing Tej.

The big cat had badly mauled Tej. In addition to the two inch laceration on his arm, his wrists looked nearly severed from his arms. He was rushed to the same hospital in Narok that had treated him for his injuries after the earlier assault by the Maasai rustlers. The difficult four hour journey and considerable loss of blood took its toll on the young body. It was nearly six months before he recovered completely. When he came home, Tej's body was marked with grim reminders of his struggle with the leopard. He had a permanent imprint on his thigh, shaped with the exact dimensions of the leopard's claw. This turned out to be quite an attraction for the European tourists passing through Maasailand. In the evenings they would sit near the outdoor fire pits and Tej would show them the claw on his thigh, the stiches on his wrists and relate the experience while they took photographs.

*"A woman is like a tea bag –
You never know how strong she is
Until she gets in hot water."*
ELEANOR ROOSEVELT

The British colonists had appointed district officers and district commissioners throughout Kenya. Harry Fosbrooke was the DC for Maasailand who had set up residence in Narok. A resident of Kenya for many years, he was a big, good-natured man with blond hair and gray eyes, seldom seen without a cigar in his mouth. Mehar met him at one of the *Mwanandas,* the cattle auction that the Maasai attended to buy and trade cattle. The two sealed their friendship while hunting together, discussing a range of subjects, always including politics. Over the years, Fosbrooke tried to engage Mehar in deeper and deeper discussion, until finally, one day, among a particularly large hunting party, including several other Asian and African friends, Harry floated the idea of a political run by Mehar.

"A political run?" Mehar said. "You can't be serious, Harry."

Mehar's friends held their collective breath and nodded their heads in agreement.

"And why not my old chap? You certainly know the Maasai district," Fosbrooke said.

"Your Swahili and Maasai dialects are as fluent as any native, not to mention that your grasp of the political needs of this area is spot on. I am absolutely serious, my dear man!"

"Even if what you say is true, I wouldn't know where to begin," Mehar said. "You begin by joining the party. Then, let me worry about the rest."

Sensing what they wanted, rather than hearing Mehar's actual decision, the rest of the group let out a cheer. Mehar never even realized he'd forgotten to say yes. After joining the Kenyan African National Union, or KANU, Mehar and Fosbrooke got to work on his platform. Because of Mehar's extensive travel throughout the region, he felt strongly about leaving the land as it was and halting all new development of farms and tourist lodges. Knowing the nomadic Maasai favored his plan, as it would allow them to maintain their cattle herds and have ample grazing land, he spent time with the *Laibonis* — the Maasai leaders — explaining the benefits of political representation. He traveled throughout Maasailand, camped in remote areas, and campaigned with help from other Sikh traders and his four sons.

In contrast to his plan to establish a moratorium in the Maasai territories, Mehar's opponent, an independent candidate named Joseph Ole Likimani, ran a campaign of race and nationality. A Maasai educated in Narok, Ole Likimani emphasized the fact that he was a native of Narok and knew what was right for his countrymen, but did little else.

In the meantime, Mehar knew what a challenge it would be to get the nomadic Maasai to register and vote. Living in remote areas of the country with no means of transportation, except cattle and donkeys, they had never voted before. So on Election Day, he and Fosbrooke arranged buses and trucks to transport the Maasai to the voting booths in Narok. The immaculately planned and managed campaign strategy worked. The large turnout made Mehar the easy winner, earning him the right to represent the Maasai in the Kenyan Parliament.

Mehar traveled throughout the Maasai district, getting to know his constituents. In time, the hard-working Sikh gained President Kenyatta's trust and confidence, which helped him fight for a number of political rights - successfully.

One such victory was a moratorium that restricted the settlers and developers from buying land in Maasailand. This preserved the land for the Maasai and their cattle. Another was an agreement between the Somalis and Kenyans over water rights. The simple and carefree Maasai were also educated about the intricacies of a political system. Mehar gained their respect and that of the other tribes. A politician had never represented the nomads so effectively. Now that he was an elected politician, Mehar Singh discarded his high brown boots and khaki safari suits. After Ole Likimani lost his election, he became a Maasai Member of Parliament. The Maasai saw what Mehar was doing for his tribe and they formed a strong friendship.

The next step in the charismatic Sikh's political career was to move up in the ruling KANU party. When it was suggested that Mehar Singh could run for the secretary's post, it was almost considered a joke. It had always been a position occupied by a black African, so a European or Asian running for a primarily black African political party was not only risky, but unheard of. Mehar, the proud and enterprising Sikh, considered it the ultimate political challenge.

Mehar Singh, helped by his entourage of young Sikhs, campaigned aggressively along with the Jaluo leader, Oginga Odinga, who was running for the vice president's post. Ole Likimani also joined Mehar in the campaign. The pair presented a formidable partnership. Over time, friendship and respect had grown into a strong personal and political bond. Mehar and Ole Likimani lobbied for support from the incumbent members of the Kenyan Legislature, ultimately forging an alliance with Oginga Odinga and the Jaluos from Kisumu, as well as the Makambas from Machakos. Together, they hoped to present a strong and united front against the Kikuyus and their incumbent candidate, Michel Kariuki.

Ole Likimani, ever a keen adversary, discovered that Kariuki had been involved in more than a few questionable dealings with some large Asian building contractors. It seemed he had used his influence to sway certain officials in awarding lucrative Kenyan government contracts.

The manipulative Asian businessmen had rewarded Kariuki with large sums of cash deposited into foreign banks, beach resort vacations, and airline tickets. Using his own considerable contacts, Ole Likimani leaked the news to the political editors at the Kenyan national newspapers. This permanently damaged Kariuki's reputation and credibility.

The morning after the election, Kariuki, the incumbent secretary general of the Kenyan African National Union, was as gracious in defeat as he had been vicious during the campaign. Dressed in his customary starched khaki pants and shirt, he conceded,

"My heartfelt congratulations go out to the Asian leader Mehar Singh Dhillon. He is a worthy and deserving winner of the contest. He knows Kenya and is a true *Wanainchi*. He knows the people and their problems. I wish him all the success and will support him."

As the newly elected Sikh secretary of KANU, Mehar would report to President Kenyatta. To his fellow citizens, President Kenyatta was simply, *Mzee,* Swahili for "old man," a title of greatest respect and affection in East Africa. Revered as a godfather and regarded as a hero to the average Kenyan, Kenyatta had become the first president of their independent Country when it broke free of colonial British rule.

After Mehar received the congratulatory phone call from the president, the crowd exploded into pandemonium. Champagne corks popped and kegs of strong beer were tapped as the celebration began in earnest. Jubilant Sikhs started the traditional Bhangra dancing, while enthusiastic Maasai danced by jumping in the air with their *makukis* and chanting, "*Kala Singha! Kala Singha! Kala Singha!*"

One of the first Sikhs who settled in Kenya was Kala Singh; to most natives, all Sikhs who wore turbans were *Kala Singhas*. The daring and adventurous young Kala Singh, from whom the name *Kala Singha* was derived, came to Kenya before Mehar Singh. They had developed a close friendship and Kala spent a lot of time with Mehar in Maasailand.

Mehar's popularity as the secretary of KANU grew by the day. His pleasant mannerisms and firmness in making decisions became a frequent subject of conversation throughout Kenya, and his neutrality in dealing with tribal matters surprised even the Kikuyus. *Mzee* liked the tall, turbaned Asian and invited Mehar to accompany him on several state visits to other countries, which proved an excellent strategy, as the multi-racial leadership representing Kenya bode well for the extremely important tourist industry, the mainstay of the Kenyan economy.

Although Mehar came to be accepted as an "African at heart," his beliefs about Africa and politics were formed mostly from his religious views, although he rarely discussed his Sikh religion with non-Sikhs. Over its five hundred year history, the Sikh religion had evolved from needing to defend Hindus from their oppressors — the Moghul Islamic invaders in India. Mehar believed Sikhism was the only religion in the history of the world that had ever fought for the human rights of another religion.

As a Sikh, Mehar recognized God as the Creator and Sustainer of the universe; he accepted the need for each person to live a life of physical, moral, and spiritual self-discipline. Devotion, discipline, and humility were the cornerstones of the Sikh faith. Sikhism taught that the true believer was a man of action with an overwhelming sense of self-reliance. Taking his religion seriously, Mehar extended that tenderness toward his fellow man from the depths of his humble heart. These efforts continued to gain him notice.

After Mehar had held the elected office for ten months, the East African Standard printed an editorial on him entitled, "The Man and His Popularity," and hinted at his prospect of becoming the next President of Kenya. Popular as he had become though, this caused quite a stir among the Kikuyus, who wanted another Kikuyu to follow Jomo

Kenyatta. Charles Lare, a Kikuyu and the vice-president of KANU, had his own ambitions set on the highest political post in the country.

> *"The dawn of a new day is the herald of another sunset.
> Earth is not thy permanent home, for life is like a
> Shadow on the wall. Even as thy friends have departed,
> So thou too must go. Thou hast lived this life as though
> It were everlasting, but the Messenger of Death forever
> Hovers near."*
> **SIKH FUNERAL PRAYER**

As Mehar's popularity grew, rumors circulated that he may well become a serious contender for the vice presidency of Kenya in the next election. The press and Mehar's constituents openly discussed the possibility that he was being groomed to be Kenyatta's successor. Lurking desperately in the background, though, lay the ambitious Kikuyu, Charles Lare, who longed to succeed Kenyatta. Lare's camp grew increasingly concerned as Mehar made front page news, complete with photos of him with Africans in remote villages, and with Europeans and Asians at sporting events and social gatherings throughout the country and with the president himself.

It became more obvious that the Asian Sikh would be a major hurdle. His popularity could even block the politically ambitious Kikuyu, Lare. His advisors held secret strategy sessions trying to develop a plan to overcome Singh's growing threat. Amid several protests, Lare decided to involve his cousin, Malefu Njoroge, a key member of the Kikuyu underground. His mission, quite simply, was to eliminate the competition. Rather than a public assassination, with too many potential variables, they agreed to hunt down their prey on his own land.

Malefu, experienced in the underside of politics, knew Mehar had a house servant who could easily be bribed. Armed with Mehar's detailed schedule, two accomplices and more than enough ammunition, Malefu arrived late one evening at the Dhillon's Kijabe estate. Without a word, Muranga, a traitorous staff member, led them to the shed that overlooked the front courtyard of the house, from where, before dawn, the murderers would set their sights on their target.

On a Friday, the sun rose on a cloudless Kenyan sky and, right on schedule, Mehar had his morning cup of spiced Indian tea and was sitting on the back terrace reading the national newspapers.

"*Mwanake*, a party of Maasai are asking for you at the front," Muranga interrupted.

"Thank you. I'll be there in just a minute."

Mehar took a final glance at a headline predicting his nomination and smiled. He stood, straightened his turban, smoothed his linen shirt, stroked his long beard and made his way to the front door. Taking three steps onto the porch he looked for the visitors. A single shot rang out, hitting him in the shoulder. Surprised, he turned toward the sound as he pressed both his hands on the shoulder, only to be met by two more shots that made their marks in the center of his chest and another on his forehead. He was dead before his sizeable frame hit the ground.

"Try getting elected now, Curryman."

Malefu sneered as he and his associates carefully made their way into the scrub and back to their car amid the confusion of the aftermath.

News of Mehar's murder sent shockwaves throughout the continent. The initial news flash on the Voice of Kenya Radio broadcast was of a robbery attempt at the Dhillon residence by a band of local Kikuyus.

"...It is believed that the popular Kenyan political figure was killed by Kikuyu bandits when he attempted to foil the robbery attempt," came the voice from the radio.

"Mehar Singh's body was discovered by his daughter, Baljit. He had been shot several times and there was blood on his forehead and chest."

Soon though, the rumors started that black Africans had carried out a political assassination. Newspapers across Africa and the world alternated stories of conspiracy with profiles of the Sikh pioneer who had made Kenya his home.

As announced on *The Voice of Kenya* Asian broadcasts and in the national papers, the *Nation* and *The East African Standard*, funeral arrangements were set for Sunday morning in Nairobi, allowing time for people to travel from East Africa, India, and the continent.

Sikhs, Hindus, Moslems, and Gujaratis throughout East Africa learned of the murder in their respective news journals. Through a flurry of phone calls, the Indians scattered throughout Kenya, Uganda, and Tanganyika and arranged a meeting at the Gurudwara in Nairobi.

Once there, they quickly made their way to the city mortuary where, according to Sikh customs, they watched Mehar's sons bathe their father in yoghurt and oil. The Sikh's compatriots then tied a new turban about his head — taking care to wrap it just low enough to cover the gaping hole left by the assassins — before dressing him in new white clothes. Together the men placed his body on a wooden platform, covered him, with first a red sheet, then the Kenyan flag, and finally a layer of roses. The Sikh Gyani recited prayers and sprinkled the body with *amrit*, holy water, before sending Mehar Singh on to his Nairobi residence in Pangani.

While the men prepared the body, Satbir Kaur and the other women of the family, and innumerable friends, began prayers at home before making their way to the crematorium. The wooden platform was lifted and placed on an open truck. The inconsolable crying and wailing drowned out the city noise as the funeral procession inched through the Capitol. Smartly dressed in white, Kenyan policemen on motorcycles led the truck, which was followed by a long entourage of cars, pickup trucks, and Lorries. The streets were lined by thousands of tearful Africans and Asians waiting to see the truck carrying the popular politician's body, and to pay their last respects. The funeral procession paused at the Sri Guru Singh Sabha Temple, where the Sikh *Gyanis* offered more prayers, and the body was laid before the Holy Granth Sahib.

In time, the procession reached its final destination, the Karioker Crematorium, on the outskirts of town. Mehar's four sons and three best friends carefully made their way through the hundreds gathered to the pyre, where they gently laid their hero to rest on the high wooden platform. The friends stepped back to allow the *Gyanis* room to recite more prayers while the sons poured ghee onto the wooden platform and the body. Then, in unison, Mehar's boys lit a torch, igniting the wooden platform. When the flame reached the ghee, the pyre burst into flames.

Onlookers stood for more than half an hour, watching the pyre burn. Eventually they began to leave in small groups, but the *Gyanis* continued praying as long as the fire burned.

When the last wisp of smoke made its way into the now-sullied sky, the mourners returned to the Sikh temple. After everyone settled in, sitting on the floor, cross-legged and hands clasped, Anarkali, a Moslem girl from a family that was close to the Dhillons, sang Mehar's favorite Shabad, *Madho, tum aysa hum ayesee*. The *Ardaas* prayer was then followed by eulogies made by prominent members of the Sikh community, by Mehar's Punjabi friends, and even by his first political opponent and steadfast friend, the Maasai, Joseph Ole Likimani. Mehar Singh's oldest son, Raj, concluded the service, emphasizing his father's honesty, integrity, leadership, genuine love for his fellow human beings, and Kenya — the adopted country he so dearly loved.

President Kenyatta had sent his aide, Makora Masharia, to extend his condolences. *Mzee* had telephoned Satbir Kaur and expressed his shock and sorrow at the loss of a personal friend and at Kenya's loss of a political giant. He promised to do everything in his power to bring justice to the murderers.

The sons of Mehar Singh, along with close friends and Ole Likimani, journeyed to the crematorium the next day to pick up the ashes. The last remains were then taken and scattered in the Tsavo River, according to Sikh customs, and in accordance with Mehar's wishes. He had worked on building the railway bridge at Tsavo and wanted his ashes to float away at that point.

One of the Kenyan journalists, Asif Khan, who was a special correspondent for the English *Sunday Times*, wrote an article on Mehar Singh:

> *If these early days in Mehar Singh's life have a message for modern times, it is surely this: then as now, man is the greatest predator there is.*
>
> *Much has been made of romanticizing the adventurous spirit of Africa's past: of Kenya's past. The man-eating lions of Tsavo stalk through the annals of our literature, assuring us that there was a time when life in Africa was wilder, freer, and more dangerous.*
>
> *Yet even then, even for Asians like Mehar Singh, who settled in what was then British East Africa, the greatest danger was never hiding in the tall grass of the Savannah.*
>
> *During those pioneering years, Mehar Singh faced down nearly all of Africa's greatest "killers." He was chased by a lioness, his son was mauled by a leopard, and the whole family was involved in the dangerous sport of hunting elephants and rhinoceroses. Yet the friends and family of Mehar Singh who were attacked by wild animals mostly survived. Nearly all whom he lost in those early years died at the hands of their fellow Kenyans.*
>
> *Our country has not lost its danger as it has embraced western culture and civilization. Rather, we have internalized the savagery; the old hatreds and tribal resentments dressed up in three-piece suits, and sent them off to the office. Beneath the thin, cracking veneer of civilization, Kenya and the Africa of today have no less death to offer the unwary explorer. It is only a more civilized death.*

So don't look for irony in the fact that Mehar Singh survived the dangers of wildest Africa, only to be killed in the supposed safety of his own compound. Now, as then, the greatest predator that man needs fear is man.

Avtar took off on his own and went to Dar-es-salaam in Tanganyika; he wanted to be independent and away from his family. The other three sons, Raj, Tej, and Ajit, took over all the businesses throughout Maasailand. They each ran some of the business entities. Life eventually got better and easier, with everyone keeping busy, but they hardly ever saw each other because the businesses were so spread out.

"Someone is sitting in the shade today because someone planted a tree a long time ago."
WARREN BUFFETT

Life went on, Amrita lived in Loliondo. Her children, Akash and Maya, were in Nairobi because of the better schools there. Mother-in-law, Satbir and Baljit, moved with them from Kijabe to their residence in Eastleigh, Nairobi. Amrita's eldest daughter, Maya, twelve, was charged with taking care of her brother Akash. Maya would get up in the morning, get her brother ready, feed him, and cook breakfast for everyone before going to school. Meanwhile, the two women, Baljit, and the mother-in-law, slept the morning away.

Tragedy struck the Dhillon household. Ajit, the twenty five year old youngest of Mehar Singh's four sons, passed away in Loliondo after getting infected with a rare fever. By the time they were able to transport him to Narok Hospital, it was too late. Ajit had been the anchor of the family, organizing all the businesses and managing them after Mehar Singh's death. He was fairly short but extremely strong and could lift a large drum full of gasoline over his head. The Maasai loved him. They trusted the Dhillons, especially Ajit. In fact, they would leave all their valuables with Ajit, without any accountability, and would return later to claim everything.

Amrita's husband and her brother-in-law Tej were heart broken. They kept saying,

"We are not going to the stores anymore. Our brother has gone. We can't go on without our brother Ajit. He did everything for us."

They all stayed at Nairobi for a fortnight after his death. Then one day Amrita said to her mother-in-law,

"Manjee, what is happening to us? Is no one going to open the business again? What are we going to do? We have children who need education, food, and clothing! If they won't go to the store, I will. I know how to run the business. I've been helping all this time. I know how to deal with the local Maasai; they must be lined up outside the store, waiting for their supplies. That's it, tomorrow morning I'm taking the turn boys and we're driving to Loliondo."

"How can you? Are you sure? Can you drive the truck?"

"I've driven… a few times before. It will be fine."

"I pray that you can do this. Go and do it my child. Something has to be done. I know my sons are heart broken. And if you can start the businesses, they will join you soon, I'm sure," Satbir encouraged her daughter-in-law.

On hearing this, Tej, her brother-in-law, quickly jumped in.

"Amrita, I will help you to set up and go to Loliondo."

Tej was an excellent shot. He liked to go on hunting safaris on his own or with tourists who wanted trophies. Accompanied by the Kikuyu, Kamau, Tej would load up his Dodge truck that had been converted into a hunting vehicle, with an open roof and no door on the driver's side. He would stock up with food and drinks, camping gear, supplies — and take off. At times he would be gone for weeks with no contact; then he would return with the prize trophies. On one of the safaris, within a week, he had shot a leopard, two elephant bulls with massive tusks, and a rhino that had two extraordinarily long horns.

Nairobi had flourished into a crowded and bustling city with buildings still speaking of a different era, optimistic but shortsighted. The growth of the city had never been anticipated. Three- and four-stories were thought to be enough. Never intended for multiple tenants, the buildings bore the scar of each subsequent resident, with windows boarded up like broken teeth, and air-conditioning units hanging from them like cigarettes from dirty mouths.

The first thing Amrita did was to go shopping for her safari clothes that were comfortable for long, uncomfortable, dusty drives. She went to Bishendas Brothers in the Indian Bazaar and looked at clothes made for the Europeans to go on safaris. After some time she picked a khaki vest that she could wear over her khaki Punjabi suit. The vest had multiple pockets, short sleeves and even had the slots to store bullets. She picked a pair of brown leather high boots that almost reached her knees, ideal for bush walks, through thick grass, deep mud, typical savannah environments including mean ants and poisonous snakes. Next, she drove to an Indian tailor and had him sew her three khaki Punjabi suits. Each was comfortable with loose salwaar and kameez. She also bought matching khaki *chunnis* that she could wrap around her neck and also covered her head. She was feeling good with the attire that she had chosen and was almost ready to tackle and challenge the world. She was confident that she could do this.

Amrita drove to the stores on Bazaar Street, Grogan Road, Government Road, and to the warehouses in Nairobi's industrial area. She shopped for all the needed goods, such as flour from the mills, sacks of sugar, blankets, beads from the Indian Bazaar shops, kerosene, and fifty-gallon petrol drums from the Caltex station. She went to Bishandas and Sons to stock up on cheese, sausages, ham, cigarettes, and cigars for the Europeans who frequented her shop. The supply shops were all owned by Indians and whenever she went to the distributors, they all knew the Dhillons and would ask,

"Where are the boys, Tej and Raj? You shouldn't be doing this."

"They are sad and sitting at home with their mother, mourning," she would reply.

Although she didn't tell anyone, she was quite apprehensive about the drive to Loliondo. Once the five-ton Mercedes Benz truck was loaded, she had the two African turn boys, Robert and Rashidi, start with her on the drive out of Nairobi to Loliondo. It was the first time she would be driving the truck over a long distance. The terrain and slopes would be difficult to navigate.

She stopped at the house, changed into her safari outfit, the khaki salwaar and kameez, along with the chunni. She looked dashing.

Satbir, Tej and Raj were home and were in awe of how good she looked,

"Now, that is one good looking truck driver. Take care my child," Satbir complemented her.

She drove out of Nairobi on the main Nakuru Road, scaled the Kikuyu escarpment, and passed Limuru twenty miles from Nairobi. African teenagers were playing soccer, barefoot, in the open fields of Limuru High School. Another few miles and looking down from the precipice, she could see the sheer and breathless drop of the Great Rift Valley. This continental divide, a literal rift through the heart of Africa stretched four thousand miles, from Mozambique to Northern Syria. This is one of the true marvels of the world.

Herds of wild animals roamed the valley floor, dotted with defunct miniature volcanoes, including Longonut, near Naivasha. The wind howled as it travelled through the valley and reached the top of the escarpment breaking up into eddies and backlashes amongst the hills and the broken ground of the rim. Looking down into the valley from the seven thousand feet high escarpment, shadows moved in the distance. Looking intensely, a giraffe took form, then two more. When some branches moved with the wind and others did not, she could make out the spiraling horns of a stationary kudu among the twisted thorn trees.

In the background, the plain beyond the river was studded with flat-topped acacia trees. Dark shadows on the golden horizon resulted from of herds of wildebeest. Giraffes, with their hides paved with bold rectangles of red-brown, fed from the thorny upper branches of the acacia trees. Their long graceful necks swayed against the brittle blue of the sky. The giraffes would dart out and pick on the thorny leaves with their eighteen inch skilled tongues. Their lips appeared to be immune to the vicious thorns. Amrita watched the progression of the giraffes across the plain. The animals with their inimitable, vegetative gracefulness appeared as if it were not a herd of animals, but as a family of rare, long-stemmed, gigantic speckled flowers advancing at a snail's pace.

She almost drove the truck into a bull elephant that stood just below the crest of one of the hills, much too canny to silhouette itself on the skyline. His bulk was screened by a new growth of leaves on the tall trees, and he blended in well with the grey rock of the slope behind him. He reached up twenty feet and sucked the air into his wide, hair-rimmed nostrils, and then rolled his trunk down and delicately blew into his own gaping mouth.

Amrita slowed the truck and brought it to a standstill. The bull had suddenly decided to cross the road in front of her. The elephant started moving slowly, clumsily it jumped over the small stream, splashing water onto the road. For a good ten minutes he stood in the middle of the road and faced Amrita and the truck, surveying the scene, flapping his ears, and moving his trunk all around. He walked toward the truck and stopped, noticing that the still vehicle appeared harmless. Sensing no danger and carrying his thick yellow ivories high, he slowly crossed the dirt track and disappeared behind the acacia and thick *lileshwa* trees. He followed a steep trail that would take him down deep over the escarpment to the plains.

With mechanical steering and brakes, the truck was difficult to handle. Amrita had to use all her strength as she started the descent to the bottom of the valley. Because she was nervous, scared, and straining, the steering put an enormous strain on her arms, shoulders and neck. Her *chunni* was getting in the way as she maneuvered the truck. She quickly had to wrap it around her neck. She gripped the steering wheel with all her might to stop it from getting ripped away from her hands. Her foot was smashed to the brake pedal continuously and she had the truck in low gear as it crawled down the slopes.

Driving downhill at such an incline was enough to put an enormous strain on any vehicle. The engine was hot, with steam billowing out the sides. The sandy edge of the road fell away toward the valley floor three thousand feet below. She took the truck into a tight turn and felt it drift sideways and heard the pop of small stones when the sliding front tires forced them over the side. An angry grinding sound cut through the truck's engine noise as they neared the valley floor. Amrita felt the second gear begin to slip. The transmission popped into neutral. The Mercedes truck began gathering unwanted speed as it ripped around another tight bend.

"Mama you are doing fine," Robert reassured Amrita. "Just keep your foot on the brake and watch the road."

She pulled on the hand brake to slow the lorry for a final narrow turn. The vehicle skidded around the corner. A burning smell filled the cabin. They freewheeled down, down, down. Fortunately, a gentle curve met them at the bottom and, as the road approached an incline, the truck began slowing. The road evened out! The truck came to a gradual stop. Amrita hunched over the steering wheel. Tears spilled from her eyes as she took deep breaths. She shook like a leaf. Robert scuttled over and put an assuring arm around her.

"You did great, *Mama Safari*. That is your name now. You saved the truck and all of us, too. You can handle this from now on, *Mama Safari*."

She wiped her tears, took another deep breath, and exhaled. Why did she have to do this? There were other men in the family who should have stepped up to be there. She waited a few minutes to gather her senses then drove the rest of the way to the bottom of the incline and stopped the Mercedes. The turn boys refilled the radiator with water from the stream that crossed the road. Amrita walked down to the stream and scooped the cool refreshing water to wash her face and arms before sitting down on a rock, waiting for the boys to get the Mercedes ready for the remainder of the journey.

After a good rest, Amrita started the drive over the hills, past the rows of *lileshwa* trees and finally onto the open Siabei plains. Going down the escarpment in Siabei, she thought of the stories she had heard multiple times from her father-in-law, Mehar Singh, and how he had navigated the same slopes with ox-driven wagons, fully loaded with supplies, for the Maasai and the travelling duka.

The tarmac road gave way to murram — degraded gravel that was dug from nearby quarries, and then crushed, spread, and rolled — making for a dusty ride, especially at high speeds. If following too closely, the vehicles driving at high speeds kicked up small stones everywhere, causing many windshields to crack. Amrita remembered her father, the doctor, telling her to drive as fast as possible on pothole-filled dirt roads, because you were halfway through the next bump by the time you felt the first one. The thought of Lal not being there, made her teary eyed again.

The truck flew down the road, stirring up a cloud of dust that must have been visible for several miles across the Savannah. This sent a large group of eland zigzagging off into the bush. Everything was strangely quiet except for the noise of the diesel engine combating the steep upgrades and the speed gained over the open plains. Blue smoke blew from the exhaust pipe. A few heavy drops of rain splattered against the windshield, but Amrita did not slacken her speed. As the rain came harder, the windshield wiper struggled on the driver's side, causing her to lean out the window as she drove in order to clearly see the road ahead.

Driving through the plains after the rains, the new short green grass was shadowed with broken glades and islands of thick green bush, and an occasional tall, flat-topped acacia thorn tree. The herds of zebras, wildebeest, Thomson gazelle, and impalas grazed along the dirt road. But when they heard the truck's loud diesel engine approaching, they would stare momentarily, then wag their tails and begin galloping away from the truck. The zebras snorted, kicked their hind legs high in the air, while the impalas jumped as high as they could and chased each other. The animals would stop behind a thicket, staying close together, believing they were safe from the strange and loud moving noise on four wheels. The scurrying warthogs would run and suddenly stop, their tails sticking straight up in the air. The little dik-dik, tiny antelopes with cloven feet, appeared out of nowhere, and then disappeared just as suddenly. Here and there, what looked like huge pieces of black volcanic rock moving ponderously through amid lesser animals, just like gray ships on the ocean, massive elephants, rhinoceros, and cape buffalos of the land wondered across the plains.

They got to the plains after Ndasegera.

"Look mama, *chui hapo*," Robert said. Amrita stopped the truck suddenly. "There are cheetahs hunting over there!"

It was an incredible scene. A fully-matured bushbuck, black with age, with spots on his haunches faded like old chalk marks, was being stalked by the two cheetahs.

Amrita, Robert and Rashidi sat and watched for what seemed like an eternity. A breeze gusted up from the plain to the north, the air pervaded with the sweet scent of the off-white and pale yellow blossoms of acacia trees. A buck grazed in the middle of a herd of Thomson gazelles, and was picking its way warily out of the thick cover near a small creek that was overflowing after the long April rains.

The bushbuck looked around, but sensing there was no threat, carried on nibbling the grass. Suddenly, his ears pricked up and his spiral horns went up high in the air, big as a pony. Stepping daintily, he came out into the open. He stopped and swung his head from side to side, usually a sign of danger. Then he trotted diagonally down the hill and disappeared into a gully. The cheetahs were waiting.

Agility, rather than raw speed, accounted for much of the cheetah's ability to catch and kill its prey. The cheetah trips its prey during the chase, and then bites it on the underside of the throat to suffocate it, because it isn't strong enough to break the necks of most of its prey. The cheetah's paws have semi-retractable claws offering extra grip for its high-speed pursuits. On the Savannah, the cheetah's favorite animals to hunt are the Thomson's gazelle, Grant gazelle, bushbucks, and impalas.

The cheetahs were lying down, their spotted bodies hiding in the high grass with their small faces popping out top. Their handsome cat-dog faces scanned the plain, watching the buck and the small, grazing, tail-flicking Thomson gazelles. The "Tommies," with their broad black insignia, wagged their tails as if the world belonged to them. The cheetahs waited. When the time was right, one sprang to life, sprinting directly toward the antelope while another ran at the back of the prey. The cat's coat shined like spun gold, the black dots highlighting the skin. The surrounding "Tommies" scattered in all directions, jumping as high as they could in flight, thankful that today the cats had chosen a different victim.

The leading cheetah — with its sprinter's build, long skinny legs, narrow hips, and deep chest holding the heart of a hunter — was gaining on the buck, which clumsily began running in a zigzag pattern in an attempt to tire and lose the big cat. The cheetah finally tripped the antelope and, as it rolled, the lead cheetah was on its throat in a flash. He was almost instantly joined by the second cat. Together, they pulled the large antelope down and began chocking it. The predators patiently waited out the flailing of its hooves as it suffocated. It took about five minutes before the cheetahs let go and started eating quickly, so other predators, such as lions, leopards, clan of hyenas or vultures couldn't catch a whiff of their kill and come running.

One of the male cheetahs had a sneezing fit, brought on from the pollen emitted by the croton trees. The sweet, honeysuckle-like scent drifted in the wind. They finished a good portion of the buck before dragging it to a safer, higher ground. There, they hid it behind some large rocks and onto a fallen acacia, where they could feast on it the next day without being bothered by other predators.

> *"If you pick up a starving dog and make him prosperous he will not bite you. This is the principal difference between a dog and a man."*
>
> **MARK TWAIN**

Amrita stopped the truck at some of the other Indian trader shops in places like Narok, Moricho, Narosura, and Ndasegera. She knew them all and it was nice to chat and get the latest news over a curried meal. She also refilled the diesel tanks with the drum that was on the truck and the radiator with fresh water. Some of the Sikh traders were married to local Maasai women, who wore *Salwaar-Kameez* Indian outfits, and had learned to cook tasty, spicy Indian dishes. Rashidi and Robert were used to spicy Indian dishes and helped themselves to extra portions.

Twice they passed abandoned *bomas* — villages of the nomadic Maasai. The thorn branch enclosures were paved with cattle droppings and spotted with low dwellings, fashioned from branches and packed blocks of cow dung. The only inhabitants were flies and dung beetles. The insects rose slowly, tired guardians, their lifeless buzzing reflecting the vanished energy of the deserted village. The huts had been burned when the Maasai moved on to a new location.

Amrita saw a number of vultures flying over an area of thick brush.

She asked Robert and Rashidi if they knew what might be going on. Rashidi asked her to stop so he could use his binoculars.

"They're after the ostrich eggs," he said.

"The vultures wait for the time when the Ostrich parents are scrabbling for food, and then, clutching sharp rocks in their beaks, they smash the shells to get the gangly chicks. It happens a lot, even though the big birds try to hide their eggs, thinking they will be safe."

About fifty miles from Loliondo, there was no choice but to cross *Mto-wa-Tembo*, the river of elephants. Recent heavy rains made the river swell with muddy water streaming in from the plains. With no bridge, Amrita had to guide the truck carefully though the river and avoid getting stuck. With the rainy season, there was also the great danger of flash floods, which could creep up quickly.

"Robert, go and walk across, be careful," Amrita instructed the turn boy.

"See where we can enter the river safely."

There were several Maasai on the other side of the river and watching curiously. They saw this every year when the rains came. Robert jumped out of the passenger door, leaving it open and waded into the water. He had to try again and again at different points, because often when he entered, his feet sank into the mushy black soil. Finally, he called to Amrita.

"Try it here, Mama! This area seems shallow and not sticky, but you have to drive fast."

Amrita reversed the truck about thirty yards to the crest of the sloping bank. Gunning the diesel engine, she lunged forward. The lorry strained at the top of the gear and plunged into the river, splashing up arcs of water on both sides. Almost halfway across, the wheels began to spin and the tires cut into the soft dark mud. The Mercedes Benz lowered itself further into the water, the engine still driving the wheels.

They were truly stuck now.

Amrita switched off the engine and opened her door. The river gushed right through the cabin and swirled out the other side where Robert had left the passenger door open. The Maasai on the other side, chatted and waved their wooden rungus, pointed fingers giving their best advice as they watched the truck sink deeper into the streambed.

Amrita asked Rashidi, the other turn boy, to fetch the thick rope from the back. She instructed the boys to reach under the water and secure the rope around the front axle. They struggled as they reached beneath the water level to find a place to anchor the rope. Meanwhile, Amrita carefully waded across to the other side of the river. Her outfit was soaked, water getting into her high boots.

"*Supa.*" She greeted the Maasai in their language.

"*Jambo! Habari n'gani,*" the Maasai replied in unison, speaking in Swahili.

"I speak your language, can you help us pull the truck?" Amrita answered in their dialect.

They looked at each other and began nodding. Soon, half a dozen Moraans and boys set aside their spears and buffalo-hide shields, and joined Robert and Rashidi. Once the rope was secured, Amrita started the engine and pointed to the Maasai to start pulling. The lorry remained stuck in place. Water lapped against the spotted round head of the leopard on the driver's door. They continued to heave the rope, but the fully-loaded truck did not move, because they were not totally synchronized. Robert decided to coordinate and get them to pull in unison.

"*Harambee, Harambee,*" he shouted.

They tried several more times, but hunched their shoulders in disappointment, realizing the task was beyond them. Slowly, the Maasai all shook their heads, stopped, and walked away muttering to each other. The turn boys were left alone pouring with sweat.

It was getting late. The evening breeze across the plain made Amrita jump up into the back of the truck to get a jacket. They were all hungry. The Maasai had started heading home and were guiding their cattle back toward their *Manyatta,* which was about a three- to four-mile walk, at the base of the Loita Hills. The concern was if it started raining again and more water came down the river it might push the truck down the river. Amrita decided,

"Robert, Rashidi, tie the ropes that are on the front axle to the nearest strongest trees on both sides, so we can protect the truck."

She felt safer seeing the truck secured, she grabbed her .303 rifle.

"Robert, you stay here and watch the truck," she said. "Rashidi, let's go find some food."

The two of them walked out of the shadow of the mountain. The sun was already turning red as it passed through the haze of dust and smoke hanging low on the horizon. The waist-high grass, which was the color of ripe wheat, moved all around them with the wind. It took thirty minutes before they came to a clearing and saw Impala and Thomson gazelles grazing and enjoying the evening sun. She spotted a male Impala with twisted horns, wagging his tail, looking dominant all by himself. He was about a hundred yards away and keeping his distance from the large gathering of females.

Amrita, closely followed by Rashidi, crawled around the scattered bushes and the acacias — away from the main group of antelopes, until she had a clear shot, within range. She walked a bit closer to the male Impala and positioned herself behind a fallen acacia tree. But she spotted red ants on the tree and quickly scurried to another spot, brushing the ants off her *kameez,* she then kneeled and took aim. Boom.

The male staggered, and the herd exploded into silent flight. Each creature danced and bounced on long skinny legs, seemingly no longer bound by the dictates of gravity. Every fluid leap blurred against the matching background of parched earth. They tumbled and shot into the mirage quivering air in a spectacular display of aerobatics, the likes of which had made the Impala unique and famous.

The wounded deer limped toward the herd as a light wind blew the tree branches behind it. Blood trickled from the animal's shoulder and ran down its foreleg, leaving a cluster of drops on the ground wherever it paused. Finally, its legs no longer had the strength to keep it upright, and it collapsed to the ground.

Rashidi ran out to the kill, pulling his long knife out of its sheath. The top of the thin blade gleamed wet as he slashed it to and fro, slitting the deer's throat.

"*Allah-u-akbar*!" he shouted in *Allah's* name, blessing it and the flesh was *Halal* — which meant it was no longer profane and was fit to be eaten by believers. He scooped up the dead Impala, with blood dripping from its neck.

"Well done, Mama," he said. "That was a perfect shot got him just below the shoulder. Proud of you."

They started back to the river with the Impala slung over Rashidi's strong back.

On the way, they saw two rabbit-sized creatures behind a pack of bushes. They each had big eyes, standing statue still except for their little twitching noses. These were *Dik-diks*, an elusive species of antelope, very shy and sensitive — and nearly impossible to approach, they were known for their tender meat. Amrita thought of going closer and taking a shot. She walked slowly toward them and watched as one of them busily covered its droppings with its back feet. As she took the next step, they sensed danger and disappeared into the thick bush.

Robert was anxiously waiting for them. He'd already started a coal fire surrounded by small rocks. Rashidi skinned the gazelle and soon had the salted slabs of meat roasting over the fire as the sun began its decline into the horizon. Soon, a full moon lit up the green hills. Amrita remembered her bottle of Dimple Scotch whiskey in the truck, and asked Rashidi to walk down and get it, along with some bottles of Tusker beer.

When Rashidi returned, Amrita poured herself a double scotch and sat next to the fire, sipping her favorite cocktail. She passed a couple of Tusker beers to the turn boys. They soon enjoyed a hearty meal of Impala meat, potatoes, and rice. Later, when the coals glowed dim and the surroundings were still and quiet, they all walked into the river, to the truck. The water level had subsided enough for Amrita to get into the cabin and close the doors. She fell asleep quickly in the front seat. The turn boys picked up their blankets and slept over the tarpaulin in the back of the truck.

The rising sun made the dust on the windshield sparkle. Amrita awoke early, but not before the boys, who said they had trouble sleeping because of the howling hyenas, the grunting of the wildebeest, and the high-pitched bark of the zebras. A lion roared nearby — the signature voice of Africa, then the sound of it died away in a descending series of moaning grunts.

Rashidi spotted the majestic lion coming toward them. They quickly jumped back into the truck and banged on the top to get Amrita's attention. Frantically, they pointed to the lion, which was crossing in front of the truck, on the exit side of the river, followed by its mate some twenty paces back. The lions were on their way from a night kill, their faces still red up to their ears from the blood of their victim.

Amrita had a spectacular view of the beautiful full-bellied male cat. Its coal black mane was long, shaggy, and dense. It had blue-grey shading down its flanks and back. The lion had drawn the eye of a lioness in heat. Amrita knew the females were most often attracted to lions with black manes. The lion strolled by arrogantly, swinging its head from side to side, to the rhythm of its stately walk. The dense bush of its mane, dark and curling, swayed and rippled to its slow, imperial stride with his half-open mouth, strong fangs glinting behind the black lips, the male lion vanished into the tall grass, slowly followed by the lioness.

After catching his breath, Robert relit the fire and made some coffee. Still in awe of the magnificent lion sighting, Amrita ate her breakfast slowly, which included a raw apple and coffee. She remembered her dad telling her that an apple freshened the mouth and kept the teeth clean. Looking through the haze, she could barely make out the outline of the majestic Mount Kilimanjaro with its snowcapped peak.

Her father, Lal Singh, had seen the same mountain as he got off the train in Tsavo on his way from Mombasa to Nairobi. Gradually, the rising light gave the peak roots in the endless plain. Amrita looked across the Savannah, admiring the clusters of thorn bush and umbrella-like trees which sprinkled in the patchy coarse grassland. She looked into the ravine of the riverbed, and across the steep opposite bank of the stream — wondering at the challenge that lay ahead of them.

Amrita asked the turn boys to remove the large khaki tarpaulin on the truck covering the supplies and to start carrying the goods to the far side of the river. The water level in the river had subsided considerably. The truck was fully loaded, so it would take some time, especially with only two of them — wading to the truck, unloading, and making their way back to the far bank. Amrita picked a flat rock under a tall acacia tree, sat down with her back against it, and watched the boys work. If only her husband had been a stronger man, then he would be the one doing all this with her. Teary eyed, she wished her dad was still alive; he never would have let this happen, he never would have allowed his daughter to be alone in the bush, driving a fully loaded truck.

Her train of thought was interrupted by the rhythmic sound of cowbells and dogs barking, as the Maasai cattle from the nearest *boma* came within eyesight. She could hear the different sound of the tinkling bells. The bush was thick and full of flowering shrubs. Goats belonging to the Maasai swarmed over the uncultivated land; they were sleek and shiny-skinned, nibbling at the aromatic leaves and juicy bark of young bushes. The tinkle of their iron bells was carried from hillside to hillside by a light breeze that stirred the bright-leaved banana trees growing in the valley.

An eight-year-old boy, wearing a red *shuka* and carrying a long stick, was looking after the goats. The young *toto* was walking and polishing his teeth with an acacia twig. His slingshot was wrapped around his neck which he used to hunt birds or rabbits. This time, almost the whole village was following the cattle; they had come to see the truck stuck in the river and how its owners would manage to get it free. It was a field trip for them.

In the distance Amrita heard a gathering sound, like the growing roar of an advancing locomotive. Threatening clouds promised a thunder storm. It was getting darker and darker, moving toward them quickly. The last thing Amrita wanted was more rain. Slowly, the water in the river was rising and becoming steadily louder.

Suddenly, a shaven-headed elder appeared wearing a thick red blanket tied at the waist, with a belt made of eland hide. His wrinkled face was mounted on the hard erect body of a young man. He had long oval holes in his swinging ears and carried a knobbed beaded staff. The *Rungu* was a symbol of authority. A clamoring host of eighty or ninety men and women walked at his side and behind him; most were men, with plaited hair and carrying heavy stabbing spears. Clusters of excited boys swarmed about them. The barking dogs ran around the goats, chasing them.

"*Supa* mama, I am the *Laiboni*, chief of this *Manyatta*," the man said to Amrita.

"My name is Ole Olamayiani. This is my village." He spoke in the Maasai dialect, gesturing with long gnarled fingers toward his followers, pointing and shaking the Rungu as he spoke. He waved away the flies that were crawling on the dried snot under his nostrils. He paused often to scratch one leg with the other while he spoke.

"*Supa Oleng, Laiboni*, I speak Maasai too," Amrita addressed the chief.

Ole Olamayiani looked at her, surprised.

"*Sidai*. Oh that is good, the water is very deep here." The *Laiboni* switched to the Maasai language, and spoke in loud, controlled tones, like a man educating imbeciles.

"Mama you know this lorry is not the first to get stuck in *Mto-wa-Tembo*," he said.

"Some small and some larger ones get trapped here when the rains come. Happens every year when the long rains come. Everyone needs help. But none have gotten stuck so far and so deep. This looks bad, and there is more rain on the horizon."

The *Laiboni* walked around and stood next to the pile of supplies that Rashidi and Robert were unloading. He lifted a *panga* from the stockpile of goods and felt its edge before cutting open a sack of ground maize and running his hands through it, sifting it between his fingers, then smelling it. He built a pile of goods beside it, including a metal bucket, tobacco, sugar, two shovels, a bolt of plain cotton from the coast, and blankets. Amrita was watching him do this and knew what he was doing.

He gestured again at the truck and spoke slowly to Amrita.

"You are so deep in the river; many Maasai must pull with all their hearts. Anyway, where are you going?"

"I have a shop in Loliondo. I am Mrs. Dhillon. They also call me *Mama Safari* now. The rain is coming and we need to hurry—"

"Oh, Loliondo," he interrupted. "I have heard of you. Wait a minute, I remember now, bless your heart, I knew your father, the old man *Mwana-ke*, Mehar Singh. I think your father-in-law."

"Yes that was my father-in-law."

The Laiboni picked a spot and sat down on a high rock with his pot-belly hanging over the edge, partially covered by the red blanket. His two front teeth were missing like most of the Maasai. The tribe frequently suffered from Tetanus, which could result in lockjaw. They pulled two of the front teeth at a young age so that in case of lockjaw, they could still be fed medicine made from tree roots and branches. A stale, rancid odor permeated from the chief. The other Maasai gathered closer, knowing the old man was about to tell a story.

The *Laiboni* started first by blocking one nostril and shooting mucus onto the ground. He wiped his lip with his right hand, took a swig of the blood and milk mixture from the *Kibui* by his side. It was made out of olive wood that had been stripped clean on the inside and used to store milk or blood or both. He then blew the snot out of the other nostril. Amrita turned down his offer to take a swig from the Kibui. He finally started his story.

"Listen, everyone. This is part of the Kenyan African folk lore. When your father-in-law worked on building the railways on the great escarpment near Kijabe, an arrogant Kikuyu named Joseph challenged the Sikh to see if he could move a huge rock that had fallen in the path of the rail line. Even though the Africans had failed moving it, Mehar Singh accepted the dare."

"'Come on *Kala Singha*, let's see what you are made of.'" All Sikhs were called *Kala Singhas*. Mehar Singh bet Joseph a month's salary that he could move the rock by himself. Bet accepted, Mehar found an iron rod, hooked it under the stone, wedging it in the ground. Then he shouted a Sikh prayer, '*Jo bole so nihal*,' and heaved against the boulder with all his might. The rod slipped in the ground. He had picked the wrong spot and couldn't get enough leverage to move the rock. The Kikuyus laughed, pushing each other, as the prospect of winning the bet excited them. As he removed the iron bar, the Kikuyus started clapping and hugging each other."

The Laiboni paused his story, rolled from one buttock to the other, drew up one knee, and clasped his arms around it before continuing.

"Quickly the Kikuyus became quiet as Mehar Singh bent down and felt the ground around the edges of the stone. He found a spot where the earth was not too loose. He stood up and positioned the iron rod beneath the stone in the new location. He yelled another Sikh cry, '*Sat Sri Akaal*,' and threw his entire body against the bar. He strained with every muscle, his feet slipping and scrabbling for leverage. After several heaves, he felt the stone move slightly. With a sudden burst of strength, he levered it over. The rock moved back and forth a few time before gaining momentum and quickly picking up speed and rolling down the deep ravine, many branches were broken as well as the small bushes in its path. The Kikuyus were amazed."

"Joseph said to Mehar Singh, 'From today, you are named *Mwana-ke,* which in Kikuyu means, a man of great strength. A sign of enormous respect.'"

Tribal names have great significance to the Kikuyu, and are rarely given to foreigners.

"He was a great man, and he did so much to help the Maasai when he was in politics. He was a leader, a great *Laiboni*. He represented the Maasai as their member of parliament and helped us in many different areas. He could have been the president of Kenya, but the jealous Kikuyus got to him and killed him; he is missed by the Maasai everywhere. You Dhillons are part of our Maasai family. Since you are a Dhillon and we know you, Mama, I can't take anything from you."

Amrita looked up at him.

"Thanks for your help. Please tell your men and boys to help carry the supplies to the exit side and then free the truck. Then we will have to load it back up again once we cross the river. Please, take as many blankets as you need, as well as spears, *pangas,* sacks of sugar for your *Pombe* and celebrations, now that the *Mwananda* cattle auction is coming up. Also, take some beads for your wives."

The *Laiboni* gestured toward the mass of Maasai waving his beaded *Rungu,*

"All of you hurry and get ready to help mama. Let's finish unloading the truck first."

The *Laiboni* quickly organized teams of Moraans and stronger boys to finish unloading the truck. But they soon realized they only had one rope, which wasn't enough or strong enough to get the truck out, once it was unloaded. The *Laiboni* picked five young Moraans and ordered them to go cut some *Ol-Dubai* to make some long ropes. *Ol-Dubai* is like a sisal plant and the Maasai use it for ropes to tie their cattle, make frames for their mud huts, and tie belongings on donkeys. When tied together, the sisal ropes are quite strong. Amrita could hear the long pangas slashing nearby at the sisal like plants. They quickly accumulated a mound full, then started slicing them into thinner strings. The Moraans then tied three layers of the sliced strings in knots to make the "rope" sturdier.

When the unloading was finally complete and all the supplies were on the exit side of the river, it began to drizzle. The turn boys tied four ropes to the differential of the truck. Amrita jumped into the driver's seat and started the engine, a plume of brown smoke burst from the exhaust. When she was ready, she gave the thumbs up sign and, with a large group of the Maasai pulling on each of the four lines, and the others pushing, the empty Mercedes truck began to rock, and rock, and gradually began to climb out of the thick mud. Slowly it moved toward the slope on the other side. Amrita brought the truck up the bank and stopped. Everyone cheered.

The clouds rolled in on the wind, changing shape, and dropping closer to the red soil.

"Quick, cover the goods on the ground with the tarpaulin," Amrita shouted to the turn boys.

They covered the goods just in time. Suddenly, it was upon them. The skies opened and the rains came hard and steady. A wall of water raged down the river valley. It travelled through the river bed like the blade of a giant plow. The flood water flashed past where the Maasai had been standing, some three feet above the river's surface, sliding on top of it like an independent force, rumbling stumps and tree trunks rolled in its path. As they always do, some of the Moraans stood on one leg, dripping wet, like storks, observing in silence. The rainwater flooded the river. The water level was halfway up the banks. There was nothing the Maasai or Amrita could do, except watch and wait. The rain came down harder and now there was hail and thunder. The noise on the roof the truck was deafening. Peeking out of the window of the Benz, she was met by the scent of sopping hide and the sight of the Maasai donkeys and cattle. The animals stood still, resigned to their fate, half asleep, their skin twitching involuntarily.

Amrita and the turn boys sat in the Benz while the Maasai took shelter under the acacia trees and bushes. After a four-hour wait and what seemed like eternity, it stopped raining. The evening was filled with the odor of rain on dry earth, a clean warm smell. Now, they had to wait for the water level to subside, as it flowed down into the Savannah and broke into smaller creeks. It was almost evening when the *Laiboni* walked across and shouted at his villagers.

"Come on, let's all help and load the supplies onto the truck before it gets dark. I think if we all join in, we can do this before dark. Form a chain link and pass the supplies. It will be quicker."

It took the Maasai several hours to load the truck. The sunset could barely be seen above the acacias. They had spent the whole day at the river, but at least they were not spending another night near the river. It was dusk when finally Amrita said her farewell. She handed the *Laiboni* the almost full bottle of Dimple Scotch Whiskey.

"*Ashe naleng, Laiboni, Ole seri Laiboni.*" Thanks Laiboini, goodbye for now."

"Never marry a woman who has bigger feet than you."
MOZAMBIQUE PROVERB

They were finally on the road again, and headed toward Tanganyika, Loliondo, and home. It was late at night when they reached Loliondo. Amrita decided to unload the truck in the morning. Just before sunrise, the Maasai were lined up by the hundreds from all the *Manyattas* around Loliondo. They had heard the truck arrive in the night, and passed the word that Mama was back with their supplies.

"Thank you *Mama*," the Maasai elders said, appreciatively. "You are an angel for us. We really needed these supplies."

The shop had been closed for two weeks, as everyone had gone to Nairobi for Ajit's funeral. The Maasai had been walking fifteen miles to Ram Singh's shop for supplies. The *Laiboni*, promised Amrita that he would appoint Moraan warriors night and day to protect her, because he was so grateful for what she had done.

The Moraans wore toga-like red sheets over one shoulder, with belts made out of eland or cow hide at the waist, allowing the skirts to flap open casually in the breeze, exposing their sizeable private assets with masculine arrogance. They wore a sheathed *Simmi*, a double-edged sword, longer than a bayonet, around their waists. All were lean and nearly naked, with streaming black ostrich plumes. Their long muscled bodies, erect, smooth, devoid of softness, yet full and long-muscled.

Their bodies were stained red with ochre and gleamed with sweat and the rancid butter they rubbed into their skin. The open loops of their earlobes swung low, stretched with beads and vials of snuff. Addicted to herding, fighting, and lion killing, alternatively passive and ferocious, the Moraans ran with their heads thrown slightly back. They ran without exertion, their greased hair flowing, plaited in fine red lines, parallel and neat, long at the back and cut in short bangs at their brows. Colored beads and copper wire circled their necks. They all seemed to have big, wide smiles and round, trance-like eyes.

Each Moraan held a devilish spear low in his right hand. Too heavy to throw far, the weapons were built to receive the charge of a lion. One iron end was heavy, squared off, and blunt — used for jamming into the ground while the kneeling warrior prepared to guide the tip into the chest of the hurtling beast. The central wooden hand hold was butter-polished and smooth. At the top, the two-foot blade was slender, but shaped for deep penetration, ready to be forced home by the weight of the blunt end. The top of the spear was decorated with a tuft of ostrich feathers. If a spear struck a man, its tip would burst out through the chest or stomach.

The young Maasai females, *Siangikis*, wore long skirts of soft hide, greased with a mixture of goat fat and red ochre, just like their faces and hair. They looked agile and feminine with their rows of copper bangles clasping thin wrists and ankles. Brass rings hung from their pendulous ears. Even their necklaces were the same rusty color. They were made of leather and wood or bone beads, piled one upon another. These circled a high proud head that suggested a starched down collar. Their bare breasts were greased with butter. They believed the shine made them attractive.

Their heads were shaven at the sides with reddish ringlets sprouted on top, like crests of exotic birds, providing an attractive feminine effect.

With the Moraans guarding the store around the clock, Amrita felt safe. It wasn't long before she had to drive back to Nairobi to get more supplies.

*"People respond in accordance to how you relate to them.
If you approach them on the basis of violence, that's how they'll react.
But if you say, 'We want peace, we want stability,'
we can then do a lot of things that will contribute towards
the progress of our society."*
NELSON MANDELA

On the drives from Nairobi to the Tanganyika border, Amrita would randomly run into Hardam Singh, who may have been Kenya's only herdsman of Asian descent. He was well and truly at home with his people in Kijabe. He led a large herd of cattle from estate to estate in search of pastures. The locals called him *"Karathinga,"* a corruption of the Swahili word *Kalasinga*, used to refer to the turbaned Sikhs.

Though Hardam Singh had lived in Kijabe for many years, the old Sikh had been an enigma to the locals who could not understand why he chose to blatantly deviate from the way of life associated with Kenyans of Indian origin. Wherever he passed with his herd, amused children shouted *"Karathinga, Karathinga."* As he directed his herd, he bore whips in his right hand while his left clasped a long sword in a crimson sheath. The lone herdsman was always clad in a coat and dirty trousers. His head was rolled in an old, sun-scorched, off-colored turban. The Sikh was eccentric in many ways.

Someone once asked him why he chose a life of pastoralism, and not business, like the majority of other people of Indian descent.

"It's tough operating a business; it's not easy," he would say. "This is the source of my livelihood. I will never engage in business."

Hardam bought his first cow in Kiangombe Village, and he now boasted of over five hundred head of cattle, not counting the calves. He was a pastoralist extraordinaire. Unlike most Indians who lived cloistered in posh estates, Hardam Singh lived in the sprawling hills of Kijabe. He had a big cattle shed on his compound and, in terms of cattle, no one in the entire town had more wealth than him. Like the Maasai, he valued his cattle immensely, and rarely sold them. When he did, it had to be a bull, for cows would give birth to more. The cattle rustlers often sneaked into his shed to steal part of his flock. He lost cattle to irate urban peasants who slashed his cattle dead on straying to their shambas.

"I don't know what has happened to people nowadays." he would lament.

"Even if you plead and urge them not to slash the cattle, they just go right ahead."

And though many saw him as an Indian with Maasai blood, he feared the Maasai greatly and avoided them like the plague.

"Maasai are very fierce. If your cattle mingle with theirs, before you know it, they become part of their flock." Hardam said he had lost several heads of cattle this way. Every time the elderly man came across Maasai herdsmen, he drove his cattle away hastily.

He was married to an African, Wanjiru; the couple had two sons, Babu and Julius. Singh, who never received a formal education, did not know their ages. He couldn't tell the age of his wife either.

"I have never bothered to ask," he once said curtly.

Hardam Singh came to the country by ship across the Indian Ocean when he was only fifteen, to join his father who had arrived several years earlier. He came from Punjab, but had never returned since then. He had forgotten everything about India and his knowledge of the country was scant. His father, a carpenter, introduced him to masonry, a skill which enabled him to earn a shilling a day; seven for the week. Singh recalled that when he came to Nairobi there were only two streets, River Road and Government Road.

"It was a very small town then," Hardam said. "But now it has grown into one big maze. Whenever I have business in the city I have to ask someone to literally hold my hand and lead me around."

He had vowed he would never get married. But when he was sixty, a time he thought was well passed marrying age, he fell in love. Soon he tied the knot.

"Marrying brings a lot of problems. Life is enjoyable when you are alone," he said. "When you come back from your work station, you cook, eat, and sleep without thinking of anyone else."

"For beautiful eyes, look for the good in others; for beautiful lips, speak only words of kindness; and for poise, walk with the knowledge that you are never alone."
AUDREY HEPBURN

Amrita and Bishan never had a relationship after she became a Dhillon. Most girls would go home to see the parents and siblings, but Amrita had no desire to return. Thakur sold all his assets in Nyeri and also moved to Nairobi. He started a building construction business with some contacts that he had established in Nyeri. Initially, he rented a house for himself, Bishan, Mohan and his two daughters, Harbans and Jagjit. Bishan's life was quite comfortable. She joined Thakur on multiple visits back to Punjab to visit the villages. Mohan was going to be in high school the following year. The girls, Jagjit and Harbans were in elementary school. Amrita did keep in touch with her brother, Mohan. They exchanged letters on a regular basis and he would visit the Dhillons when he was allowed by Bishan.

But sadly, after several years, Davinder left the army and began drinking heavily. He moved from one town to the next, never settling down or developing roots. Bishan ignored him, for she was quite happy with her life with Thakur. In Davinder's mind, his mother and stepfather had ruined his life.

Amrita continued making the long and exhausting trips from Loliondo to Nairobi a number of times, driving the truck back and forth.

With her inner strength and willpower, Amrita had single handedly rescued the Dhillon businesses after Ajit had died. Her long trips through the wilds of Kenya and Tanganyika demonstrated her determination and self-discipline to succeed and ensure the businesses kept running. This insight into her character overshadowed her husband's weaknesses being indecisive and tentative throughout his life.

"Ok," her husband finally said. "You have proven yourself, *Mama Safari*, and shown us what the men should be doing. You can go and stay at the shop and run it. I will supply the goods from now on."

Life remained as it was for several years. Amrita was glad to be back in the store and they were doing well financially. Being the ultimate entrepreneurs, the Dhillons decided to start a bus service all the way from Loliondo in Tanganyika to the capital of Kenya, Nairobi. They converted a Dodge truck into a bus that seated forty passengers and had a driver and a conductor. The bus stopped at a number of small towns throughout Maasailand, all the way to Narok and Kijabe, and then on to Nairobi. Soon, the postal service approached the Dhillons, and their bus became the mail delivery service, proving to be a profitable venture.

Amrita became pregnant again and gave birth to a healthy son. This time she went to Nairobi and the baby was born at the Ngara Maternity Hospital. Satbir Kaur, the mother-in-law, was very happy. The matron was especially excited, because the baby weighed a healthy eleven pounds. She invited all the visitors to see the infant, pointing out how healthy he was. One day the mother-in-law was present at visiting time, and noticed that many people were being allowed in to see her grandson.

"Do not invite everyone to see my grandson," she told the matron. "I am not happy about this. Some of these people have bad vibes and could put a curse on him."

Amrita stayed in Nairobi for a month and then went back to Loliondo to manage the store. The baby boy and Amrita were both there, alone. Raj had managed the store in her absence, and soon went back to running the other shops. He drove down to Loliondo with supplies once a month.

A burly South African farmer, Keith Miller, who always dressed in a faded corduroy coat, a big hat, and high black boots, used to come to the store to buy supplies for his workforce. Keith was a hunter and had a contract with the British Government to supply meat to the workers who constructed the roads, as well as to the prisons. It was not uncommon to see him drive in with a truck full of dead zebras, antelopes, and wildebeest. He had a daughter, Jennifer in her teens who played with the baby whenever she came to the store. The baby was always very calm and happy, so Jennifer nicknamed him Jolly.

The next year, Amrita was alone with Jolly while her husband was away in Nairobi getting supplies, when Amrita began hearing frightening stories about swarms of locusts. They were said to have come from Ethiopia. After that land faced two years of drought, the locusts supposedly travelled south, eating all the vegetation in their path. Before anyone saw them in Tanganyika, there were strange tales circulating in the country of the devastation they had left behind. It was said that maize, wheat, and fruit farms were a vast desert where the locusts had passed through. Swarms were said to blacken the sky, descending on crops and pastures; leaving behind barren stalks and earth stripped of all vegetation. Tree branches were broken beneath their weight. Trains had even halted because the tracks were being smothering by locusts, making them too slick for train wheels to grip. The locusts were leaving behind a generation of hoppers, which advanced in huge greedy swarms, that devoured everything the swarms had left behind. Then they would invade new territories, where they turned into adult locusts and started the cycle all over again.

On all the farms in Kenya, the settlers had stockpiles of firewood and maize stalks ready. When the locusts showed up, they set fire to the stockpiles, and sent all their laborers out with empty tins and cans, telling them to shout and yell and beat the tins to frighten the insects from landing, but it was a short respite. No matter how much the farmers frightened the grasshoppers, they could not keep them in the air for long. The most they could do was drive them to the next farm. The hungrier the locusts got, the more desperate they became, and they would simply settle in on the next farm in line.

"Mama, *Ol-maati, Ol-maati* , Mama *Ol-maati*." The Maasai Moraan was shouting and running toward the shop. The Locust are coming!

Amrita looked out over the valley and virtually lost her breath. All along the northern horizon, a dark shadow approached in the sky, like a long stretch of smoke. She shouted to the servants in Swahili, "*Nzige. Nzige*. Close all the windows and doors. Hurry. Get inside, hurry!"

Her two Alsatian dogs, Simba and Pumba, saw the approaching dark cloud and not knowing what it was started running back and forth, toward it, barking loudly,. Amrita again shouted to the servants, "Get the dogs in, quickly. *Upesi, Upesi*."

Before everything was battened down in the buildings, a few grasshoppers, the lead party, perhaps twenty in all, landed on the lawn in front of the shop. The house boy tried to kill them, but it was a losing battle. Through the window, Amrita could see the dark cloud in the distance, getting closer. Jolly was sitting on her lap, cuddling her, but then the noise from the mass of grasshoppers was getting louder and scaring him. He began to cry. Amrita hugged him tighter and started singing to him to take his mind off the impending cloud. The noise grew louder, almost like a hurricane with winds gusting at over a hundred miles an hour.

There was a gap in one of the doors and some of the insects started coming into the house, the dogs started barking at the intruders. John, one of the Kikuyu servants, went and checked the dogs and quickly ran back with a piece of wood and nailed the opening shut. Then he had to run around and kill all the locusts that had made it inside.

Finally, late at night, it grew silent. Amrita hoped and prayed the locusts had moved on to the next farm. She was scared to go outside and check. She decided to wait till morning and went to sleep holding Jolly in her arms all night. She hardly slept a wink.

In the morning the servant, Raphael, woke her up early and urged her to look outside. She looked through one of the windows in the main shop. She blinked, and blinked again. The whole landscape was the color of pale dull terra-cota. The trees, lawn, and main yard in front of the house and shop were all that she could see. They were covered with the dye, as if in the night a thick layer of terra-cota colored snow had fallen on the land. The grasshoppers were sitting in the maize and wheat farm that belonged to the Dhillons, finishing off whatever was left on the ground.

"Don't open any doors or windows," she told the Africans. "Let's wait it out. Stay indoors."

The Maasai were outside in the distance, patiently sheltering behind some buildings, waiting to come in and buy their regular supply of flour and sugar. It was about 11 in the morning when the locusts started stirring, and the whole landscape began quivering. As if the locusts had been given a signal, they lifted off the ground. The atmosphere fluttered loudly with the buzzing noise of wings. They were leaving. In ten minutes, they were gone.

All you could see on the farm were small twigs and a few laps of dry leaves from the broken stalks. The grass was bare and the red soil visible. The vegetable garden, which had been irrigated and kept green, was like a dust heap. Some of the dead grasshoppers were on the ground. They were about an inch and a half long, brownish grey and pink and sticky to touch. They had broken several big trees in the yard, simply by sitting on them. Amrita thought they must only have weighed a tenth of an ounce each. She began to realize the magnitude of the damage, was unthinkable, in relation to their size. She could not conceive the sheer number of them.

Worst of all, they had laid their eggs in the soil. Next year, Amrita thought, after the long rains, the little black brown hoppers would appear, grasshoppers in the first stage of life that could not fly, but crawled along eating everything in their path.

She finally mustered the courage to go outside and survey the damage. Then, teary eyed, she opened the shop; and the Maasai started trickling in. The natives shopped for their groceries, but they sat there much of the day, discussing with Amrita the trauma of the past twenty four hours. At least there was some comfort in that.

*"Darkness cannot drive out darkness: only light can do that.
Hate cannot drive out hate: only love can do that."*
MARTIN LUTHER KING JR.

Lalita was now always on the front line whenever they attacked, alongside the men and she soon became notable. She was frequently invited to go on missions headed by the Mau Mau leader himself, Field Marshall Dedan Kimathi. By now, she had been on countless missions, attacking Kikuyus loyal to the British Government, killing and mutilating them, burning their huts and villages, attacking European farmers and Indian traders. She was always with Sungura, who had been promoted to Field Marshall and now was second only to Dedan Kimathi in the hierarchy.

Jeevan Singh was over seven feet tall, a Sikh from the same village as Mehar Singh and towered over everyone including the Maasai. He was a strikingly handsome man and always wore stylish, bright colored turbans and kept his beard impeccably neat. The ceiling in his shop was low for him and he had to sit down or bend to work in the shop. The rest of his house was higher. Jeevan had his regular customers and was a regular stop for the Dhillon's bus that carried passengers from Nairobi, Kijabe and Narok through to the Tanganyika border and Loliondo. The Mau Mau had gradually begun to infiltrate the Maasai district, moving from the Aberdare Mountains.

One cool summer evening, Lalita and Sungura's gang decided to target Jeevan Singh's shop in Ndasegera. As usual Jeevan Singh had already finished his three large drinks of Johnny Walker whiskey and he was settling down for a fine curried dinner of curried *dik dik*, a small antelope that he had shot that evening, close to his shop. He had the wood fire burning in a pit in the ground and the hot sweet smoke drifted towards where he was sitting. The walls were covered with corrugated sheets around wooden frames. There was no chimney, just a small black hole in the wall. The black Alsatian, Max, was dozing off next to his feet. Every evening, Jeevan would go walking through the plains around his shop, where an abundance of antelopes and zebras roamed. He would shoot one of the animals and get the Maasai to help him carry it back to his store.

It was around eight at night, when Lalita, wearing a bright red scarf around her face and neck, came down the green slopes along with Sungura and three others. There was a hyena laughing. The sound seemingly closer than it was. Sungura and the others circled the *duka* a few times to make sure that Jeevan had no visitors. One of the fighters stood outside, keeping watch.

Once they were certain that he and his wife were alone, they slammed the side door open and rushed into the kitchen, circling Jeevan. His wife Meena, was in the bedroom and when she heard the noises and shouting she hid under the bed. Jeevan started to run towards his rifle, but the two Kikuyus grabbed and held him down. Max started barking; Sungura aimed his revolver and shot the Alsatian.

"*Kala Singha*, we need food, money, bullets and guns, now. Or we kill you." Sungura shouted.

"Go to hell," he replied back.

Physically strong and with an aggressive nature, Jeevan was well known for his temper. With his strength, he managed to free himself and tried to run into the bedroom where he kept his .303 rifle. One of the Kikuyus, who had a long scar across his face, swung at Jeevan as he was making a dash to the bedroom, catching him on the forearm and forcing a deep cut with his sharp *simmi*. As Jeevan stumbled, the two Kikuyus and Sungura jumped on him and started hitting him with their wooden *rungus*.

Meena heard her husband's moans. She knew where the rifle was kept. As quietly as she possibly could, she crawled from under the bed and got to the rifle and carefully peeked into the living room. They were still beating up on Jeevan Singh and he was starting to bleed from around his temples and mouth, his teeth were starting to fall out. Meena realized she had to do something quickly. She opened the bedroom door and without really aiming, fired two shots in the direction where she saw shadows moving. Blood started spurting as the bullets made an impact and Sungura fell backwards. He was shot in the chest.

Lalita screamed and kept screaming as she reached forward and held his head in her lap,

"Sungura, oh my god, Sungura, *mpenzi wangu*, my love, what has she done to you."

She shouted at the nearest Kikuyu,

"Bring the lamp over here, I can't see where he is hurt."

She saw the deep hole in his chest and blood pouring out and knew the inevitable. Sungura looked into her eyes and his attempt at a smile said it all, farewell and the sadness. Sungura had difficulty breathing and was in a lot of pain. He leaned towards Lalita and tried to whisper her name and say something, but the words failed. His eyes were half closed. He looked at her and his love for his beautiful Kikuyu soul mate was clear in his eyes as he reluctantly bid his farewell. He was gone. She was still holding his head in her lap. Lalita had no words to say, tears ran down her soft and delicate sharply etched cheeks. Suddenly, she realized who had the rifle, she looked at Meena,

"You did this to my Sungura."

It didn't take long before she emptied the whole magazine into the Sikh woman's body and into the almost lifeless Jeevan's body.

Lalita was devastated as they carried Sungura's body back into the forest. She had lost the cause and reason for her living. She was angry but had taken her revenge, killing the Sikhs. Her hatred of the British was now coupled with a mounting dislike for the Indians too. They took the guns, all the groceries they could carry as well as many blankets. They rounded the goats that were in a corral in the backyard, tied them together and quickly started back into the hills with the animals.

Around midmorning, the next day, the Dhillon bus from Nairobi made the usual stop at the Ndasegera shop and found the gruesome site with flies hovering all over the two dead bodies and Max. A couple of jackals were following a group of giggling hyenas which sounded very much like human laughter. The predators were getting ready to go into the shop. They scattered when the bus stopped and the passengers got off. The bus driver instructed his turn boy to stay at the shop while he drove to the next town and sent help.

"Make sure you keep the hyenas and jackals away," he instructed the turn boy.

Jeevan Singh and Meena's bodies were transported to Nairobi in an open British Thames Trader truck. The bodies were placed in beds on the truck and covered by white sheets, but as the bumpy journey progressed, the sheets turned into a dark red.

Once the news got around, nearly all the Sikh traders in Maasailand accompanied the sad procession to Narok and then onto Nairobi, stopping at the Sikh temple in Kijabe. Some of the traders sat on the lorry with the bodies, praying and reciting from the holy Sikh Granth sahib. The others followed in their jeeps. The nearest person to the bodies would waive the flies off as they sat or hovered on the bloody sheets. As oncoming vehicles approached, the procession would stop and traders going in the opposite direction would climb up on to the lorry, lift the sheets and tearfully pay their last respects.

They had robbed and killed Jeevan Singh in his shop in Ndasegera, which was only fifty miles north of Loliondo. The district commissioner requested that everyone leave Loliondo and the surrounding small towns and move to Narok, or go and sleep at the nearby store. Amrita refused. Some of the Gujaratis decided to pack up and move to Nairobi where they would be safe in the midst of a larger community. Most of the Sikh traders decided to stay in Maasailand.

"The store is worth a lot with so much stock," Amrita said. "Someone may break in. I am not giving in to them."

Amrita had wire grills hammered to the windows to stop anyone getting in. Every night before she went to bed, Amrita would pour herself a shot of Dimple whiskey, sit on the leather sofa and turn on the radio, listening to The Voice of Kenya, cracked and fizzing with distance, and the latest updates on the violence. She would then talk to her son, Jolly,

"If we are alive in the morning, we will get up. It is god's wish."

Amrita used to get up at 5 a.m., have her breakfast, and prepare some food for lunch, bathe, and feed Jolly, then open the store. By that time, some of the Maasai elders would be there waiting for her to open. Knowing she was alone, they were very protective. In the evening, they would wait for her to close before they left for their *Manyattas*.

Amrita had an eerie feeling when she went to bed that night. She heard on the radio that another loyal Kikuyu chief, a supporter of the British presence in Kenya, had been ambushed in his Land Rover, near Limuru and in cold blood killed on the road. The Governor, Sir Evelyn Baring, called the chief "a great man, a great African and a model citizen of Kenya, who met his death in the service of his own people." There was an expectation that more violence was to follow. The governor had declared a state of emergency a few months earlier which he announced on the radio,

"A state of emergency has been declared throughout the colony and protectorate of Kenya. This grave step was taken most unwillingly and with great reluctance by the Government of Kenya. There was no alternative in the face of the mounting lawlessness, violence and disorder in parts of the colony. As a result of the activities of the Mau Mau movement, the government is taking drastic action in order to stop the spread of violence."

Her premonition and fear turned out to be true. She had difficulty sleeping because of the Kikuyus but she also kept hearing the grating call of a leopard, low and like a saw being drawn roughly through wood. She wasn't sure if this was a real leopard noise or the Mau Mau. They were known to mimic animal noises to signal each other. She finally dozed off with the .303 rifle, fully loaded, by her bedside.

They came, a dozen Kikuyus, sworn Mau Mau freedom fighters. Jolly and Amrita were in bed, but with the hot weather, she couldn't sleep for long. The windows were slightly open to let the cold air in. After midnight, Amrita heard the dogs barking. Then a loud yelp and the sound of a dog whining. They had killed or crippled one of the dogs. She didn't turn the gas lamp on, but turned on the battery powered light and walked to the window. She saw shadows moving quickly across the paved yard, followed by a shattering sound — broken glass.

They were in the house. Jolly was still sleeping peacefully.

Amrita scooped up the sleeping baby and frantically looked around before deciding to hide in the walk-in closet and behind her long Indian dresses. She heard footsteps and heavy breathing. The Kikuyus had entered the house and seemed to be searching for her. They knew she was alone — the servants must have been forced at gunpoint to tell them. She saw a light through the shuttered closet door. She could smell the pungent, sour smell of home-brewed beer mixed with the stale odor of sweat. They carried kerosene-ignited lanterns which they must have grabbed from the servants quarters and were creeping from room to room looking, rushing, searching, and knocking things over. Jolly was starting to wake up. Amrita's heart pounded as she covered his mouth with her hand and moved to hide deeper behind the clothes.

One of them was close. The closet door ripped open. Amrita opened her eyes and she was looking into a mouth with broken teeth and a face with a long scar that ran from the right eye all the way down to his chin. The dark bright eyes of a tall Kikuyu stared right at her with a raised *Panga* about to strike her.

"I found them!" the Kikuyu shouted. "Here, they are here!"

He looked at Amrita's frightened face and Jolly's half-open eyes.

"We don't want to kill you *Muhindi*, but I will if you don't help us."

Amrita was in shock. She could barely speak. The Kikuyu repeated what he had said only louder this time, pointing his rifle toward her face, almost touching her nose.

She was shaking. Jolly started to cry.

"What, what do you want?" Amrita managed.

"Mama, we are hungry," the man's eyes glared. "We want food, bullets, guns, alcohol, money, and blankets."

"Don't harm us, please," she said.

"Here, Here are the keys to the store, help yourself to whatever you want."

"That is better. Now, come with me and show me where everything is."

It took a while, with Amrita walking around the shop, showing them what they were demanding.

Finally, one of them shouted to the leader.

"We got everything. Let's kill them now. We don't need them."

The first person, walked around, looked up and down, and then back at Amrita, and especially at Jolly. She was the skinny, tall fair skinned woman that wore a long red scarf covering her head and face. She was carrying a revolver in one hand and a *Panga* in the other hand.

"You help the British, all you Indians, we don't need you here."

She raised her revolver, aimed then suddenly stopped,

"Wait, I know this *Muhindi*,"

"Amrita, is that you?"

"Who are you, I can't see your face," Amrita mumbled, still scared.

The woman took the scarf off and Amrita screamed as she recognized the face,

"Lalita, Lalita, oh my god, what are you doing with them?"

Showing no feelings, Lalita arrogantly replied,

"This is your lucky day since I recognized you. I will spare you and your son. It is a long story but now, I am one of them and fighting for our freedom from the British, we have to run now before someone finds out."

"Leave them, " Lalita instructed the others. "They are my family."

The leader shouted,

"Family? With *Muhindis*, Whatever, just leave them and let's go. We might need them the next time."

He turned to Amrita. "We are going to spare you and the boy now as long as you keep quiet and help us the next time we come here, you can thank Lalita for today," he warned.

They started to leave with sacks full of supplies, heading toward the valley.

Amrita took a few steps towards them and said,

"Lalita wait, I want to talk to you. It is very important."

"What?"

Lalita walked over and Amrita asked her to sit next to her in the living room. The others had stepped out and were ready to leave.

Lalita shouted to the others,

"You all go ahead, I will catch up."

Amrita held Lalita's hand,

"I promised your mother after she was gone that I would look after you, my sister."

"I don't understand, who is your sister,?"

"You are, let me explain."

Amrita related to Lalita how Lal Singh had saved Wamboi after her accident and how she had lived with him for weeks to recuperate. Wamboi then worked with Lal at his practice. She started seeing him regularly, as a result the affair and her pregnancy.

"This means all of us, you, me, Kirpal, Davinder and Mohan are related."

"Wait, let me think. This is not possible. I am still confused, I never thought of this, is that why I am fair skinned with curly hair?"

Lalita was in shock.

"Why don't you stay here now with me and I will take care of you. The Mau Mau movement is too dangerous for you," Amrita pleaded.

"No, I have taken the oath and nothing will stop us till we get our freedom from the British."

Amrita assured her,

"Well, now you know where I am, so anytime you need help, contact me."

Lalita tied the scarf around her neck and head. She was gone in a flash, shaking her head in disbelief and not quite comprehending it all. This all happened too quickly. She didn't have the time to hug or say her goodbyes to Amrita. She was sad to leave Amrita, her childhood friend, a half-sister. At least she was there to save her life. She was deep in her thoughts of Sungura and his seed that was growing in her body now.

Amrita couldn't sleep thinking of Lalita with the Mau Mau and how she was so different now, so angry. She got up, in the morning, to the baby's screams and knocking at the door. It was the Maasai, waiting to buy their flour, sugar, tobacco, and necessities. Amrita went to find the African servants; they had been locked up in their rooms by the Kikuyus, their mouths stuffed with grass. Amrita let them out.

It would take months before Amrita could sleep again, because she would hear every noise at night, and imagined seeing shadows in the house. Listening to the radio every night, she heard that Jomo Kenyatta, the Kikuyu leader had been arrested on charges of leading the extremist wing of the Mau Mau movement. He was charged with inciting hatred and violence against the Europeans as well as the creation of the Mau Mau oaths. This was only going to intensify the fight and strengthen the freedom fighters. British troops were being flown in from the Middle East, a cruiser had arrived with more troops in Mombasa and the Kenyan Police reserve and Home Guard were being mobilized in greater force to tackle the threat. The news was that thousands of Kikuyu had fled arrest and were now living in the forests and the highlands.

Coincidentally, the same week, one of the Mau Mau gangs visited the Dhillon's saw mill in Mau Narok. The mill foreman had been warned by the fighters, so he informed Tej, who happened to be there that week. They were coming in the evening. Tej had stock piled the supplies that these fighters might need and had instructed the foreman to give them whatever they wanted and not to have any confrontations. They came around two in the morning and in a couple of hours after feeding themselves and taking blankets, more food and a few guns were gone. Leaving a note,

'Asante Kala Singha', thanks.

A month later, Amrita was walking from the shop to the backyard to go check on the dogs, when she noticed a large snake following her; Loliondo was famous for its snakes. It kept following her until she went to the bathroom to wash her hands. It stopped, when she came out, it followed her again.

Amrita watched the large snake with its zebra like coloring and an arrow shaped head as it made its way to the dining room. From there it started moving into the space between the wooden boards and corrugated sheets. Amrita kept looking as to where it was going and in the meantime told Raphael, the house servant, to go next door and call the Sikh at the next shop. Quickly, Gurdial Singh Bhalla came with his shotgun, peeked through the opening in the boards and fired a shot through a hole, even before the explosive sound had cleared the air, he fired again. It did not kill the snake. It was still moving. He reloaded the shotgun. They carefully pulled a few more boards, so they could spot him and finally Gurdial managed to hit him with another two shots. The second one caught the snake in the neck so that it jumped sideways. Bits of flesh spat into the dust around the wooden boards along with bright splashes of its blood. It turned out to be a thick cobra, twelve feet long! The Sikh cut its head and dipped it into methylated spirits.

"You keep these marble like stones," he said to Amrita. "If anyone gets bitten by a snake, this marble will suck all the poison from the wound."

*"A man's greatest glory doesn't consist
in never falling, but in rising every time he falls."*
ANONYMOUS

Whenever Raj was in Loliondo, Amrita would go hunting with him, the neighbor, Gurdial Singh Bhalla, along with two native workers and a couple of German Alsatian dogs. They would always walk to the clear flowing Loliondo River about a mile away from the valley where they could shoot guinea fowls and partridges. Frequently, they would see a family of weavers at work near the water, hovering frantically with twigs in their beaks while they built a hanging nest suspended from the limb of a tall acacia tree.

Raj's cousin, Sang Singh, who had come from Nairobi to visit, joined them on this hunting trip. They walked to the river as usual. Climbing up the slope, almost like humans, a family of six long-legged red monkeys was gathered together protectively. The two adults stood on hind legs, using their stiffened tails for support. Standing at full height they peered through the bush. The female, perhaps half the size of the male, clutched a small lizard in her hand. The male ascended into an acacia. His ruff stiffened with alarm. He stared at the hunters like a lookout in a crow's nest. His small rounded ears flattened against his head. His close-set eyes glared out from under long black brows. He bared his canines and jumped down with a shrill scream. The female led the young monkeys off while the father drove his family before him; soon they disappeared into the tall Savannah grass.

Walking another mile or so, they saw the heads of three Giraffes peering toward them in curiosity over some fresh leaved shorter acacias. Islands of bamboo extended into the forest like fingers reaching from the moorland. Every now and then the forest opened into sudden grass clearings. The glades were patchy with sunlight, and rich with wild grasses, and long petaled pink flowers.

The Maasai guide, Raphael, was on the lookout for signs of rhinos, because he said they frequented this part of the landscape. The latest deposit of dung had been within the preceding twelve hours. The spoor indicated a single bull. They followed the freshest tracks, hoping for a sighting. They'd gone only half a mile when, just beyond the wall of grey impenetrable bush that flanked the narrow trail, there was a sudden hissing. Then there was an outcry of alarm calls and a cloud of brown ox-peckers rising above the scrub. The noisy birds lived in a symbiotic relationship with the larger African game animals, feeding exclusively on the ticks and bloodsucking flies that infested such animals, and in return acting as wary sentinels to warn of danger.

Following the alarm there was a deafening chuffing and snorting like that of a steam engine. With a crash, the bush parted and an enormous grey beast burst onto the path, not thirty paces ahead of the hunting party. It peered over its long polished double horns for something to charge. Aware that the rhino's weak eyesight could not distinguish a motionless man at more than fifteen paces and that the light breeze was blowing directly into the rhino's face, the leading guide stood frozen and motioned everyone else to move slowly to his left.

Raphael was poised to hurl himself to one side if the charge came his way. The rhino switched his grey bulk from side to side with startling agility. The guide reached for his *rungu*, a large wooden stick. The rhino sensed the movement and trotted half a dozen paces closer, so that the guide was on the periphery of his effective vision. The guide was in serious danger. Using a short underhanded flick, the guide tossed the *rungu* high over the rhino's head into the ebony thicket behind it and there was a loud clatter as it struck a branch.

Instantly the rhino spun around and launched its huge frame in a full and furious charge at the sound. The bush opened as though before a centurion tank and the clattering, crashing charge dwindled swiftly as the rhino kept going up the side of the hill and over its crest in search of an adversary. The relieved guide raised his hand and signaled the rest to follow him in the other direction. They walked for another hour before they came to a thicker hilly section of the forest, darkly shaded, with dampness heavy in the air.

"Be quiet," whispered Raphael, the tall Maasai guide. "I see something moving there."

They all stopped and waited for him to go ahead. They crouched low under the cover of fallen bamboos. Raphael stepped into a narrow rocky stream that was knee deep. After a few minutes, he waved back for the rest of them to follow, but also to be quiet. The moving water covered their sound and their tracks while they followed the guide into the thickest section of the forest.

When Amrita and the rest of the group caught up to Raphael, they came upon a new born buffalo calf with no one else around. The Maasai walked around searching the area and found the horns of a dead buffalo. Apparently, a pride of lions had attacked the buffalo, but missed the calf. The buffalo herd had moved on, leaving the young calf behind. This must have happened in the early hours of the morning.

Raj named the calf *Mbogo*, a Swahili word for a buffalo. He instructed the Africans to pick up the calf and bring him back while he ran to get the Land Rover. Raj met them halfway, and they brought the calf back with them on the back of the Rover.

The problem was how to feed the baby. Amrita put some cow's milk in a bowl, but no luck. Everyone was coming up with ideas, but there was no response, even though the calf was obviously very hungry. Finally, Sang Singh suggested that they fill a large Coca-Cola bottle with milk and attach a pacifier to it. After some coaxing, and repeatedly pushing the bottle into the hungry calf's mouth, *Mbogo* finally started sucking on the bottle and the hungry calf finished the milk in no time.

The calf was fed for weeks before it started going out and grazing on its own around the shop. It took about two months, and then it started following the Dhillon's cattle herd, walking right behind the Maasai Moraan, named Kimani. *Mbogo* became a huge tourist attraction and would pose for photographs and allow everyone to pet him, as long as they had some salt for him to lick.

Years later, a Maasai from a different area got scared of *Mbogo,* not knowing it was a pet, and speared the buffalo. *Mbogo* was treated by a local veterinarian. For a while it seemed he had recovered. The external wound was fine, but the internal one became infected and several months later, *Mbogo* grew ill and died.

"You can search throughout the entire universe for someone who is more deserving of your love and affection than you are yourself, and that person is not to be found anywhere. You yourself, as much as anybody in the entire universe deserve your love and affection."

GAUTAM BUDDHA

Kimani, the Maasai herdsman, had lost his mother when he was a baby. He had been brought up by his father and the women in the *Manyatta*. Now that he was a Moraan, his locks were long, impeccably plaited, and stained with red ochre. These were his marks of being a Moraan, a warrior. He walked tall and with an air of swagger about him. The elders in his *Manyatta* had decided it was time for him to become an elder and give up the life of a Moraan. Since his mother was not there, it was very unusual, but he asked Amrita, a non-Maasai, to be his mother and to shave his locks.

This was an honor that surprised Amrita.

"I am honored to do it," she said. "But it has to be in the *Manyatta* right?"

"Yes, thank you so much," Kimani said. "This means so much to me."

Come nightfall, the Maasai men herded their cows into the *boma*, the area in the center of the Maasai village, where livestock were guarded against predators overnight. The *Totos* followed with their goats, which leapt and tripped to get inside, as though they knew, that once the thick thorn branches from acacia trees were pulled into place, they would be safe from darkness and the predators beyond.

Amrita arrived that night and slept in the tent that was set up by her turn boys. As she drove up to the *Manyatta*, cattle were spread out grazing on the sweet grasses of the high table land. Beyond the cattle, she picked out the pattern of the huts and cattle pens that formed the *Manyatta*. Goats, chickens, and naked herd boys scattered as her Jeep approached.

Kimani spent the night in a hut in the *Manyatta*. He awoke before dawn, his nose full of the strange, familiar smell of smoke, dung, and animals in the mud hut. He was led to the *Boma*, in the middle of the *Manyatta*. The women were ululating, making a long, wavering, high-pitched vocal sound resembling a howl, with a trilling quality. The sound was produced by emitting a high-pitched loud yell, accompanied with a rapid movement of the tongue and the uvula. The other Moraans chanted a deep, breathy, rhythmic song.

When Amrita awoke, she went inside the *Manyatta* to see Kimani. He appeared, ducking out of the low doorway of the mud hut, and walking toward her. She laid out a freshly tanned calfskin especially prepared for that day. He knelt before her, bowing his head in submission for one final time. After the greetings, where she patted his head, she took a gourd filled with milk and spirits and poured it gently over his head. The flies were everywhere, on his face and head. She kept waving them away. The milk ran down his cheeks. Kimani sat down on a wooden stool and Amrita stood over him, commencing the cutting, tugging each lock as she applied the blade, taking it back to the skin.

When she had a clear patch, she would start to shave and the taste of milk changed to a taste of blood as she cut into his scalp. It was a sign of honor to bleed without flinching and, because Amrita knew that was expected, she had to cut him gently where a small vein ran high on his temple. He bled profusely, but without pain.

When she had finished, he arose and washed his head with water from a *Kibui*. He looked down at the small, bloody pile of locks in the center of the calfskin. He rubbed his hand over his scalp, which had not been bare since boyhood, and he felt the breeze on his skin. It was as though his past had been cleansed from him and his future was his to determine. He had become an elder and would no longer be the herdsmen for the Dhillons and Amrita. Now, he could be married and buy as many wives as he could afford. He had saved quite a bit of wealth working for Amrita.

"Now that you are going to get married to many wives, I am going to give you ten head of cattle. So you can get someone you really want," Amrita offered.

He happily bowed his head for Amrita to bless him, hugged her and then ran away to join his fellow friends who had gone through the same ceremony in the *Manyatta*.

*"Strange, is it not, that of the myriads who
before us pass'd the door of darkness through, Not one returns to tell
us of the road, which to discover we must travel too."*
OMAR KHAYYAM

The Dhillons had an outhouse in the big yard outside the shop and the main residence. The Alsatian had given birth to six black and grey puppies. They were kept in the yard not far from the outhouse. One of the servants had gone to the outhouse and accidentally left the door open. The puppies followed each other and tripped into the deep hole in the ground. Their barks were so low that they were hardly able to get attention and were going to drown for sure. Their mother started barking loudly and running back and forth to the shop to get attention and running back towards the drowning puppies. Raj was in the shop and realized that something was wrong. He followed the dog to the outhouse and heard the desperate yelps coming from deep in the hole. He quickly called one of the turn boys and constructed a wooden box with a long pole that could be used to pick up the little dogs, before they drowned. Amrita lit the kerosene lamp so she could shine the light into the deep hole and look for the pups. The heads were barely visible as they swam in the smelly swamp. After repeated attempts they were able to get all the pups out but only three of the six survived. The well was sealed over and the outhouse taken down to avoid future mishaps.

"Unlike the scriptures of other creeds, they do not contain love stories or accounts of wars waged for selfish considerations. They contain sublime truths, the study of which cannot but elevate the reader spiritually, morally, and socially. There is not the least tinge of sectarianism in them. They teach the highest and purest principle that serve to bind man to man and inspire the believer with an ambition to serve his fellow men, to sacrifice all and die for their sake."

MAX ARTHUR MACAULIFFE ON SIKHS

Raj and Amrita were awakened early one morning by the *Laiboni* banging on the door to their shop in Loliondo. Raj opened the door.

"You have to help us," a voice urged. "Early today, before sunrise, the lions came, jumped over the *Boma* fence and killed three of our *Ngombes*."

"The lions have recently moved into this area," the locals continued. "They were near the villages at Ola-la and now they are here! We need help killing them — with your guns. They ran away once we started beating drums, throwing stones and fire sticks, and shouting at them. You have to help us."

"How many were there?" Raj asked.

"A large male, probably five or six year's old, very cunning, with a reddish mane. He has a scar across his forehead, probably from a fight over a female. The lioness is younger, not as experienced but very quick and strong; she has two grown cubs. Her hide is clean and unscarred by claw or thorn. Across her back she has a sleek olive tan shading down to a buttery yellow at the throat with fluffy cream on the belly. She is the dangerous one."

"Not a problem, we will do what we can to help," Raj promised the Maasai.

"Give us a couple of hours. We have to pack and arrange for the shop to be run in our absence."

Amrita packed the Land Rover with drinks, clothes, and enough food for several days. Raj gathered up his binoculars, his rifle and slung his cartridge belt around his waist. The *Laiboni* and the others jumped in the four wheel driven vehicle. Amrita shivered in the cool air of the morning, the sun hadn't broken yet above the tops of the trees. The Land Rover had a canvas roof, there were no windows and the air was cool and damp against Amrita's skin. She reached into the back of the Land Rover and drew out one of the red Maasai blankets and pulled it over her shoulders. They drove, juddering, over the uneven grass of the Savannah heading towards the *Manyatta* with their two Alsatian dogs. An eagle pushed up from the branches of an acacia, beating its black wings into the white sky above them. They climbed out of the valley and emerged onto a ridge that overlooked the Maasai village. Almost everyone in the village was standing outside the *Manyatta* waiting for them.

In front of them, a committee of vultures was resting on a dying Acacia, dipping their long necks to try and get to the dead cattle. A family of jackals was crouching down in the high grass, waiting for their chance to feast on the meat too. The first cow was lying in the middle of the corral; its stomach had been eaten out. The other two kills had not been eaten. Raj told the *Laiboni* to go ahead and skin the cattle and salvage the meat and hides.

After the Maasai had given chase, the lions then ran to the far side of the stream across from the *Manyatta*. They found a safe spot and the lioness, leaving the cubs there, crossed the stream with her mate. The mating season was just beginning. Shaking water from their bodies with fierce shuddering spasms, the male lion snuffed at the lioness, drumming softly in his throat. Then he lifted his snout to the bright white stars. His back arched reflexively at the tantalizing musk of her pale blood-tinged discharge.

She led him by about a half-mile, leaving the cubs far behind and up one of the thickly wooded tributary valleys. Then she crept into the heart of the thicket of tangled bush, a stronghold guarded by the menacing two-inch wickedly hooked thorns. There in the dawn, he covered her for the first time. She crouched low against the earth, hissing, and cracking with angry snarls. When he came over her, he bit at her ears and neck, forcing her to submit. Afterward, she lay close against him, licking at his ears, nuzzling his throat and belly. Turning half away from him, she nudged him flirtatiously with her hindquarters, until he rose and she crouched down submissively and snarled at him while he mounted her once again. They mated over and over again before leaving the thorn thicket and wandering back to the cubs.

The *Laiboni* had assigned two of his best trackers, Lemaron and Simel, to accompany the Sikhs. After walking around the dead animals and checking the tracks, the guides confirmed that a lion, a lioness, and two large cubs had been there. The hunting party accompanied by several of the Maasai dogs and the two that the Dhillons owned, started after the fresh tracks. The tracks led along a paddock fence for several hundred yards. The lions went underneath the fence and finally away in the direction of the hills. Because the young cubs were in tow the lion family was probably not too far away, the hunting party followed Lemaron closely, knowing he was bound to be in the right place at the right time. With the dogs barking, the Maasai guides spread out over the terrain and worked the spoor with the same instinct, superhuman sense of sight, smell, and hearing as one of the animals they were tracking. Up on the plateau the grassland rose and fell beneath them as they climbed the low round hills and dropped into the valleys. The grass around them moved with the wind. The waist high soft dry grass was the color of ripe wheat. The spoor was hot. The stink of the animals seemed to steam as the day grew later and hotter.

At about 4 p.m., with the sun blazing overhead, Amrita and Raj were resting on a shelf of dusty rock by an oasis of brambles. Both of them had dark patches of sweat on their khaki Safari suits. Raj opened a Tusker beer. A tsetse fly circled around his turban and finally settled behind his ear and bit into the softness of his neck. Raj quickly brushed it away.

Suddenly, there was a great commotion — a crash directly beneath them. The lions were close! Raj shoved a round into his 9.3 mm rifle. Amrita broke open the barrels of her shotgun and removed the fat red cartridges from the breeches one at a time. She examined them for blemishes and polished them on her shirt before slipping them back into place. She snapped the barrels shut and tucked the butt of the loaded weapon under her right armpit.

With all of the thrashing and growling erupting, it seemed as if everything was going to explode. The dogs began to maneuver into position, barking, closing in all around. The skirmishing noises were punctuated from time to time by sharp coughs and then the shrill yelp of a dog being thrown into the air. With all the commotion around them, the lions were panicking.

One of the confused cubs, almost fully grown, streaked past the rock, in full view of the Maasai Moraans. Instinctively, two of the young warriors, aimed and almost simultaneously sent their spears into the air. Both found their target. The spear from one of the *Makukis* struck the cub in the gut and knocked it a few feet out of its way. The other spear found the cub's neck. The cub rolled over with blood spilling out from the two deep wounds. The two Moraans would now be among the elite in all the regional villages when word got out they had killed a lion and proven their manhood.

Another cub skidded into the ground on the right and within range of Amrita's gun. It was growling and crawling back on its belly for cover. Amrita took aim with her double-barreled shotgun and fired both cartridges. The recoil threw her back. Her ears hummed. Gunpowder filled her nostrils. She hadn't missed. The dogs ran to the fallen cub and surrounded it, barking, and trying to tear pieces of the golden skin from the downed cub. Seeing her cubs dying, the lioness came into the open, snarling, and nonchalantly picking up a dog and tearing its chest open. Amrita quickly reached for the cartridges in her safari suit and started reloading.

Raj saw it just before the lioness started coming toward him with its yellow fangs protruding from behind wet lips. Its furry pink tongue arched across her open throat and her eyes filled yellow with hatred. She screamed a wild high ringing sound. Then she launched into her charge, which was unbelievably fluid. In fact, her flowing speed turned into a yellow rushing blur. She snaked in low, the sand spurting beneath her paws, all claws fully extended, the lips drawn back in a fixed silent snarl, the teeth exposed — long, white, and pointed.

Raj knew he would only have time for one shot, so he took his time, knowing he could not miss. Calmly as possible, he took aim, pointing just above the elbow, hoping to rake both her lungs and get to her heart. He fired. The bullet was 230 grains in weight, and the bronze jacket of the slug was tipped with a grey blob of lead so it would mushroom on impact, causing massive damage through the lioness's chest cavity.

And that is precisely what happened.

The yellow eyes of the lioness blinked tightly at the jarring shock as it slowed and its head wrenched backwards. Her arched body lost its grace and lightness, turning heavy and shapeless in midair. It fell like a sack at the Sikh's feet, with tiny droplets of brilliant red blood spattering Raj's khaki safari suit and his white turban.

The lioness lay on her side with her mouth open. She let out a soft moaning grunt before panting for air. Her chest pumped like a blacksmith's bellows, and her eyes were half closed. The bullet had hit her high in the shoulder, but far forward, cutting in through the heavy muscle and grazing the big joint of the shoulder. It lacerated sinew, and shattered the extraordinarily small floating bone, found only in the shoulder of a lion. — The lucky bone so prized as a hunter's talisman.

The bullet had missed the artery as it plunged into the neck and lodged there beneath the skin, a lump the size of the top joint of a man's thumb. Flies quickly swarmed joyously into the mouth of the wound, and she lifted her head and snapped at them, and then mewing softly at the agony that movement had caused, she began to lick the bullet hole carefully. The long tongue rasping roughly against her hide, curled pink and dexterous as it cleansed the fresh little trickle of watery blood that had sprung from it. Then she sank back wearily and closed her eyes again.

The male wasn't far behind.

"Mama, look over there, *Simba*," one of the Moraans shouted.

The majestic male cat was already in full charge, rushing at the hunters, grunting in short staccato bursts, like the steam pistons on a speeding locomotive. Its black mane was fully erect and with rage the long tail was swinging from side to side. He was enormous and growing bigger as he closed the gap between them with every stride. Amrita had reloaded and was ready. She aimed and fired her shotgun, letting go of both barrels. The impact of firing both barrels shoved her backward; she had missed! The bullets, hastily aimed, flew over the lion's back and kicked up a spurt of dust yards behind it. Amrita thought she had winged him.

In the meantime, Raj had reloaded. The lion kept boring straight in, a yellow blur of speed, grunting, kicking up dust, and slashing its tail. Raj fired. His bullet clipped the lion's right shoulder. The impact pushed the lion back and it fell on its right side. But he rolled to his side and quickly stood up, swung away, and bounded across the open ground toward the safety of the thick, tall grass.

Raj and Amrita looked at each other relieved, and smiled. They had been close to death — and very lucky. They walked over to the lioness. Raj touched her open staring eye, but the fierce yellow light was fading and there was no blinking reflex of the eyelids. He closed her eyes and sat down on the grass next to the lioness. Amrita did the same. They both sat next to her as they stroked their open palms across the soft thick golden fur. It was quiet except for the remaining dog barking and running around the dead lions, and the Maasai whispering to each other.

The *Laiboni* told everyone to head back to the *Manyatta*. The wounded lion would probably show up again in a week or two, hopefully, marauding another *Manyatta*. For now, the *Laiboni* was satisfied that his *Boma* wasn't in danger. He instructed five of his Moraans to go after the lion and kill it before it attacked a nearby village.

"Lemaron, you are the leader, take four others with you."

Raj looked at Amrita,

"I am going after the lion with the Moraans. I can't leave a wounded animal out there, I should have shot better."

"You don't have to go, they will take care of it." She paused for a second. "But if you insist on going, then I'm going with you."

"You know the Maasai and the *Laiboni* won't let a foreign woman go with them," he said. "They don't even allow their own *Siangikis* to accompany the Moraans when they are hunting."

Raj turned to the *Laiboni*,

"I am going with the Moraans to finish something I should have done earlier."

"Well, you can go if you want to, just be careful. That is a big lion out there and extremely dangerous with the wound you gave him."

"I know, I am going to dress like a *Moraan* and kill him with my *Makuki*."

"Why, use your gun as you know how to kill with it. Do you know how to throw a spear? Have you ever thrown one?"

"Yes, I can do it; I know I can. Just get me a *shuka*, a *Makuki*, a *Simmi*, and the sandals that your *Moraans* wear."

The sandals were sold at the Dhillon's store. They were cut out of old truck tires and formed into the shape that fit the feet. Then, the Maasai would cut *ol-dubai* in the form of laces to tie the shoes. The *Laiboni* looked at him from head to toe, doubting the Sikh's ability to be a Maasai hunter. He turned to the Moraans who were not part of the chosen five.

"The *Wahindi* wants to risk his life. Let him be with the Moraans. One of you who is the same size as him, give him whatever he needs."

"Please don't go, there is nothing to prove," Amrita pleaded once more. "Let's just go home."

"No, I have decided. I will be back as soon as I finish the kill."

Raj, being a Sikh, had long hair that had never been cut; it fell way past his shoulders. He went behind the Willy's jeep and changed his attire. He took his turban off and tied his long hair in a braided pony tail. He took all his clothes off, and dressed as a Moraan. He even painted his face and beard with red ochre. He still wore his *Kada*, one of the symbols signifying that he was a Sikh. The other Moraans had their hair plaited in thin braids and their faces painted with symbols that extended down onto their chests beneath long necklaces of colored pearls.

When he appeared from behind the Jeep, a roar went up from all the Maasai. He was dressed in a red tribal shuka, the skirt was belted around the waist, and the tail was thrown back over his left shoulder; he wore sandals that he borrowed from a Moraan. The brown skin on his upper torso and libs was exposed. The hair on his arms and chest was black. His shoulders were wide, his chest broad, and his limbs, hard and muscled. He had a *Simmi* on a sheath attached to his belt, the shining *Makuki* in his right hand, and a brown painted rawhide shield in his left.

The Maasai looked at each other and kept smiling, they had never imagined a *Wahindi* to dress as one of them. Ready to go, he said his farewell to Amrita and the *Laiboni*, and joined the other five hunters. One of the long-standing rituals of the Maasai culture was the killing of a lion to signify the final rite of passage to becoming a warrior. The government had outlawed the killing of lions, but the tradition continued for some time among the Maasai.

The Moraans, who were left behind, skinned the dead cubs and the lioness, which they would take back as souvenirs and proof of their bravery. When they returned to the *Manyatta,* villagers sprinkled the heroes with milk as they walked by, and offered them cows. Women showered them with beautiful beaded necklaces and bracelets and offered themselves.

The five young Moraans accompanying Raj, led by Lemaron, were dressed in red leather kilts decorated with ivory beads and cowrie shells. Their naked torsos gleamed with a coating of Eland fat and red ochre with hair, dressed in an elaborate style of coiled plaits. They were lean and long-limbed, hard and elegantly muscled. Their features were handsome and hawkish, with eyes bright and rapacious, showing their eagerness for the hunt to begin. They formed a single rank, shoulder to shoulder. At their lead was Lemaron, who was more experienced than the others, and had five lion tails in his kilt, one for every Nandi tribesman he had killed in single combat. His war-bonnet was the headskin of a black-maned lion, further proof of his prowess. He had a signal whistle made from the horn of a reed buck hanging on a thong around his neck.

Evenly spaced, they formed a long, sinous serpent, which wound down a grassy slope. The sunlight reflected in bright sparks off the steel of their *Makukis*. They carried on their shoulders long rawhide shields, each painted with a single large eye of black and ochre, with the eye's pupil glaring white. Raj was second in the line.

Not far into the hunt, one of the Maasai fell tripping over a small rock, his ankle swelled right away so that he could no longer keep pace with the rest. They told him to head back and catch up with the rest of the villagers before dark. The trackers kept tracking the male lion till late and it was getting difficult to see the spoor. Lion spoor, unlike that of hoofed animals, is light, and it takes a keen eye to follow it, especially across hard, ground. The Maasai are unique in that they follow the spoor on any surface.

The sun sank, seeming to touch the earth and erupt in an explosion of green and crimson. Then it fell away to change the world into sudden darkness. The mountains were an inky blue and seemed to shrink and flatten against the distance. The four Moraans and Raj decided to settle down for the night. The warriors fetched wood and arranged it together on the sandy earth to form a sort of bed. The Moraans had speared a reed buck on the way. They lit a fire and piled the cut pieces of meat onto a pyramid built of sticks. While the meal was being prepared, Raj and the Maasai sharpened the spears on the *Makukis* so fine that they could shave the hair off their forearms with the keen edge.

There wasn't much talk or laughter from any of them. The chatter was subdued as they each thought of the challenge ahead. They slept on the grassy ground with just the red *Shukas* covering them. The silence of the night was broken by the howling and squealing of a pair of jackals, followed by the sounds of nearby hyenas. The mosquitoes from the stagnant pools buzzed around them all night. Frogs croaked away in the reeds on the bank of a rain-filled stream close by.

At first light, they headed off again. The sun had come up and showed its rim above the horizon directly in front of them, bright as molten metal from a furnace. It shown in their faces and dazzled them. The bee-like sting of the Tsetse flies annoyed them, but for some humans and animals, the sting was more than a bother as it carried the dreaded sleeping sickness disease. They had to keep waving their hands to keep the pests away. A jackal barked somewhere close to them in the bush. Moments later something moved ahead of them in the thorny scrub. They all stopped. All they could hear was the chattering noises of the weaver birds making their nest in the acacia. A buffalo's charge is dangerous having gored more hunters than any other animal. A flock of guinea fowl burst out of the bushes producing an explosion of cackling sounds as they ran ahead. The buffalo, there might have been more than one, had moved in a different direction. They were safe for now.

It wasn't long before they spotted blood markings on the grass; they were on track. The lion was bleeding from the shoulder wound, but not heavily. They found where the lion had killed an Impala earlier. The wounded cat didn't have the strength to ward off the scavengers following him as they had wrested the antelope away from the lion. The scavengers had cleaned the area effectively as there were only a few splinters of bone that had fallen from the crushing jaws of a hyena. Also remaining were a few pulled tufts of shred of dried skin and part of the skull with the twisted black horns still intact. Unfortunately, the spoor was cold. Wind and trampling feet of the many scavengers, including jackals, hyenas, vultures and marabou storks had wiped away all signs. The hunters continued slowly on up the valley making wide tracks back and forth, casting carefully for any signs.

Finally they picked up the spoor again. The morning chill had given way to dull, humid heat, as the sun streamed down through the thick foliage. The male lion was moving slowly, and the spoor ran hotter by the hour. They found where the hungry lion had stalked a prey and then where its deep driving back claws had raked the earth as he leapt to the back of a full grown zebra without success. Twenty paces further, he had fallen heavily from the zebra, dislodged by the stallions plunging and kicking. The zebra had struck the lion's shoulder first. The zebra had run away, but must have been bleeding from the long slash of the lion's claws. The lion had moved slowly and lain under a thorn tree for a long time, before rising and going back, slowly and desperately looking for another victim. He was hungry and desperate.

It was mid morning when the lead hunter saw the tops of the grass move — and there had been no wind to make it move. They were close enough to hear the rasping of the lion's tongue against its paw, as the lion groomed himself. They spotted the dark mane and then heard him growl. It was a scary sound that struck the hearts of the hunters. Their legs became weak, and made each advancing pace a conscious step as they approached the wounded prey.

A downpour of recent rain had forced the lion to move in close under the shade of an umbrella thorn. The flat-topped mass of foliage spread from the tree's straight trunk. The lion was lying in the shade on his side, exposing his thick mane. Perhaps some deep sense of survival instincts warned him of the hunters' presence, because his head moved in a flash of yellow. This was an extraordinary swift reaction that is so characteristic of all the big cats. He stared fixedly downwind.

The lion arose suddenly, to his full height, swinging his tail from side to side. He snarled at the hunters, his lips peeling back from his long, bright fangs. The Maasai with Raj in the middle started to curl in around him, surrounding him and leaving him no escape route. The lion swung his head from side to side, surveying the hunters as they closed in. His head stopped swinging and his tail began to lash from side to side, the black tuft on the end of the tail whipping each of his own flanks. Raj, being in the middle, was in the place of honor and was close enough to see the lion's eyes. They were yellow, bright burning yellow, and fastened laser like directly on him.

"He is mine, let me get to him first," Raj whispered to the Moraans.

The four Moraans nodded to each other as they narrowed the circle around the cat. They positioned the shields in front of them in their left hands, with their spears half-raised in their right hands. Shuffling forward slowly in unison, they closed in on him. The lion couldn't get away from the ring of shields and spears around him.

The leader, with the black-mane headdress, blew a blast on his buckhorn whistle. They all dropped to one knee behind their shields. The points of their *Makukis* aimed at the center of the lion's chest.

The lion fell into a crouch as he gathered himself for his charge. His tail stopped lashing. He held it straight out behind him, rigid, and slightly curled upward. Then the tail flicked twice and he came charging straight at Raj as he and the cat faced each other. The lion came snaking surprisingly low along the ground, so fast that he surprised Raj. Everything seemed to snap into slow motion and the air seemed to grow dense and heavy which made it difficult to breathe. It was like being trapped in a thick mud swamp. Every movement required a deliberate effort.

Raj braced behind the rawhide shield and raised the point of his Makuki. The sunlight caught the burnished metal and sent a bright splinter of light into Raj's eyes. The form of the lion swelled up before him until it filled his active vision. The lion's chest pumped as he deafened Raj with his killing fury with mighty gusts whie running at full throttle.

Raj braced again, stiff, positioning the rawhide war-shield in front of him. Then he screamed the Sikh prayer, *Jo-bole-so-nihaal*, and at the same time repostured the point of the *Makuki* at the charging lion.

The beast took the spear in the center of his chest. It burried so deep that Raj's right hand, which held the shaft, was covered in the coarse black fleece of the mane; the lion's heart was pierced cleanly by the razor sharp steel point. The lion's jaws gaped wide as he roared, and from his throat shot a fountain of bright blood that sprayed all over Raj's face, beard, head, and shoulders.

The dying lion fell on top of the Sikh and bore him backwards to the earth and crouched on top of him, racking the shield with his claws while bellowing his rage and agony. Then suddenly the lion's whole body stiffened and he arched his back. With his jaws wide open he vomited a copious gout of his heart blood all over Raj, drenching his head and entire upper body. The Maasis quickly dragged the lion off the Sikh.

Raj had done it.

Raj threw the shield aside and bounded to his feet, bellowing triumphantly, his face contorted under the glistening coating of the lion's blood. The Moraans stepped forward and stabbed their *Makuki* blades in to the corpse, a gesture of staking their claim. Then, they gathered around the Sikh, hugged him, picked him up on their shoulders and congratulated him. They celebrated by drinking blood and milk from their *Kibuis*. Raj joined them, slowly gulping the mixture. Lemaron as the leader spoke to Raj,

"We are so proud of you, that as a non-Maasai you hunted with us and as a Moraan. We have decided that you keep this lion skin as a momento and a special memory for you."

"Thanks, I feel privileged and honored to be with you and the hunt. I will treasure the skin forever."

The Maasai skinned their trophy and headed back to the village with the skin and the thick mane. The mane started two inches above the opaque yellow eyes and ran halfway down the broad back. Wave after wave of dense black hair, extended over the skull and neck, over the massive shoulders, under the chest until it ended midway in the middle of its back. This was a prize lion.

All of the Moraans sang the lion song, which was taught to the young Moraans when they got circumcized. The initiates accompanied it with a stiff-legged dance, bounding high into the air, as effortlessly as a flock of birds taking flight. Their red toga-like *shukas* spread like wings around them.

We are the young lions,
When we roar the earth shivers,
Our spears are our claws,
Fear us, O ye beasts,

Fear us, O ye strangers,
Turn your eyes away fro our faces, you women,
You dare not look upon the beauty of our faces,
We are the brothers of the lion pride,
We are the young lions,
We are the Maasai.

It was also the song that the Maasai sang when they went out to plunder the cattle and women of lesser tribes. It was the song they sang when they went out to prove their valor by hunting the lion with nothing but the stabbing *Makuki* spears in their hands. It was their battle hymn. The excitement showed on the happy warriors' faces as they thought of the *Manyatta* and the warm welcome they would receive from the *Laiboni*, the villagers, and the pretty *Siangikis*. As tradition would have it, they would now have the right to place their spears outside the hut of any woman in Maasailand. Raj couldn't wait to get home, clean himself, and be in Amrita's arms where, together they would share large glasses of Dimple Scotch Whiskey and relate their extraordinary hunting adventure.

The Moraans were so excited they almost ran all the way back to the *Manyatta* to celebrate and to share their success. They slaughtered an ox to celebrate. In the middle of the *Manyatta*, six Moraans tried to wrestle the ox to the ground from the side. The terrified animal, with eyes wide open and sensing danger, thrust about with its horns. After several attempts, the warriors managed to grab the horns and turn its head to one side, and the beast slowly sank to the ground. Immediately, its legs were tied, and three of the men set about slaughtering it while the others held its legs.

For the Maasai, that was the only way they knew how to kill their cattle. When the ox stopped moving, it's main artery was cut and all the men stood around to drink the blood. It was a great delicacy for them. There was a lot of pushing and jostling with all the Moraans in the village. Then the butchery began. Old men, women, and children lined up for their fill. The best bits went to the old men, and only then did the women and children get their share. Four hours later, there was nothing left but a pool of blood and the splayed out hide. The women withdrew into their huts and began cooking. The old men sat in the shade under the trees, drinking home made beer, and waiting for the cooked meat to arrive.

In the cool of the evening, with bellies full, everyone gathered around a large pit of glowing embers in the middle of the *Manyatta*. Some of the younger males started their celebratory dance where they jumped high into the air and sang songs.

As Raj walked into the shop at Loliondo, Jolly and Amrita both screamed at the same time when they saw him, fearing that he had been hurt,

"You have blood all over you. What happened? Are you all right?" Amrita shouted running towards him.

He hadn't bothered to wash himself. The lion's blood had dried thickly in his long untied hair and on his brown skin. His face and beard were a mask of dried blood. He was still wearing the Maasai *Shuka*, which was now a darker red with the mixture of red ochre and dried blood. Amrita inspected him from head to toe, thankful he had returned home safely with no apparent wounds.

Raj looked at Amrita proudly,

"Go look in the back of the Jeep."

Amrita inspected the large lion skin,

"Well, this is impressive, but I am glad you survived dressed as a Maasai and hunting with just the *Makukis*."

The Lion skin was treated and preserved. Decades later, it now hangs in Amrita's grand daughter's home in Ohio.

> "I want nothing to do with any religion concerned with keeping the masses satisfied to live in hunger, filth and ignorance. I want nothing to do with any order, religious or otherwise, which does not teach people that they are capable of becoming happier and more civilized, on this earth, capable of becoming a true man, master of his fate and captain of his soul."
>
> **JAWAHARLAL NEHRU**

As usual, it was dusk and Amrita was sitting in the outside patio in Loliondo, sipping her scotch whiskey, she was listening to the news on The Voice of Kenya when something attracted her attention,

> Last night, a band of terrorists thought to be some two hundred strong, attacked a location of professed loyal Kikuyu at Lari. It is believed that one hundred and fifty peaceful Kikuyu were murdered. Women and children were sadistically butchered and whole families, who refused to open their doors, were burned to death. The leader of the group was identified as a woman, Lalita daughter of Wamboi, highly ranked in the Mau Mau hierarchy.
>
> She was killed later that night, after leaving Lari and walking into a trap set by The Black Watch Company at Narok, about seventy miles West of Nairobi. Laying the ambush were two sergeants under the command of an African Company Sergeant-Major who had spent two weeks tracking the woman's movements in the Maasai area. When she was challenged to halt and surrender, Lalita, who was dressed in a Khaki jacket and a Sam Browne

> belt, raised her gun and opened fire on the Company in a bid to fight her way out of the ambush. The soldiers fired back killing her instantly. This was a significant loss for the Mau Mau as Lalita was one of their front line leaders.

Amrita was shocked, not believing what she had just heard. Although it was inevitable because of the life Lalita had chosen for herself. Losing her half-sister was just another blow to Amrita after seeing her father die and then Wamboi.

All the Dhillon businesses were successful and especially the shop in Loliondo was prospering. Amrita had hired a driver, Krishan Aggarwal, one of the sons of Chunilal Aggarwal, who was from the same village as Mehar Singh. Krishan made weekly trips from Loliondo to Nairobi to pick up supplies for the shops and saw mills; he was extremely reliable.

The Maasai had complete trust in the Dhillons. They would leave their valuables, mainly silver shilling coins, with the Dhillons and reclaim them when needed. All their purchases were paid with silver coins, because they didn't trust paper currency. There would be times when Amrita and Raj would pack all the silver coins the Maasai had spent, and load them into empty sugar sacks. The sacks would sometimes get so heavy that it took four or five men to load them into a truck to take to the Barclays Bank in Nairobi for deposit.

After the youngest Dhillon, Ajit passed away from a serious virus infection and Avtar had gone out on his own after Mehar Singh's murder, there were only two brothers left in business together. Raj had joint business bank accounts with his brother Tej in two different banks, which held cash from all the businesses that had been sold or were in operation. The checks had to be signed by both brothers, but with the unconditional trust they had in each other, each brother had blank checks signed by the other one. So, once the check had both signatures there was no limit on the amounts that could be withdrawn.

Tej had never finished his high school education. He had been suspended and reprimanded for being a bully in class and then assaulting his teacher. This behavior had been repeated a few times and finally Mehar Singh took him out of school and made him work in the businesses. Tej had a severe temper and throughout his life he had many confrontations. Since, Raj was educated and was always favored by Mehar Singh over the other sons, in time Tej developed a jealous hatred towards Raj. Whenever, he had the chance he wanted to get even and hurt Raj and his family. Tej saw an opportunity as this time to get even and really hurt his older brother.

Raj had gone to the Barclays Bank to make a routine cash withdrawal on a Monday morning. The teller then said to Raj,

"I'm sorry, my friend. There is a problem." He asked Raj to wait as he called for his manager, Kundan Lal Vohora.

Kundan Lal appeared, looking a bit sheepish,

"I am sorry Raj. There are no funds in your account."

"What are you saying? I don't understand," said Raj. "There has to be a mistake in the account numbers or names, please check again." Raj felt light-headed and began looking pale.

"I made sure," Kundan said. "Your brother Tej signed the check last week and has withdrawn all the funds."

"Has to be a mistake," Raj muttered as he rushed to the other bank, Standard Bank of South Africa, and came head-on with the same situation. No funds.

Raj's hard work and life savings were gone. His brother had stolen everything. The trust they had as brothers was broken. He sat on the bench in the bank for a long time before heading home to break the news to Amrita. He was devastated, as was his family when he shared the news with them.

Tej would not discuss the situation when confronted by Raj. Their mother, Satbir Kaur, tried in vain to get Tej to explain what had happened, but Tej ignored her. She even begged him by bending down and touching his feet, but he nonchalantly pushed his mother away. With his vicious temper, he would end up shouting and screaming, ready to hit someone. After a number of family arguments and fights, with the matriarch being there, Tej and Raj agreed to get legal help. They both engaged attorneys and picked a date for the meeting with a neutral mediator.

The Nairobi courthouse is an old, imposing brick building that occupies a full city block; the entrance is off to the side, down a set of steps. As they sat in the large room, the chill of the air-conditioning soothed them but tempers were right at the edge of blowups. The beautifully carved plaster ceiling echoed their voices sharply in the marbled interior.

The mediator, Paddy O'Connor, an Irishman, was disheveled and shapeless, with baggy linen trousers and an undersized blue shirt that barely covered his pinkish stomach. He had white stubble on his patchy red face, and a crown of wispy white hair. He called everyone to order.

Each discussed the assets of the properties and businesses that were left. The topic of Tej withdrawing all the funds came up often,

"I am sorry, Mr. Raj Singh, you, had counter-signed the checks and there is no provision to question the withdrawals," O'Connor informed Raj.

There were further arguments and Tej threw, tantrums, as expected but the milder-natured and timid Raj sat through it. Finally, with the mediator intervening constantly, and Raj feeling hopeless and giving in, they reached agreement.

Tej got the shop in Loliondo, the one Amrita used to run, while Raj was left with just the Mercedes truck and the Mercedes Unimog truck. Raj also had a half-share of the family house in Nairobi west. All the saw mills and other businesses had been sold earlier and all the funds had been in the banks that Tej had withdrawn from. Tej had most of the family funds now. Even then, Raj could not believe his brother had signed the checks and taken everything.

Amrita and Raj were in a serious financial bind now. There was nothing in Maasailand left for them, Tej had the Loliondo shop and Raj only had the two trucks. To support the family and generate some income, Amrita began a driving school in Nairobi for ladies using an old Volkswagen. She named the school, Jolly Driving School. The name was written across the side of the bright yellow car. She advertised in the Sikh Gurudwaras and Hindu temples, and received a great response from Indian women wanting to learn how to drive. The earnings helped the finances. Maya, the eldest, was still finishing her teacher training classes. Akash was going to turn fifteen and graduate from high school. Raj spoke to his friend who was the branch manager of the Barclays Bank, Government Road branch, to see if he could hire Akash as an apprentice in the bank. As a favor for his old classmate Harbans hired Akash. So at the tender age of fifteen Akash started supporting the family. He had ambitions of going to college and then university to become a physician but those dreams had to be put on hold because of the family financial situation.

The landlord of the driving school office building, Parminder Singh Sian, was a contractor who built homes and commercial properties across Nairobi. He suggested to Raj that he find a driver to drive the Mercedes truck they had, so they could supply sand and building materials to his construction sites. Raj rented two seven-ton trailers, which both could be hooked to the powerful Mercedes Unimog four-wheel-drive vehicle. Raj started driving the convoy himself from Muthaiga to Nairobi, transporting cement bags from the cement factory, which was close to the exclusive Muthaiga Country Club with its glittering lawns and expensive cars bringing the local and expat Europeans.

The founder of the Country Club was Berkeley Cole, an Anglo-Irish aristocrat who wanted to create a place where a bell would summon a drink on a "spotless tray." The club, a peachy-pink, low-rise building with Doric columns and tennis lawns was an oasis with pebbled walls. Guests basked by the tennis courts with their tall glasses of gin and tonic. The sitting rooms were all done in dark hardwood flooring with Persian carpets and framed hunting trophies. In the latter years, they added soccer, rugby, hockey fields, cricket pitches and a golf course to the facilities.

The fifteen-mile trip from Muthaiga to the Nairobi industrial area took two hours after the heavily loaded Unimog trucks crawled up the long slopes towards the capital. After the time it took to unload the cement, Raj could only make one trip per day. The compensation was limited but did help the family budget.

> "It is a common experience that a problem difficult at night is resolved in the morning after the committee of sleep has worked on it."
>
> **JOHN STEINBECK**

Although Amrita's driving school was doing well, it wasn't enough to help maintain the family budget. At the same time, a few plots of land were being allocated to the Indian traders in Ngorongoro in Maasailand in Northern Tanganyika.

"Let's try and get a plot in Ngorongoro and set up a *Duka*, we know the area and the Maasai," Raj suggested to Amrita.

"We will be better off than what we have now," she agreed.

A plot had been allocated to a Sikh from the same village as the Dhillons, named Bhag Singh. His nickname was *Malefu*, the tall one. He stood six-feet, six-inches tall. He was kind enough to let Raj rent his plot.

Raj and Amrita had a meeting with the manager, Kundan Lal, at the Barclays Bank branch in Arusha and presented their plans to start a new shop in Ngorongoro. Kundan Lal had known the Dhillons for decades and opened a line of credit for them. With his usual entrepreneurship, Raj built a shop, plus a two-bedroom house with a kitchen and bath. The shop overlooked the crater and was on the main road between Arusha and Loliondo so the Maasai customers could easily stop there. With his bare hands and help from the locals, he raised the wooden structure, complete with aluminum roof and sidings. At the time, they did not have enough money to fill the shop with goods, so they got help from some of the big stores in Arusha. The store owners trusted them as they knew them from the time they had businesses in Loliondo and extended them credit for 90 days.

Within months, the shop was flourishing. Amrita spent most of the time at the store. She could hear the dull ringing of Maasai cattle bells as they came up the slopes, out of the crater, at the end of their grazing time and stopped at the *Duka* for groceries.

They were quite comfortable and happy. Surjeet and Jolly went to Indian Public School under their grandmother Satbir's supervision. The eldest daughter, Maya, was now teaching at the Indian School in Arusha. Akash had transferred to the Barclays Bank in Arusha from Nairobi.

For one of the first times since her father passed away, Amrita was happy and content. They were on their own and the children seemed settled. This carried on for two years — until Tej struck again. He was bitter and jealous to see his brother, Raj's family so happy, so he decided to do something about it. This time he approached Bhag Singh *Maleju*, who was running Tej's other shop in Loliondo. Tej told him to evict Raj and repossess the lot on which Raj had his shop In Ngorongoro. Raj had rented the plot from Bhag Singh, who in turn had rented Tej's shop in Loliondo. Sadly, Bhag Singh had no choice but to agree to Tej's request in order to protect his interest in Loliondo.

Raj was issued a twenty four hour eviction notice to leave the store in the middle of a political coup in Dar-es-salaam, the capital of Tanganyika. For a number of months there had been reports of dissatisfaction over the country's critical economic position. Already ranked as one of the world's poorest countries its imports had been severely cut because of an acute shortage of foreign exchange. There were serious food shortages, with commodities like milk, basic grains, soap, and even meat in short supply. Blamed were a breakdown of the socialist central distribution system and poor results in the collective farm operation. The revolt was planned and triggered by a number of highly placed army officers. This was an opportunity for looters to go on a rampage; and it was a time when shootings were prevalent.

A cattle auction, *Mwananda*, was being held in Ngorongoro, where the Maasai brought a few of their cattle to sell and live on the profits. In those days Maasai did not understand the value of paper money. As soon as they received any monetary notes they would rush to the shops and exchange them for coins, and deposited them with the traders who acted like banks for these nomads. Raj suggested that Amrita go to Arusha and meet the magistrate, Mr. Amir Sheikh, and request him to give them some additional time for them to vacate the shop, as twenty four hours was just so unrealistic.

Amrita asked an old man, Nahar Singh, who had a small shop near Ngorongoro, to accompany her to Arusha. Raj was at the *Mwananda*. It was too risky travelling alone.

Nahar Singh, an old family friend, was an impressively large man. He was hairy faced, proud of bearing and slow of stride. He had beady, penetrating, but unusually self-contained eyes highlighted by bushy eyebrows. His immaculate, all Khaki attire consisted of a buttoned shirt and loose trousers, cut wide at the top, narrow at the bottom. He and Amrita left Ngorongoro for Arusha, knowing that they were risking their lives on the way because of the unrest triggered by the coup.

She drove on the off roads, through deep thickets. They had to lean in to avoid the acacia branches which snapped against the sides of the Jeep. To make Amrita's trip even more stressful, as she was going down the escarpment at Ngorongoro, she turned into a narrow "S" curve. Immediately she saw a huge grey wall in front of her. It was an old elephant bull with sizeable tusks. Although she slammed on the brakes, the four-wheel-drive Jeep skidded then it veered severely toward a deadly drop-off.

Amrita tried the handbrake, but that only made the skid more severe. She turned the steering wheel to the left and, by some miracle; the vehicle came to a stop, hanging over the edge of the escarpment wall against a fallen tree. A few feet further and there would have been nothing there to stop the Jeep. It would have plunged head first over the edge.

Amrita was shaken, but Nahar Singh kept calm and encouraged her. She engaged the four-wheel-drive and gradually maneuvered the vehicle back onto the road. A little way down the road, they approached the bull elephant. They stopped about fifty yards away, looking at the bull's enormous backside. Just then, the surprised elephant tried to turn around on the narrow road. Amrita quickly threw the Jeep in reverse and retreated another twenty yards. By now the bull was facing them and was with his big eyes staring at the Jeep. Amrita was wondering if this day would ever end.

The elephant swung his trunk high in the air and trumpeted, the long powerful tusks making him even more threatening. Amrita decided they were too close and retreated further. They were now back up to the point where the bend made it too dangerous to maneuver. They could still hear the elephant breaking branches and chewing. It took about an hour before it was all quiet and Amrita inched forward and saw the road was clear. The bull had taken the trail down the slope into the crater. Greatly relieved, Amrita and Nahar Singh continued their trip to Arusha.

Police and military roadblocks were stationed every few miles with stones piled on the road; they were checking everyone, from Africans and Asians to Europeans. Some of the heavily armed officials were drunk and arrogantly demanding to see identification papers for individuals and vehicles, and then asking why people were travelling. If they were not satisfied, they forced the individuals onto buses that were transporting people to the Monduli prison outside Arusha.

Women were interrogated excessively; some were abused. Some travelers got through by handing Tanganyika shillings to the uniformed men; there were stacks of the bills at the checkpoints. Amrita had to sidetrack through the jungle and negotiate dirt roads in the direction of Mount Meru, the fourteen thousand feet, landmark towering over the small town of Arusha. The two-hour trip took five hours. She had to drive through sand drifts, and muddy narrow winding unused tracks. When they finally arrived in Arusha and went home, her mother-in-law was shocked to see her.

"What are you doing here at night?" her mother said. "No one is going out of the house because of the coup and the fear of guns."

"*Manjee*, with the cannon which has struck us today, there is no fear beyond that," Amrita said. She went on to explain to Satbir how her son, Tej, was scheming for them to be thrown out of the shop at Ngorongoro.

Amrita left Nahar Singh with Satbir and went to the magistrate's house. It was 9 p.m. Everyone in Arusha knew Amrita because she ran the booking office there and dealt with the traders. She was not afraid of approaching anyone. She was one of the first Indian Sikh women to drive a vehicle in Arusha. If any of Amrita's friends wanted their servants to come to their house, they would say, go to the lady's house that drives the car.

Amrita knocked on Mr. Sheikh's door. The magistrate was a small, thin man with a rough chin and narrow moustache. He wore white pants and a loose shirt with a fluffy scarf on his head. He was surprised, but politely opened the door and asked her to sit down.

"This is quite late. Are you ok Mrs. Dhillon? What can I do?" he asked.

Amrita explained the situation and what her brother-in-law was up to.

"How much time do you need?" he asked.

"As much as I can get but I think a month should be enough."

He wrote a letter and told Amrita to give it to the person sitting at the store in Ngorongoro, with the summons. The next morning, she drove the same route back through the dirt tracks, side tracking the main roads, avoiding the military and the police roadblocks.

Within the month reprieve, they started packing the contents in the shop. Meanwhile, Raj had applied for another plot two miles down the road. To their pleasant surprise, they received a letter stating that the plot had been allocated to them. They pitched two tents there, one big one for the business and a smaller one to live in. They made the full-time move there within the month.

The tents were on the edge of the forest on the escarpment and were frequented by elephants surrounding the tents at night. They could hear the big bulls scratching the fabric and trying to break through the canvas with the tips of their tusks. They would feed on seedpods from the branches above the tent; as they shook the branches, the pods would come raining down on the tents. It was nerve racking, as the great beasts gingerly moved around the tents. Entire trees shook as their ceaseless browsing and shuffling enveloped the tents in mini dust clouds. The smell of elephants rich mildew odor filtered through the mosquito gauze, and the noise of them communicating with each other via their deep rumbling belly growls echoed all around.

After several months had passed, they got word that Tej had ended up selling his shop to another Sikh trader named Joginder Singh. He just didn't want his brother Raj to have any success.

Gradually, Amrita and Raj built another shop, on the new plot, all over again with wood and aluminum and moved from the tents to the new structure. The manager at Barclays Bank in Arusha, Kundan Lal, extended them a second line of credit to get back on their feet. They had paid the first one off.

Most of the Maasai customers, who were loyal to the Dhillons, followed them there. The Maasai like to deal with people they trust, including the traders. They had great faith in Amrita. Fortunately, Amrita and Raj did not lose any customers. The other shopkeepers were surprised. The Maasai, in their typical habitat, would hang around the shop all day, talking and exchanging ideas with Amrita and Raj.

"Only after the last tree has been cut down,
Only after the last river has been poisoned,
Only after the last fish has been caught,
Only then will you find that money cannot be eaten."
AMERICAN INDIAN PROVERB. CREE INDIAN PROPHECY.

Time passed and the new shop was doing well when Amrita and Raj were approached by the Ngorongoro conservation officer, a Maasai named Ole Saibulu, who had a business proposition for them. A government house located nearby the shop where a forest ranger had resided, had ten rooms and a large lounge. With the recent influx of tourists coming to Ngorongoro from all over the world, there was a great need for additional lodges and beds on the crater rim.

Saibulu asked Raj and Amrita if they might be interested in converting the structure to a rest house or lodge for the tourists. He suggested they could get four-wheel automobiles to drive the tourists into the Crater Game Reserve like the Ngorongoro Crater Lodge. The building would be leased from the government on a renewable three-year lease.

"We should do this. It will be a challenge but we can handle it. It could be really lucrative, just look at the Ngorongoro Crater Lodge and how they have expanded," Amrita tried to convince her ever hesitant husband.

Ngorongoro is the Maasai word for cowbells. The Ngorongoro Conservation Area, often called the eighth wonder of the world, boasted a blend of landscapes, wildlife, people, and archaeology unsurpassed in all of Africa. A world heritage site situated at the eastern edge of the Serengeti in northern Tanganyika. The area boasted the largest unbroken ancient caldera crater in the world. The crater is rimmed with steep walls and sheltered forests, grasslands, fresh springs, and a large soda lake at its center.

The Ngorongoro volcano, before it exploded and collapsed two million years ago, was one of the world's tallest mountains. The crater it left measured about twelve miles across. The rim is two thousand feet above the crater floor. There is a steep and rough trek that curves down the slopes onto the floor of the crater. The only vehicles permitted are four-wheel-drive Jeeps or Land Cruisers.

Inside the crater there is a lake and the Larai forest with tall acacia trees scattered amongst dense bushes. The lake and its surroundings are home to a large number of hippos and beautiful African flamingo birds. These birds added color to the scenic environment with their bright pink feathers. The Larai forest is the favorite stopping ground for herds of elephants that come down the crater on a regular basis from the rim of the crater. These large animals almost tumble their way down the steep slopes then struggle against gravity as they climb up on the other side after visiting the crater floor. There is a large picnic area outside the Larai forest where all the tourists break for lunch.

Raj reluctantly agreed to the proposal and now they were in the lodging business.

Another Sikh trader, who was from the same village as Mehar Singh, had a small *Duka* in the town of *Mto-wa-mbu*, the Swahili word for the River of Mosquitoes. This river flows into Lake Manyara in the Great

Rift Valley. The lake is located at the base of the escarpment leading up to the Ngorongoro Crater. Gurchand Singh lived with his African Chagga wife, Mary, and their two sons, William and Balwant. He agreed to buy the shop at Ngorongoro, which made it easier for Amrita and Raj to pack up and start the tourist business.

Tucked into the upper crags of the Ngorongoro Crater, Raj and Amrita started converting the ranger's house. They named it Dhillon's Lodge. Cradled in the dense forest, the lodge had an unusual look and atmosphere while offering the advantage of being in the midst of the animal habitat. The scenery was spectacular. The circular driveway allowed guests to stop and check-in before parking their vehicles. They were greeted with fresh fruit drinks and baskets of cool damp towels upon arrival. The open area next to the main building featured umbrellas and chairs where visitors could lounge and enjoy a beer, unwind while taking in the magnificent surroundings.

Amrita worked tirelessly on the interior design. Though primitive looking from the outside, the interior boasted a lavish array of silk, leather, mahogany, beaded furnishings and dressings. The lodge provided for every luxury, from full baths to private guided safaris down the winding road to the base of the crater. They hired a chef named Suleiman, an Arab who had worked for German, French, and English families in East Africa. He was also an expert at making Indian curries. Frequently, guests from other lodges in Ngorongoro would come and dine at the Dhillon's Lodge with its assortment of cuisines. This was the highest compliment for the local chef.

The cedar-paneled bar was tucked away in the corner facing the salt lick and a clear view of the visiting animals. Above the bar, mounts of the "African big five" animals looked directly down at the guests. In the beginning, they only had twenty beds and a large dining room with a fireplace. But gradually they added another building with fifty beds. The rooms had double beds and fluffy mattresses, covered with soft cotton sheets and thick, white duvets. The walk-in, slate-lined shower contained soaps, sugar scrubs, and shampoos laced with herbs. Bottles of mineral water were placed on the double-sink vanities. All the rooms had the zipped-up mosquito netting and some had private patios complete with chairs looking out into the open areas. The large living room was outfitted with safari-chic décor highlighted by rich earth-toned upholstery, antique wooden furniture and pillows covered in animal prints. A stack of *National Geographic* magazines were available as well as other periodicals and books about Africa. A dominating large fire place would be crowded on cold evenings as the wood fire spit and crackled in the stone hearth. The air was sweetened by the smell of burning *leleshwa*. The armchairs gathered round the fire, draped with zebra and cattle skins.

As tourism to Tanganyika and its unique game reserves was being advertised around the world, the demand for lodging increased by the day. Amrita managed the booking office, which was at Arusha, with the help of a young Ismaili man, Dawood, who also kept track of the accounts. Raj managed the lodge and vehicles. They had acquired eight Land Rovers and had African drivers, ranging from Kikuyus, to Chaggas, to Maasai. The cooks and waiters were also all Africans. The bedrooms were cleaned and managed by young Maasai girls.

Life was indeed getting better for Amrita and Raj; they were moving up and their extraordinary effort and hard work was becoming fruitful and prosperous. Tourists would stay overnight at the lodge and then take early morning day trips to the crater with Raj or one of the other drivers. Raj was a master as a storyteller and a tour guide. Visitors loved him and he became quite a legend; everyone wanted to travel with him. Whenever he took tourists down the crater, he would add that extra touch by relating a lifetime of experiences with the animals that he loved and grew up with.

On busy days when Amrita was at the lodge, she also drove down into the crater in her Toyota Land Cruiser and entertained the tourists with her knowledge of the animals and the scenery. The trips always started before dawn so they could be on the base of the crater as the sun was coming up. It was the best time to see animals. On most days, a low bank of mist would hang over the lake water. The dawn would be windless and the lake a polished grey. Skeins of luminous pink flamingoes, which resided in the salt lake in the crater, would fly in long, wavering images along the lake. The unruffled grey waters reflected their perfect mirror images — a magnificent site.

In the crater, all day and night there was constant movement occurring. The animals were noisy, but it was a concert, from the grunts of the gnus, to the songs of the grasshoppers and cicadas. There was the roar of the lions, to the high-pitched bark of the zebras and the excited laughs of the feeding hyenas. The many sized birds sang and fed, adding richness and fine texture to the grand stage. Sounds and activities were everywhere. The ground seemed to be alive. It invigorated and recharged the human spirit right at its ancient roots.

At the base of the crater, the excited foreign tourists photographed and filmed movies of animals in their natural habitat. They witnessed the lions stalking their kills and elephants knocking down the bigger trees to reach the tender top leaves. Elephants, buffalos, and lions that fed during the night were quenching their thirst at the water holes and seeking shady spots for sleep. Herds of zebras, antelopes and wildebeest fed during the day. All of them, grazing or browsing, would look for shade under the trees before the sun got too high. The Land Rovers had thick metal braces holding up the roofs and an opening at the top where passengers could stand and get a higher view of the animals. The clients were able to take photographs at close range. Occasionally, tsetse flies would get inside the vehicles and stick to the roofs and the tourists would have to wave them off constantly.

At times, cheetahs could be seen hunting a gazelle or a zebra. Leopard sightings were rare, but they could be seen as they jumped out of trees, hunted, and moved to different locations. Ngorongoro, at that time, had a population of about twenty black rhinos, which could be seen over the entire crater. Recognizable by the shape and length of their horns, Raj had named each one and would refer to them by name. When he spotted them he would relate stories about that particular animal.

At the lodge, in the evenings, the guests would sit on the fenced patio under the stars, around the large fireplace and listen to Raj reminisce various experiences about hunting and travelling in the wild. Amrita would join her husband, with a glass of Dimple Scotch whiskey, and narrate her own experiences. She had a great sense of humor and would have the tourists laughing and enjoying her Indian and African jokes.

Facing the patio, Raj had placed salt which was poured daily to attract waterbucks, elephants, rhinos, buffalos and occasionally a lion or cheetah. The elephants especially loved this area and the taste of salt. The fireplace was quite close to the salt lick area. The guests were able to look for and take photos of animals that stopped by. Raj had placed some floodlights at strategic points to highlight the animals' markings. A well-trodden winding path led the tourists through the thick river bush toward the main dining area, a wooden building with a thatched roof and a wide shady verandah overlooking the salt lick.

Tourists would be guided back to their rooms after dusk by armed Maasai Moraans, because of the danger of wild animals lurking about. In East Africa, darkness falls within half an hour. With the millions of stars looking so close, one might feel that they could pluck them from the sky. At night it was common to see elephants and buffalos walking through the lodge grounds to visit the salt lick. In the morning, tourists would get excited to see elephant dung outside their rooms and realizing how close they had been to the wild animals.

Over the years, quite a few celebrities and world leaders, including Prime Ministers such as Indira Gandhi, Golda Meier, Dr. Adenauer from Germany, a number of film stars, and others stayed at or visited

Dhillon's Lodge. Many wrote complimentary notes in the visitor's book. Depending on the time of year, the tourists would leave Ngorongoro and drive to the Serengeti Plains to see the great migrating herds of wildebeests and zebras. Many felt that perhaps this migration was the most impressive sight in Serengeti.

For many visitors the sounds, smells, changing light and the constant theater of primal Africa in the Serengeti remained vivid in their memories. The Maasai, who grazed their cattle on the vast grassy plains for millennia, named the Serengeti, *Siringitu* — "*The place where the land moves on forever.*"

In the evenings, as the shade began to spread over the Savannah, zebra mothers and foals migrated through pastures on an endless journey. Some grazed while others were constantly alert looking for predators. Several of the stronger zebra stallions went for each other's throats in battle, but caused no serious harm. Such fights often ensued when a rival would try to filch a filly from another male's family. A stallion reigned over a group of up to ten females and their offspring. On the other side of the herd, bathed in dust and light, a zebra rolled on a rough patch of ground scratching and cleaning its skin. Others waited their turn to romp and roll on this favored spot.

Lionesses eyed the grazing zebras for hours, weighing their chances of taking one down alone. With cat stealth, chest low, they would slink closer, ignoring nearby wildebeests, and watchful gazelles. Suddenly, bursting into full flight they would leap toward their prey. As startled animals scattered in panic, claws tore into the victim's rump, and it would stumble and fall to the lions attack.

The plains are the great sanctuary of the Maasai people and they harbor more wild game than any similar territory in East Africa. In the season of drought they are as dry and tawny as the coats of the lions that prowl the area and during the rains the plains provide the benison of soft grass to the animal herds.

Early in the year, usually late February or early March, the plains near Olduvai and Ngorongoro Crater are green with fresh grass and bright with wildflowers. Rainwater collects in clear reflecting pools and thousands of wildebeests drop their calves.

The Indian Prime Minister, Indira Gandhi, with her extensive entourage, stayed at the larger Ngorongoro Crater Lodge, but she arranged to have lunch at the Dhillon's Lodge and meet the Sikh owners. Raj and Amrita laid out special tables in the open yard next to where the animals normally came for the salt lick. All the cooks, drivers, and workers were dressed in clean Khaki uniforms with the Dhillon logo. Tables were set for fifty guests, including local dignitaries and Government Officials. The cook prepared an assortment of Indian dishes, along with African ones, and fresh fruit including papayas, tangerines, bananas, peaches, mangoes, and pomegranate. The matriarch, Satbir Kaur, traveled from Arusha to join the function.

Indira Gandhi hugged the Dhillons warmly when she was introduced. After the tour of the lodge and drinks of fresh juices, she sat for lunch. She sat opposite the matriarch Satbir Kaur, and had Amrita and Raj on each side of her at the table. Indira Gandhi was sincerely curious as to how their grandparents had arrived and settled there from India.

As if it was orchestrated, a large elephant bull trailed by a few females and babies from the herd, strolled by and moved to the salt lick area, scattering the water bucks and the small *dik-dik* that were already there. The shy antelopes moved behind the bushes to wait and take their turn after the larger animals left. The large bull flapped his ears and raised his trunk a few times as he looked toward the lodge, as if he was greeting the Indian Prime Minister. All the animals looked inquisitively at the setting with the tables, but they were about seventy yards away and felt quite comfortable carrying on with the licking. The younger elephants scooped water from the stream that flowed nearby. The stream brought clear, cold water from the higher elevations. They used their small trunks to mix the water with mud and playfully pour on each other, before lying down and rolling over in the grass. Most of the guests had their cameras out and were busy capturing the unique moment and scenery.

Indira Gandhi addressed the hosts and Satbir Kaur.

"*Manjee*, Raj and Amrita, I am so happy to be here and see what you have done. What a beautiful site to come to and the special welcome, including the wild animals. Thank you. You have certainly picked a beautiful spot to live. The crater is so unique and it feels like paradise with all the animals around us. I want to know everything about both your ancestors, how they came here, from which part of India, and what they did in these countries. Also, what you and your families have been doing."

Raj related Mehar Singh's life story and how he became a politician and nearly the president of Kenya and how he was murdered. He then talked about his life with Amrita followed by narrating Lal's arrival in Somalia, moving to Kenya, and also how she became part of the Dhillon family. Indira Gandhi was genuinely interested and asked a number of questions. She presented the Dhillons with an Indian flag as a memento of her visit to Ngorongoro. Raj had a lion skin that Mehar Singh had shot years ago in the Maasailand when he first started setting up "*dukas*" there. He presented it to the Indian leader to remember them by. It was an unforgettable day and established the Dhillons as the primary lodge on the rim of the crater.

As time passed a number of Indian movies were filmed in and around the crater. The cast and crew stayed at the Dhillon's Lodge, with Raj arranging their tours into the crater. Indian mega super star, Shashi Kapoor, was one of the famous actors who made several movies at this location.

"It's not whether you get knocked down; it's whether you get up."
VINCE LOMBARDI

With the political situation changing in Africa, countries gaining independence, and new rulers altering their attitude toward Asians, Amrita decided to send her children to England. Most of the Asians had chosen to keep their British passports and not take up Kenyan, Ugandan, or Tanzanian citizenship. The name had been changed from Tanganyika to Tanzania after Zanzibar and Tanganyika became one country. British passports were issued to the Asians with a "D" prefix that distinguished them from the ones issued to white settlers from Zimbabwe, Hong Kong, Kenya, and other colonies. The "D" marked the holder as inferior to the white immigrants, and was subject to control under the Commonwealth Immigrants Act.

In 1972, thousands of Ismailis, Moslems, Sikhs, Hindus, and Gujaratis were among the Asians expelled from Uganda by the dictator, Idi Amin Dada. For the longest time, the Asians could not believe it. No one could. How could a dictator wake up one morning, report a vision from God, and throw them out of their own country.

Yet they had watched from their homes in Kampala and other cities and towns, the fateful day that President Idi Amin Dada told the country's eighty thousand Asian residents that they had ninety days to leave Uganda and go into exile; Ugandan citizens included. Africans had celebrated in the streets, singing, tying tin cans to their dusty cars, and flying Ugandan flags. The locals fully expected to take over the businesses and homes owned by Asians that would be left behind, and achieve instant prosperity.

Almost overnight, Kampala became a city of queues for injections, passports and for the tiny amounts of currency that they were allowed to take with them, less than fifty British pounds per family. No family could take more than two suitcases of possessions. This came after a lifetime in Uganda for most of them. Toward the end of the ninety days, more than thirty flights a week were leaving Entebbe for London. More than once, Amin turned up at the airport with his massively decorated chest puffed up. He could be seen laughing at the Indians who had once seen him as their protector. They were now leaving his country.

It is rumored that Amin, with his lavish taste for women, fell for one of the wives of a rich family of Asians. He wanted to marry her and when the family quickly sent all their women abroad, he expressed his anger by deporting all the Asians. The airport immigration officials harassed and interviewed the Asians with "D" passports excessively. Finally, the "D" immigrants after years of living in Britain were eligible to get European Union passports.

The Indians in Kenya and Tanzania were fearful that they might be next to be asked to leave their countries. For some they would be asked to leave the country of their birth. Soon, a movement to regain African identity after the effects of colonization dominated these countries. The Africanization movement focused on giving Tanzania an African outlook and character. This involved a modification of geographic and personal names to reflect an African name. The movement was also used to increase the indigenous presence in the civil service. This had been underrepresented during the colonial era. All youth were compelled to provide two years of national service. Economically, Africanization was manifested in the nationalization of key industries, assets and properties. Many of these nationalized assets belonged to ethnic non-Africans. Nyerere's Africanization policy was part of a larger pan-African movement, which sought to define post-colonial political, social, and economic values in an African context.

Under Africanization policies, the future was bleak for young Indians in East Africa. For that reason, Amrita wanted to send Akash out of the country. He had already made plans with two of his friends, Kishore Pradhan and Nini Gidoomal, to go to London.

"Why do you want to send them to England?" Raj complained to Amrita.

"Why can't they just be here with us? Akash is doing great at Barclays Bank, a prestigious posting, and Maya is a successful teacher in Arusha. What are they going to do in England? Tanzania is different."

"Papa, it is only a question of time before they Africanize the teller and clerical positions in the banks," Akash pleaded with his dad.

"I need to do something before that. You have to understand this country is changing by the day."

Amrita always did what she thought was best for the children. Other family members were very upset when they found out that Akash was going to England. However, Akash did go to London. Amrita saw him off at the airport in Nairobi and returned home. The next day, she went to the bank where he worked to deposit some cash. One of his co-workers said to her, "Auntie, how is he?" Amrita could not control her tears; she had to step outside for a while. He had gone away too far, some place she had never been.

Akash flew to London with Kishore Pradhan and Nini Gidoomal. The three of them initially stayed with the Barwa family, who had a four-bedroom house with a terrace in Kingsbury. They rented furnished rooms with meals. Kishore's dad knew the family from Africa and had arranged the accommodations. There were eight people living in the house, with one bathroom being shared by everyone. Breakfast and dinner were cooked by the landlady.

It was a grand opportunity for them to learn the English culture and live on their own. Akash and his two East African friends lived there for a year, but then moved closer to the city and rented individual single-room bed sitters in South Kensington. Akash applied for jobs all over London before joining the sales department at the Hertz Rental Car Company in the fashionable London district of Knightsbridge, not far from the famous Harrod's store. One cold winter morning, four long haired, giggling young men walked into the sales office. One of them, in a thick Liverpool accent, addressed Akash. "Can we rent a car, mate?"

"Sure, what size would you like," Akash asked.

"How about a Mini Cooper, please?"

"Who will be driving?"

"I will. My name is John Lennon." He looked around at the others in his group.

"Who else wants to drive?"

"I will," said another. "Put me down as Paul McCartney."

While not knowing who the four gentlemen were, Akash was first exposed to the four Beatles, John, Paul, George, and Ringo. That was before they turned the music world upside down with their unprecedented music, lyrics, and style. Those were exciting times for the music industry in England, with The Beatles, The Rolling Stones, Searchers, Gerry and the Pacemakers, Manfred Mann, The Animals, and a host of others. These groups were playing in small clubs before becoming household names around the world. With their English girlfriends, Akash, Kishore and Nini frequented nightclubs in Chelsea, Earls Court, Hammersmith, and Bayswater, where they had the opportunity to see the Beatles and many others live on stage before they became world famous.

George Haskell, a tall cockney with an abrupt manner, was in charge of the Hertz accounts department in Knightsbridge where Akash worked. One day George posted a memo stating that Hertz had just acquired Data Processing Equipment from IBM, and that they were going to automate some processes. Hertz was looking for keypunch operators. This intrigued Akash and he knocked on George's office door.

"My name is Akash. You have seen me around. I was wondering about this punching job."

"I will explain the position," George said, "but normally we employ young women to do that."

"I want to learn, if you can show me what the job is. I can do it. I like to learn new things."

George walked Akash over to the keypunch machines, the label Stated IBM 026 Printing Card Punch. George demonstrated by feeding a blank card in and pressing some keys. He had typed the word, Akash. George took the card out and showed Akash the holes in the card that signified the different letters of his name, with two holes being punched for every alphabetical character.

"We punch data, such as names, addresses, sales, and payroll information onto these cards. Then we verify on that machine, The IBM Punch Verifier, before processing the information."

"This is fascinating," Akash said. "So I basically transfer the data from a paper format and key it into cards."

"Yes, you got it."

"What happens after the card is punched?" Akash inquired.

"It is verified by using the 056 machine," George said. "The 056 is programmed to check the values. Now, I know you are going to ask me the next step. Let me tell you, we get the verified card decks and then feed those to the bigger IBM machines, The IBM Tabulator and Accounting Machine, 421. The Tabulator is 'programmed' with a plug board to read certain columns off the card deck, do some calculations if needed, then punch another card deck or print a report. We can get payroll checks printed and sales analysis reports based on the information punched onto the cards."

"I am fascinated, I want to learn. Please give me the opportunity and you won't be sorry."

George offered Akash the position the next day, and trained him over the upcoming weeks. After a year at Hertz, and being proficient on the data processing equipment, Akash was ready to move on to another position. Honeywell Limited was introducing its line of computers in Britain and was looking for staff. A friend of Akash's, Sunder, was working at Honeywell and introduced him to some key people.

Akash joined Honeywell Controls in Brentford, Middlesex, as a computer operator. This marked the beginning of a career in an industry that, for him, would last decades in countries around the globe. He was trained within Honeywell Inc., as a system analyst and programmer. In later years, he would become an expert as a data base administrator, network analyst, systems consultant, computer performance expert, applications designer and developer, and manager at all these levels.

As Akash grew up in the industry, he was able to work on operating systems from different computer vendors that were extremely basic, running a single program at a time, to the most sophisticated equipment, which processed thousands of processes concurrently. He worked on an assortment of programming languages and databases.

Akash and Amrita exchanged letters on a weekly basis for the first five years he was in London. He wrote letters to his mother every fortnight. Amrita always replied to Akash's letters as soon as she received them. She shared all the local news and told him how the country was changing politically, and how it was not safe anymore.

With the political climate changing, it was getting unsafe for non-African girls in Arusha. An incident happened on the island of Zanzibar where acid was thrown on two Sikh girls, causing severe burns. They were flown to the capital Dar-es-salaam and then to London. The motive appeared to be that the primarily Moslem community wanted other religious sects to leave. The incident was applauded in other towns and cities throughout Tanzania by the locals.

Amrita decided to send Surjeet to London. Again, the whole family was against the idea. Amrita's older sister-in-law had a big row over her sending Surjeet out of the country. Raj agreed with his sister. Amrita had no one to accompany her to Nairobi Airport, except her daughter Maya. They both decided to go to Nairobi and see Surjeet off. It was going to be very late at night for the return journey. So, Amrita asked one of their family friends to come with them.

Fortunately, Akash was at the other end to receive Surjeet. He knew two sisters from Nairobi, Jyoti and Reena, the daughters of Bakshish Singh Dhillon. The young ladies were nurses in Greenwich at Miller General Hospital. Surjeet had shown interest in being a nurse, so Akash introduced Surjeet to them. His younger sister ended up enrolling at Miller General Hospital as a trainee nurse and she shared a three-bedroom flat with Jyoti and Reena. Surjeet was a great cook and the three of them got along well.

Back home, Jolly was fourteen and attended the Arusha Secondary School. He had just gone back after the Easter holidays, and came home with blisters on both hands. Amrita asked him,

"How did this happen?"

Jolly informed his mom that the students were told there would be no more academic lessons, and that all the students would now be required to work in the schoolyard and cut the grass. They had to use garden scissors, *pangas*. This was the result of the new socialism being preached by President Julius Nyerere, affectionately known as the *Mwalimu*, the teacher. He was also known as *Baba wa Taifa*, Father Of The Nation.

Nyerere had created a single-party system with the Tanganyika African National Union, TANU, and used "preventive detention" to eliminate trade unions and all opposition. He mandated that everyone worked for the community and worked the land. Some of the land was forcibly confiscated from Indians and Europeans, and assigned to local Africans. The schools had more classes in which students actually did hard labor on farms.

The central government created collective farms and encouraged people to move into large villages in which food and other goods would be produced collectively for the whole community. Nyerere and his ministers made a regular practice of public relations stunts where they would grab a shovel and pitch in.

However, over time, Nyerere's policies led to economic decline, systematic corruption, and shortage of goods. Nyerere ordered his security forces to forcibly transfer much of the population to collective farms and, because of opposition from villagers, often burned villages to the ground. This campaign pushed the nation to the brink of starvation and made it dependent on foreign aid for aid.

"There is no future here for us, especially the children," Amrita said after seeing her son suffering and crying.

"You are not going to school tomorrow. You and I are going to London."

The next morning she went to the Aggarwal Travel Agency and had them book two tickets for her. Then she asked the bank manager to get her some travelers' checks by that afternoon.

"It is a bit late now, but don't worry I will do my best for you," he said.

She received the checks just in time. On Saturday, they left for Nairobi. The ever-enterprising Amrita got one of her friends, Shabana, to drive them to the Embakasi Airport in Nairobi. On Sunday evening they were on the flight, set to arrive in London on Monday. Amrita phoned Akash at work and told him what was going on.

"Where are you?" he said.

"Heathrow," she said.

"What, mum, you can't do this? Akash said.

"This is not Africa. I am living in a bed-sitter with two friends. Where are you going to stay?"

"We'll talk about it when we see you," she said.

"Wait for me where you are and I will be there shortly."

Akash picked them up and took them to a hotel.

"When you get up, go downstairs and turn left, there is a restaurant a few yards away, have tea or something to eat and come back the same way, otherwise you will get lost."

They went back to the apartment and waited for Akash to return. He came in the evening and informed them that he had found a bed-sitter not far from where he lived. They all went there. It was on the 7th floor, but no elevators. Amrita had to rest several times before she could get to the top.

> *"You are either alive and proud or you are dead,
> and when you are dead, you can't care anyway."*
> **STEVEN BIKO**

Eventually, Amrita went back to Arusha, leaving Akash, Surjeet, and Jolly behind in London. Jolly was enrolled in a private school near Farnham in Surrey. Initially he was happy, but then some bullies started taunting him, using racial slurs, and beating him up. They would throw his books and clothes in trash cans, and call him derogatory names. Jolly was scared to go back to school. Akash brought him to his house in Hayes on the weekends; he would beg not to be taken back to the school. Finally, Akash confronted the principal, explained the situation, and told him he was going to take his brother out of the school and complain to the school boards.

"Give me a week and I will sort this out," the principal assured him. "Your brother will be looked after."

He suspended the three bullies, and the taunting did stop. Jolly was never the same, and never really did fully recover from this dark period of his life.

Meanwhile, one of Tej's three sons, Amarjeet, the oldest, was taking over the businesses that his father owned. Amarjeet was twenty one, tall, handsome, and enterprising. With his charming personality and wit, he had taken over the entire tire retreading factory, and had also started a tourist business where he led safaris into the game reserves. He had so much in front of him to be a success in life.

Tragedy struck one weekend in November when Amarjeet and some friends were visiting the coastal town of Tanga. There were five of them in a Datsun pickup truck. Three sat in the front while Amarjeet and his friend Jamal sat in the back. Approaching Tanga, the vehicles ahead of them stopped suddenly. They pulled the Datsun off to the shoulder of the murram road when they saw a fifteen passenger van on its side, split open like a coconut. Another similar vehicle was sideways in a ditch, its front end smashed inward. People were stopping, getting out of their vehicles, and rushing to help the bodies on the grass while other passengers were trying to crawl out of the van.

Amarjeet and his four friends were getting ready to get out when a heavily loaded seven-ton Volvo truck, driving way over the speed limit, failed to stop. The driver tried to steer toward the shoulder, but the speeding overloaded truck plowed into the pickup in which the boys had been traveling. All were killed instantly. The Volvo finally came to a stop yards after the impact. The driver quickly jumped out of the truck and ran into the bushes, before he could be stopped.

After being contacted, Mohan Singh, a local prominent Sports Shop owner in Arusha, drove over to Tej's house,

"There has been an accident." Sadly he gave them the news.

"What do you mean, who," Tej asked him but deep down feeling the worst.

"All the boys are gone, it happened near Tanga. I am sorry."

Tej's wife, Manjeet started screaming and running out towards the road, Tej dropped to his knees and sat down on the ground.

When the news got around Arusha, the whole town was in shock.

Nothing like this had ever happened in their small town, where everyone knew each other. The main Babati Road was lined with people on both sides when the open truck came back with the five young corpses.

Tej and his wife never recovered. Manjeet died one year later from a broken heart. On top of all that, the matriarch, Satbir Kaur, passed away in the fall. She couldn't bear the loss of such a young and energetic grandson.

Tej became even more bitter and nastier than ever. He would start drinking as soon as he was out of bed in the morning till he passed out at night. He paid no attention to his two younger sons. They ended up not going to school and started drinking excessively at early ages.

Tej, who had always been the cunning and constantly jealous brother, was always looking for any opportunity to take down his older brother, Raj. When he heard the three-year government lease on Dhillon's Lodge was up again for renewal. He again started planning on how he could hurt his brother and get the lodge away from him.

Tej approached the head of The Ngorongoro Conservation Authority, the Maasai, Ole Saibulu.

"Saibulu, hey old friend, I need to discuss some business with you," Tej said.

"What is it?"

"Need some private time over a few Tuskers. You won't be sorry; I have a deal for you."

Saibulu was willing. "Meet me at the Crater Lodge bar tonight."

After they had downed several cool beers, Tej leaned close to the Maasai.

"I know the lease is up on the Dhillon's Lodge and it is up for tenders."

"Yes, in two months we will renew. The request for applications and submission of tenders has been publicized. What is your angle? You plan to bid, too?"

"I want that lodge. I will do anything to get it."

"But your brother has it now."

"I know, but I want to take it away from him — family issues."

"I don't understand you *Muhindis*, I thought all you people cared about families," the Maasai said. "Family means nothing? So what did you want me to do?"

"I will take care of you, just let me be the last to bid and I will be the highest tender after you give me the figure."

"I can't do that, this is not ethical."

"Ethics. Saibulu that is a joke in Africa. You know that," said Tej. "How much are your ethics worth? Name a price."

"Don't insult me, I do have ethics."

"Think about it. I am telling you — you won't be sorry."

Saibulu hesitated. "Let me think about it. This does not seem right."

It took a week and a lot of soul-searching, but the Maasai, Saibulu, finally arranged a meeting with Tej.

"I have been thinking about this," he said.

"It is risky. I could lose my job, although I could use the money. For the risk I want two hundred thousand shillings."

"Wow, you want the moon, don't you," Tej smirked.

"This is a pretty high price."

Tej already had a number in mind,

"I can pay you one hundred fifty thousand."

Saibulu did not hesitate. "Okay, it is a deal. Done."

There were six tenders submitted. The deadline was midnight on a Monday. Saibulu gave Tej the figure for the highest bid. Whoever bid over that amount would take the lodge away from Raj and Amrita. Tej had won, for the time being.

Raj and Amrita were heartbroken. Again, they were given a time limit to pack and move. They had started the lodge from scratch, built it up to become a world-renowned facility, and now it was being stripped away from them. They appealed to the conservator, and even wrote to the president of Tanzania, Julius Nyerere, but to no avail. Once again, they had to move and start their lives all over.

Amrita was totally devastated, all her life since her father died, she had worked hard, built businesses, drove trucks, and took care of her children, husband and her in-laws. Everytime she made some progress, it seemed that she had to take a step back. She was tired now and seemed to have lost the will to start all over again. Her husband's brother just would not leave them alone.

Within ninety days, they had to pack up a lifetime of belongings and leave the lodge. The decision had been forced on them. Amrita started finding buyers for the four-wheel-drive vehicles and the furnishings in the lodge. She wasn't interested in selling any of the furnishings or anything connected to the lodge to her vicious brother-in-law.

Once the news spread, the contacts the Dhillons had in Kenya within the government approached Raj and Amrita to see if they would be interested in starting a new lodge in a location within the many game reserves in Kenya. It was a lucrative opportunity with the experience they both had. They thought about it for a while. Amrita was all for it. She was always the entrepreneur, ambitious, and fearless. Raj, who was more reserved, was adamant that he had spent his whole life building businesses from scratch and wanted no part of another startup business.

They agreed to move. This was *Kismet*. They should have moved to Kenya and started a new lodge. It turned out ironically, that Raj, who didn't want to send his children to Europe, would now be there with them.

"I am an African, not because I was born in Africa but because Africa is born in me."
KWAME NKRUMAH

Amrita now, had a window seat next to Raj on the British Airways 747 bound for Heathrow in London from Nairobi International. The plane was half-full, with a number of Kenyan students going back to colleges in England, some wives, and children of Kenyan diplomats in London. Like the Dhillons a large number of Indians were leaving Kenya for good, to start new lives. Their jobs had either been "Africanized" or their businesses had been taken over by African citizens. A mixture of Swahili, Gujarati, and Punjabi conversations filled the cabin.

Raj, with his head down and teary eyed, reminisced about his whole life in Africa. Should they have taken on the new lodge in Kenya? Raj was worn out. He had put his heart and soul into the one at Ngorongoro, started it from scratch, and spent his whole life in that region with the Maasai. He just didn't have the desire or energy to start over with a new lodge or another enterprise especially after developing the famous, world-class Dhillon's Lodge. How could anything else compare? The pressure would be immense to attempt to replicate it.

He was deeply burdened to leave the country of his birth, where his father had settled, despite all the hardships. This was where his children had been born. He was now leaving for a continent that would be completely foreign to him.

Amrita too thought of the East Africa she was leaving, where she had been born and where her father had settled, coming from Somalia. She thought of Nyeri, her birthplace, Wamboi and Lalita, Davinder, Kijabe, where she met the family she married into, the Dhillons, the Maasai, Narok, Loliondo, and Ngorongoro — along with all the other game reserves and all the friends she was leaving behind. The carefree young Amrita had envisioned a totally different life for herself when her father was alive. She had pictured herself going to Europe, becoming a doctor, and having a house full of everything she would ever want. She had imagined being with her father until he was a very old man and taking care of him. Her dreams had been shattered, starting at the tender age of eleven when her father passed. Her life had been one filled with hardships, one after the other,

The plane jerked slightly and began backing up.

Now, they were going to start a new life in Europe.

The pilot said they were next in line as the 747 taxied towards the runway and ready to launch them toward their new life.

At least they would see their four children often and there would be grandchildren; a pleasant thought that made Amrita smile.

A final airplane meal was announced by the hostess, a tall attractive English woman — goat curry and rice, pork chops, or a vegetarian dish. They ordered but both Amrita and Raj just picked at their food. They finally managed to get some sleep. At last, the tarmac hugged the screeching tires on the British Airways jet as it wobbled, slowed and wound its way to the gate at London's Heathrow International Airport.

Amrita peered eagerly out the window, trying to get a glimpse of their new home, but she could barely see the silhouette of the airport terminal buildings as the London fog rolled in. She reached out her hand to Raj. Their eyes locked. She squeezed his leathery hand.

A tear leaked out of the corner of her eye.

Raj squeezed her hand back.

Amrita took solace in the fact that her husband and children would be by her side, as well as many friends who had already moved to England. Even her brother Mohan would be there with his family.

She was going to make it.

They were about to start anew.

A beep sounded and the captain said they could stand.

"Come on, old man," she said to Raj. "Akash will be waiting for us. Let's get this new life started…"

EPILOGUE

Thakur Singh had passed away in Nairobi after suffering from a cardiac arrest. After his death, Bishan decided to stay in Nairobi with her and Lal's two daughters, Harbans and Jagjit. They attended the Duchess of Gloucester High School in Pangani. After their graduation, Bishan moved back to India to her paternal village.

Kirpal retired in Nairobi. He was a prominent member of the Sikh community in Nairobi and was a decent tennis player playing for the local Sikh Union Club. He died alone in Kenya. His wife had passed away years ago and his three children were living in London.

Amrita's youngest brother, Mohan graduated from high school and moved to London. He was married and had four daughters and a son. Davinder, Amrita's brother died at age 75 in Moshi, Tanzania, single, homeless, penniless, and in dire ill health. He had served in the British Army in Kenya and was qualified to immigrate to Britain and receive the financial retirement benefits, but he chose not to go there.

Tej would eventually be all alone, having lost his wife, oldest son Amarjeet and his mother. He had his two younger sons with him but paid no attention to them. He died an alcoholic with a severe liver infection. A tragic life which had so much potential. He lived through a leopard attack in Loliondo, survived a Maasai attack with the cattle and the fire in Eastleigh where he had been working on the Thames Trader truck that had caught fire. He had the foresight to reverse the truck out of the driveway and also drive the jeep out onto the street before the flames got to the fuel tanks. He had severe burns on his face, hands and arms but once again came through the ordeal. But he died alone, miserable but relentless in thinking of ways to hurt his brother, Raj.

Bishan and Amrita had never reconciled. Amrita never forgave her mother for marrying Thakur and not caring for Lal's children. Bishan was in love with Thakur and never cared for Lal or her children with him. After Thakur's death, Bishan spent time between India and London where she stayed with Mohan and his family. She passed away in London at the age of one hundred and two. A ripe old age that again had so much potential but she spent it the way she wanted it with Thakur as her mate. Her daughters with Thakur, Harbans and Jagjit were married and settled in Leicester, England.

Amrita and Raj settled down in London and started working part time jobs to get out of the house and get to know the life in Britain. Akash got married and moved to California. Jolly moved to Sydney where he lives with his wife, Nina and two sons Taran and Manveer. Maya lives in London with her husband and son. Surjeet also lives in London with her husband, three daughters and son.

Raj passed away in 1985 from a cardiac arrest in London. Amrita died in 2010 in London from heart complications.

Amrita's life had started with so much promise in Nyeri but changed completely with her father's passing. The family she was married into was never appreciative of how hard she worked and how much she did to keep them together. Her brother-in-law Tej was bent on destroying Raj and Amrita and any progress they made. He was there to make sure they didn't succeed.

Amrita's mental strength and will power was always the pillar that made them survive in Kenya and Tanganyika despite all odds. Raj was the weaker link, but once Amrita decided that they would overcome all obstacles, there was no holding her back.

Amrita and Raj always believed in *Kismet,* destiny. She remembered how Lal Singh had taken her and Davinder to Kijabe and the hot water springs and then to the Dhillon house where unknowingly she had met her future relations, father-in-law Mehar, mother-in-law Satbir and husband Raj. Spending their last decades in East Africa and then moving to England was a blessing in a way. Raj and Amrita were able to spend the rest of their lives with their children and grandchildren and away from Tej. An ending that could have been so different but was never meant to be. Now they could see their descendants prosper with renewed challenges in the western world.

DHILLON'S LODGE NGORONGORO CRATER

INDIAN TRADERS IN MAASAILAND. PHOTO TAKEN IN KIJABE, KENYA IN 1930S.

(STANDING BACK ROW)	FAZAL AHMED, BHAG SINGH, JIUN S. CHIURA, CHET SINGH
(MIDDLE ROW)	SHAMBUDATT UNKNOWN UNKNOWN MELARAM SUCHA SINGH
(SEATED)	BAGA SINGH DHARIWAL, KISHAN SINGH AMLI, RAM SINGH, KEHAR SINGH DHILLON, HARNAM SINGH, RAJA RAM, SARWAN SINGH DHILLON

AKASH WITH HIS MAASAI FRIEND AFTER A HUNTING SAFARI

DHILLON'S PET BUFFALO "MBOGO" IN LOLIONDO, TANGANYIKA

READY FOR A SAFARI

AUTHOR BIOGRAPHY

Pally Dhillon, a retired computer professional, born in Kenya now lives in Westlake, Ohio. He enjoys writing historical fictional novels. *Kijabe*, his first novel was based on his grandfather, Mehar Singh's, migration from India to Kenya in the early part of the twentieth century when the British colonialists were recruiting laborers to work on the railways in Kenya. The story narrated his adventurous life as Mehar Singh settled in Africa and then his untimely murder. *Kijabe* was then translated in Punjabi and is available as *Surkh Haneri*.

His second novel, *Walk with Pride*, is a well-researched historical novel encompassing three generations and the unfolding of their lives in India, Iran, Canada, Tanzania, Uganda and Kenya. The theme of this manuscript is how genocide keeps getting repeated in different countries at different times. The Sikh religion is well depicted in terms of the historical sacrifices made by the Sikh Gurus.

Whispers from the heart, is a short manuscript that is a compilation of romantic love poems and passages that touches one's heart. It commands the reader to react emotionally to the joy, sadness and despair that love can bring.

This novel, *Footprints on the African Savanna*, is his mother Amrita's story, most of it written by her before she passed away. It depicts her father's life in Somalia and Kenya and her life from being born in Nyeri in Kenya, getting married and then the multitude of adventures and the hard life that she endured in Kenya and Tanganyika.

Dhillon's interests are reading, sports and technological innovations and trends. Involved in field hockey all his life, he has been active in USA field hockey on the west coast as president of the hockey association and as a player, coach and organizer. He has traveled all over the world to play hockey and to watch Olympics, World cups and other sporting events. He organized the medal ceremonies and announcements for hockey at the 1976 Montreal Olympic Games and then at the 1984 Olympics in Los Angeles. Golf is now his sporting love in Ohio.

SYNOPSIS

Footprints on the African Savanna is the story of a Sikh woman, Amrita Kaur Dhillon, who wrote fifty pages in her own handwriting about her childhood, her parents, her in-laws and her life growing up and then surviving in East Africa. Unfortunately, she passed away before she could finish writing and publishing her story.

Amrita belonged to a generation of pioneering Sikh women in East Africa who were born there in the early part of the twentieth century, and worked tirelessly to raise their families. This is her story, from birth to a glorious childhood which ended abruptly when she married at the age of fourteen and was thrust into the busy and demanding life of a large Sikh family who were one of the early settlers in East Africa.

The manuscript narrates the intriguing life experiences of Amrita's father and father-in-law, who were pioneers, professionals, hunters and business owners. The reader will be engrossed in her struggles, hardships, and daring adventures as she attempts to support her husband, his family, and her own children in the vast, raw, and often turbulent countries of Kenya and Tanganyika. She was a big game hunter, ran businesses in the nomadic Maasailand and drove large trucks to transport goods through the roughest terrains in East Africa.

The story narrates her father's life who was a surgeon, was born in India and then spent his life in Somalia and Kenya. The story also encompasses her father-in-law Mehar Singh was also born in India and then moved to Kenya to work on the Railway line in Kenya from the coastal town of Mombasa to Kisumu, the town on Lake Victoria. Mehar becomes a successful entrepeneur and then goes into politics.

The storyline reflects Amrita's inner strength and willpower when with all the odds against her she fights her way through and ensures the survival of her extended family and her children.

Printed in Great Britain
by Amazon